THE BIOGRAPHIES OF ORDINARY PEOPLE

VOLUME 1: 1989–2000

Nicole Dieker

Copyright © 2017 by Nicole Dieker
Cover image © Canva

Ebook interior design by Pronoun
Ebook distribution by Pronoun

Paperback interior design by Veronica Ewing
Paperback distribution by Ingram Book Group

ISBN 978-1-5080578-5-7 (ebk)
ISBN 978-0-9986743-0-8 (pbk)

"Natalie takes Kindergarten Readiness" was originally published in Boing Boing on November 5, 2015.

This is a work of fiction. Names, characters, organizations, places, events, and incidents are either the product of the author's imagination or are used fictitiously. Opinions stated by the characters should not be assumed to be those of the author's.

To my Patreon supporters.
This book would not exist without you.

CONTENTS

SUMMER 1990

FALL 1990

WINTER 1990

SPRING 1991

SUMMER 1991

FALL 1991

WINTER 1991

SPRING 1992

FALL 1998

SPRING 1999

SUMMER 1999

FALL 1999

WINTER 1999

SPRING 2000

FALL 2000

AUTHOR'S NOTE

You're going to ask me how much of this book is true. I'm going to say none of it—and stick to it.

Yes, I grew up in a town very similar to Kirkland. Yes, my parents are musicians. Yes, I wrote a novel and was in a community theater performance of *Into the Woods* and did a lot of the stuff that Meredith and her sisters do in the book.

But that doesn't mean this book is a true story.

I did want to be as true as possible to the feeling of what it was like to grow up in rural Missouri in the 1990s: to spend summers at the community pool, pushing ourselves out of the water like Ariel; to practice piano and collect gold star stickers and play "Joy to the World" at a Christmas Eve service; to see the internet for the first time and then watch it change everything.

So I drew from my own memories and experiences, but please don't believe that these chapters represent what actually happened. Let the Grubers and the Seths and the MacAllisters and the Dillards be themselves, and take what happens to them as fiction—the most honest fiction I know how to write.

THE BIOGRAPHIES OF ORDINARY PEOPLE:

VOLUME 1: 1989–2000

PART 1: 1989–1992

SUMMER 1989

1. ROSEMARY'S THIRTY-FIFTH BIRTHDAY.

The last night before they left was Rosemary Gruber's thirty-fifth birthday.

It had, of course, been her birthday since the morning, and the girls had duly remembered to call out "Happy birthday, mommy!" when they came out of the bedroom. Meredith did the bulk of the remembering, and had written it on her chart by the door, but after they were finished the chart came down and was thrown away, and Rosemary dug her nails gently at the bits of Scotch tape stuck to the hollow door's wooden veneer, because they did not want to lose their security deposit. Jack had assumed they would lose it, with the three girls, but Rosemary knew better. Teach a child that food is only served at the table, and they'll never try to eat it over the carpet. It hadn't been like that in her house when she was a child, but she had made this home with her own words and will. (And now she was unmaking it and stacking it in boxes, and that chart was finally coming down.)

"Were you born on a Friday?" Meredith asked, as Rosemary brushed her hair.

"No," Rosemary said. "I was born on a Saturday." She was pretty sure of this. It sounded like it could be true. She was thinking about everything that still had to be finished before they left, and only partially thinking about Meredith's hair, and it was a good thing the mirror had been packed away or her daughter would have noticed.

"Saturday's child works hard for a living," Meredith recited. *That's true enough,* Rosemary thought, with the part of her mind that wasn't worrying about packing and cleaning and whether it was worth it to bathe all three girls one more time before they left. "What day was I born on?" her daughter continued.

"Tuesday," Rosemary said, and this she *did* remember, because she had been watching *Laverne and Shirley* in the hospital while she waited for her contractions to continue.

"Tuesday's child is full of grace," Meredith said, and smiled at herself, and at the idea of being graceful. It was a real smile, because Meredith was happy, not one of the posed ones she put on for pictures. Rosemary's oldest daughter was not yet eight years old and she would tilt her head and widen her eyes whenever anyone pulled out a camera, imitating the child models she saw in Rosemary's issues of *Ladies' Home Journal*. Rosemary had thought about tossing the magazines out before Meredith could get to them, but her weirdo kid read everything that came into the house, often before Rosemary herself could read it. She'd be making dinner and the kids would have PBS on and Meredith wouldn't be watching; she'd be squatting on the carpet in front of the sofa with one knee tucked under her chin, studying "Can This Marriage Be Saved?"

"What day was Natalie born on?" Meredith asked, and Rosemary said "Sunday," because she remembered that day too—and then she suddenly remembered she was wrong about Meredith, that she had gone into the hospital on Tuesday but Meredith had been born at night, when it was Wednesday.

"Nat, hair," Meredith called out, and Rosemary's second daughter took her place in front of what would have been the mirror but was now just a blank wall, with a mom and her little girl cross-legged on the carpet and facing the empty space. Rosemary did not need to look in the mirror on her thirty-fifth birthday; she had not showered that day and probably wouldn't until the evening, and she had stopped wearing makeup years ago, but she was still thin, and Jack smiled when he looked at her, and nobody else really looked at her besides her daughters.

"Sunday's child—no, wait, the child that's born on the Sabbath Day is blithe and bonny and good and gay," Meredith sang, and Natalie echoed "blithe and bonny" the way she always imitated her sister, and Rosemary looked at her happy baby, the one who came home from preschool with stories about new friends and games, and thought again: *true enough*. Her middle daughter had Rosemary's own golden-brown wavy hair, though the girls only knew that from photos because Rosemary had cut it all short right before

Meredith was born. All three of her children had been born with hair that clustered in tiny dark sweatlocks, but Natalie's hair was the only one to thicken and curl.

"Blithe and bonny," Natalie continued to sing, turning the words into nonsense, and Rosemary could see Meredith stiffen slightly with frustration. The two of them were close, but Meredith very much wanted to be her own person. The nursery rhyme was something *she* had memorized.

"When was Jackie born?" Meredith asked, over Natalie's song.

"I don't remember," Rosemary said, even though it would have been easy enough to count backwards; Jackie had just turned three a few weeks ago. On a Tuesday.

"We don't know who you are yet," Meredith said to Jackie, and Rosemary thought this was also true; she was pretty sure she knew who her two older daughters were, but Jackie was still toddling between babyhood and personality. Watching the two girls who had already gone ahead of her and figuring out how she was going to be similar to—and different from—them.

Her mother called in the afternoon, while Rosemary was sitting on the carpet playing Lotto with Jackie and Nat, and Jack was using Meredith's help to hold boxes together as he taped them shut. Rosemary stretched the phone cord out and called to the girls, and they took turns standing by the phone to say hello to Grandma.

"Well, I'll be looking forward to seeing you all in the new house," her mother said, when it was Rosemary's turn again. "You still haven't seen it yet?"

"Just the photos," Rosemary said. Sometimes she wondered if her mother even understood how the world worked, anymore. Of course she couldn't fly out to Missouri with Jack just to see a house. He had brought back a roll of film, and she had come out of the grocery store a week later with the image of a front porch, where a swing could go.

"What if you don't like it?" Rosemary's mother's voice had started to pick up that quaver that old women had. It made Rosemary a little uncomfortable to think about it, so she focused her irritation on the question.

"I'm going to like it," she said, because she had already decided she was going to like it. If it hadn't been long distance, and her family hadn't been within earshot, and her mother had been a different person, Rosemary might have explained about the porch swing, and the picture her mind put over the photograph that Jack had taken. A future that already

3

felt like a memory. Her girls, on that swing, in matching dresses.

There were presents after dinner, small because they were moving, and small *because they were moving*. Jack cut open an avocado, squeezed it into a china soup bowl that had been part of Rosemary's wedding set, and added the last scrapes of the mayonnaise jar, so it would serve five. He offered it to Rosemary first, and Meredith and Natalie watched her with hungry eyes but were quiet, because it was her birthday. Because having a birthday was kind of like being a guest, and Rosemary had taught them how to behave when they had guests.

But at this party Rosemary was both a guest and a host and a mother, and so she took a small portion for herself and gave the rest to her girls.

"Guacamole is my favorite food," Meredith said.

"Salsa is my favorite food," Natalie said. "And guacamole."

Jackie said "Salsa!" and laughed, and that seemed to settle it.

Later Rosemary would wash the china bowl and the plates and the forks from this last dinner in their Portland apartment—because paper plates, even for the last day, cost money—and later she would put the girls to bed in sleeping bags on the floor, and later she would do one more load of laundry and make sure all the suitcases were ready for the morning.

But first her daughters had a surprise for her, and she already knew what it was.

Meredith hauled the cassette player out of the bedroom, one of the few toys that hadn't been packed away because they were going to need it on the long car drive from Oregon to Missouri. Their Volvo's tape deck had died two months ago, with Natalie's cassette of *The Muppets Take Manhattan* still inside. The girls talked about that cassette sometimes as if it were a lost historical artifact, and argued over who remembered the correct words to the songs.

There was a bit of whispering over where to stand, and then the three Gruber children decided to form a line in the doorway. Meredith ran to the cassette player, pressed Play, and hurried back into place.

The three girls sang "So Long, Farewell" from *The Sound of Music*, accompanied by the soundtrack that Meredith and Natalie had created by holding the cassette recorder up to the the television while the movie was playing. Meredith and Natalie acted out most of the parts—and Rosemary knew that Meredith had negotiated the choice role of Liesl by allowing Natalie to play "all the other girls"—and at the end the two girls scooted out of the way to let Jackie take center stage and sing Gretl's final verse. Natalie sang along from the side, since Jackie was a little unclear on the words (this had also been part of Meredith's negotiation), and Meredith furiously pantomimed putting her head on her hands until Jackie finally picked up that she was supposed to pretend to be falling asleep. Then Meredith, still playing Liesl, paraded in to carry her offstage.

It was a birthday gift and it was a goodbye to their apartment and their old life. The next day they would get into the car and drive, for five days straight, to Kirkland, Missouri. A town that Rosemary had never seen; that none of them had seen except for Jack, when he went down to Kirkland College for his final job interview.

She knew whatever was coming had to be better than what they had now, in this tiny apartment where she didn't even like to have the girls outside, because of the neighbors and the voices calling out and the people who gathered in the parking lot, just to stand there. So far she had made a quiet and structured world for them indoors, with PBS and *The Sound of Music* and Meredith's to-do list on the wall—although that had been Meredith's idea, and honestly Rosemary thought that Meredith could do a little without whatever it was that prompted her to make lists, but it was much easier to say "in this house, we eat food at the table" than it was to say "in this house, seven-year-olds don't read Mommy's magazines or tape handwritten charts to the door." She could have canceled the subscription, though, or taken down the charts when they were sleeping. It was part of her job, making the right kind of world for her family. It was exhausting. (She would shower the next morning, before they packed everything away. She would put the earrings Jack bought her in her purse, by the door.)

Now they were going to make a different world for themselves, Rosemary and Jack and the three little girls in their sleeping bags with the nightlight plugged into the wall, the one thing Rosemary would forget to pack when they left the next morning. Her girls would discuss it like a lost treasure, this piece of plastic shaped like a castle that they no longer owned. It would be a reminder that there once was another bedroom and another city, and that even if they spent the rest of their lives together in this small Missouri town, they would always have come from somewhere else.

2. MEREDITH IN THE CAR IN IDAHO.

Meredith sat in the car and held the silence in her mouth like an egg. She knew all the things that would make it better—she could read to them! they could sing!—but she also knew that sometimes you had to wait for someone else to tell you what to do, even though they would just say something that you had already thought of.

They were not lost. It sounded like they might have been lost, but they were not lost now. They were on the highway, and they were in Idaho. They were on the highway in Idaho and they were all quiet, and Meredith could tell that her parents wanted it to be quiet because they were not saying anything.

At the beginning, her mother had said "wave goodbye to the apartment!" and they had sat quietly listening to both parents talk about highway exits until they were safely out of Portland, and then they had listened to the radio, and then they had listened to *The Sound of Music* cassette that they had taped off TV, the whole thing. And they sang. And then Meredith read from the torn yellow-covered copy of *Little House on the Prairie* that she had in her backpack, which she had packed because of this trip, which she was waiting for her chance to read aloud.

The last time they went on a long drive, to see Grandma in Fresno, Natalie had felt carsick and Mom—Meredith thought the word "Mom," even though she still said "Mommy" because her sisters did—had asked Meredith to read to her. Meredith had been reading *Matilda* then, and she started over from the beginning, and it made Natalie laugh.

So now Meredith knew that reading could be a way to make the car feel a little better, to get everyone talking again, but she kept her mouth tightly closed around the silence because she knew it was not the right time to ask.

Natalie was watching her. Natalie wasn't looking carsick right then, they were on a pretty straight road, but Natalie was looking for something to do. They could play. They couldn't move around much, with Natalie in her booster seat and Jackie's car seat in between them, but Meredith could lean over, her seatbelt shoulder strap flat against the backseat of the car because it was safer. They'd have to play something that would be okay to play in the car, that they wouldn't mind their parents overhearing.

"Do you want to play?" Meredith whispered.

"Okay," Natalie said.

Meredith looked at Mom and Dad. They hadn't responded.

"What do you want to play?" Meredith asked.

"Orphanage?" Natalie suggested.

That was going to be hard, in the car. At home—no, at the place that *used* to be home—"orphanage" required nearly every paper doll they had, because part of the game involved assigning their paper dolls secret personalities, designating whether they were going to be nice or mean or smart or silly. They would line up the paper dolls against the wall, and then each take on the role of a parent, meeting the orphans and deciding which ones to adopt without knowing who these children really were.

"Can I play?" Jackie asked. Meredith and Natalie had started giving Jackie small roles, like the family dog, so she could participate without derailing the storyline. Sometimes Jackie forgot there were paper dolls and just ran around the room barking. Their old room. Not the new one that was still four days away.

Meredith nodded and whispered "yes" just as her mother called back "Let Jackie play." So they were paying attention. Meredith would just have to pretend that they weren't, otherwise she wouldn't be able to make up the story.

They didn't have a lot of toys with them, but each girl had been allowed to bring one doll into the backseat of the Volvo, so they stood the dolls up on the sides of Jackie's car seat and then Meredith said, knowing she was speaking loudly enough to be heard by everyone in the car, "Well, honey, here we are at the orphanage." She mumbled the last word just a bit, to blur it.

"Let's go look at the kids," Natalie said, taking on the mother role. Meredith generally let Natalie play the girl parts. It was their agreement. Meredith was the one who put the story together and created problems for the characters to solve, so she got the part she wanted, too.

"Let's look at the kids," Jackie echoed. Both of her sisters ignored her.

"Who are you, little girl?" Meredith asked, directing the question to Natalie and her doll.

"My name is Sarah," Natalie said. "I like to ride horses and play baseball."

Already Meredith was drafting a scenario in which Sarah had to bravely ride a horse to save her snobby adopted sibling's life, and then her mother interrupted: "What are you playing?"

"Orphanage," Natalie said, and Mom said "What?" and Meredith felt a little embarrassed and sad, that she and Natalie were playing orphans with their parents sitting right in front of them. This was why she always hated it when people listened to them play. Why, on the rare minutes when Jackie was in bed and Natalie was in the bath and Meredith could play by herself, she moved her paper dolls around and kept all the words inside her head.

But her mother only asked "are you letting Jackie play?" and so they continued, Meredith weaving a story of three new sisters, Sarah and Anna and Jackie, because that was what Jackie wanted her doll to be called, as they got in a train to go to their new home. Then the train went off the tracks and Anna got hurt and Sarah had to ride a horse to get help and rescue her, and Jackie rode on the back of the horse too, there was enough room on a horse for two sisters. The three girls bounced their dolls up and down and started laughing, and Jackie learned how to call out "giddyup" and "woah," and from the front seat Rosemary heard her three daughters playing and was glad of all of them, and glad the road was straight, and glad Jack was driving so she could close her eyes and rest, with her children's laughter in her ears like peace.

3. JACK PLAYS THE NPR GAME IN KANSAS.

Jack Gruber was John Gruber on paper and Dr. G in the classroom. At school he had been one of the Gruber kids, and even in college people put together that it was him, his sister, and his younger brother, even though they all had different majors. Now he and his sister had PhDs and tenure-track jobs, and his brother was smoking pot somewhere outside of Eugene, although he had come to that last dinner with the family to say goodbye, and had gotten down on the floor to play Memory with the girls.

This was an adventure to him, in a way that he didn't think it was to Rosemary. She had grown up in California, but Jack had never lived outside of Portland and, until he had flown to St. Louis and driven the rental car to Kirkland for his interview, had never been to Missouri or any part of the Midwest. It had been only the second time he'd been on a plane.

There was a while when everyone wondered if Jack and Christopher would both end up going to Vietnam, but that ended before either of them were old enough. So this stretch of Kansas highway was his big trip into the unknown.

Plenty of it was known, of course; he would have a 3-4 teaching load and be responsible for woodwind lessons as well as conducting the band and the chamber orchestra that was slightly larger than a string quintet but gave the college a bit of a cachet. Anyway, he could recruit more people, there had to be smart kids with violas who wanted college scholarships, that was practically why smart kids picked up the viola in the first place.

He thought for a minute about what his three kids might end up playing. He'd start them all on the clarinet, of course, the way Rosemary had sat them each in front of the

9

piano. But he suspected Meredith might switch to oboe, or maybe bassoon if he could convince her—a female bassoon player, that was like a walking college scholarship—and maybe Natalie would take after her mother and be a pianist after all. Though they would all be in band. Gruber kids always played in the band.

And Jackie, his namesake, the goes-without-saying-last-chance-for-a-son: Jack got a strong flute vibe off her. She went with the flow.

Jack turned on the radio, which was perpetually kept at the low end of the dial because that was where you always found NPR. He caught the overtones of a symphony buried beneath noise, and pushed through static to see if there was a better signal. There. Not a symphony, a concerto.

"Who can name what instrument this is?" he called to the backseat.

Rosemary, in the passenger seat, opened her eyes and then closed them again.

He realized quickly that he had stumped them all. They knew how to tell a violin from a clarinet, and a flute from a trumpet, but Meredith looked like she was actually thinking about this one, and not holding back so that Natalie could answer.

"Is it singing?" Natalie said.

"It does sound a little like singing," Jack said. "But it's an instrument. A brass instrument."

"Is it a baritone trumpet?" Meredith guessed.

"Do you mean a baritone horn?" Jack easily transitioned into the same voice he used as Dr. G, the "have you forgotten about the E flat?" nudge that was supposed to guide a student in the right direction. "It isn't a baritone, but you're on the right track."

"Is it a trumpet?" Natalie called out.

"Nope," Jack said. "Jackie, do you have a guess?"

"Trumpet trombone," Jackie said from her car seat, and Jack grinned because even his three-year-old could name instruments from the brass family. They were all Gruber kids, to be sure.

"It's a French horn," he finally told them. "This is Mozart's third horn concerto, second movement. How do you know it's the second movement?"

This time he could feel Meredith wait, to see if Natalie had an answer before she said hers. "It's slow."

"Correct," he told her. "Andante."

"Probably larghetto," Rosemary said, her eyes still closed.

"Your mom thinks it's larghetto," Jack said to the back seat. "Guess we'll find out."

Then they were all quiet again, to listen to the Horn Concerto No. 3 in E Flat, K447, and Jack kept the car steady on the highway and drove forward into their adventure. The road was unchanging, but every minute of it was something he had never seen before.

4. THE GRUBERS MEET THEIR NEW HOME.

"I'm thirsty!" Natalie called out, and Jack said "just suck on your spit and swallow it," and Rosemary thought *how can you even say such a thing*, the anger of being away from home for five days and being crammed next to each other in this car and having to explain to the girls that they couldn't go swimming in the motel pool because they didn't have swimsuits, and then wondering if she should have packed swimsuits so her girls could have this "first time in a swimming pool" experience which they might set down as a memory. But she knew that drying out damp swimsuits over the motel bathroom shower curtain would have been more work than she wanted, and they wouldn't have dried completely anyway, and the next night she would have had to tell the girls that they couldn't go swimming because their suits were still wet, and Meredith would have wanted to try drying them with the motel's hair dryer, which didn't even dry hair.

And Jack was right. They had passed a sign that read "Kirkland: 25 Miles," and she knew that he wasn't going to stop. Still: *suck on your spit?* Who says that to a child?

They were very close to their new home, but the view from the window was the same as it had been for the past two days. Cornfields and grass on both sides, green with yellowing tips, and no trees. Rosemary recognized she was being unforgiving. There were trees. There just weren't enough of them to be counted as a group.

She was thirsty too, and she started thinking about everything she would need to do before the day was over. They'd want to see the house first, and then they'd need to find somewhere to eat. Rosemary wondered if the electricity had been set up, if they could go to a grocery store instead of a restaurant and bring food back. She wondered if Jack would be willing to sit with the girls while she did the grocery shopping, because she could not imagine taking three of them in to the store, not when it would be after 7 p.m. and time for them to be going to bed. Not when they would all be hungry. Maybe it would be better to find fast food for now, and then put the girls to bed, and then she or Jack could go out and get food for the next day.

Rosemary leaned in to Jack, so the girls wouldn't hear her. "Should we stop at a McDonald's first?"

"There aren't any McDonald's here," Jack said. "We're in the country now!"

Rosemary fell back against her seat, irritated at Jack for not having prepared her for this, exhausted at the thought of all the work to come. She was sick of this car, sick of sitting, sick of wind-blown rest stops where she pulled wet packages of meat and cheese out of the cooler. Jack felt like he was playing pioneer, even though the real pioneers had gone in the other direction.

"Are you ready, girls?" Jack said, and Rosemary knew he meant all four of them. "That's the sign up there. Meredith, can you read that?"

It was so far away that Rosemary could barely read it, but Meredith had sharp eyes. "Kirkland, Missouri. Population 2,053." Then: "Did they change the sign after you got the job, or are they going to change it after we move in?"

"It's an estimation," Jack said. "They estimate that there are 2,053 people living here."

"The three is weird," Meredith said. Nobody responded to that, and she wanted to explain that the three was weird because it didn't fit with what she had learned about estimations on *Square One TV*, and she wanted to know why they didn't just count everybody. It would only take an afternoon to count everybody. She could count to two thousand in her head in five minutes.

But nobody asked her, and she thought about saying it again, but they had already passed the sign. And then they all saw houses.

The first houses were small and rectangular, like Grandma's house in Fresno, but after they passed Dad's college the houses got bigger, like the ones from *Mary Poppins*. Some of them had shutters and fancy porches. One of them had a tower.

"Which one is our house?" Natalie asked.

"We're almost there," Jack said, and then he was pulling into a driveway and Meredith saw a white house with a stained-glass window and a blue front porch, and she suddenly remembered having seen it before, when Mom showed her a photograph. It looked bigger than the picture.

Rosemary thought it looked smaller than the picture, and the siding was dirty, and the photo hadn't shown that the first porch step was rotted through. The stained-glass panel in the front window was pretty, though. She thought of Christmas, and putting a tree in front of that window, and the way the lights would shine through the colored glass.

"We're home, girls," Jack said.

Home was the blue-painted porch and the stained glass in the front window; home was a living room and a kitchen and a yard; home was an upstairs with three big rooms that the girls immediately claimed as their own.

"The three of you will share this room," Jack said, picking Jackie up so she could touch the ceiling. "But the room in the middle can be your playroom." He and Rosemary had already planned this, when they talked about the house and looked at the photos: a bedroom, a playroom, a guest room. They had already planned where the girls would go, and where the television would go, and where the piano would go. They had talked about everything.

"You didn't tell me there weren't any doors," Rosemary said.

Jack stopped, with his daughter in his arms, and looked around. He looked, and he began to laugh, and Meredith and Natalie ran out of the room that would be their bedroom and down the stairs—and Rosemary thought *are they going to run down the stairs without asking?* and realized they would—and then Jackie kicked to be put down because she could hear her sisters laughing and calling "No doors!" without her, and Jack let her down and Rosemary scooped her up before she could run, and carried her down the stairs to see Meredith and Nat running smudges on the hardwood floors, running and laughing in the empty rooms that had no doors, this wonderful big place that was their home now.

5. JACK FINDS A FRIEND FOR MEREDITH.

It was exactly like *Little House on the Prairie*, Meredith thought, because that home had no doors either, and Pa had put up a blanket the same way her dad put up a sheet as a door for her parents' bedroom. The girls' bedroom was left as it was, the light from the stairwell shining in to serve as the nightlight they now knew had been forgotten.

It was also like *Little House on the Prairie* because her mother had hurt herself when the moving van arrived and she and Dad were not careful with the boxes. Dad had to go to the store to get some ice, because they didn't have any yet in the freezer. It was easy to go to the grocery store here because it was just two blocks away. Not like in Portland where you had to get into the car and drive.

But today was going to be like *Betsy-Tacy*, because today she and her family were walking towards Daddy's college to meet a friend.

"I've found a friend for Meredith," Dad had said a day earlier, and Mom had said "just for Meredith?" and Meredith had gotten very quiet, so she could hear them. The friend was named Alex MacAllister, and she was Meredith's age, and she was smart. Her mother was a math professor. They were all going over to meet the MacAllisters, to see if they could be friends.

Meredith was wearing a pink dress and she had asked her mother to French braid her hair. Natalie had asked for a French braid too, but she was wearing shorts and a T-shirt that read "Duck Deli" on it. That wasn't the kind of thing you wore to meet a friend. Not the person whose name would be put next to yours like mush and milk.

She wondered if they ate mush and milk in Missouri. It was much closer to where Betsy and Tacy had lived than Portland. Once Meredith had asked her mother if Milwaukie was the place Betsy had made her song about, and her mother said no, the Oregon Milwaukie wasn't the same as the Wisconsin one.

Meredith and Natalie still had to hold Dad's hands as they crossed streets, and Mom came behind with Jackie, who was slower. They saw a tan house with green windows and a cement porch, and a girl sitting on the porch steps, reading a book.

"That's her," Meredith said.

"I think it is," Jack said. "I thought you might get along."

The girl had enormous red-framed glasses and tangled hair. She was not wearing shoes. By the time they got close enough to say hello, Meredith could see that she was reading *The Phantom Tollbooth*.

"Hi," she said. Her hair was the color of the freckles that covered her face and arms. "I'm Alex." Then she turned and leaned into the open screen door. "Mom! They're here!"

Mrs. MacAllister looked like Alex, only with brown glasses and paler hair. She came out onto the porch without shoes on. "Y'all must be the Grubers," she said.

"Most of us," Dad answered. "My wife is bringing up the rear with our three-year-old."

"Ah, that's right," Mrs. MacAllister said. "You've got three little girls. This is Alex. Say hello, Alex."

"I said hello," Alex said, and Meredith felt another pull of similarity towards this girl who was also told to do what she had already done on her own.

"I'm Meredith," she said.

Natalie immediately followed with "I'm Natalie," and by then Mom and Jackie were there, which meant it was time for the grownups to talk and the kids to stand there and stay quiet. They had spent a few afternoons on their trip to Kirkland visiting people, and Mom and Dad talked while Meredith and her sisters sat next to each other and waited. Sometimes Meredith tried to find the entire alphabet in the room, in bookcases and newspapers on the table and magazines. If there was a newspaper left open, and she was close enough to read it, she tried to find the alphabet in order, starting at the top of the page. Meredith was good at knowing how to stay quiet.

Except Alex wasn't like that. She said "come on," and left her book on the porch and started walking away like she expected Meredith and Natalie to follow her. Natalie did, and Meredith turned to look for Mom's permission, and Mrs. MacAllister said "oh, they're just going to the backyard," and so it was okay.

The backyard included an enormous white dog who ran up to them and began barking, and put his feet on Meredith's dress. "It's all right," Alex said. "That's just Newton." Meredith thought "like *Newton's Apple*," but kept the words inside herself because her mother had taught her not to say the names of TV shows or books that other people might not know.

Newton left them alone after it was clear neither of the new guests were interested in him, and they sat in the rubbery swings of Alex's swingset and talked.

"Where are you from?" Alex asked.

"Portland," Meredith said.

"I'm from Portland too," Natalie said.

They quickly worked out that Alex and Meredith were both going into second grade in the fall—and that Natalie was starting kindergarten—and that they both liked reading and watching PBS. It felt exciting to be in the backyard all by themselves, with a whole house between them and their parents. When they swung the swings high enough, the metal pole came out of the ground just a little.

Then Mrs. MacAllister came through the back door, to ask if they wanted cookies and juice. They went inside and Meredith saw that Alex's house was messy, but it was mostly messy with books and magazines, which she liked. She could definitely find the entire alphabet in here. The cookies were Chips Ahoy.

"How about I take the three of them swimming this afternoon, so you can have an afternoon to yourselves?" Mrs. MacAllister said, and Meredith and Natalie both turned to listen.

"They don't have suits," Mom said, but then Mrs. MacAllister said "Oh, I'm sure I've got some of Alex's old suits somewhere for your older girls, and nobody will mind what your youngest one wears, we can just put one of Alex's old T-shirts on her and she can splash her feet in the baby pool."

There was a little bit of discussion to figure out, but Alex grabbed one more cookie and ran off to her bedroom without waiting for the grownups to finish talking; she dug around in a drawer and tossed out two swimsuits for Natalie and Meredith to put on, and in a few minutes they were dressed to go, and ten minutes later they—and Mom, who didn't want to leave them alone—were at the Kirkland community pool.

The water looked blue from above but looked like nothing once you were inside, the same way it felt cold when Meredith first put her feet in and then stopped feeling cold once Alex laughed and said she had to put her whole head under the water, and then counted to three so she would do it. The swimsuit was a little too big, and Meredith kept one hand busy pulling it away from her stomach, feeling it slowly detach from her skin and make a floating balloon as the water came in to fill the gap.

Jackie was in the baby pool, and Mrs. MacAllister had introduced Natalie to a few friends her own age, so it was just her and Alex in their own little corner of the pool, deep enough that Meredith had to bounce on her toes to keep her head and shoulders above the surface. It was like being a ballerina; she could even stand on her toes and feel nothing but two tiny prickles of concrete under her skin. Alex quickly taught Meredith how to hang onto the side of the pool and kick, and how to turn a somersault under the water. Alex knew how to swim, but you didn't need to know how to swim to turn a somersault. Meredith figured out on her own that you needed to come up out of the water with your face first and your hair back, otherwise the wisps from your braid would stick to your forehead and get into your eyes.

Every once in a while somebody in the pool would scream "horsefly!" and then everyone would dive under the water and come up warily, looking around. Meredith knew what a horsefly was only from books, and did not know if it could sting or bite you. Once she came out of the water and said "Rocking-horse fly!" in an imitation of *Alice in Wonderland,* and Alex laughed.

Alex laughed a lot, and Meredith laughed, and then she had to go into the pool toilet because of the water and the laughter, and Alex came with her, and the two of them kept laughing. The pool toilet had curtains instead of doors, and it had signs that read "You Must Shower Before Entering Pool," and Alex laughed and said nobody ever did that. And then they turned the shower on anyway and jumped in and squealed, because the shower water was so cold, and the pool they were running back to—"No running!" called a lifeguard—was comfortable and warm.

By the end of the afternoon, Meredith and Alex were best friends. Meredith went home that night knowing that she would go back to Alex's house the next day, and maybe this time she wouldn't be scared of Newton. It was exactly like *Betsy-Tacy*, because they were friends and because she had brown hair and Alex had red hair. As Mom was getting Jackie and Nat ready for bed, Meredith pulled books out of the box labeled "Books" until she found *Betsy-Tacy*, and then she sat, with her chin resting on her knee, to study how to be a friend. She wanted to be ready for tomorrow.

6. MEREDITH AND ALEX GO TO THE LIBRARY.

Meredith had never met another person who had read the same books she had. In her old school there had been a library and the books were lined up on shelves by grade, with the kindergarten ones nearest the floor and the big chapter books at the top. They had told her she could only select books from the bottom two shelves and Meredith remembered feeling terrified, the way it was in her dreams sometimes when everything was wrong and she couldn't move.

And then a librarian came and asked if she could help, and Meredith couldn't remember how she had explained it, even though it had only happened two years ago. All she could remember was that the librarian reached up to the highest shelf and took down a book called *All-of-a-Kind Family*, and asked if Meredith would like to read that instead. There were five little girls on the cover, in dark dresses and white pinafores. Meredith said she would.

Now she and Alex went to the Kirkland library every week and used a stepstool to climb up to the highest shelves and checked out anything they wanted. When Meredith discovered that this library had a copy of *A Little Princess*, which she knew existed but had never seen, she kissed it. Alex laughed, and said "I've never seen a person kiss a book before," and Meredith didn't know why she had done it, except she had been wanting to read this book for such a long time and there it was, right on the shelf in her new hometown.

Alex's family turned out to be kind of like library books; they were spread out all over Kirkland, but they all came from the same place and you could recognize them if you looked closely. Alex's mother, who asked Meredith to call her Donna, was a Cory, and when the three of them would go to the library or the drugstore, they'd see one of Donna's cousins or half-sisters or uncles. Sometimes Donna would stop and talk, and Alex and Meredith would get to go on ahead, running into the drugstore to order phosphates. Alex picked different flavors every time, but Meredith tried a vanilla phosphate the very first time and found it perfect. She was nervous to try cherry or lemon or chocolate or any of the mixtures Alex dared them to make, because she didn't want to give up the chance to taste what she already loved best.

Sometimes Meredith worried that Alex didn't think she was brave. The first time Donna suggested Meredith go out into the backyard without shoes on she cried, because she hated the feeling of the dry grass under her feet but she knew she was supposed to do it because a grownup had said. But Donna didn't mind. She scooped Meredith up and took her into the bathroom and washed all the dead yellow flecks of grass off Meredith's feet, and then she gave her a hug and sent her back out in her sandals. Alex didn't say anything about it, and Meredith knew that meant they were friends.

Meredith had never had a friend who wasn't a sister. She had never known anyone like Alex, who walked down the sidewalks saying hello to everyone, who climbed up on a library stepstool without asking, who ran towards her father every evening shouting "Daddy, daddy, daddy!" Mike MacAllister was big and red-headed and he would lift Alex off the ground or tousle her tangled hair.

When Meredith went back to her own home she said "Hello," and whichever parent was in the living room said "Hello," and asked her how her visit had been, and Meredith said that they went to the library, or they went to the drugstore, or they played in Alex's room. Alex was good at playing. She liked making up stories too, so Meredith didn't have to always know what was coming next, and that was exciting. Sometimes when they played the story got so exciting that Meredith's head started buzzing and she stopped being able to see Alex's room clearly; she just saw Alex's face, and it was like Alex really was dressed like a princess and they really were going to escape the castle together, by rowing the boat that was also Alex's bed.

But Meredith didn't say that to her parents. She just said they played, or they went somewhere, and then her mom or her dad asked her to go play with Jackie or help set the table, and Meredith did that, because her parents had said, and later they would say grace and eat dinner and clean up and play a game and read stories and sing the good-night song and go to bed. This room didn't have a door and her chart had been thrown away, but Meredith could still run the chart in her head, and then she stopped because she was old enough not to need it anymore.

7. ROSEMARY SUGGESTS DINNER WITH THE MACALLISTERS.

Of course they started talking as soon as the song was over and their parents kissed them and went down the night-light stairs. Meredith was on the top bunk, and Nat was on the bottom, and Jackie was in her big-girl bed which was smaller than theirs but still retained its name. The three of them lay in the sticky Kirkland heat on top of neatly folded bedsheets, wearing nothing but T-shirts and underwear, and whispered to each other until they were asleep.

Below them, on the sofa that was slowly being covered with matched socks and dishtowels, their parents were talking too.

"We need to have the MacAllisters over for dinner," Rosemary said. "Meredith spends so much time there."

"I can ask Donna about their schedule," Jack said. "I'll see her at the faculty meeting tomorrow. Do you think Friday would work?"

"I think so," Rosemary said. "Do you think maybe pork chops and salad and rolls? Do you think that'll be enough?" She remembered the way Alex grabbed handfuls of cookies, and how Meredith's stories upon coming home always seemed to involve food. Donna was fat, with hips that stuck out on either side like chicken drumsticks, and Mike was tall and broad. She didn't want them to sit at her table and leave hungry.

"We could just get pizza," Jack said.

"I don't want to just get pizza." Rosemary wanted to fill this new home with something that came from her own hands, something that was identifiably hers. She had already begun to realize that living in a small town meant being known for things, the way the librarian had talked to her about Meredith's reading, or the way she had been stopped, on the street, by an older woman who wanted to say hello to the mother of those three pretty girls. She had seen Rosemary and the girls in the grocery store the other day, and they had been so well-behaved!

So whatever they served at this first dinner gathering would be something they'd become known for over time, something that Donna or Mike might mention to someone else at the college, something that would establish them as one of the smart people, or whatever it was they wanted to be. Jack had come home the other day saying they needed to start going to the Methodist church, not the Baptist church or the Catholic one. It had been a piece of advice he had heard from someone else at the college, someone who had already recognized Jack as being "one of the smart ones," because even in colleges there were people who were smarter than others.

And Rosemary knew it all mattered, where they went to church and whether she brushed her girls' hair and what they served at dinner. Donna MacAllister could let Alex run around with slept-in hair and dirty feet because she was a Cory, and because she had already done the work of leaving Kirkland, going to graduate school, and coming back with a husband. She'd always be one of the smart ones.

"I'd like to paint the kitchen," she said. "I'd like to do it in stencils."

The kitchen was not stenciled by the time the MacAllisters came for dinner, but Jack had gone to the Nearly New store while Rosemary watched the girls and come back with an angel food cake pan, which Rosemary had asked for, and a grill, which was a surprise. Rosemary watched through the kitchen window as Jack washed the grill down with a wet rag, cleaning off the dust and spiderwebs. She loved him so much.

Alex hadn't come over to Meredith's house as often as Meredith had gone to hers, because going to Meredith's house meant playing with Natalie and Jackie as well, and Natalie was fun but Jackie was way too young and it felt more like minding her than playing. Meredith's house was the only place Alex had been in that had a whole separate room just for play. Everyone else played with their toys in their bedroom, or sometimes in the basement, but upstairs the Gruber girls' bedroom was tidy and empty, the three beds always made. Everything else happened in the playroom.

Sometimes there would be a toy that made it downstairs, usually one of Jackie's, and Alex could tell because it would be in a wicker basket next to the sofa that Meredith called the "go-upstairs basket." That night there was a toy phone in that basket, the familiar white phone face with the blue wheels that Alex had played with too, when she was a baby.

Now Alex looked at that phone and wondered why they couldn't just go up to the playroom like they usually did, why she had to stand next to her mother the way Meredith and her sisters were standing next to Mrs. Gruber while the grownups talked. All three sisters were wearing dresses, and they had matching barrettes in their hair, pink ribbons with a rose in the middle, that Alex's aunt Tracy sold at the Dollar Store.

Donna wondered if she should have dressed up for this. She was wearing a T-shirt from that spring's Missouri Math Olympiad, and she was very aware that Rosemary had put on lipstick and she was wearing a shirt that featured a multiplication sign with eyeballs. Rosemary seemed to be trying to do the good-wife thing. Showing off the piano Jack had bought for her, with the back to the wall so no one could see that "Kirkland College" was still painted on it. It was something everyone already knew, though; that Jack had asked the department chair where he could buy a used piano for his wife, and the music department not only sold Jack this one, they also sent along the brass professor to help Jack get it up the porch steps. The joke was that both sides thought they had gotten a great deal.

They admired the piano and then all eight of them walked through the house to the back porch to admire Jack's new grill. Donna already knew about that too. Her cousin Linda had told her about Jack coming in to buy an angel food cake pan, and how she saw him looking at that old grill and sold it to him. People started passing her news about the Grubers, because they saw Meredith and Alex together and assumed she would want to know.

They sat down to Jack's freshly-grilled salmon and a bowl of salad with two wooden tongs sticking out, the four girls on little pink plastic chairs around a card table, and Jack said grace and all three of his girls said it along with him, reaching out to take Alex's hands. Donna knew they were nice people, you could already tell that they were going to bring more than their share to the faculty potluck and that Jack would be the kind of professor that President Barnes called "an asset to the school." She already knew this from getting to know Jack, and from the news people passed to her about this new family, but now she was seeing a bit into their private everyday. Rosemary had used that pan to make an angel-food cake from scratch, and Donna could picture her making the orange glaze too, standing over the stove and stirring a saucepan of melting sugar. Donna would have used can frosting, or bought a white cake from the store.

Afterwards, when the MacAllisters were gone and the girls were in bed, Rosemary said "I think that went well."

Jack was reading a spy novel on the sofa. He said "Oh! Um-hmm," like he hadn't expected to be having a conversation, and also like he hadn't expected it to go anything *but* well.

"We should do it again," Rosemary said, settling in next to Jack with her magazine. She liked that they were already becoming a different family in Kirkland. They had enough money to bring home a surprise grill, they had started saying grace, they had three well-behaved girls, and she had worn lipstick and a skirt and hosted another family at her table. Donna had complimented her orange glaze, and Rosemary wondered if that meant the beginning of becoming a person known for her cooking, even though she also knew that Donna hadn't seen the first batch, the one that burned. Donna hadn't heard her swear, and then look behind her to see if any little ears were listening. Donna hadn't seen that Rosemary had done all of this in her nightgown because it was so hot that she wanted to wait until afterwards to shower, and she hadn't seen that in the middle of this Rosemary's mother had called and Rosemary had been short with her because she was cooking and in a hurry, calling to the girls to say hello to their grandmother and then half-listening to her mother talk before quickly hanging up the phone. Donna hadn't seen Rosemary scrape the glaze into the garbage and start over again, and tell Natalie that it had been "for practice," and no, they couldn't taste it.

But Rosemary also knew that practice was a part of becoming. She would teach her girls how to practice the piano the same way she had learned, and she would practice her orange glaze until she was known for it, and she would figure out what else she wanted to be known for. She felt, as she turned the pages of the *Good Housekeeping* she had bought at the store, that she could become any of these women. They were so new to this town that she could become anybody she wanted.

8. NATALIE TAKES KINDERGARTEN READINESS.

Natalie wore a red-and-white checked dress with strawberry buttons, and she could feel the ends of her hair brush her chin. She held on to Mommy's purse with one hand as Mommy pushed the stroller and Meredith walked a few steps ahead, in her dress that was blue.

Yesterday Mommy had given them afternoon baths and then asked them to go out on the front porch and sit still while she cut their wet hair. She asked them not to put their feet near the broken part of the step because Daddy hadn't fixed it yet. Then Mommy put one knee on each side of Natalie to hold her in place as she cut and combed and cut again, and pulled Natalie's hair straight with her fingers to make sure it was even.

They all had just-alike hair now, all new-school just-alike hair and different colored barrettes that had come from the same package. Natalie's barrettes were red, and Meredith's were blue, and Jackie's were yellow. Mommy had let them toss the old hair in the yard, for the birds. Meredith had not been happy.

Now they were going to school for Orientation. They were close enough that Natalie could see the tent. She had never seen a school with a tent before. When they lived in Portland, she had gone to preschool.

They stopped at the crosswalk and looked up and down the empty street for cars, because Rosemary knew you had to do it every time or one of her girls would forget, when they were older. She said the sing-song they had made up—"left, then right, then left again"—and heard three voices sing it along with her. Then they crossed, all together,

27

Meredith not bothering to seek out her mother's hand.

Rosemary knew Meredith was mad about the haircut. She had been watching the girls' hair in the Midwestern humid heat, seen enough long sticky strands attach themselves to a sweaty neck or arm. Nat's hair was like hers, which meant it looked thick and shiny no matter what, but Meredith and Jackie had Jack's hair, which brushed out fine and smooth but ended up clustered in limp locks like the wax on a melting candle.

Now they all had neat hair, cut off their neck in sweet little-girl bobs, and Rosemary was the one who needed a haircut, but that would have to wait until after the girls were in school. She had used one of the girls' elastics to pull her hair back into a ponytail, wondering if it made her look younger or just made her look silly. She hadn't known what to wear to this event, so she put on a jean skirt and a T-shirt with pink stripes that felt nicer than the other ones. As she led her three girls under the tent she saw that most of the other moms were wearing shorts, and most of the kids were wearing shorts too. People in Kirkland only seemed to dress up for church.

"Rosemary!" Donna was in shorts, and the Kirkland College graphic on her T-shirt was coming apart in rivulets. "Hello, girls! Natalie, don't you look just like Strawberry Shortcake."

Meredith knew that Natalie didn't look like Strawberry Shortcake; Strawberry Shortcake had a bonnet and red hair and a pink dress with a white apron. Natalie had strawberry buttons down the front of her dress. And Donna hadn't said anything about her, which Meredith knew to mean she didn't look like anything. Her dress was blue checked, like Dorothy's, but nobody would say she looked like Dorothy anymore because she didn't have braids. She had short hair.

Meredith hated her hair because she no longer knew who to be. Sometimes when she was at church, or when her parents went shopping and they had to stand still and be quiet, she would pretend to be someone else and imagine what life would be like as them. What would Mary Ingalls be able to tell about the Methodist church just by listening to the people and feeling the rough fabric on the chairs?

And now it was harder to imagine herself as Dorothy, stepping out into a world of color, pretending that the grocery store was Oz and she hadn't seen any of it before, staring at the shiny green apples next to the ones with the little brown spots. Not even when she was wearing a blue checked dress.

After she had gotten her hair cut she had gone upstairs and looked at the picture of Betsy in *Betsy-Tacy and Tib*, because she wanted to see someone whose hair looked like hers. Mom hadn't let her keep a lock of hair, which would have made it a little better because she could have felt more like Betsy. Betsy's hair grew back, and it didn't stop her from making up stories.

Then Alex came running up, and she was wearing a blue dress like Meredith's except hers had a fish print on it. "Do you want to meet our teacher?" she said. Meredith looked at her mom, hoping she would say yes. "She's right over there," Alex said, pointing to a blonde woman in a green jumper with an apple stitched on the pocket.

"Stay under the tent," Rosemary said, "where I can see you."

"You know," Donna said, after they had gone, "she wanted to wear a dress today because of Meredith. They are already such a pair."

Rosemary watched the two girls talking to their second-grade teacher and thought how grown up Meredith and Alex looked, engaging in this conversation. She saw Alex say something that made them all laugh, and then she saw Meredith say something that made them all laugh, and she saw her daughter smile again, the real smile that seemed so rare. Alex was a good friend for her, a nice smart girl who might help her kid relax a little.

"You make those dresses, right?" Donna asked. "That must be hard."

"It isn't that hard," Rosemary said. She had been making clothes since she was a teenager. She and her best friend had spent Saturday afternoons picking out fabric and patterns for their prom dresses, and then cutting and sewing and taking turns pinning up each other's hems. Rosemary remembered how quiet and tidy her friend's home was; how she looked around at the ballerina figurines and the mugs stacked upside-down in rows, dripping dry next to the clean sink, and decided she would have a home like that when she grew up. Except now she knew ballerina figurines were tacky. "Do you sew at all?"

"Never picked it up," Donna said. "Except for one summer in 4-H. I made a pillow."

There was a general rush of excitement under the tent; a man was wheeling up a white box with a metal lid, and the words "Sno-Cone" stenciled on the side.

"Better get your girls in line for snowcones," Donna said, as Rosemary watched every child under the tent begin to cluster around the man and the white box. She wondered if the snowcones would cost money, and if she'd have to be the mean mom if they cost too much, but as the first kids started peeling off, gripping sticky colored ice in paper cones, she realized they must be free.

So she took Jackie's hand and walked Jackie and Natalie over to the end of the line, but they were stopped by two women—one of them short and round, in the general "apple and schoolbooks" outfit that designated her as a teacher, and the other tall and thin with a stiffly-sprayed cluster of gray curls.

"You must be Rosemary Gruber," the older woman said. "I'm Peg Howard, the principal, and this is Deanna Cory, our kindergarten teacher."

"Hi," Deanna said to Rosemary, and then she squatted down to Natalie's level. "I'm Miss Cory. Are you going to be in kindergarten with me this year?"

"Yes," Natalie said, with one eye on the snowcone line.

"We need to do Kindergarten Readiness," Peg Howard continued. "Most people do it at the beginning of the summer, but you hadn't moved here yet."

Natalie knew the women were talking about her, but she also knew that all the other kids were over there, in a line, and that they were coming back eating something that Natalie had never seen before. Something with red or yellow or purple ice in it. Natalie wanted one, and she wanted to be where the other kids were. Some of the kids she remembered from the pool, and they were waving, and she waved back, and then she felt Mommy's hand come down on her shoulder, to hold her in place.

Then the woman with gray hair asked Natalie to come with her, and walked her away from the snowcones and the other kids. They walked up to the school and opened one of the big doors with the gray bars. Inside it was quiet, and the lights were off, and Natalie's sandals made slapping sounds against the floor.

The woman took Natalie into a small room with white walls and said that she was the principal, and that she wanted to ask Natalie a few questions. She asked Natalie if she knew her name and her address and her telephone number, and then she asked Natalie to say the alphabet, and then she took a book from a basket next to her desk and asked if Natalie could read it.

Natalie could read but she didn't like it. She kept her eyes wide open and tried not to blink. This book had big letters, though, and it had pictures that helped her guess. Cat, dog, ball.

Then the woman asked if Natalie could count for her. Natalie counted to ten, and then stopped.

"Do you know any numbers higher than that?" the woman asked.

Natalie knew from PBS and from Meredith telling her that numbers went all the way to infinity. She nodded.

"Can you keep counting?" the woman prodded, and so Natalie continued, working her way up past twenty and thirty and then fifty and eighty and ninety. She could feel sweat on the back of her neck. She did not like the sound of her voice in this quiet school. She wondered what she was missing, under the tent outside. All the other kids were there and she was here. She wanted to be there too. She wanted a snowcone.

When Natalie reached one hundred, she paused and looked at the gray-haired woman. The woman didn't say anything. Natalie suddenly thought that the test must not end until she reached a number she didn't know. She thought of all the snowcones and the kids in line. There wouldn't be any left.

"Two hundred," she said, watching the woman to see if she could tell. "Three hundred. Four hundred. Five hundred."

"Thank you," the woman said. "You can stop now." She made a note in a book, and then walked Natalie back outside. There were still snowcones, and the man put a squirt of both orange and red in hers. She saw the kids she knew from the pool, and she clutched her snowcone in its wet paper and ran over to them, forgetting anything else existed except these new friends and the taste of cold sweet ice in her mouth. She ran out from under the tent into the sunlight, dripping snowcone onto her red checked dress and its strawberry buttons.

FALL 1989

9. MEREDITH WRITES ABOUT HER WORST FEAR.

Meredith's hair almost brushed her shoulders as she leaned over her desk and wrote about her worst fear.

She had thought about picking a second-worst fear, like the wasps that appeared in the corners of the playroom windows and then flew in threatening swoops over her and her sisters' heads. They could not play in a room where there was a wasp; they would run to the bedroom and hope it would not follow through the open doorway.

But Meredith had always understood school as a place where you tried your hardest, and even though it was easier to try your hardest at spelling tests or Around The World—another game where the buzzing would take over Meredith's head as she heard herself shout out "15!" and walk to the next desk—she was going to try her hardest at writing this paragraph. She would not only name her worst fear, she would make sure everyone else understood just how scary it was.

When they were done, they all had to read them aloud. This was Meredith's least favorite part of second grade; they spent hours every day taking turns listening to each other read. Sometimes when they read chapter books Meredith would keep one finger in the page they were on while she lifted up the corners of the other pages so she could read ahead. When Miss Anderson walked around to her cluster of desks, Meredith would put all of the corners back but keep a second finger in her new place.

Meredith listened to Kristin L. and Kristin B. and Andy and Sara read about spiders and haunted houses and bad dreams. When it was her turn, she read aloud what she knew would be scarier than all of that, if only because she had written it better:

> *Last Saturday Alex and I went to Alex's cousin's house to play Atari. He had a game called Countermeasure. The game is about shooting tanks and finding codes. Once I finished the level without finding the code, so when the screen asked what the code was I just guessed. Then the TV screen went dark. I did not know what was going to happen. Out of the darkness came a scary laughing skull. I leapt up and turned off the TV. I never want to play Countermeasure again. The laughing skull is my worst fear.*

Meredith wondered if Miss Anderson would respond—she sometimes did, when Meredith read her paragraphs aloud—but instead Miss Anderson said "Thank you, Meredith. Jeff?" and the readings continued. The whole classroom was by then tired of these stories, but there were two more clusters of desks to go.

And then it was Alex's turn.

> *My worst fear is death. Death is frightening in two ways. When someone you love dies, that person is gone forever. You can never talk to them again. When my grandpa died, I was sad because I loved him and now I will never get to see him again. Death is also frightening because someday I will die. I will be gone forever too.*

Meredith's head buzzed and her body tingled and she felt her heartbeat inside of her and she sat very still so nobody else could see. Someone else was reading but she wasn't paying attention, not even the half-attention she usually paid when people read aloud.

She had never thought to be afraid of death, but she knew, as soon as her head quieted down, that it was the worst fear. She understood that the reason the laughing skull had been scary was because it was a symbol of death. Everything goes dark. You are gone forever. Being scared of wasps was just being scared of getting stung, which was different. That was why wasps had been a second-worst fear.

Meredith was also jealous that Alex had known this and she had not. She and Alex had always been the fastest readers, the best spellers, the quickest voices in Around

The World, and Alex's paragraph had been so much better than hers. It wasn't fair. Meredith would have written about death too, if she had known it was the worst fear.

But now she knew. And she sat in her second-grade classroom, trying to figure out if everyone else had just learned it too.

10. JACK REHEARSES THE KIRKLAND COLLEGE SYMPHONIC BAND.

When Jack was alone in his office, he sang. Sometimes when he ran down the back staircase to get to the band room, he kept singing, his feet making the 6/8 rhythm on the stairs as he hummed the trumpet fanfare in Lincolnshire Posy. He loved everything about Kirkland College: the students whom he was teaching to master the Circle of Fifths, the woodwind students who arrived weekly for private lessons, the chamber orchestra that was making their way, one measure at a time, to the end of Schubert's Unfinished Symphony.

He had big plans about growing his chamber group, which was not only the weakest of any of Kirkland's choirs and ensembles, but was also well aware of the fact. He spent his afternoons coaxing music out of students who, had they been more talented, would have spent their adolescent afternoons practicing while dreaming of scholarships and symphony orchestras. Most of them wanted to be elementary or high school music teachers, and since each music major at Kirkland was required to perform in two ensembles, the chamber orchestra was mostly made up of students who couldn't sing.

The band, on the other hand—that was an immense group, and it made a powerful sound. There was still a bit of fuzz around the edges, where the first and second chair instruments couldn't quite cover up the sound of the third chair ones, but Jack spent a lot of time tuning and retuning the group, focusing his eyes on the students who needed the most help, so they would see him paying attention and be inspired to pay attention in return.

"You make us tune between every piece, Dr. G!" a student had said, but in a way that made it clear, to the rest of the band: *we like Dr. Gruber.* There were always a few students who made that decision, and the rest of the classroom followed.

Jack had been a little worried when those same students had complained about Lincolnshire Posy being "hard," because it wasn't that hard at all, the entire thing could be sung or whistled as you ran down a flight of stairs. What he really worried about, though, was how these students didn't seem to be musically curious. There were a few who were, of course, like the skinny, floppy-haired freshman who sat in the Listening Library half-conducting with one hand while his shoulders twitched, unconsciously, to the rhythm of whatever came into his headphone-cupped ears. This was the student who would come bounding into Music Theory class announcing that he had discovered this great new composer named Anton Webern, and the rest of the class would shift in their seats and make their decision: *we don't like you.*

Eventually they would all play Carmina Burana together, the band and the string kids and the two choirs. He'd get the theater kids to build a set and come up with some costumes and dancing. That was Jack's plan, for three years down the road. It would be the sort of performance that would become part of his tenure portfolio.

Until then he would work with what was in front of him. Today, he and the band would put their instruments down and just clap rhythms, the melody against the countermelody, one section at a time until Percy Grainger's lost lady was finally found.

11. ROSEMARY GOES TO THE BANK.

Rosemary's piece of cake had a blue flower on the edge, the kind that cracked into pieces when you stuck a plastic fork into it. There were bits of blue frosting resting on top of the bank lobby's maroon carpet, waiting for an accidental misstep to grind them into the fibers.

"Ro, honey, you don't have to do that," Bobbie Jo said, as Rosemary bent over to pick up a piece of hardened blue petal. Bobbie Jo was one of the Kirkland women who kept one eye on everybody else's whereabouts, moving her glasses up and down her nose as needed.

"It's like she works here," Marcie said. Marcie was only an afternoon away from not working at the Kirkland Central Bank, and the sheet cake that read "Welcome Baby Stiles" was in her honor. The flowers over the chocolate half of the cake were pink, and the ones over the vanilla half of the cake were blue. So far more people seemed to think Marcie was going to have a girl, or else they just preferred chocolate.

Rosemary had started stopping by the bank after walking the girls to school. Natalie and Meredith were in the big building, the one the entire town called "Rix" since the Kirkland school served students who lived both in Kirkland and on Rural Route IX. Rosemary had heard that some farm kids rode the bus for 45 minutes every morning, but she had not yet been in Kirkland long enough to drive the rural route and see the farms. She wanted to, though. She wanted to know more about where they lived, and whether they came home from their long afternoon bus ride and went straight into a red-painted barn, to feed the animals.

Jackie went to the Sunshine Day Care and Preschool, in a quonset hut right behind Rix that shared the school's playground. When Marcie came back from her maternity leave, she'd drop Baby Stiles off at Sunshine and walk the two blocks over to the bank. Then, around noon, she would take her lunch break and walk over to Sunshine with the other working moms, to nurse her baby and feel the warmth of tiny baby fingers around her thumb.

Rosemary saw the working moms, wearing their hair salon smocks or grocery store name badges, as she and the other stay-at-home moms came to pick up their kids from preschool or morning kindergarten. Noon at the quonset hut was a cluster of Kirkland mothers, and Rosemary had only started to learn their names—though they all knew who she was, because the Grubers were still "the new family."

But Rosemary knew Bobbie Jo and Marcie and Carolyn. The three of them took turns staffing the two teller stations at the Kirkland Central Bank, and Rosemary stopped into the bank nearly every day to say hello. At first she had actual business to do, getting the accounts set up and dropping off Jack's paychecks. She'd come by, ready to add a new set of sums into her bank passbook, and then Bobbie Jo would say "Ro, don't you need to get your girls?" and Rosemary would run over to the quonset hut because it was past noon.

Bobbie Jo acted like she was in charge, but that was only because she was tall enough to hover over the rest of them and old enough to have photos of her grandkids in her wallet. She referred to herself, sometimes, as "grandmaw," in that Midwestern twang that only seemed to carry in the voices of older people. Carolyn was actually in charge. She worked her teller shifts, scheduled the other teller shifts, and was the person who gave reports to the bank president. Even on her days off, she'd often stop by to see how things were doing. Rosemary suspected that Carolyn stopped by for the same reason she did: because it was fun to stand around the lobby and chat.

Rosemary both liked and admired Carolyn. She had walked into the bank on that first day and had been a little intimidated by both the tall, gray-haired woman with the beak-like glasses and the shorter, brunette woman in an eggshell blouse, and then the older woman had said "You must be Rosemary Gruber," and the shorter woman smiled and came out from behind the teller station to shake Rosemary's hand and introduce herself.

And that was Carolyn. She was unmarried, she had no children, she wore a skirt suit and pumps nearly every day (though the jacket spent most of the time hanging on the back of her chair), and she lived with her parents. Rosemary had seen them come in to the bank; a quiet woman who did not seem to know where she was, and a man with long, straight hair. Carolyn's hair was cut just above the shoulder, and she often wore it pulled back in a gold clip. She was one of the few people in Kirkland who always looked dressed up.

Over time, Rosemary learned that Carolyn thought of it more as "my parents live with me," since she was the one paying for the small house they rented on the north end of town. She learned that Carolyn would laugh sometimes about "dating in your 40s" but never seemed to go on any actual dates. Carolyn laughed often, as if she were happy, but there was a briskness to it, as if she were in a hurry to get her laughter over with and move on to the next thing.

One morning, when there was no one else in the bank lobby—Carolyn and Bobbie Jo were at the teller stations, but Bobbie Jo was taking her smoke break—Carolyn told Rosemary that she felt a bit like a parent, too. Like she was a parent to her own parents. Rosemary knew that it wasn't quite the same but didn't want to correct Carolyn because it would seem rude, just like she knew that most of the questions she wanted to ask Carolyn about her life and her heritage, like whether there had ever been more American Indian families in Kirkland or if she'd ever felt discriminated against, would seem rude.

And now Rosemary stood in the bank lobby with a crumb of blue frosting clutched in a napkin, and Marcie was smiling at her as if she knew a secret, and Carolyn said from behind her teller window, "Well, how would you like to work here, Rosemary?"

"Just while I'm on leave," Marcie said. "I want my job back."

"I don't know," Rosemary said. "I hadn't ever thought about it." But she could tell, by looking at Bobbie Jo and Marcie and Carolyn, that they had thought about it, and that they had already decided she would say yes. Which, she realized, she probably would.

"Come back to my office," Carolyn said, "and we'll talk."

Rosemary hadn't known until that minute that Carolyn had an office. She felt a shaking sugar nervousness in her stomach, as if all of this were happening too quickly for her to make a thoughtful decision, but her mind covered that feeling with an image of herself in a skirt suit, walking into an office of her own.

Carolyn explained that the job would be four days a week, 9 a.m. to 3:30 p.m. It would pay $4.75 an hour, and Jackie and Natalie could go to day care on the afternoons Rosemary was working. Three minutes later, Rosemary was fishing her drivers' license out of her purse so Carolyn could make a photocopy, and writing down her Social Security Number and address on the tax forms. She started to write their old Portland address and had to reshape the first two numbers, drawing over them in heavier ink.

After they were done and Carolyn had shaken Rosemary's hand, Rosemary wondered if she should have asked Jack. Not asked him, that wasn't right, but called him. Just to make sure there wasn't any reason for her not to take this job. But she thought, as she walked to the quonset hut to pick up Nat and Jackie, that he didn't know what she did with her time most mornings anyway, so it didn't matter—and tonight she would be able to surprise him with her good news, the way he had come home to announce that he had gotten the job at Kirkland College.

She also realized that she finally had a question to ask Carolyn that wasn't rude. She could ask her where people in Kirkland went to buy office clothes.

12. ROSEMARY'S MOTHER VISITS KIRKLAND.

Meredith turned eight on November 11, and on November 9, her grandma arrived. Dad drove all the way to St. Louis to pick her up from the airport, and she was sitting in the living room when Mom walked Meredith, Natalie, and Jackie home.

It was hard for Meredith not to look at the couch, because it was covered with presents. She couldn't stop herself from looking, even though she said "Hello" and "I love you too" and let herself be squeezed in to her grandma for a hug. Grandma didn't have a special name like Grandma Gruber had. She was just Grandma, short and soft and slightly sour-smelling. The hugs felt like love but Meredith always held her breath until they were over.

"Well, don't you look grown up!" Grandma said. Meredith thought Grandma might be referring to her birthday, except she said the same thing to Natalie and Jackie. "They're all getting so big!" she finished, turning towards Mom, who was sitting on the arm part of the couch because there was no space next to the presents.

Rosemary knew that her mother had brought birthday presents for all the girls, to make up for her not being able to see them on each of their birthdays, but she still felt angry about all the Barbies and ponies spread out next to her. She had heard the girls talking in their bedroom the other night, chattering about how Grandma was going to bring them a lot of presents, and she felt like it was wrong somehow, that this was what they wanted *and* what they had received. With their Grandma Gruber they baked cookies and read stories and played the same faded version of Chutes and Ladders that Jack had once played. Her mom showed up with piles of plastic garbage, and on a Thursday, too. She couldn't wait until the weekend, when Jack wouldn't have had to cancel two classes and a rehearsal to drive the six hours round trip to pick her up.

At least there were books. She had asked her mom to bring books, and everyone who knew Meredith understood that she'd rather get books than Barbies, but as she watched her mother hand out pink ponies and blonde dolls and a boxed set of *The Chronicles of Narnia*, she heard Meredith say "Thank you, but we already have these books. You should give them to someone else." There was always something she had forgotten to teach them. She'd have to talk to Meredith later and explain how she had been rude. Then Meredith would mope around for the rest of the day, because she had accidentally done something wrong. It was so stressful, having your mother in your home.

When Grandma gave Jackie a white box that had both a My Little Pony *and* a girl doll inside, Jackie clutched the box to her chest and began to turn around the room in a little circle. This was hers. It was not Natalie's or Meredith's. When they played, she would get to hold this girl doll and make it say things.

Jackie began singing. "I'm a girl and I'm a pony, these are both my friends." She stopped, held the box out, and looked through the plastic at the two toys inside. "These are both my friends," she sang, louder.

"Jackie, be quieter," she heard Mommy say.

"Do you want another—"

"I think she is happy with what she has."

"THESE ARE BOTH MY FRIENDS!"

She saw her mother's hand come down on her new box. "Jackie, I asked you to be quiet and you are being loud. Do we need to take these away until you can be quiet?"

Jackie felt her whole body tense, the last bit of awareness she had before the tears and screams came out. "NO! NO! NO! I WANT THEM! DON'T TAKE THEM AWAY!"

She heard her mother say "I've got this," and kept screaming because now she was being picked up and carried away from Grandma and her sisters and her new toy. She screamed because she wanted to be back downstairs, not upstairs on her big-girl bed with Mommy sitting in the doorway. She screamed until it was just crying, and then she cried until she felt sleepy instead of sad.

"Are you okay?" Mommy asked. Jackie nodded her head and ran her sleeve across her face to make her nose feel better. "No, Jackie, let's get a tissue." Mommy stood up and took a tissue out of the box on the dresser. "Do you need me to help you blow?" Jackie shook her head and tried really hard to blow into the tissue. Then she used her finger to get the rest out.

"Do you know what you did that was wrong?" Mommy said.

"I was loud when you said to be quiet," Jackie said.

"Are you going to do that again?" Mommy asked.

"No," Jackie said, because that was what you had to say to grownups. She knew she would be loud again. At preschool they kept asking her to use her inside voice, and she didn't understand how to make her voice what they wanted.

"Give me a hug," Mommy said. "Let's go wash your hands and see what Grandma and your sisters are doing."

When Rosemary returned Jackie to her sisters and her grandma, she said "This town has changed her! She used to be my quiet baby!" by way of apology. She felt like she had to apologize to her mother, because her youngest daughter had a temper tantrum within ten minutes of being in her presence. Not that preschoolers weren't supposed to have temper tantrums sometimes, but... well, it was true, a little bit. Meredith had been her intense baby, demanding and angry until she taught herself how to read. Nat had been her happy baby, and still was. Jackie, arriving after Rosemary had her hands full with two toddlers, had been the quiet baby. It was hard not to miss that, the little girl who was content with whatever her two older sisters offered her. Rosemary didn't know if it was Kirkland or the afternoons in day care or just a phase.

Now the couch and the floor were covered in cardboard and plastic, and Natalie and Jackie were picking up each new pony doll in turn, discussing their attributes and giving them personalities, and Meredith appeared to be reading two books simultaneously. Rosemary's mother, crouched down in the middle of the detritus, looked so happy to have provided this. Rosemary felt Jack come up behind her—where had he been during all of this, anyway?—and put his hand gently on her arm as if to say *I know how you feel. It'll all be okay, and your mother will leave in five days.*

WINTER 1989

13. CAROLYN HOSTS A CHRISTMAS PARTY.

Carolyn had the party at the drugstore, hanging a little wreath on the Kirkland Central Bank's door that read "Back in one hour!" while keeping one eye on her watch to hold them to it. She had thought about holding the party in her office, but that wouldn't have seemed like much of a party, and she had thought about holding the party in the living room of her house, but she felt embarrassed at the idea of inviting these women who all had husbands and children and grandchildren of their own to come into her small, quiet home, with her parents sitting in their side-by-side recliners. She didn't know how they imagined she lived—she was pretty sure they didn't imagine it at all—but she did not want to give them a picture of her reality.

So she picked the drugstore with the painted snow on the windows, now several shades whiter than the real snow on the edges of the sidewalk. She and Bobbie Jo and Rosemary and Marcie crowded into a booth, and Marcie pulled out the newest photos of baby Cody, and Bobbie Jo pulled out photos of her grandchildren on Santa's lap.

Rosemary did not have any photos of her girls on Santa's lap. It felt like a waste of money to pay someone to take a Polaroid and slide it into a white paper frame. Bobbie Jo had driven her grandchildren 40 minutes to the mall Santa in Delacroix, but Rosemary had been waiting until the bank's Santa was scheduled to arrive. It was the bank president in a Santa suit, of course, but Carolyn had told her that he would let kids sit on his lap and then give them a miniature candy cane afterwards.

Maybe Rosemary could get a picture then. It would be something nice to send to the grandparents, if she could get them developed in time. She was already late on sending her Christmas cards out, because it seemed like every evening was full of school concerts or church caroling parties—and the ones that weren't had to be filled with homework and piano practice and sewing the girls' matching red velvet Christmas dresses together, and doing the dishes that had started to pile up, and decorating the tree and putting an electric candle in every window.

There was also the business of trying to reconcile the presents she and Jack had already purchased for the girls with the lists that each girl brought home from her respective classroom, "letters to Santa" in various states of handwriting. Rosemary had never had the Santa talk with Meredith, but she suspected that Meredith had figured it out, because this year Meredith seemed to be much less interested in making sure Santa got her letter. Maybe Alex told her.

Meredith had not told Natalie and Jackie, though, and Rosemary would have to thank her for that later, after she was sure Meredith knew. This was the first year Jackie had picked up on the idea of Santa as a magical gift dispensary, which Rosemary knew was directly related to her attendance at the Sunshine Day Care and Preschool. Jackie could not stop talking about what Santa was going to bring her, and what she would say when she got to meet Santa, and how many days there were until she got to sit on Santa's lap. Jackie knew that some of her day care friends had already gotten to meet Santa, and she was very excited about her turn.

Natalie's holiday wishlist still held the expectations that Grandma and Grandpa Gruber had set: Santa brings candy, small dolls, the types of things that can actually fit into a child-sized stocking. This was the first year that the family would not be spending both Christmas Eve and Christmas morning at Jack's parents' home; the first year that Rosemary and Jack would be playing Santa for their own kids. It was also the first year that Rosemary had received a wishlist from one of her children that included the words "Barbie car."

Well, Jackie wasn't getting a Barbie car, and Meredith wasn't getting an Atari— nice try, though, especially the way her daughter paired it with "and peace on Earth"— and she knew that each girl already had their Grandma Gruber hand-selected six-inch

Doll of the World ready to go, the package had arrived a full month in advance with a holiday card that featured a Nativity on the front and "from Santa" on the inside.

But Rosemary did not want to just copy the Gruber Christmas. Yes, she'd put the dolls in their stockings, but she had spent so many years asking Jack if they couldn't have Christmas on their own, and take the girls to see his parents afterwards. When would they get to make their own Christmas traditions, instead of having to spend every holiday sleeping on a pull-out sofa, having Christmas brunch with the Grubers, and then driving 14 hours to make it to Fresno by midnight?

Now Rosemary had gotten exactly what she wished for—as sure as if she had asked Santa for it herself—and she still felt like her holiday was taken from her by other people. The preschool teachers who let Jackie believe that Santa would bring her a Barbie car and a Little Miss Makeup (and she'd have to do her part to make sure her mother never knew that toy existed, otherwise Jackie would end up actually getting one), the other kids who went to the mall Santa and came back with stories, the school concerts and church parties and everything at the college, whoever it was that told Meredith that Santa wasn't real. It all felt unfair, like everything about Christmas got decided before Rosemary even had a chance to say what she wanted.

"Are the girls excited about Friday?" Bobbie Jo asked, as they sipped their hot cocoa with candy canes sticking out of each mug. "Santa, Santa, Santa!"

"Jackie can't talk about anything else," Rosemary said.

"You look tired, though," Marcie said, who was currently as tired as any human being had ever been.

"I just feel like it's all getting away from me," Rosemary said. "I wanted a quiet Christmas this year."

"Ain't no such thing as a quiet Christmas," Bobbie Jo laughed.

Carolyn thought that she could tell Bobbie Jo and Rosemary a bit about a quiet Christmas. She'd sit on the couch, next to her parents in their two recliners, and her father would say "well, should we go see the lights?" Then they would bundle up her mother and get into the car and Carolyn would sit in the back seat as her father drove them around and around, turning onto every street like he was playing Pac-Man. It wouldn't take long.

That made her think of her watch again. "It's time to get back," Carolyn said, and three of them waved goodbye to the drugstore clerk before crossing the snow-puddled street to open up the bank. Marcie stayed in the drugstore just a bit longer, since she had not officially gone back to work yet. She would sit in the booth until she had finished her candy cane, and then she might sit five minutes more, and then she would go get her baby.

14. MEREDITH ON CHRISTMAS EVE.

The thing Meredith liked best about the Methodist church was that nobody asked her to consider her sins. In Portland they had gone to church with Grandma and Grandpa Gruber sometimes, and it was a big church with ceilings so high that Meredith couldn't even read the words at the tops of the stained glass windows, and when you turned around to walk out of the sanctuary you had to face an enormous statue of Jesus nailed to the cross, with red painted blood dripping from the hole in His side. Meredith tried to look everywhere else but at that Jesus. She focused her eyes on Grandma Gruber's purse instead.

But before that you had to kneel down and think about your sins, and Meredith felt like she was in the wrong place because she didn't have any sins. She didn't steal, she didn't lie, she didn't cheat, and she didn't try to hurt people. What was she supposed to think about, in the silence? She thought about her parents and her grandparents, and she was pretty sure they didn't have any sins either. Why were they all doing this?

The Methodist church never used the word "sin." When they said the Lord's Prayer, they used "trespasses," which Meredith liked because you could hear the "s" sound come out of a hundred mouths at once, and there were plenty of "s" sounds in "Forgive us our trespasses, as we forgive those who trespass against us." It was her favorite part of the prayer.

Meredith had asked Dad what "trespass" meant, because she knew about "No Trespassing" signs from books but thought they probably weren't talking about that.

"It's sort of the same thing," Dad had told her. "Think about it like going into someone's space when you aren't supposed to. Like when you're playing, and you want a Barbie that Natalie's playing with, and you get her to give it to you even though you know she doesn't want to."

Meredith had definitely done that. She hadn't even realized it was bad. So she also liked this church because it helped her become a better person.

Now she stood next to Natalie and Jackie and Alex, wearing red velvet to match her sisters and shaking hands with the grownups in front of them and behind them. Some of them said "Peace be with you!" and some of them said "Merry Christmas," and one of them asked if they were excited for Santa, and Jackie said "Yes!" so loudly that everyone laughed, which Meredith thought was a little unfair. Jackie didn't know yet about Santa, and it was mean of them to laugh at how excited she was.

Meredith had figured out Santa when she checked out *Little Town on the Prairie* from the library. She asked Alex if she knew, and Alex talked about footprints in the snow and half-eaten carrots next to the stockings, and Meredith said that at her house, Santa didn't leave any footprints or carrots. They put it together like the Boxcar Children solving a mystery, and then Meredith decided not to tell Natalie or Jackie. Laura Ingalls hadn't told Grace, after all.

After everyone shook hands and sat down, it was time for Special Music. Meredith and her sisters walked to the piano in their matching dresses, Natalie carrying the music book under her arm with a paper clip in the right spot. The two of them made sure the book wouldn't tip forward, and then they carefully lined up their hands on either side of Middle C, while Jackie took her place next to Natalie and stood very still like Mom had taught her.

Meredith counted, trying to do it so no one else could hear. "One, two, three, four—"

"JOY to the WORLD, the Lord is come!" Jackie sang out as Natalie and Meredith shared the melody between their fingers. Meredith also had a few chords to play with her left hand, and she concentrated on what Mom had told her: be the accompaniment, not the solo. She kept her fingers curved and her wrists loose. It all made a difference, even though it was hard for Meredith to hear what the difference was.

After they finished, the congregation clapped, which embarrassed Meredith because she knew you weren't supposed to clap at church. She didn't know whether they should bow, but they hadn't practiced bowing, so she didn't. The three Gruber sisters stayed very still, like Mom had taught them, until the applause stopped.

Then Jackie and Natalie went back to their seats and Alex sat down on the bench next to Meredith. They moved the piano book pages forward to the next paper clip, and played "What Child Is This?" They had picked this Christmas carol because it sounded like castles and princesses. Dad had explained that it was also a folk song from England, and pulled out a record called "Fantasia on Greensleeves," which Meredith wished he would play again, as soon as it was over. She wanted to write a story about a girl who listened to that record and closed her eyes, and when she opened them again she was in a magical forest. The instruments made sounds like trees and rain on leaves and waterfalls.

The other reason Meredith liked "What Child Is This" was because it was both happy and sad, so it really felt like Christmas. It was easy to think of all her trespasses tonight, and all of the ways she had been trespassed against. Even though she didn't believe in Santa anymore, she still wanted to be good. She wanted to get everything right.

Then it was time for the candles. There had been candles in wicker baskets when they walked into church, and now everyone took their candles and one of the ushers turned off all the lights and the pastor lit her candle from the big Peace Candle in the center of the room. Then she walked to the first row, and the candlelight began spreading throughout the sanctuary.

Everyone sang "Silent Night" with no piano or organ, just voices. It was all voices and the steadily growing light, and Meredith half singing as they began a second verse and she realized she didn't know any of the words. It felt like forgiveness, like it was okay that Meredith had read an extra chapter of her library book instead of cleaning up the playroom and Mom had come up the stairs and said "Meredith! What did I ask you to do?" or like it was okay that she had sat on Santa's lap and pretended he was real. It was okay that they had called Grandma and Grandpa Gruber that afternoon, and Meredith had nothing to say except she was fine and school was fine, and she felt like she should have said more because it was a special day and she wanted them to know she loved them. It was okay that the congregation had clapped at their music, even though it had felt so embarrassing to sit quietly while it was going on.

Christ was born. Meredith looked at Alex in the candlelight, and Alex made a face, and Meredith tried not to laugh—and then she made a face back and Alex did laugh, but covered it up with her hand. Meredith looked the other way and saw Natalie leaning into Mom's side, and Mom's hand reached around to hug Natalie's red velvet shoulder. Dad was helping Jackie hold her candle, as Jackie kept singing the one verse of "Silent Night" that she knew, over and over. When all the verses were finished, the ushers turned on the lights and the pastor called out "Merry Christmas!" and it was.

SPRING 1990

15. MEREDITH AND ALEX SEE *TIED TO THE TRACKS.*

When the musical was over, Alex stood up right away. Her cousin Sharon was one of the first people out to bow, and her babysitter Marina was one of the last. Marina held hands with Becky because the two of them had shared the lead role, the same way the other three main characters all swapped actors between Act I and Act II. There was a note in the program explaining that this was to give more of Kirkland's talented high school students the opportunity to perform.

Meredith didn't stand up until enough other people did that she was sure it was a standing ovation. She had made that mistake at one of Dad's band concerts, jumping up after the very first piece because it had been so fast and triumphant and wonderful, and hearing her mother whisper "sit down, Meredith." Mom and Dad explained it to her afterwards. They had a lot of talks about performing, and how there were certain times you were supposed to clap and certain times you were supposed to stay silent. She kept one finger on her program to keep track of the movements, and Natalie would watch her finger, knowing it would be time to clap when she finally took it off of the page.

The biggest question was whether there would be cookies afterwards, because sometimes there were cookies afterwards. Mom liked to take Natalie and Meredith and Jackie to piano recitals at the college, since they were all taking weekly piano lessons now, and sometimes Alex would come along too. Afterwards there would be a table with little cookies covered in white sugar crystals, and pink punch in a big glass bowl. They were allowed to each take two cookies, and Meredith always picked the rectangle cookie and the one shaped like a pretzel.

But when Meredith and Alex walked out of the gym, they only saw rows of lockers and clusters of parents.

"They're waiting for the cast to come out," Alex said. She had been to high school musicals before.

So the two of them waited, too, and when the cast members appeared they walked down the line and shook everybody's hand and told them they had done a good job. A lot of the students knew Alex, and Meredith watched as Alex gave one of the girls who had played Dakota Melody a hug. Meredith wanted these older students to like her as much as they all seemed to like Alex, and to talk to her in the same familiar, smart way.

"Marina is my babysitter," Alex said after they got out of the line. "We watch *Golden Girls* together."

Meredith turned to look at Marina again, who was now accepting a huge bouquet of pink and yellow flowers from a boy. She wondered what it would be like to have a babysitter like Marina. Her mind created an instant story: Marina in jeans and a big white sweater, making macaroni and cheese and then singing songs from *The Sound of Music* and *Mary Poppins*. They would all sing together, and then it would be bedtime and Meredith would read the chapter of *Little House in the Big Woods* to her sisters because her parents weren't there, and Marina would say that Meredith was a natural actor, and then the next year the high school would do a musical version of *Mary Poppins* and ask Meredith to play Jane. Maybe Meredith and Alex could both play Jane, since the high school liked to cast two people in each part.

Meredith imagined all of this as if it were something that had already happened, the way she pulled up pictures of the past in her head sometimes. When she tried to focus on the images, they went away, but if she let her brain just bring them up, they felt as real as movies. Like she had the words and the way everybody looked and the feelings all at once.

Alex looked behind her and saw that her mom was still talking to a group of the other parents. They were going to be there for a while. She had an idea.

"Let's go explore the school in the dark," she said. Alex whispered it, because it was kind of like a secret, and definitely like the kind of thing you should whisper.

"Okay," Meredith whispered back. The two of them looked once more at Mrs. MacAllister, who was smiling and leaning against a wall in a way that suggested she wasn't planning to leave any time soon, and then they began walking quickly down the hallway. They passed the music room and the art room, and by the time they were in the lunchroom they were running and laughing, their shoes making squeaks and echoes against the floor.

On the other side of the lunchroom were the elementary school classrooms, and they both stopped and began walking more slowly, because the only light was the little bit that came through the window in each classroom's door. It felt like trespassing in a sacred space, walking down the same hallways they passed through every day, seeing the same drawings and handwritten paragraphs lined up on the wall, turned holy and sinister by the darkness.

They stopped in front of their second-grade classroom, currently displaying the class's drawings of Fern from *Charlotte's Web*. They had all been asked to fill in an outline of Fern's face, the same outline as the one on the book cover, and they could see the eyes and mouths if they looked closely, the white paper just barely reflecting the lines back to them.

"Your drawing is the best," Meredith said. It was the sort of thing she could only have said when it was dark enough not to have to look at Alex while she said it.

"Yours is next best," Alex said, and Meredith knew that was true too, and that they didn't often say who was best and next best at piano or math or drawing or acting. They both wanted to be the best, and they both wanted each other to be next best, which was almost as good. As close to best as possible.

"We'll both be the leads in the musical, when we're in high school," Meredith said. It was something she didn't have to imagine as a future; she knew it would be true. Of all the drawings on the wall, only Alex and Meredith had understood that Fern's outline had been drawn in profile. Everyone else filled in two eyes and a nose and a mouth, even though Fern's nose and mouth were clearly already part of the drawing. Alex's drawing was best because she had drawn the eye in a way Meredith did not realize was correct until she saw it. From the side, an eye doesn't look like an oval with points on the ends. It looks more like a scrunched up triangle.

"I'll be the lead in Act I, and you'll be the lead in Act II," Alex said. Meredith wondered if that was Alex's way of saying which of them was best and next best, because Act II was always where the most dramatic parts of the play happened.

"We'll be roommates in college," Meredith continued, wanting to plan their whole life together as they stood side by side in their Christmas dresses—the red velvet one her mother had made, and the black velvet one Alex's mom had bought at the store.

"Yes!" Alex said excitedly, and Meredith created another instant story that felt like it had already taken place: the two of them, tall with long hair, side by side on one of those skinny dorm beds that Meredith had seen when Dad took them on a tour of the college. She had come back and tried to play "dorm" with her sisters, but Jackie kept messing up the pretend dorm by bringing her toys into it. The room she had seen was empty and beautifully clean, with two matching beds and two matching desks. That was the game she was trying to play: the game of being grown up and sitting at a desk and writing something very important. Now she saw that room again, only with her and Alex together, sitting on the same bed so they could talk about their roles in college plays and the books they were reading. Then they would sit at their matching desks and be the best at their own specific things. Alex would draw, and Meredith would write, and both of them would sing and act and dance.

Meredith started singing, because she was happy and because the musical's songs were stuck in her head, and Alex joined in and their voices made the kind of echoes that never happened in the daytime, only at night in secret magical places. They jumped up and down, making noises they knew no one else could hear, coming up with as many lyrics as they could both remember until they were laughing too hard to carry the tune.

Then the two future leads of the Kirkland High School musical ran back through the hallway and the lunchroom to find Alex's mother still chatting with the other parents as if they had never been gone. As if they had never had their own private adventure.

"Can we get ice cream?" Alex asked, and Mrs. MacAllister said goodbye to the other parents and they got their coats off the rack and went out into the nearly empty parking lot, and instead of saying "it's too cold for ice cream" like Meredith's dad would have said, Mrs. MacAllister drove them down the block to the drugstore and let them sit at the counter and each choose a single scoop. Alex chose something new called "rainbow" that turned out to be sherbet, and Meredith had vanilla with a squirt of strawberry syrup, because it was her favorite.

"We explored the school in the dark," she whispered to Alex, and they both started laughing again.

16. EASTER SUNDAY ON THE GRUBERS' FRONT PORCH.

Rosemary heard the three sets of feet running down the stairs, the alarm clock that drove most of her weekend mornings. On the weekdays it was reversed; she climbed the stairs and called out "good morning," or sometimes Jack went and said "up and at 'em!" but on weekends she liked to stay in bed as long as she could before wrapping herself in the quilted blue robe that Jack had given her as a Christmas present. She had asked for a bathrobe, and thought about saying something to Jack afterwards, asking for the receipt, but the girls had already seen her take it out of the box, and she wanted to model *you get what you get and you don't get upset.*

And no, the girls were not upset to see that the Easter Bunny had left each of them a chocolate rabbit the size of their hand and a stuffed white rabbit the size of their other hand. Rosemary wondered if they would be, after hearing Bobbie Jo describe the squirt guns and Disney movies that her grandkids were going to receive—but Easter, unlike Christmas, was done quietly; kids didn't spend the first day back at school comparing their loot. Rosemary hadn't ever thought of the Easter Bunny as someone who brought loot, anyway; you get some chocolate and a small present, because Christ has died, Christ is risen, Christ will come again.

Jack had done the Easter shopping, and if Rosemary had been able to fit it into the schedule she would have driven the 30 miles down the road to the Delacroix mall, so she could go into B. Dalton and buy them each a book. Instead, Jack went to the Dollar Store downtown and came back with the kind of toys that would get one afternoon of play before being dropped into a toy box, which would be fine except the girls would then refuse to ever throw or give those stuffed rabbits away, because they were theirs and because they were a gift from the Easter Bunny.

But Meredith didn't believe in the Easter Bunny anymore. Jack had also hidden a dozen plastic eggs around the house, each of them with their own foil-wrapped candy egg inside, and Rosemary watched as Meredith saw the first egg, said "It's an Easter egg hunt!" and then paused.

Rosemary often didn't know how to feel about her daughter; certainly there was a sense of pride and love and accomplishment in the idea that she had raised the kind of child who would hold back, whose sharp, smart eyes would case the room for eggs and then help her younger sisters find them. But she also felt a little sad, watching this, because she saw her daughter growing up and doing exactly what she and Jack had taught her, *think before you speak and before you act*—and she worried that Meredith thought too much. She'd have to tell Meredith later that she had seen her share the egg hunt with her sisters, and that it had been the right thing to do, but it was also right to search for eggs for yourself.

Then it was time to get everybody dressed for church, and Rosemary carefully undid all of the rag knots she had put in her girls' hair so that they would have special-day Easter Sunday rag curls. "Cover your eyes," she said, and each daughter covered her eyes so Rosemary could spritz their curls with hair spray.

Before they left, the girls sat side-by-side in the porch swing that Jack had installed the previous weekend. The swing had arrived as a Valentine's Day present, the kind of present they both discussed beforehand before calling the number on the catalog. Then they had to wait for the weather to get warm enough, and then they had to wait until there was a free weekend between band concerts and piano recitals and grocery shopping trips that took all afternoon.

Rosemary took a photo of her girls, side by side in matching dresses and matching hair, each of them with a 5-inch stuffed white rabbit on their lap. Jackie looked as if she had just been visited by magic—which, of course, she believed she had. Natalie looked ready to jump off the swing and run to church. She was bouncing slightly, trying to see if the swing would bounce with her, and Rosemary said "Natalie, sit quietly. Eyes ahead, hands on lap."

Meredith already had the eyes and hands ready to go, because she knew her mom wanted to take a picture. Meredith also had her stuffed rabbit with her, which she had picked up once she saw her sisters were going to carry theirs, because she knew the photo should match. She smiled, tilted her head slightly to one side, and waited.

After the church service there was an egg brunch and a second Easter egg hunt on the church lawn, nobody seeming to care that they were bringing the Easter Bunny into the celebration of Christ's resurrection. The church held the egg hunt in stages; first they let the pre-K kids wander around and pick up the largest eggs, then the kindergarten and first graders, and then the second and thirds. Rosemary saw Meredith and Alex line up with the other kids and then take off running as soon as the pastor said "go!" She watched her daughter and Alex working together, shouting at each other that they had thoroughly searched this bush or that sign, and Rosemary finally felt like she could relax.

"It took all morning for her to act like a kid," she said to Donna, who was standing next to her. "You should have seen her pretending she didn't know where we hid our eggs so that Nat and Jackie could find them."

"No, this Easter Egg Hunt is great," Donna said. "I don't even think they'll find all of them. We used to do it the other way, but the Baxter boys would grab all the eggs before the other kids had a chance. So now we split up the grades and make sure to hide some of the eggs really well."

"Does Alex still believe in the Easter Bunny? Meredith stopped, this year."

Donna laughed. "Yeah, they were talking about it before Christmas. Alex came to us and thanked us for all of the work we had done as Santa Claus, and let us know that our services would no longer be needed—but she'd still like the presents, of course."

"She fired you? As Santa?" Rosemary watched Alex run ahead of a bigger boy to claim a thumb-sized egg that was tucked behind a tree root.

"It was like she was trying so hard to spin it," Donna said. "Like she wanted us to know it was okay that she knew, and of course she wanted the points for having figured it out. But I think she was crushed."

"I couldn't tell if Meredith was disappointed or not," Rosemary said—and then she understood the feeling that had been bothering her all day. She couldn't tell whether

Meredith was disappointed, or happy, or just being patient. She couldn't tell whether Meredith was glad to be helping her sisters find Easter eggs, or whether she was doing it out of duty. It seemed like Meredith was happy right now, in this moment where she and Alex were comparing the number of eggs each of them had found, but Rosemary wanted to be able to give her daughter moments like that too.

So when Meredith and Alex ran back, baskets piled high, to ask if Alex could come over and play, Rosemary said yes—and that afternoon, after everyone had changed out of their Easter dresses and the rag curls had mostly gone limp, the four girls were on the front porch playing a story that Meredith and Alex had made up together, one where a parade of Barbies and ponies and stuffed white rabbits were acting out some kind of Narnian-esque adventure on the porch steps and the railings and the arms of the new porch swing.

Rosemary went into the house through the back door, to get her camera. She came back and began taking photos, filling up the roll of film, because she wanted to remember the four girls together like this: Jackie with a pony in one hand and a doll in the other, Natalie holding her white rabbit in the air and dive-bombing it onto the porch swing, Meredith saying something that made everybody laugh, and Alex squatting barefooted on the porch to assemble the next wave of characters. She wanted to catch this moment of happiness, and if she took enough photos, one of them might look like what she and her girls were feeling.

SUMMER 1990

17. NATALIE PLAYS LITTLE MERMAID WITH HER FRIENDS.

The shallow section of the Kirkland Community Pool had steps along one side, and if you put your hands on the second step and pushed, you could come out of the water like Ariel. Natalie and Jenna and Kimberly and Chrissy all took turns, and then they lined up against the steps and tried to do it all at once, four little mermaids flipping their hair out of the water simultaneously.

Sometimes the lifeguard would blow his whistle, if he thought they were getting in the way of mommies and babies trying to get into the pool, and the four of them would giggle and scatter, running in that slow way that you had to run through water until they came to the rope that separated the shallow section from the deeper one. Then they would duck their mermaid bodies under the rope and start swimming.

Natalie loved swimming. Daddy had taught her, at the beginning of the summer. He had put his hand on her stomach to hold her up, and then he took his hand away and she kept on floating just like he had promised would happen. Now she could kick her feet off the bottom of the pool and swim to the other edge, or to the ladder next to the waterslide, or anywhere she wanted—except she wasn't supposed to go to the part where she couldn't touch the bottom of the pool with her toes. They all had that rule. Kimberly was the tallest, and sometimes she would go out to where she could still touch and dare them to come closer. Natalie and Jenna would bounce, carefully, kicking their feet under the water to make sure nobody could see that it would for sure cover their chins if they stopped moving. Chrissy stayed behind. She was one of those girls who worried about rules and told on herself if she broke them.

Jenna was Natalie's best friend, and Kimberly was her next best friend and Chrissy was also her next best friend, and when Mandy came to the pool she was a best friend too, and they set their pool towels next to each other so that they could sit together during Pool Check. Natalie liked Pool Check because it meant buying candy at the canteen. Daddy would give each of them fifteen cents, and Natalie could pick whether she wanted to split up her nickels and use them for three Laffy Taffys at three different Pool Checks, or buy a single string of Sixlets. Daddy told her that if she saved up all her nickels and didn't buy anything, at the end of the week she'd have 75 cents, and if she did that he'd give her 25 cents more and she could buy an ice cream sandwich.

Natalie bought the Sixlets instead, so she could share them with her friends. They all took turns figuring out what a Laffy Taffy would taste like if they dipped it in Fun Dip powder, or whether you could really tell the different kinds of Runts with your eyes closed. Natalie always hoped she would get banana, because that was the one she knew for sure.

Sometimes Jackie or Kevin or Brad or other younger siblings came and sat with them, and everyone was always nice if it was someone else's little sister or brother. Then when Pool Check was over Daddy would go back to splashing with Jackie in the shallow end, and Natalie and her friends would run over—"no running!"—to go down the waterslide. It was the most fun to enter the pool from the waterslide, because that way you got used to the water with your whole body, instead of feeling the cold inch up your legs and belly until it got deep enough to put your head in.

They went to the pool almost every afternoon with Daddy, because Mommy was at work. Mommy worked at the bank, and when they came back Natalie would tell her all about how Jenna tried to go down the waterslide head first and the lifeguard said she had to spend ten minutes standing next to him as punishment, or about how Mandy got a green Laffy Taffy that had the funniest joke on it, or about how they had played Marco Polo and Kimberly made it not fair by going out to the end where they couldn't reach.

Sometimes when none of her friends were there, Natalie would play with Alex and Meredith. Alex liked to play swimming teacher, and show Natalie how to do the butterfly. Alex was on swim team, and Natalie wanted to be on swim team as soon as she was old enough next summer. She practiced her swimming, going from one side to the other on the part of the pool where she could still touch, and Alex and Meredith counted Mississippis to let her know if she had beaten her previous record.

Meredith couldn't swim. Daddy had tried to give Meredith swimming lessons, and Alex tried too, but whenever they took their hands away from Meredith's stomach, she sank. Jackie could probably swim, although it was hard to tell because Jackie wasn't allowed to go beyond the rope that separated the shallow end from the rest of the pool. She could float, though. Natalie and Jackie had floating contests in the shallow end, holding their faces into the water and seeing who could go the longest without coming up for breath.

Jackie liked playing Little Mermaid too, but she would always start singing "Part of Your World" instead of just practicing the hair flip. Or she would say "I'll be the Sea Witch!" and start waving her arms and legs around and trying to get Natalie to play like they might play at home. Natalie didn't play like that with her friends. They never made up stories together the way she made up stories with her sisters. Instead, they lined up side by side and tried to make an arc of heads and water splash out of the pool at the same time. Or they ran to their pool towels and tried to sunbathe, letting the sun dry their wet skin until they were bored.

Meredith and Alex still played that old way, even in the pool, and Jackie still played that way because she was little. But when Natalie was with her friends, they didn't have to play anything. They were just themselves. They all wanted to be on swim team next year, and wear the blue and silver uniforms. When they played Little Mermaid, they didn't have to agree on who would be Ariel and who would be Flounder. They could rise out of the water together, all of them mermaids at once.

18. BOBBIE JO INVITES ROSEMARY AND CAROLYN OVER.

Bobbie Jo's kitchen had two themes: chickens and grandmas. A row of chicken-printed china hung on the wall next to a wooden plank painted with the words "Grandma's Kitchen. Today's Menu: Love." A dusty crocheted chicken covered what Rosemary assumed was a teakettle, and the refrigerator was adorned with as many magnets extolling the benefits of being a grandmother as it was with pictures of Bobbie Jo's grandchildren.

"What can I get y'all?" Bobbie Jo asked, bending to look into her fridge. "There's some Mountain Dew, we've got Pepsi, Jonetta's got a thing of wine coolers in here"—she stood up and turned around—"and I've got Jim Beam."

"Water's fine," Rosemary said. She would have asked about tea, if she weren't put off by the condition of the chicken.

"You know what? I've got some Crystal Light." Bobbie Jo pulled out a scratched Tupperware pitcher and began running the tap. Rosemary glanced at Carolyn as if to say—well, she wasn't sure exactly what she wanted to say. She thought it might be a moment for a silent, shared smile, but she wanted to look at Carolyn first to gauge her reaction.

"Thank you," Carolyn said. "Your home is lovely."

"Aww, it's a mess," Bobbie Jo said, dumping handfuls of ice into the full pitcher. Rosemary would have done it the other way around, and she would have washed her hands first. "We haven't had much time for cleaning, lately."

The timer on the oven went off, and Rosemary heard "I got it" from the living room, over the sounds of the TV. "Oh, you can sit, Jonetta," Bobbie Jo called back, but Jonetta was already in the kitchen, putting on an oven mitt patterned with chickens and pulling out a long glass pan. Rosemary could see a layer of cornbread on top, covered with cheese.

"You think it's done?" Bobbie Jo asked.

"I'm checking it," Jonetta said, and she yanked open a drawer to grab a fork. "It's done, mama."

"Well, sometimes you don't let it cook all the way through." Bobbie Jo turned back to Rosemary and Carolyn. "Jonetta and Stephanie are living with me while Jonetta gets her D-I-V-O-R-C-E."

"She can spell, mama," Jonetta laughed. She turned to Rosemary. "I've seen you around Rix, right? Your girls are going into first and third grade."

"They are," Rosemary said. She had stopped being surprised at how everyone in Kirkland knew everything about her family. She didn't know what grade Stephanie was going into, so she said "Is Stephanie excited about school starting?"

"She doesn't get a choice about it," Jonetta said. "But she's excited to see her friends. She has Miss Anderson this year. I went down to the school and made sure. Who'd you ask for?"

"You can ask?"

"Oh, you have to ask," Jonetta said, getting a stack of plates out of her mother's cupboard. "You don't want your kids stuck with one of the mean teachers, or not getting to be in the same class as their friends."

"What if all their friends are in the class with the mean teacher?" Rosemary said, and Jonetta laughed. Rosemary hadn't gone to Bobbie Jo's house expecting to like Jonetta—even after a year in Kirkland, she still felt out of place around other Kirkland moms—but there was something about Jonetta that made her feel almost comfortable, or at least as comfortable as she could in Bobbie Jo's chicken-and-crumb-covered kitchen. She looked again at Carolyn, to see if she was enjoying herself too, but Carolyn stood quietly and politely with her glass of Crystal Light in her hand.

"I'll make a plate for Steffie," Jonetta said, and Bobbie Jo said "no, I've got it," and as soon as Bobbie Jo left the kitchen Jonetta said "She *loves* having her grandbaby in the house."

"She talks about her grandkids all the time," Carolyn said. "I like seeing the pictures."

"You wanna see the real thing?" Jonetta smiled, then called out "Steffie! Come in here!"

The little girl who appeared shyly in the doorway was recognizable as one of the teased-hair children Bobbie Jo pulled out of her wallet, although her hair was combed smooth now.

"Stephanie, this is Rosemary and—"

"Carolyn."

"Can you say hello?"

Stephanie did her part and said hello, although she looked like she hoped she would not be asked to say anything else.

"Okay, baby, go eat your dinner," Jonetta said, and Stephanie ran back into the living room, relieved. "We help ourselves in this house," Jonetta said, pointing to the plates and the glass casserole dish. They each spooned out a plate of cornbread casserole, and then both Rosemary and Carolyn sat at the table awkwardly until Bobbie Jo returned, smelling more-than-faintly of cigarette smoke.

"Girls' night!" Bobbie Jo said, looking at the three of them together, with only one bite taken out of their plates of food. "My favorite girls all in one place."

"Mama," Jonetta said. "Sit down. We're hungry."

"So my daughter is living with me," Bobbie Jo said as they began eating, "because she married a dumbass. Which I believe I told you when you married him."

"You said he was a nice man," Jonetta said.

"Nobody ever says someone is nice when they could say something better about them," Bobbie Jo said. "But at least you can get divorced. I had to wait for your father to die." She looked over her glasses at Rosemary and Carolyn. "Dillard women don't know how to pick 'em."

Rosemary watched as Bobbie Jo continued to make jokes about her daughter's divorce and how glad she was that her other children were sons—"because I raised 'em right, not to be fools"—and wondered what she would do if one of her daughters got divorced someday. She had never thought about that, although she had thought about each of their weddings, in the early days when she was walking each of them back and forth across the living room floor, hoping they would sleep, and later, when she could see enough of what they would look like as adults to imagine how each of them might style their hair. (Meredith would have to pull hers back into a smooth chignon, maybe with flowers. Natalie would have the long, flowing curls. Jackie might be able to wear her hair straight, under a Juliet cap.)

But she couldn't imagine them getting divorced. If they did, she hoped she wouldn't treat them the way Bobbie Jo was treating Jonetta, although she got the sense that it didn't seem to bother Jonetta much; that this was a house where people used words like "dumbass" and "fool" regularly and it didn't matter. She thought of Stephanie, sitting alone with her dinner and the television. If it were her grandchild, she would be in the room.

After dinner, Bobbie Jo went out to smoke again, and Jonetta said "y'all want a fuzzy navel?" and when she took one of the wine cooler bottles for herself even after Rosemary and Carolyn both said no, Rosemary understood that maybe Jonetta hadn't been as comfortable as she had been making everyone else feel.

"So what do I need to do next year, to make sure my kids have the right teachers?" Rosemary asked.

Jonetta smiled. "Well, first you gotta start getting in good with Peg Howard."

19. JACK AND ROSEMARY DISCUSS THEIR DAUGHTERS' EDUCATION.

That night Jack put the girls to bed. He sat on the floor in the middle of the bedroom, the way Rosemary did, and read aloud from *Caddie Woodlawn*. Afterwards Meredith and Natalie both wanted to explain to him how this chapter was different from the movie—"since you haven't seen it," Natalie said authoritatively.

"Well, sometimes they change things when they turn books into movies," Jack said.

"Did they cut Clara and Hetty out of the story because they didn't have enough money to pay the actors?" Meredith asked. "I know PBS is always asking for money."

Jack tried not to laugh. "I'm sure they had their reasons."

Once the lights were turned out, Jack went downstairs and opened up his music stand. He took out the score to Shostakovich's Festive Overture and began conducting, humming the parts himself and practicing the page turns. School started in two weeks, and he hoped that all of the recruiting he had done this spring would pay off with a Symphonic Band that was ready for this challenge. Otherwise he'd have to program Emperata Overture instead.

Rosemary came in the door timed with a cymbal crash, and the music kept going in Jack's head even after he stopped conducting. "How was it?" he asked.

"It was good," Rosemary said. "I met Bobbie Jo's daughter Jonetta."

"Does she go to school here?" Jack asked.

"No, she's our age," Rosemary said. "She's getting a divorce and she and her little girl moved in with Bobbie Jo."

Rosemary kept talking as she took off her shoes and changed out of her denim skirt and blouse into her oversized sleep T-shirt. Jack watched her through the open door, because he would always watch Rosemary unhook her bra and raise her arms to pull the loose shirt over her head.

"I think that's why Bobbie Jo had us over," Rosemary was saying. "Because Jonetta needed a friend. I wonder what happened to her old friends."

"Maybe she didn't have any," Jack said.

"She doesn't seem unfriendly," Rosemary said. "I liked her."

"Maybe she cheated on him."

"Oh, I don't know," Rosemary said. "Bobbie Jo said he was an asshole."

She came out of the bedroom and went to sit on the couch. Jack followed and let Rosemary put her feet up on his lap. It was too warm of an evening to sit much closer, so they sat on either end of the couch and he stroked her legs with his fingertips.

"Jonetta said that a lot of the parents ask Peg Howard to put their kids in certain classes," Rosemary said. "So that they don't get stuck with the bad teachers. It's too late for this year, but I'm going to start asking around to see where we should put Meredith and Natalie next fall."

"We shouldn't ask for special treatment," Jack said.

"It isn't special treatment if all the other parents do it," Rosemary said.

"Well, what do you mean, *bad teachers?*"

"I don't know," Rosemary said. "Jonetta said that some of the teachers are mean."

"You want our girls to go through life never having to deal with a mean teacher?" Jack asked. "I say get it over with and let them learn how to survive."

"But what if it affects their grades?"

"It won't affect their grades," Jack said. "Our girls are going to do well in school because they're smart, and because they're Gruber kids. And because we'll help them."

"Natalie still isn't reading very quickly."

"She's six. Not every kid's going to read like Meredith. She'll figure it out."

Rosemary's legs had tensed up in Jack's lap; he stopped stroking them. "I want to give our kids the best possible school experience."

"They are going to be fine," Jack said. "I've got a doctorate. My sister has a doctorate. My father went to college. That's their predictor of school success, not what teacher they get in first grade."

"But how are they supposed to learn, without those teachers?"

"They learn by *being in the world*," Jack said. "They learn by being smart kids who are curious about things. The rest is just homework."

Rosemary knew that there was something in Jack's argument that wasn't right. Homework had to be important; you wrote down your spelling words the same way you practiced your scales, and that's how you learned how to spell and how to play the piano. And he couldn't say that teachers weren't important, not as a teacher himself.

"So what do you do if Meredith comes home one day crying because her teacher was mean to her?"

"That's not going to happen," Jack said. "Meredith is the type of kid teachers love. She's smart, and she knows how to behave."

"What about Natalie?"

"Come on, Rosemary," Jack said. "Going and asking for a special teacher just teaches kids that the rules don't apply to them. We don't need to do that."

Rosemary didn't say anything.

"Our girls are going to be fine," Jack said. "They're going to college, and they're going to go for free, and after that it's up to them."

"I'm still going to ask which teachers are the mean ones," Rosemary said. Then she took Jack's hand and squeezed it softly, to let him know the argument was over, and when she let go he began gently stroking her legs again.

FALL 1990

20. JACK BRINGS HOME A MOVIE.

When Dad picked the movie it was usually about boys; he brought home *Pinocchio* once, and Meredith watched it patiently, silently, waiting for a reason to care about boys who lied and smoked and turned into donkeys. Once he rented *The Three Stooges* and all three of his children rebelled; they looked at each other and shifted position on the sofa until Natalie finally said "this is boring," which freed them from watching the weird men try to hit each other in the face. They went upstairs, wrapped their Barbies' legs in pink and green ribbon, and played *The Little Mermaid* again.

This time he came home from work with a movie called *Fiddler on the Roof*, which was the musical the college was putting on that year. The front cover had an old man on it, which did not look promising, but the back had a group of women, which at least meant there was a reason to pay attention to the story. Meredith watched girls and women to see what happened to them, but also to look for pieces of herself, and to see what the characters who carried her pieces might do with their lives.

They all had their places, in the living room: Dad in the recliner, Mom on the end of the sofa nearest him, and the three of them next to Mom, with Meredith on the far end where she could dangle her arm over into the tantalizing magazine rack. She could read two articles during a commercial break, and if Mom hadn't put a new magazine in there, she would just re-read one of the old ones. There was a story in one of them about a mom who felt sad because she didn't get to do anything fun, and then she joined a choir, which meant that for 45 minutes every Wednesday she got to do something fun.

Meredith re-read that article to remind herself that the most important thing she needed to do when she became an adult was to make sure that there was something fun in *every single day*.

The movie started, and it did look like it was going to be mostly about an old man, and Meredith was nervous about the two thick videocassettes worth of old man story ahead of them, and then it was suddenly BOOM BOOM BOOM and the TV screen changed with every beat of the drum and she stared as hard as she could to see everything before it became something new.

Her cheeks started to heat up and her skin got all prickly. The song kept going: images of bread dough and strange churches and hammers going clang and knifes going into meat and flutes playing so fast they sounded like the air inside of her.

The fiddler was almost as fast as the flutes, and Meredith was already sad that she would only get to hear this once; that they didn't have the tape recorder set up next to the TV. She listened so hard she forgot to blink, hoping her brain would keep as much of the music as possible and put it in the same place where she kept the numbers for Around The World, so she could let herself go all buzzy and remember every note.

Fiddler on the Roof turned out to be about girls after all. All of the good stories were about girls and women. Meredith liked Chava and Hodel the best, because they were smart and brave and liked dancing. Chava was the one with the books, but Hodel got to dance with Perchik, who looked like a real-life Prince Eric and was also the smartest boy.

Still, when she told Nat and Jackie "Let's do a play of 'Matchmaker,'" she knew she would be Tzeitel. There were three main sisters in the movie just like there were three sisters in the Gruber family, and so she had to play the oldest one. The two younger sisters would be saved for later, when they took out their paper dolls and created the story that the movie had not written for them.

It was hard to remember all of the words, and Dad had already taken the movie back to the college, but all three of them could sing the chorus, and they put together the rest of the song in a way that felt like what they remembered. They took old T-shirts out of the drawer and tied them around their hair, and Mom let them borrow her aprons, and they took baby blankets out of the toy box and practiced swinging them around.

When it was time, they invited Mom and Dad to come upstairs and sit in the doorway of their bedroom, because they needed a bed for the end of the song, so they could fall backwards and then sit up at the same time. Jackie always giggled during that part, because it was so much fun. Natalie didn't giggle. Meredith thought that Natalie wasn't really enjoying this play as much as she had enjoyed the other ones; that any minute she would say "this is boring" and it would be over.

But she didn't, and they did their play, and Mom and Dad clapped, and Meredith thought that she couldn't wait until the college put on *Fiddler on the Roof*, so she could hear all of its music again.

21. THE GRUBER SISTERS PLAY PRINCESSES.

"What do you want to play?" Meredith asked.

"Princesses!" Jackie said.

Meredith looked at Natalie, who said "I'll play princesses," and they opened up the box of paper dolls. They had to pick dolls that matched, and Meredith knew that Jackie would probably want Disney, but she took out the *Godey's Lady's Book: 1840–1854* paper dolls anyone, the ones that had been a ninth birthday present from her sisters. They were still new.

"Let's play with these," she said, and her sisters didn't object.

It was easy to tell what each paper doll might be like, if she were a princess; Pauline was clearly the oldest sister, with her wise eyes and folded arms; Emma was the smiling one, the friendly one, the one who felt like Natalie, so Meredith handed her over—and then there was Alice, the one who looked like Alex, with her red hair, and Meredith kept that one aside to be the best friend.

Clara had an upturned nose, so she was the villain, and Meredith kept that one aside too; and Jackie of course wanted to be Daisy, the littlest one, and that left Flora, who looked shy and weak and would probably have a very good heart but would also support the plot by getting in the other characters' way, and Netty, who had a plain face and a servant's name.

"Pauline and Emma and Daisy are sisters," she said, standing her paper doll up against the wall. Natalie and Jackie stood their paper dolls up next to hers.

"Emma! Daisy! Are you dressed?" Meredith began, sorting through Pauline's clothes as she spoke. "We have guests coming this afternoon. We need to welcome them to the palace and treat them like the princesses they are."

"Are they princesses too?" Daisy asked.

"They are," Pauline said, "and they're from Germany. They are visiting us while their parents take care of some important political matters. Netty!"

Netty appeared, in her simple brown dress and red jacket. "Yes, princess," she said.

"I'm so glad you're here," Pauline said. "I need you to look at Daisy's hair. It's a mess. She's been out horseback riding all morning and we have to prepare for our visitors."

"I've been horseback riding too!" Emma said.

"Then you had better take a good look at both of them," Pauline said, and she left the room to take care of something very important.

Netty began brushing Emma's hair, as Daisy twirled around the room in her prettiest dress. "Have you heard about these two princesses? The ones that are coming to visit? Their maid wrote me and told me to watch out."

"Why?" Emma asked.

"They're not very nice," Netty said. "At least that's what I heard. The older one's as old as Pauline, and she'll boss you around for sure."

"I won't be bossed around," Emma said. "If they're mean, I'll play tricks on them."

"I'll put a jar of spiders in her bed!" Daisy said.

"You'll mess your hair up even more if you go hunting for spiders," Netty laughed. "Come here and let me comb out those rag curls. Emma, you are so lucky that your hair curls naturally."

Pauline returned with Alice, who was dressed in an everyday gray dress, not one of her ball gowns. "Look who's here!" she said. "Alice's father is going to be at the meeting this afternoon, since he's the Prime Minister. So Alice will be spending the rest of the day with us."

"I didn't realize you would be meeting two princesses today," Alice said. "I didn't dress for it."

"You look fine," Pauline said.

"Better be careful," Netty warned. "I heard that older princess is very particular on clothes."

Pauline crossed her arms. "Netty, have you been receiving gossip about our guests?"

"It's only gossip if it ain't true," Netty said. "And I'm going to bet it's true."

Netty left, and Alex—sorry, Alice—went to say hello to Emma and Daisy. "What have the two of you been up to this morning?"

"We went horseback riding!" Daisy said.

"Oh, I would have liked to go riding with you," Alice said. "I had to spend the morning practicing the piano. Did you race?"

"Yes," Emma said, "and I won."

"You did not!" Daisy said.

"I'll have to watch you later," Alice said, "to see who really is the fastest. Would you like to race again this afternoon?"

"Yes!" came from both Emma and Daisy, and then they were interrupted by a knock at the door. Netty entered, bringing Pauline and two strangers with her.

"May I present the Princess Clara and the Princess Flora, of Germany."

Flora smiled, but Clara sneered at what she saw in front of her. "To whom am I being presented?"

"I am Princess Emma, of England," Emma said.

"And I'm Princess Daisy!"

"And I'm Alice, the Prime Minister's daughter," Alice said.

"Hmm," Clara said. "I thought you were a servant. You dress like one."

"She looks just fine," Emma said. "And she's our friend."

"Then perhaps you have poor taste in friends," Clara said. "The two of you look adequate. It is clear you put some effort into our arrival."

Flora took a shy step forward. "Clara, you're being mean. We are their guests."

"If there's one thing princesses need to learn, it's that appearance is everything. We are representing our country and our family. When guests arrive, it is important to look our absolute best."

"I think they look pretty," Flora said.

"I think you look pretty too," Daisy said.

"Thank you," Flora said. She walked to Daisy and Emma and whispered "We'll talk later."

"I heard that," Clara said, pompously.

Pauline stepped in, since she knew it was about time to move the plot forward. "We would love to entertain you for the afternoon," she said. "Daisy and Emma were thinking about horseback riding."

"I am excellent at riding," Clara said, "although Flora is quite poor at it."

"Well, we should change into our riding clothes and go to the stables," Pauline said, and Netty entered to help the princesses and their guests remove their fine dresses and put on simpler clothing that was more appropriate for riding.

"I told you," Netty said.

"She's so mean!" Daisy said. "We should play a trick."

"Let's give her the bad horse," Emma said. "That way, it'll drop her into the mud."

"Did I hear you talking about playing a trick?" Flora asked. "I'm sorry, but I'm not sure that's a good idea. If Clara realizes she's been tricked, she'll be very angry."

"Don't you ever play tricks on your sisters?" Emma asked.

"No, never," Flora said.

Daisy laughed. "Then what do you *do* all day?"

"I sing, sometimes," Flora said.

"I like to sing too!" Daisy said, and she began singing the song from *Sleeping Beauty*, which was okay because Mom and Dad had said it was actually by Tchaikovsky. Emma and Flora joined in, and when the song was finished, Flora said "I didn't realize you English princesses knew the same songs I did! Where did you learn it?"

"From a movie!" Daisy said.

Emma corrected her. "She means from a play."

"From a ballet," Pauline wanted to say, but she wasn't in the room.

"Oh, I love the theater," Flora said. "I would love to see some Shakespeare while I was here. Will you take me, later?"

"Of course," Emma said. "We own all the theaters in England."

Netty came back in with Pauline and Clara. "The horses are ready," she said.

Alice—who must have been there the whole time—said "I didn't bring my riding clothes, so I'll have to watch."

"It is clear you do not think about your clothing at all," Clara said cruelly, and the seven of them went to the stables.

"Which horse is mine?" Clara demanded. "I want the best one."

Daisy laughed. "We'll give you the best one."

"His name is Mister Ruler," Emma said. "Because he's the best."

She leaned over to Flora. "Actually it's because he kicks everyone off."

"Into the mud!" Daisy added.

Clara examined Mister Ruler. "He appears to be good enough," she said. "Not as good as my horse at home."

"Well why didn't you bring your horse from home?" Emma asked.

"He gets seasick."

"Let's get the horses ready to race," Emma said, and she and Daisy and Clara all lined up on their respective horses.

"My horse is white because she's special," Daisy said.

"If she is so special, maybe I should ride your horse instead," Clara said. "In fact, I demand we switch."

"No!" Daisy said. "She's mine!"

"You have the best one," Pauline said. "I usually ride Mister Ruler, but I'm letting you ride him."

"Girls! Dinner!"

"He's the fastest for sure," Emma said.

"Fine," Clara said. "But if I am unhappy, we are switching horses afterwards—and if I like your horse best, Daisy, I may take him back to Germany with me."

"Girls!" Dad's voice was closer; he was at the bottom of the stairs now. "Come down for dinner!"

Meredith, Natalie, and Jackie stopped talking. They were each holding a paper doll pressed against the torso of a My Little Pony.

"We'll finish the race after dinner," Meredith said, the way Pauline would have.

22. MEREDITH AND ALEX GO TO THE VIDEO KNIGHT.

It usually took about an hour to pick the movie. This was okay because a lot of people came in to the Video Knight while they were there, and Alex's mom liked to talk to each of them, and so Meredith and Alex had plenty of time to make their decision.

They started at New Releases, even though they weren't allowed to rent any movies that cost more than 99 cents. They picked up the empty videocassette cases, flipped them over, and read the backs like books.

Pretty Woman was one of the newest releases, and Meredith and Alex held the case between them, their bodies pressed together to hide it from observers. They were only allowed to rent PG movies, but Alex's mom hadn't said anything about reading the back of the case.

They re-read *Pretty Woman* nearly every time they came to the Video Knight. They had already made up a game like *Pretty Woman* and played it in Alex's bedroom, where both of them were grown-up women with important jobs who came back to their shared apartment to talk about the successful moguls they had met. Then they took turns playing the moguls and going on dates together. The one playing the mogul took Alex's jewelry box and held it open like the picture on the back of the case.

Meredith liked looking at the front of the case as much as she liked looking at the back; the back had Julia Roberts' hair and that dress with the white polka dots—she liked it a lot better than the red one—but the front had Richard Gere looking right at her, like he might open up a jewelry box for her someday. Not him, of course. He was too old already. But someone like him, when Meredith was old enough to look like Julia Roberts.

Alex was also eager for *Ernest Goes to Jail* to make it off the New Releases shelf, and Meredith was less interested in the Ernest movies but she let Alex rent the movies she wanted sometimes, the way Alex let her rent *Big Business*. Both of them had been disappointed in *Big Business*, but at least it was a story about women.

After they finished the New Releases section, they spent some time looking at titles in Action and Drama, but that was just for fun; they both knew they were going to rent something from Comedy. Comedy was the best section. When *Pretty Woman* made it off the New Release shelf, it would end up here, along with their other favorite movies: *The Princess Bride* and *Clue*. They could still look at it, the way they still occasionally picked up *The Witches of Eastwick*—rated R, of course, so it was off limits—and tried to imagine the kind of story adults would tell each other about witches.

This was one of Meredith's favorite parts of Movie Night with Alex: getting to see the kinds of stories adults made for each other. She loved *Clue* because it had jokes about numbers and Kipling, and because she and Alex would both shout the dialogue along with the characters, but she also loved *Clue* because of Mrs. White's cape and Miss Scarlet's dress and the way everyone talked about their jobs in this casual grownup way that she still didn't quite understand, even though she and Alex had rented the movie three times already. She wanted to go to a party like that someday and lean against a desk and make jokes and have a roll of negatives from her job that everybody wanted to see.

That night they rented *¡Three Amigos!*, which didn't look like it had any women in it but it did have what Alex excitedly called "the best comic actor in the world," so they ended it up taking it to her mom for approval and then waiting as she dug the 99 cents out of her pocket and the clerk went into the back room to find the video that went into the case. Then they got into the car and drove back to Alex's house and Alex's dad put a frozen pizza in the oven, the kind where the pepperonis curled up like those toys they got at the school carnival, the little half-circles that flipped over when you pushed on them.

Alex's mom gave them each a glass of Mountain Dew with ice and let them go into the TV room with the pizza and a roll of paper towels and a half-eaten package of Oreos, and Meredith loved being at Alex's house so much because the two of them were able to sit in this room together with their pizza and cookies and paper towels and this grownup movie that Natalie and Jackie would never be allowed to watch, rewinding the parts they liked best so they could memorize them. Meredith never felt embarrassed for saying "I want to see that again," because Alex would always say "Okay."

Because watching movies with Alex wasn't about getting to the end. It was about rewinding the "My Little Buttercup" song four times so they could learn all the words. When the movie was over they went back to that part and practiced the dance, Meredith scooting backwards with Alex's hands on her hips. Alex was Steve Martin because he was her favorite, and because she was taller than Meredith. Meredith grabbed a paper towel and put it on her head like Martin Short, and the two of them pointed out to an imaginary audience and demanded they sing along.

23. ROSEMARY TEACHES PIANO LESSONS.

On Wednesday Rosemary taught piano lessons. She started with the John Thompson books that she had carried with her in the bottom of a box from her childhood home, packing and repacking through college and marriage for the children she knew she would have someday.

She hadn't expected that one of her children would have a best friend who would also want piano lessons, but Alex asked, and Donna and Mike let Meredith come over so often, and gave her dinner, and Rosemary felt like it was a fair exchange.

She also hadn't expected that she would have a friend with a daughter who would be old enough to take piano—that wasn't the kind of thing she dreamed of when she carefully put the Thompson books in the bottom of another cardboard box—but when she helped Jonetta move into a tiny apartment with pockmarked walls, Jonetta had said that she wanted to buy a piano someday so Stephanie could take lessons. Now Stephanie practiced on a cheap keyboard that she sat on her lap, but she was a good student, and she didn't need the full eighty-eight keys yet.

So Rosemary talked to Carolyn about her work schedule, and after that the five girls all came to the Gruber house after school on Wednesdays. Rosemary gave them each a glass of milk and two cookies, and at 3:45 p.m. the lessons began.

Jackie was first, and she sang everything she played; Rosemary had tried to talk with her about how real pianists didn't sing along, but Jackie—it wasn't that Jackie didn't listen, it was more like she considered her mother's perspective and then did her own thing.

She was still in preschool in the mornings and day care in the afternoons, and Rosemary thought how her daughters were so different, and how Jackie would eventually outgrow the singing, because every pianist except Glenn Gould outgrew the singing.

Jackie also liked to make up songs. Her father had told her about Bach spelling his name on the piano even though there was no H key, and so Jackie had decided that she could create a J key, and then she realized that she could call it a Jac-key, and Rosemary listened every week to the new song Jackie had created for her—or, more accurately, the song she created in the moment:

> *This is the jac-key*
> *It sounds so pret-ty...*

She was making her way through Thompson, though, and she could read music if it stayed on the staff. That was good enough for four years old.

Next, Natalie and Stephanie shared a lesson, since they were at the same level in the Thompson books. Natalie had the head start, but Stephanie was a quick learner, and when Rosemary played music flashcard games with them, Stephanie usually answered first.

When they played their pieces, Natalie was generally note perfect but Stephanie paused every few notes, to look up at the music and then down at her hands. Rosemary thought about her sitting in that dimly lit apartment with her little keyboard on her lap. She hoped Jonetta would get her piano soon.

She also wondered how much of Natalie's note perfect talent was her ear. When she gave them a new piece, Natalie was just as hesitant and halting as Stephanie until Rosemary played it through for them and helped them find the right place to put their fingers. When it was Stephanie's turn, she looked at the music before pressing each key; when it was Natalie's turn, she—well, it was like she felt the music in her fingers, stretching them out to find the third or the fourth. Rosemary thought that Natalie would eventually outgrow that too, as the music got more difficult; she wondered if she should drill her a little harder on the flashcards.

Then it was Meredith and Alex, one of them antsy on the bench and the other one straightbacked with perfectly curved fingers, both of them wanting to prove that they had practiced the hardest. She barely needed to pull out the flashcards for them; they had all the notes memorized, and when she spent an evening writing out one of those fill-in-the-blank music stories about cabbages and bags, they came back the next week with a story they had created that was even cleverer. Ace was a cab driver in a faded jacket, with an aged face and a banged-up badge. (How did they even know what cabs were? She didn't think either of them had ever been in one.)

They were past Thompson before she had time to teach it, so she went up to the Kirkland College music library to find books she could check out on their behalf, Kabalevsky etudes and Schumann's Album for the Young. They were both note-accurate and quick-fingered, but she had trouble talking to them about nuance; they preferred to play fast, and their dynamics were technically appropriate but they chunked through them as if they were picking up and putting down different-colored crayons. There was no shading, not yet, and no subtlety.

But they would learn, right? They all would learn. Rosemary had put in the hours and she had learned, and even though she couldn't remember herself as a beginning piano student she wondered if she had done all of these things that her five students did before learning how to sight-read and sit still and follow a musical phrase from beginning to end. She didn't have to think about any of it anymore, and she didn't know how to teach her students how to think about it. She could teach them notes, and what all the markings on their music meant, and she could play for them how the piece should sound and hope they were listening. They were all beginners, and that would do for now.

24. THE GIRLS TAKE BALLET LESSONS.

On Thursdays Meredith waited in the hallway outside the elementary school bathrooms until she saw Natalie come out of her first-grade classroom. Sometimes Natalie waited if her class was let out first. The two of them walked to the quonset hut behind the school to get Jackie, and then the three of them walked the block over to the Kirkland Central Bank.

The bell rang when they pushed open the door, and even when their mom was busy with a customer she would take a second to look over at them and smile. Sometimes Bobbie Jo would have a glass candy dish at her teller station, and they always checked for it; it was the second thing they looked for after walking in the door and meeting their mother's eyes.

"Y'all want some Tootsie Rolls, girls?" Bobbie Jo would ask, and if Mom was busy with a customer they would have to wait until she was done to ask "May we have a Tootsie Roll?" She would say "Yes, but only one," and Meredith would take the candy dish off the teller station and hold it where Jackie could reach it. Afterwards they would all say "Thank you," because if they didn't, their mother's voice would come over the teller partition as a reminder: "What do we say?" It was a lot of work, just to get a Tootsie Roll. At first Bobbie Jo only had hard candy, the kind that came in colored wrappers and tasted like the perfume people wore in church, but she changed it after Mom said Jackie couldn't have any.

Alex often came into the bank with them on Thursdays, and since her mother did not work at the bank she did not have to ask anyone's permission to reach into Bobbie Jo's candy dish—but after the first time, when her candy was unwrapped and swallowed while the Gruber sisters stood waiting for their mom to finish counting out dollar bills, their bodies tensed and focused on their mother's movements, she held back too. That was one of the reasons Meredith and Alex were best friends. They talked, in Alex's bedroom, about the Gruber way and the MacAllister way.

It was like they were two characters living in two different books, Meredith thought. She had taken her dad's copy of *David Copperfield* off the shelf one day, when she had finished all her library books and was tired of re-reading Mom's magazines, and had put the book back after a few chapters because there hadn't been any girls in it. But she did remember the opening sentence. She wrote down in her diary, after she read it, that maybe she wasn't Betsy and Alex wasn't Tacy; that each of them were their own stories, and if hers was like *Betsy-Tacy* then maybe Alex's was like something else. She felt for sure that Alex's book was newer than hers, like *Sweet Valley Twins* or *The Baby-Sitters Club*. In that story, Alex was Kristy and she was Mary-Anne.

After the candy, and after they went over to their mom's teller station and told her that school had been fine, they walked two doors down to the Kiwanis building. They could hear the music as soon as they opened the door at the back of the hall, the one that led up a set of dark and dusty stairs—Meredith held Jackie's hand—to the dance studio.

Every Thursday, Liz Coburn drove 45 minutes down a rural highway to teach ballet in the studio above the Kiwanis hall. She taught two classes: K–2 and 3–6, but she was more than happy to make exceptions, which is how Jackie ended up in the kindergarten class. Her rules were pretty simple: if you gave her five dollars, you could dance. It was Meredith's job to get the $15 check from one of her parents on Thursday mornings and carry it in the inside pocket of her backpack all day long. It was also her job to make sure Jackie and Natalie made it to class safely.

Once the money had been handed over and once her sisters had been absorbed into the cluster of girls changing into ballet slippers, Meredith had an hour free to do whatever she liked, which nearly always meant running down the stairs with Alex and racing her to the library. With no other Grubers around, they both did things the MacAllister way: only looking twice, instead of three times, before they crossed the street; making piles of library books next to them instead of putting each one back; scraping their fingers against the seams at the bottom of their backpacks to see if they had enough dimes to go to the drugstore and share a scoop of ice cream in a cut glass bowl.

When the clock said they had five minutes left, they ran back up the stairs to put on their ballet slippers and leotards. Some of the girls wore swimsuits, but Grandma had given all three Grubers black ballet leotards and shiny pink tights for Natalie's birthday that past August. So when it was their turn to line up at the barre, Meredith was dressed like a proper ballet student. Alex was behind her in a black leotard but ordinary tights, the white ones with little red hearts on them that Meredith also had in her dresser drawer. The Gruber way and the MacAllister way.

They always started ballet class with the same piece of music, and Meredith liked it because it was the same music they played on *Garfield and Friends* when it was time for U.S. Acres. She had asked Dad what it was, and after she hummed a few bars Dad said it was Mendelssohn's Spring Song. Meredith could hear Jackie humming along from the pile of books and toys Liz Coburn had put in the corner, to keep siblings occupied during the lesson.

But Meredith kept her focus on her toes, and her fingers, and making sure each part of her body was in the exact place it should be. It was not hard for her to move along with the rhythm, so she focused on each tendu and dégagé, to see if she could hit the same spot with her feet every time.

They did pliés, relevés, tendu and dégagé, and rond de jambes at the barre, always in the same order and to the same music, and Meredith loved that she knew what was coming next because it was like practicing piano; since she already knew how it should go, she could practice doing every movement perfectly. But Mom gave her and Alex a new piece to practice every week, and Liz Coburn never gave them any new ballet steps. Meredith knew from Noel Streatfeild's *Ballet Shoes* that dancers practiced the same steps every day, but she also knew that the three Fossil sisters learned more steps as they grew older. She had checked out a ballet book from the library, to look at pictures of elevated rond de jambes and battements.

If this was the 3-6 class, it meant she might not learn any new steps for three years. She had to learn more at some point, if she wanted to be a ballerina when she grew up. She already knew that it would be hard to say this dream aloud; that when she thought about growing up to be a writer like Betsy Ray, she could take her purple notebook with the shiny unicorn on the cover and write the first chapter of a novel about a girl who goes back in time to help slaves travel the Underground Railroad—but when she thought about growing up to be a ballerina, there was nothing she could practice besides the same five dance steps she already knew. She wrote in her diary about how she wanted to ask her parents to send her to a dance academy like the one in *Ballet Shoes*, but she did not know how to ask that, because it seemed more like a story she was making up about herself than something that could really happen.

After the barre exercises, Liz had everyone practice châinés turns down the length of the studio. Sometimes she would swap out her classical music tape for the *Little Mermaid* soundtrack, which meant Jackie would get up from the toy station and take her place at the end of the line, singing and spinning her way across the floor.

Jackie was like Posy, Meredith thought, even though Jackie's turns were more energetic than accurate. Maybe Jackie's book was *Ballet Shoes* even though she hadn't read it yet. That meant Natalie, who did not get up, was Petrova—and that made her Pauline, which made sense because she was oldest and most responsible and the one who liked to put on plays. Even if she couldn't grow up to be a ballerina, she could work hard and become an actor who danced in musicals. She could be like the college students who performed *Fiddler on the Roof.* The Chava dance only used châinés turns, not pirouettes or pointe work or anything she didn't know.

But she still wanted to learn more. She imagined, waiting in the line before she spun, the day when Liz would invite her for special ballet lessons. Maybe Alex too, and Jackie when she was older. Meredith saw the picture in her mind, the three of them in tights, elevating their ronds de jambes, as she waited in line to perform her turns and show Liz Coburn she was ready.

WINTER 1990

25. ALEX PLAYS DR. MARIO.

Alex's parents always left the hall light on. The Christmas tree was plugged in too, blinking red and blue and yellow light on the piles of boxes and wrapping paper that had been there for the past three days and the stacks of typewritten pages from her mom's dissertation that had been there for a month. There was almost enough light that Alex didn't have to leave the refrigerator door open, but she kept her foot ready out of habit, kicking herself a bit more light as she took a scuffed pink plastic bowl out of the cupboard and poured herself a bowl of Christmas Crunch. When she put the milk back, she lifted the foil on the corner of a baking dish to grab two squares of fudge. She liked it cold, the way her teeth felt going through the cool resistance of the chocolate. The way the fudge pushed up into the roof of her mouth, smashing against that place with the infinity-shaped ridge that she traced with her tongue, sometimes, when she was bored at school. It always tickled when she licked it.

The Christmas Crunch was too rough to eat right away, so Alex took it back to her bedroom to let it soak in the milk while she played Dr. Mario on her Game Boy. She kept the sound turned down, not as much to keep her parents from hearing the music as to allow her to hear them if they woke up. She'd have from when she heard footsteps on the stairs to hit pause and put the Game Boy face down under the covers as she pretended to sleep. She had the whole plan ready to go, even though she had never had to put it in action.

Alex had a lot of plans that she never got to test out. She and her cousins had gone to see *Home Alone* over Thanksgiving, and since then she had planned out exactly how she could rig her own house to trap would-be robbers. It would be easy to take glass Christmas ornaments off the tree and hide them under the torn wrapping paper on the living room floor, but Alex thought bigger: a trip wire that pulled the string on her talking Big Bird doll, so the voice would startle the robbers; another trip wire that released a balloon covered in a sheet like a ghost; Newton's stinky dog poop smeared behind door handles. Covering the basement stairs with newspaper, so when a robber tried to go down the stairs he would slip and fall.

She and Meredith had planned to go caroling that winter; they had talked about how they would ask Meredith's dad to ask the theater professors to let them use some of the costumes, and then they would walk from door to door by themselves, singing the old-fashioned Christmas songs that fit the costumes and then announcing that they wouldn't leave until they got figgy pudding. They didn't figure anyone would actually have figgy pudding, but maybe they'd get candy, like at Halloween.

But Meredith never asked her dad. Instead, the Grubers had gotten in their car and driven to St. Louis to fly back to Portland for Christmas. Alex had never been on a plane. She had never been to Portland. She had been to Missouri, and Illinois, and Iowa.

So they made a new plan, and Meredith wrote Alex a letter every day. The letters didn't arrive every day; Alex's most recent envelope had contained three letters at once. Meredith called her *My dearest Alexandria*, like the library, and signed them *Meredith of the Sea*, because they had looked up their names in a book, and because Portland, where Meredith was born, was near the ocean.

Her cereal was soggy enough to eat now, and she paused her Game Boy because it was hard to both eat and play Dr. Mario. She had seen a cousin do it, shoving food in his mouth with his right hand while his left hand moved the D-pad, always bringing his thumb back to the A and B buttons in time. That was the same cousin who dared her to see who could eat a piece of pecan pie the fastest. She chewed through the stickiness of the Karo syrup and the impossible-to-dissolve nuts and tried to swallow as fast as she could. They had to open their mouths afterwards to prove they were done, and her cousin won, and then they all ran downstairs to play World Class Track Meet on the Nintendo until they had stitches in their sides.

None of her family members called her Alexandria. Getting letters from Meredith felt like reading a story Meredith was writing about both of them, the brilliant girl in the library and the mysterious girl of the sea. Meredith always wanted to make things into stories. It was another game, like the *Home Alone* game and the caroling game or the stories they acted out together. Nobody else she knew played games like that, except for her and Meredith.

She had half a letter written, so far, to give Meredith when she returned. It was the start of a response to what Meredith had written about what it felt like to see her grandparents again, how she felt older and wondered if they had changed too. Alex wanted to write about what it was like to spend Christmas at her grandma's house, sleeping next to cousins in sleeping bags even though their homes and beds were a few blocks away. The farting contests and the laughter and the one cousin who sat up and cried "You're sinning!" because they were talking after their parents had turned the lights out. The paper was sitting on her desk, with *I bet nobody farted at your Christmas* at the top of the page.

After she finished her cereal she was tired again, and she put her bowl on her nightstand and turned off her Game Boy. It was dark now, except for the hall light which was always on. The Dr. Mario theme circled itself around in her head until she fell asleep.

SPRING 1991

26. THE KIRKLAND R-IX TALENT SHOW.

Jackie lay on her back in Miss Opal's office. If she looked out of the bottom of her eyes, past the blurry part of her nose, she could watch her stomach rise and fall.

She could also look out of the side parts of her eyes at her sisters, to see if their stomachs were rising like Miss Opal said they would. She knew she had to stay still and quiet for Miss Opal, so she didn't move, except for breathing in and out as Miss Opal counted to ten. Sometimes she didn't quite make it to ten, so she had to take a quick breath to catch up. Her stomach jerked then, and she wondered if Miss Opal saw it.

They were taking voice lessons for the Kirkland R-IX school talent show. At their first lesson Miss Opal had asked them to sing something they knew really well, so they sang "The Sound of Music," Jackie singing the high part at the end of each line just like the movie, and Miss Opal had asked them if they wanted to try singing in harmony.

That was three Saturdays ago. Now they practiced "Sing, Sing, Sing" every night, right before each of them took their turn practicing the piano. They visited Miss Opal's office at the college every Saturday morning, and she had them practice other things too: breathing so their stomachs pushed out instead of their chests, standing up straight, making sure they put the Gs at the ends of the words.

"Otherwise, it would be a very different kind of song," Miss Opal said, and Meredith laughed.

Jackie thought the song was like a surprise, because they started out singing the same melody and then split into harmony. Miss Opal said the audience would be surprised too.

"They'll call you the next Andrews Sisters," she said, and then she ran her finger against the records on her shelf until she found the right one. There were three women on the cover, and when she slid the record out of its paper and put it on the record player Jackie could hear the three women sing the same song they were working on. The Andrews Sisters sang all of their Gs.

The version on the record was longer than the one they were going to sing for the talent show. Miss Opal gave them special sheet music with parts crossed out, and an extra copy to take home so Mom could play along on the piano. Mom would play the piano during the talent show, but Miss Opal played for them in her office, her long fingernails making clicking noises on the keys. She had lived in New York once, and sang opera. Some of the posters on the wall had pictures of Miss Opal in them.

Jackie wanted to ask Miss Opal about the pictures, but Miss Opal did not like distractions in the middle of their lessons. She did not like Jackie to touch anything in her office. She did not like it when they breathed at the wrong part of the song, or when their vowels—never their notes—flattened.

"Just because we're in rural Missouri doesn't mean we have to sing like it," she said, and Jackie could hear her Ts and Gs as if she were singing every word.

On the day of the talent show, Meredith sat a few rows ahead of them because she was doing her own act with Alex before they were singing their song. Jackie and Natalie kept the seat next to them saved, so Meredith could come sit in their row when she was done. Everyone performing in the talent show sat in order, so they knew when it was their turn to go on stage.

Rosemary was sitting with the other parents, on the aisle so she would have access to the piano, in plastic chairs that had scratches on the seats from years of high-school use. She sat slightly forward so her pantyhose wouldn't catch on the edge of the chair and run. She was wearing the same basic outfit she might wear to work, the skirt and blouse she had chosen after talking to Carolyn, and everyone around her was wearing jeans. Donna and Mike were next to her and Jack, and although Mike had also come from work and had hung his jacket over the back of his chair, Donna still looked exactly like she always did; the messy-haired math professor in her novelty T-shirt.

Jonetta was a few rows back. Stephanie was playing in the talent sho
had asked her if she wanted to perform something on the piano, and n
in the middle of the third row with her piano book on her lap. Stephanie was dressed up
too, with her bangs teased out over the top of her head. Rosemary watched her tap her
fingers against her piano book, practicing the song one more time before she had to play
it in front of everybody.

After Peg Howard welcomed everyone to the first Kirkland R-IX talent show—
Rosemary noted that Peg did not say *first annual*—and reminded them that the real reason
they were there was to donate money to help the school replace the gym floor, she turned
the event over to the high school choir director. He immediately made a joke about how
he wished the money could be used to support the arts, "but since the choir performs in
the gym, maybe it still counts!"

"He's not coming back next year," Donna whispered, having heard all the good Rix
gossip from her network of Corys. Rosemary nodded. She could ask Bobbie Jo for the
full story tomorrow.

The choir director introduced the first act: three seventh-grade girls "performing
Technotronic's 'Pump Up The Jam!'" The girls walked on stage—technically a raised
platform placed on the substandard gym floor—carrying a basketball and a cassette player,
and did something that was a cross between a dance and a basketball drill. They were better
basketball players than dancers.

"Did that song say what I think it said?" Rosemary whispered back in Donna's
direction during the applause. She felt like she owed Donna a comment, since Donna had
made one in her direction.

The acts continued, and Rosemary was astonished at how few of them included any
real talent. She had almost told Meredith that she couldn't do her act with Alex because it
hadn't seemed appropriate, but after she saw the basketball-passing girls and the teenage
boy who read jokes from index cards while staring at the ground, she realized they might
be one of the highlights of the evening. At least they'd practiced.

Meredith and Alex stood in front of the audience in blue jeans and white
blouses, with strips of red fabric tied under their collars. Rosemary had let them have that

fabric from her scrap pile, and she'd let Meredith have the strip of brown fabric that was currently hanging out of her back pocket. She had no idea why they wanted to do this act, when they could have played a piano duet or done something that showcased their actual abilities, but Donna and Mike and even Jack had said "oh, let them have fun," and she had been outvoted.

The two of them, singing "My Little Buttercup" from ¡Three Amigos!, looked like they were having fun. They waved their arms over their heads, did jumping-jack motions with their legs, and tied that brown piece of cloth around Meredith's head. They got to the part of the song where they asked the audience to join in, and enough people responded that Rosemary knew their act would not be a failure. She still felt a little embarrassed, though, watching them sing and shuffle around and slap their hands on their knees. It wasn't as if she hadn't seen Meredith do this kind of thing before—how many times had Meredith come running up to her saying "Mommy! We have a play to show you!"—but it felt wrong watching Meredith and Alex play in public. Because that's what it was. That's why it was different from the three girls singing an Andrews Sisters song, and why it was different from the teenage boy with his index cards. They were playing, and calling it a performance.

Jack had initially wondered if he might see someone during this talent show whom he could recruit to Kirkland College's music department, but so far the talent was proving negligible except for one flute player who was using the talent show as her rehearsal for the upcoming Junior Miss Something beauty pageant. He'd talk to the band director afterwards and find out her name. He wished the talent show had programs, so he could take quiet notes on his knee between the acts without it being obvious that he was working. It seemed like the school had budget issues.

By the time it was Stephanie's turn, Meredith had changed into her Easter dress so she could match her sisters, and had taken her place in the chair they had saved. She felt excited and flushed and buzzy from her performance with Alex. It felt funny to have imagined and planned the performance, to have thought about it for so long and written about it in her diary, and then to have it happen just like she wrote it. It felt like having a new kind of power. Like being able to predict the future by writing it down.

They knew the Mexican Hat Dance by heart, since they heard Stephanie play it every week at her piano lesson. Natalie had also learned the piece, and one night when the three of them were in their three beds, talking as they always did before they went to sleep, they came up with words:

Oh, the things about chips that are neato
They are either called Fritos Doritos
Or sometimes they are even called Cheetos
Oh, why is it that all chip names rhyme?

Natalie mouthed the words as Stephanie played, and she saw Meredith smile.

The three of them went on at the very end, when there were only two acts left and nearly everybody wanted to go home. Some of the parents had already left with their kids, and there were holes of empty chairs in the rows where families had stood up and apologized and pushed their way out.

But the Gruber sisters stood up straight, like Miss Opal had taught them, and breathed through their diaphragms, and sang their Gs. They started in unison and split into harmony, the big surprise of the night, and all three girls could feel the shift of attention towards them, the way the faces under the gym lights stopped looking at nothing and started looking in their direction. They sang together, taking quick breaths at the same time and stopping the very last note as if they were one voice, each of them knowing in a way that was both instinct and practice. Someone from the back whistled, once, before everybody began to applaud.

Jackie smiled so hard the outsides of her mouth hurt. She bowed exactly the same as her sisters, because Miss Opal had made them practice that too. She wanted there to be a talent show every month, so she could keep singing like this forever.

27. NATALIE NEEDS GLASSES.

Jack knew who it was because her knock was a series of fingernails tapped against the door frame. "Jack," she said, her voice deep and resonant the way sopranos always sounded after years of practice, her higher registers saved for performance. "I wanted to ask you something."

"Sure, Opal, what is it?" This was Jack's last semester before Kirkland College would decide whether to promote him from assistant to associate professor. There were just a few weeks left before he would know their decision, and until then he had time for any faculty member who walked into his office.

"This is going to sound strange, and I know I am speaking out of turn here, but I wanted to ask you if you'd had Natalie's eyes checked."

"Her eyes?" Jack asked.

"I noticed, when I was teaching your daughters, that she was very cleverly following along without actually reading the music. That in itself is not particularly surprising for children of her age, but then I realized she wasn't reading the words either."

"Natalie can read," Jack said. He'd heard her do it.

"I'm quite sure she can," Opal said, "but we were working off a standard SSA arrangement, and I began to wonder if the text was too small for her to read clearly. Perhaps she is nearsighted. Or farsighted, I can never remember which is which."

"The school's never mentioned anything," Jack said.

"Well, she's figured out how to get by," Opal said. "She listens and repeats what she hears. Perhaps her teachers haven't noticed. Or perhaps I am being a busybody for no reason."

Jack smiled. Nobody could be a busybody in the last few weeks before the department decided whether to promote him. "I'll ask Rosemary about it," he said. "Thank you."

He called Natalie into the living room that evening. "Nat, can you read this?" he asked, pointing to the cover of one of Rosemary's magazines.

"Good Housekeeping," Natalie said.

"What about this?" he asked, pointing to one of the smaller headlines. He saw Natalie's face tighten, as if she were working on each letter. "Ten easy summer sal—" Maybe she didn't know the word. "Salads," he said.

He opened the magazine. "How about here?" he asked, pointing to one of the columns of text that ran down the page. Natalie looked up at him. "Where?" she asked. "Where it begins *Beverly's not the type of person who worries about her figure*," he said. "Start there."

"Beverly's not the type of person who worries about her figure," Natalie said. She repeated the words slowly, as if she were reading them aloud, and then she looked up at her dad for another hint.

"Nat, has the school ever given you an eye exam?" he asked.

"I don't know," Natalie said.

"Well, I think it might be time to see if you need glasses," Jack said, giving Natalie a little squeeze on the shoulder to let her know that was a good thing. "To help you with your reading."

"I can read," Natalie said.

"I know you can read," Jack said. "But we might be able to get you reading even better. Would you like that?"

"I don't know."

"It's okay," Jack said. "Glasses are cool. You can wear glasses like your cool dad."

He brought it up with Rosemary after the girls had gone to bed. "So Opal came into my office today to tell me that Natalie needs glasses."

"What?" Rosemary said, just like he had that afternoon.

"She said Natalie wasn't able to read the words on her sheet music. Has the school ever mentioned anything?"

"I don't think so," Rosemary said. "They always say she's a joy to have in class."

"Yeah, that's teacher code for *keeps quiet and bangs the erasers*," Jack said. "So no one's ever mentioned this? It took one of my colleagues to tell us our kid needs glasses?"

"Maybe they thought she was just following along," Rosemary said.

"That's what Opal said too. That she was just following along. Why didn't any of them notice she was just following along?"

"I don't know!"

"Well, you're over there more than I am," Jack said. "Are those teachers doing their jobs?"

"I don't know," Rosemary said, knowing it sounded like whining, wondering why she wasn't saying *I thought they were!* instead. "You're the one who always says I shouldn't worry about what goes on at the school, that they'll be fine because they're smart."

"And she was doing fine *because* she's smart," Jack said. "I bet she has everything memorized as soon as her teachers say it."

"She's like that in piano lessons. She picks it up after someone plays it for her."

"Well, fine, we'll make an appointment for her to get her eyes checked. No big deal."

"We should make an appointment for all of them to get their eyes checked, right?"

"Oh," Jack said. "Sure. Of course."

Two weeks later Natalie sat in a chair and held a plastic spoon over her left eye, reading off the same chart Meredith had just read. She knew the letters because Meredith had already said them. She wasn't sure if she wanted glasses or not. She knew she didn't like this chair, and she didn't like the way her mom sat on the side of the room, like she was waiting for Natalie to do something wrong.

"Okay," the doctor said, and he projected a different chart on the wall. "Can you use your hand to show me which way the Es are pointing?"

Natalie didn't have any practice with this kind of reading. She got the first few, but she couldn't remember what Meredith had said and she started crying.

"It's okay," the doctor said, stepping in front of her so she could see his face. "This is all perfectly normal, Natalie. We're just figuring out if you need glasses, and then we're going to make sure you're able to see everything on the chart, all the way down to the bottom line. Do you know what people always say, when they get glasses for the first time?

They go outside, look at a tree, and suddenly they can see all the leaves."

Natalie already could see the leaves. She could read. She could do everything that everyone else could. She wanted to say that, but she couldn't stop crying.

"Natalie," Mom said, her voice both comfort and warning. Natalie sniffed, and the doctor handed her a tissue.

"Let's start at the beginning again," he said. "And then we're going to do something fun."

It did turn out to be fun, when he moved the lever on the metal mask in front of Natalie's face and she suddenly knew which way the Es were pointing. It also turned out to be fun to try all the different glasses on and laugh at the ones that made her face look silly. The word *astigmatism* was silly too, and Natalie and Jackie stood next to Mom and whispered it to each other, while they were waiting for her to be done at the counter. Three days later, when Mom drove Natalie back to the eye doctor and he gave her the brand-new purple glasses, she went outside and she saw the leaves. She saw the sidewalk, which looked further away than usual and made her feel like the time she wore Mom's high-heel shoes. She blinked, looked around, and saw everything.

28. ROSEMARY AND JACK GO ON A DATE.

Rosemary liked counting back the dollar bills so they all faced the same way. She liked the rules of banking; putting one bill after another into an outstretched hand, saying "and ten $10s make $100," knowing that ten Alexander Hamilton profiles were looking in the same direction. Bobbie Jo teased Rosemary about her drawer, but Carolyn said she was doing a good job, and every time Rosemary got a stack of cash she took a few minutes to fold out every corner and stack the bills like matching rows of towels.

She had taught Meredith how to line the towels up in the closet, the rounded outer folds making dunes you could run your hand over. When Jack did the towels, he put them in whichever way they came out of his hands, the edges with their loose threads hanging down and reminding Rosemary that, even though they had more money now, they still didn't have enough. There were still holes and threads on the corners of everything they owned.

That day Rosemary was wearing pantyhose that didn't yet have nail polish painted over its runs and snags; her underwear didn't have little bits of elastic popping out of the seams. She and Jack were going on a date.

It felt silly to say that, even though the latest *Ladies' Home Journal* she had grabbed at the grocery store had asked its readers "are you still dating your husband?" and advised them to put weekly date nights on the schedule. Before she had read that article, she would have said that she and Jack were going out to dinner. That's what her mother had called it, the nights when Rosemary had been left alone to practice the piano and eat a peanut butter sandwich while watching TV.

116

Well, her girls would be taken care of while she and Jack were on their date. Jonetta and Stephanie were coming over, and they were going to play board games and eat the leftovers Rosemary had set aside in the refrigerator. "Oh, I can make something," Jonetta had said, but Rosemary felt awkward asking Jonetta to cook for her kids, in addition to watching them. It was an unspoken exchange for the free piano lessons.

"Where are you and Jack going to dinner?" Bobbie Jo asked, as Rosemary closed her drawer and opened her purse to make sure her checkbook, driver license, and keys were still inside.

"Dos Bandidos," Rosemary said. Kirkland had opened its first Mexican restaurant that spring. It sat on the edge of town, hoping to entice people off the highway.

"Oh, that's real good," Bobbie Jo told her. "They give you the margaritas in those big ol' glasses."

Rosemary nodded, and then quickly remembered to smile at this. Margaritas in big ol' glasses weren't going to be part of either her or Jack's dinner order, but she didn't need to mention that.

After Jonetta and Stephanie arrived, and after Rosemary had hugged all of her girls with the strange sensation that she might be saying goodbye to them forever—she whispered *I love you* into each of their foreheads, just in case something happened while she and Jack were away—she got into the car with Jack and they drove past the college and the small houses and the apartment where Jonetta lived and parked at Dos Bandidos. The sign was large and lit up, so that drivers could see it from the road. There were three other cars in the parking lot.

"Ohio plates," Jack said. "Looks like the strategy is working."

Rosemary was reminded of what she had loved about Jack when she met him: his eye for detail; his ability to notice that an out-of-state car probably meant someone pulling off the highway, hungry. This attention did not extend to folding towels, or putting mugs in the cupboard so the handles all faced the same way, and that was the sort of thing you didn't realize until after you married someone; that their interest in noticing the bits of life around them was an intellectual curiosity that only extended into the physical world in certain cases: cars, barbecue grills, and—of course—music.

Jack had probably not noticed that he was putting on weight, for example. His stomach had started to turn into a belly, poking forward over his belt, and he still ordered the Bandidos Combination Platter, cheese and chicken enchiladas and a tamale plus the rice, beans, and salad that came with every meal. Rosemary ordered a tostada. She dipped chips into the salsa slowly, putting her hands in her lap between each chip, thinking of the "Ten Tips to Save Money—and Calories!—While Dining Out" that she had read in the *Ladies' Home Journal*.

"Congratulations," she said.

Jack smiled. The promotion had come two weeks ago, and they had known it was coming, but the dinner was a celebratory one regardless. It was also a birthday present for Jack, in addition to the waffles-and-presents family party Rosemary had put together last Sunday afternoon. The girls had drawn birthday cards, and Rosemary had put an apron over her church dress to fry up bacon.

"I'm excited," Jack said. "Next year we're increasing ensemble enrollment by thirty percent. We're starting to get string students who are actually interested in strings."

"That's great," Rosemary said. She started to lift a hand, under the table, and then decided to wait for her tostada.

"It might be a good year for us," she said. "I'll have been working at the bank for two years this fall, so I should get another raise."

"To us," Jack said, holding up his water glass.

"To us," Rosemary said, taking her glass and clinking it against his.

"So I was thinking about this summer," Jack said. "We could make a big road trip out of it, drive up into the Dakotas, see Mount Rushmore, hit Devil's Tower, maybe go into Canada for a day or two."

"I mean, I don't think we should take a *lot* of time," Rosemary said. "Two weeks at the most." She knew Carolyn would give her as much time as she needed, but she didn't want the bank's summer schedule to be determined by her family's vacation. Bobbie Jo and Carolyn couldn't take any days off while she was gone.

"Well, we could get over to Portland in four days if we really hoofed it," Jack said.

"Couldn't we just fly?"

"For five people? That's so expensive."

"Maybe if we mentioned to your folks that we wanted to fly their way, they'd help out."

Jack did not want to ask his parents for help. That wasn't something that the Gruber kids did. He couldn't imagine calling up his dad and saying "look, we want to visit you this summer, but we can't afford it." He'd rather make the drive and pack a tent if they had to. Besides, camping would be fun. He hadn't gone camping since his days in the Boy Scouts. He remembered wrapping up a potato in tinfoil, and how good it tasted when he took it out of the fire pit. He could show the girls how to cook beans in the can, and eat them with a spork.

He knew they wouldn't really like it, though. They might enjoy one meal of beans and potatoes and s'mores, but Meredith would not enjoy getting her hands dirty and Jackie would need to be walked to the bathroom, and she probably wouldn't want to shut herself into a dark port-a-john every time she needed to do her business. Natalie might have a good time. Would they have to get a tent big enough for the five of them, or would Rosemary be willing to let the girls sleep in a tent by themselves?

"Jack," Rosemary said, her voice softly teasing.

"I'm sorry," Jack said. "I was doing the math in my head on camping."

"There's no way we're going camping," Rosemary said. The food arrived, the plates wide and oval and overflowing with rice and refried beans. "Careful, they're hot," the server reminded them.

"Thank you," Rosemary and Jack said in unison. That was another thing Rosemary had loved about Jack, when she met him; he knew his manners. "What if we asked your folks to fly out here?"

"I don't know," Jack said. "They've never been on a plane before."

"My mom does it," Rosemary said. "And it'd be a lot better if we could stay here. I could work, Nat could do swim team—"

"I thought we weren't going to do that," Jack said.

"No, it's okay," Rosemary said. "Jonetta and I will take turns driving them. Or I can drop them off before work and Jonetta can pick them up."

"She'll have meets every weekend, right?"

"Not every weekend. And we took the girls to the pool pretty much every day last year."

"I don't want to spend every afternoon at the pool this summer."

"So we'll trade off with Jonetta or Mike or Donna," Rosemary said, knowing the "we" didn't really include her, since she was already scheduled to work in the air-conditioned bank during most of the summer afternoons. But she'd take turns when she could. "Look, if we don't sign them up for something, one of us will have to spend every day watching them, and it's probably going to be you. At least this way they'll be supervised for a while."

"So does that mean no vacation?" Jack said.

"No," Rosemary said. "We can figure out something small. If we get your folks to fly out here, maybe we can spend a long weekend in St. Louis with the girls. Or we could drive out to meet your folks at the airport and go to the zoo!"

Jack thought of walking, with his parents on one side and his kids on the other, through the St. Louis Zoo. He saw his mom standing in line with the girls to buy cotton candy, and his dad standing back, next to him, the two of them watching. It wasn't a vacation.

"Can we talk about this later?" he asked. "I want to enjoy our dinner at the Two Bandits."

"Of course," Rosemary said, and she smiled at him. She wiped her fingers on her napkin before pushing a stray piece of hair behind her ear.

She looks so beautiful, Jack thought again, noticing that she had painted her nails a pale pink, that they looked almost the same color as the blouse she had on. But that wasn't what made her beautiful. It was that she was Rosemary that made her beautiful. It was that she loved him.

SUMMER 1991

29. DONNA WELCOMES THE SETHS TO KIRKLAND.

"One pepperoni, one cheese, one veggie, and one Hawaiian?" Mike asked, the phone in one hand.

"That should do it," Donna said. She didn't know if the Seths ate meat, and she didn't know if she should avoid beef, and asking seemed like one of those things that would sound inappropriate. *Do you fit into the mental stereotype I have of an Indian person?* Donna knew that just because some As were square didn't mean every square was an A. Even her freshman students could figure that one out. Of course, theories were easier to apply to math than to people.

So. Jackie and Natalie would eat cheese and pepperoni, Alex and Meredith would eat cheese, pepperoni, and Hawaiian, the Seths might eat everything or they might only eat cheese and veggie, or they might only eat cheese, veggie, and Hawaiian, under the assumption that the pepperoni might include beef—Donna wasn't too sure on that herself—and the adult Grubers and MacAllisters would eat whatever was left over. She also put out two bags of Ruffles chips, popped the lid off a jar of sour-cream-and-onion dip, and broke the plastic packaging on the edges of the bags of Oreos and Chips Ahoy, sliding each tray of cookies out halfway so they'd know they were meant to be eaten. Then she took two Oreos and put one in her mouth.

By the time the Seths and the Grubers arrived, the first row of each tray of cookies had been eaten. Donna stuck a spoon in the onion dip last minute, after seeing Alex start to dunk a chip directly into the jar. The pizzas covered the dining room table, lids still closed, the scent filling the house.

And there they were, the familiar Grubers and the unfamiliar Seths, Donna knowing that within a year this new family would be as much a part of their lives as the Grubers had become. Anand Seth was officially teaching computers, but he was also picking up one of the introductory math courses, so they'd see each other. Plus, they had a son who was Alex's age, which probably meant they'd want the kids to get to know each other, the way Jack had suggested introducing Alex to Meredith.

The boy was short—more Meredith's height than Alex's—and he had dark hair and dark glasses. He wore a button-down shirt tucked into a pair of navy blue pants, even though it was July. They also had a younger daughter, whose dress had ruffles around the sleeves and hem, and who removed her shoes on the MacAllisters' front porch.

"Priya," Anand Seth said, picking up the little Mary Janes. He looked to Donna, the only face he knew. "We take our shoes off at home."

"Sure," Donna said, knowing she had only put on sandals because guests were coming. "We don't wear our shoes much around here, either."

Anand was dressed like a larger version of his son, and his wife—whose name Donna couldn't remember—was wearing a long silk blouse over loose pants, and dangling gold earrings. Donna was wearing shorts, because it was summer. She remembered the first time the Grubers came over, and the way Meredith and Rosemary had dressed up.

"Should we do introductions first, and then pizza?" Mike asked.

Anand's wife's was Preeti, and their children were Daniel and Priya. Daniel was nine, like Meredith and Alex, and Priya was five, like Jackie.

"You'll both be in kindergarten together," Rosemary said. "Are you excited?" Jackie said "Yes!" and Priya put her head against her mother's thigh.

"She's my shy girl," Preeti said, smoothing Priya's dark hair.

Donna had thought that the kids could go eat in the TV room, but Priya wanted to stay with her mother, and then Jackie wanted to stay with Rosemary, so the four older kids took their pizza and sat cross-legged on the floor.

"Which teacher do you have?" Alex asked.

"I don't know," Daniel said. He put his pizza down, got up, and came back with the answer. "Mrs. Donovan."

"That's who we have," Meredith said. "We'll all be in the same class together."

"My mom asked for us to be put in that class," Alex said, "because Mrs. Donovan's the best fourth-grade teacher."

Meredith looked at Alex. "She asked for me too?"

"Yeah," Alex said, "I asked her. My cousin Deanna says sometimes they don't like to keep friends together in the same class, so I told mom to ask for both of us. I threw myself on her desk and said *don't separate us!*"

Meredith laughed. Daniel laughed, a little. He had already spilled pizza sauce on the bottom of his shirt.

"Deanna teaches kindergarten, so your sister will have her. She's nice. She's going to get married this winter, and I'm going to be a junior bridesmaid. They timed the wedding over Christmas break."

"Do you celebrate Christmas?" Meredith asked.

Daniel wiped his hand on his mouth. They had forgotten to grab napkins. "Sort of," he said. "Because everybody else does."

"Christmas is my favorite holiday," Natalie said, "because of Santa."

Daniel saw the two older girls look at him, sharp and pointed. He had no idea what that was about.

"We love Santa too," Meredith said, trying to put both meanings of the sentence into her voice. She looked at Daniel again, hoping he wouldn't spoil everything.

"This Christmas I'm going to ask Santa for a Nintendo," Natalie said.

"I have a Nintendo," Daniel said. "At home."

"What games do you like?" Alex asked. "Do you have the Power Pad?"

"No," Daniel said. "I like Final Fantasy and Ultima: Exodus, but Ultima is hard. You have to map out all the dungeons on paper. I can use the maps in Nintendo Power for Final Fantasy."

"What's Final Fantasy?" Meredith asked.

"Have you ever played an RPG before?" Meredith shook her head, so Daniel continued.

"Okay, so it's like a big story where you get to be all the characters. And you go around and find things, like missing crystals or a witch's crystal ball."

"Wait, is it like Mixed-Up Mother Goose?" Meredith said.

"It's way better than that. Mixed-Up Mother Goose is for babies. You get to be mages and ninjas and thieves and you can cast spells and fight monsters."

"I want to play this," Meredith said. "My dad lets me play games on the computers at the college sometimes. Have you played Hitchhiker's Guide to the Galaxy?"

"Yeah, but I've never beaten it. I always end up dead."

"Me too," Meredith said, "but then I checked out the book from the library. You're supposed to lie down in front of the bulldozer at the beginning. I still haven't beaten it though. It's really hard."

"There's a book? Like a game guide?"

"No, a real book, like a novel," Meredith said. "It's hilarious. There's this whole bit at the beginning about Jesus—" and then she stopped herself. "I mean, I can show you where it is at the library, if you want to borrow it."

"Final Fantasy II is coming out, so maybe I can let you borrow my old Final Fantasy," Daniel said. "I have to ask my mom."

"We don't have a Nintendo, though," Meredith said.

"Well, your sister just said Santa was going to bring one," Daniel said, grinning in a way that meant he was in on the joke, and Meredith suddenly realized that she liked Daniel, that she wanted to know more about Final Fantasy, and that she was glad the three of them were going to be in the same class at school. It would be like Anne, Diana, and Gilbert Blythe.

FALL 1991

30. MEREDITH ASKS JACK A QUESTION.

Meredith looked over the top of her book to see if Dad was still working. The big scores were spread out over the dining room table, so he probably was. Dad often worked on Sunday afternoons. Meredith worked on Sunday afternoons too, but all of her homework was done and now she was waiting. She wanted to ask before one of her sisters ran down the stairs and demanded she come play ponies with them, or before Mom woke up from her nap and asked her to unload the dishrack. She could unload the dishrack now, maybe. Maybe if she walked past the dining room table Dad would look up, and smile at her, and it would be just enough not-working that Meredith could ask the question without interrupting.

She was another two chapters in before he stood up, stacked a few of the scores together, and walked into the kitchen. Meredith heard him open the cupboard and turn on the tap. She kept her finger on her page and listened for the little echo of glass against metal as he put the dirty water glass in the sink. He came back; he walked past the dining room table; he walked past the couch and Meredith wondered if she just missed her chance. He opened the front door and stood on the porch, and after counting to thirty to see if he'd do anything new, Meredith looked back at her book just long enough to memorize *page 153* and then left it on the couch and went outside.

"Can I ask you something?"

"Sure, Mer, what's up?"

She paused. It felt like a request that would change everything if she said it aloud. She thought through it one last time, confirming she wanted to make that change.

"Can we start going to different churches?"

The summer humidity had finally been blown out of the air, slowly pushed away to wherever it went; Meredith crossed her arms over her cardigan. "It could be for my birthday."

"Which church do you want to go to?" Dad asked.

"I want to go to all of them," Meredith said.

"Well, you can't really go to all of them," Dad said, beginning to joke in the way that Meredith didn't like; the way that meant he had already decided. "Not unless you invent time travel."

"You could if you went to a different one each week."

"Oh," Dad said. "Sure. I guess if you wanted to go to a different church one Sunday, with a friend, that would be okay—but we go to the Methodist church, and it's one of the things we do as a family, and I don't think we're going to change that."

"We went to a Catholic church in Portland."

"Yes we did," Dad said.

Meredith didn't like that response, either. "So why aren't we going to the Catholic church now?"

"Because when your mother and I moved out here, we decided we wanted to try the Methodist church."

"But we didn't try any other churches."

"No," Dad said, "we liked the Methodist one. Do you not like it anymore?"

"I like it," Meredith said, not quite sure that was true but feeling like it was the answer she was supposed to provide. There were a lot of things she liked about the Methodist church, like the music they sang together and the people who shook her hand during the Passing of the Peace. She liked sitting next to Alex at Sunday School, and she liked the cookies in the Fellowship Hall at the end.

"But you're curious about what other churches are like," Dad said.

"Yes," Meredith said, smiling because he finally understood. "I want to know why everyone believes different things."

"Well, most churches are about the same thing," Dad said, "and they just talk about it in slightly different ways. One of the reasons we go to the Methodist church, for example, is because they use language like God the Creator instead of God the Father. They don't think of God as a man with a big white beard sitting in the sky."

"But we still say *Our Father, who art in Heaven.*"

"You know what that's about, though," Dad said, looking down at Meredith like he was leading up to a joke. "Tradition!"

Meredith didn't know how to say how serious she thought all of this was. She felt embarrassed to hear her dad doing fake movie voices on the front porch. She sat down on the porch swing and tried to put words together, sorting sentences in her head and taking out the parts that didn't accurately describe her feelings. Then she erased all her sentences and said something else.

"Some people don't believe any of it is true," she said. She didn't say *Daniel.* She didn't say *Douglas Adams.* She didn't say herself. "And Jewish people don't believe in Jesus, and Hindu people don't believe in Jesus or God."

Dad sat down beside her. They swung back and forth slightly, not far enough that Dad had to take his feet off the ground, but enough that Meredith knew Dad was thinking, too.

"God is a metaphor," he finally said.

"For what?"

"For the Great Mystery," Dad said, still rocking his feet carefully back and forth, just enough to keep them moving.

Meredith thought of the song she had heard Miss Opal sing at the faculty recital last spring. *Ah, sweet mystery of life, at last I've found thee.* She wondered if Dad was thinking of the song too. Sometimes someone would say something, like at dinner, and it would put a song in her head that would stay there while she cleared the table—and she'd hear Dad, in the living room, humming the same melody.

They talked about it for a while longer; how people use the word "God" to describe what they don't yet understand, and how so many stories are the same story with different names. They talked until the sky started to get dark and Meredith felt cold and Natalie came to holler through the screen door that it was dinner time and Meredith had not been there to set the table and she had done it for her.

Later, after dinner, Meredith waited and watched until everyone else was busy and then walked quietly into her parents' bedroom, knowing she was breaking a rule. The books sat next to each other on her parents' bookshelf, and Meredith kept her hands behind her back so she would not touch them: *Primitive Mythology*, *Oriental Mythology*, *Occidental Mythology*, and *Creative Mythology*. She had always assumed these books were about Greek gods or the myths she read about at the library. Now she knew they were also about Methodists too.

She saw *The Hero With the Thousand Faces* and thought of the stories she was writing in her notebook: princesses on quests, poor girls who realized they were royalty, the abandoned novel about the Underground Railroad. They were all the same story. They were the same story that everyone had been trying to tell, since the beginning of time. Meredith thought about asking Dad if she could read the book, and then decided she didn't want to. Her stories might be the same as everyone else's, but as long as she kept that book closed, they could still be hers.

31. THE GRUBER GIRLS GO TO AN AUDITION.

After everyone had arrived and the moms and older kids had filled out the forms, they all sat in the front row of the auditorium. Jackie swung her legs because they didn't touch the floor yet, and because she was excited, and because she liked her new back-to-school shoes. Mom would have said "sit quietly," but Mom had to stay in the back, where she couldn't see. When Jackie swung her feet forward, she saw pink sneakers with white laces. She swung back and kicked the metal under the seat, and heard the noise and stopped. Miss Opal looked at her, and Jackie wondered if she had heard the noise too.

Miss Opal looked so pretty, with her white hair and all the bracelets on her wrists. She was the only old person Jackie knew who was pretty. She asked all the kids to join her onstage, and Jackie went up with everyone else and stood as close to the piano as she could, so Miss Opal would see her.

Natalie stood next to Jackie, but when she saw Stephanie standing by herself, she waved her arm to let Stephanie know she could stand with them. None of her friends from school were there. A lot of her friends had quit ballet lessons too, but Natalie still went every week, and she still practiced the piano, and she stood next to Stephanie so they could share the photocopied piece of paper that Miss Opal handed out.

"I'm going to teach you the song that the Siamese children sing," Miss Opal said. "It's called 'Getting to Know You.'"

Jackie already knew the song. They had practiced it at home, and they had practiced it that morning before they left for the auditions. The college was putting on *The King and*

I, and they were all going to be in the play.

Dad had said if they were in the play, they would get to wear a costume and color their hair black, and they would have to do exactly what the director said. He said that during the auditions, people would be watching to see if they did what they were told to do, so Jackie watched Miss Opal and stood very quietly and didn't look at Natalie, because when they were waiting to drive up to the college they had sung the song in silly voices and started laughing, and Mom had said they couldn't do that during the audition.

They sang the song a few times, then Miss Opal had them divide into groups of four and gave each group a chance to sing the song together. Then their part of the audition was over, and most of the kids went home.

The Gruber girls stayed, because Meredith was auditioning for one of the speaking parts. There were two parts for older kids: Louis Leonowens and Prince Chulalongkorn. They were both boy parts but Dad had said it was okay for girls to audition. So Jackie and Natalie went to the back to wait with Mom, and Meredith walked by herself back onto the stage.

Meredith had hoped there would be a chance for her to be alone before her audition, the way Pauline had always found a moment to be alone in *Ballet Shoes*. She wanted to stare at herself in the mirror until she stopped seeing herself and started seeing Prince Chulalongkorn. Whenever her sisters were busy with something else, she practiced walking around the bedroom with her head held high, catching her reflection in the full-length mirror, waiting for the moment when she would see someone besides herself. Sometimes she thought she did.

"My name is Meredith Gruber," she said, "and I'm going to be singing 'Whistle a Happy Tune.'"

It was a little complicated to sing Louis' song when you were hoping to get cast as the Prince, but everyone who was auditioning for one of the speaking parts had been asked to prepare that song, so Meredith sang it as though she were a child of royalty. She tilted her head up and kept her back straight and tried to sing as if she were commanding people to kneel before her.

When she was done, she bowed and waited. She knew Miss Opal and Dr. Barney and everyone who would be making the casting decisions. She saw Dr. Barney writing on her form.

"Thank you, Meredith," he said. "Do you have something to read for us?"

"Yes," she said. "Puck's speech from *A Midsummer Night's Dream*."

Meredith did not quite understand Puck; she knew he was a fairy, but when she pictured him she always saw someone like Dr. Barney, tall and thin with his cigarette behind the stage door. Someone who always looked at you as if he were judging you, even when he liked you. It was hard to see Puck as a little naked boy like he was in the movie; it didn't match up with the words. So Meredith thought of Pauline Fossil playing Puck instead. She knew what it was like to feel like Pauline.

When she finished she bowed again, and left the stage, and then it was Alex's turn. Alex sang, and grinned, and recited "Jabberwocky," and looked exactly like Alex. She should play Louis and Meredith should play Prince Chulalongkorn. They had talked about this at school, Meredith's lunchbox next to Alex's hot lunch tray. Alex had even said she would cut off her hair for the part, to look like a boy.

Daniel had started sitting with them at lunch, and he said that his parents were making him audition, too. They had sent him to the audition wearing a tie, and when it was his turn he held his copy of "Whistle a Happy Tune" and sang it like he had never sung alone in public before. Maybe like he had never sung alone at all. His eyes looked up from the music to follow the sound of his voice as it echoed into the auditorium, and then jumped back down because he had lost his place.

"Do you want to try that again?" Dr. Barney said.

"I don't know," Daniel said.

"Maybe one more time."

The second time was better, and Meredith watched Daniel's eyes as he focused on the paper in front of him. He sang to the end of the piece and then looked up, a little surprised that he had made it, and then he smiled.

"Do you have something to read for us?" Dr. Barney asked.

Daniel stopped smiling. "No, I didn't know I was supposed to bring anything."

There was a pause and some whispering, and then Miss Opal's voice came calmly up from the darkness. "It's all right, Daniel," she said. "Can you read the lyrics on your paper? Don't sing them. Just read them like you were telling us what you do when you are afraid."

Daniel began, and Meredith could hear him putting the rhythm of the song into the words, and then they started to smooth out into sentences. He even did the pose, just like the song said, and everyone laughed, and Meredith laughed, and Daniel turned his head quickly and met her eyes, and then he found his place again and kept going, standing straighter and speaking more clearly and looking like... and Meredith suddenly realized she knew what would happen.

After Miss Opal called that night with the news—Daniel had been cast as the Prince, Meredith had been cast as Louis, Alex and Natalie and Jackie would all be playing Siamese children—Meredith stood in front of the mirror and tried to see Louis Leonowens. She saw herself. So she took her diary out from under her mattress and sat at the foot of her bed and wrote about how she felt excited but also sad, because this was the part that Alex had wanted; but she didn't feel sad that Daniel had gotten the part she wanted, because she knew he would be good at it. It was strange that he was good even though he hadn't practiced. *I wonder if I am good at anything that I haven't practiced.*

Meredith thought of all the things she might like to be good at: tap-dancing, sailing, gymnastics. There wasn't any opportunity to test those things out, not in Kirkland. She stood in front of the mirror again and did a few tap dance steps she had seen on television, quietly, so nobody downstairs would hear her bounce. Then she put her diary away and went to find her sisters.

32. *THE KING AND I.*

Daniel and Meredith sat in the wings, notebooks open on cross-legged laps, Meredith's math book between them. It had been Meredith's idea to use the same book, even though they had both carried copies from school to rehearsal; it had also been her idea to race to the end of their homework. They were doing long division.

Daniel knew to keep his eyes on his own paper, so he did not look at Meredith to see how many problems she had completed. He could feel her, tense and focused, her breathing interrupted by a pause, as she thought—and then the air came out of her nose in a little snort and he could hear her writing numbers down.

Daniel was also fast at math; his father drilled him at home after dinner, and he had participated in a state Math Contest at his old school, when they lived in Boston. Everything seemed strange and small here; the whole town like a penny in the middle of a field, something you might find only by looking, something that only seemed to have value if you were close enough to pick it up.

He had told Meredith about Boston one night, during another break when they were not needed onstage, and she had told him about Portland. They talked about riding the MAX and the MBTA, the memory of standing in the middle of a crowd of people as the city went by. Daniel's memories were newer than Meredith's, though only by six months since she had been to Portland that past Christmas. She had flown on a plane, but Daniel had flown on an international plane to India, one of the flights where they show movies on a tiny screen at the front, and bring you dinner on a tray. His parents had told him to close his eyes and sleep, even though that meant missing the movie.

"Do you feel like Kirkland is your home?" he asked, and Meredith had said "No. I'm a Portland girl." Daniel was a Boston boy and an Indian boy, even though he had only been to Delhi once in his life, to see his grandparents. They talked about the strangeness of seeing grandparents only rarely, the awkwardness of the long-distance phone calls and the ache of not being able to say anything more than "I'm fine. School is going well. How are you?"

Daniel was good at math, and he could solve any individual problem just as fast as Meredith, but he could never get through a string of problems in a row without getting distracted. He was distracted now, watching the actors on stage rehearse the scene where Tuptim tries to escape. They did not have a whip, not yet; so the actor playing the King waved his hand and the stage manager said "crack! crack!" in a dull and professional voice.

"I'm done," Meredith said, exhaling and leaning back on her hands. She looked excited. "I hate showing my work. Do you ever just solve the problem and then go back and write your work down the way they want?"

She was wearing blue jeans and a brown sweater. On the days they came to rehearsal, Meredith dressed like a boy, with her hair pulled back in a low ponytail. Daniel did not dress like a Siamese prince. He already knew what it was like to wear kurta pyjama, which was not the same thing as the costume they had measured him for, the pants that gaped over the legs like bells and the fitted blouse with its gold trim, but when the student who pinned fabric around him asked "Is this like what you wear in India?" he said "Yes." The distance between India and Thailand was incomprehensible in Kirkland. It was like trying to explain that the triceratops and the stegosaurus could never have been friends in *The Land Before Time*, back when he was interested in dinosaurs.

While Daniel finished his homework, Meredith crawled forward, getting herself as close to the stage as she dared without being visible. They had all been told, during one of the big Siamese children rehearsals, that if you could see someone in the audience, they could see you; so Meredith kept herself just out of sight of where she knew Miss Opal and Dr. Barney were sitting. Her dad was in the band room rehearsing the pit orchestra; during their breaks, they would go out into the hallway and hear the orchestra practicing the songs they had just finished singing with the rehearsal pianist. The college students sang along with the orchestra too, trying to make their voices heard through the band room wall.

She watched Tuptim's face; the fear, the defiance, the little wince she made every time the stage manager said "crack!" even though Mrs. Anna stepped in before she was actually whipped. Then she watched Mrs. Anna, who had the more difficult part in this scene, and Meredith listened for the grief and anger and confusion and shame that were written into her lines, to see how the actress made the emotions come out and whether she missed any. Meredith thought of how she would say the lines, if the role were hers to play. How she would have to make a single sentence communicate so many different feelings. It was a lot easier to think of everything that a line should contain than to say it. Something always disappeared when she opened her mouth, the way a memory reduced itself to simplicity when you tried to tell it to someone else. She and Daniel both agreed that, when you flew on an airplane, the clouds looked like cotton balls. They didn't, of course. They didn't look like cotton balls at all.

Natalie liked a lot of things about rehearsals. She liked Alex, who stood with her and Stephanie when they sang "Getting to Know You" together. She liked singing, well enough. She very quickly learned the dance, where they all held hands and walked in a circle around Mrs. Anna, and then turned around and walked in the other direction.

But Natalie still thought all of this was silly. After they watched the movie for the first time, she sang "Getting to Know You" in the scoopy voice that Mrs. Anna had, and Jackie laughed, and Dad laughed, and he sang in the same silly voice right back at her. Meredith and Mom didn't laugh. Meredith thought the whole play was wonderful.

There was a part Mrs. Anna sang, in the middle of the play, where she made fun of everything and waved her butt around, and that was what Natalie told her friends the play was like, at school. Then she didn't want to talk about it anymore. She wanted to talk about what they were doing, and about Kimberly's upcoming birthday party at the roller rink. Natalie didn't know yet if she would get to go, because of *the play*, but she wanted to so much that every night she prayed at the image of her and Kimberly and Jenna racing around the rink together, and Kimberly picking the two of them to sit with her in the big skate when it was time for her special birthday song. Chrissy still sat with them at lunch, but she sat at the end of the table.

Jack was glad that Meredith and Jackie were enjoying the rehearsals so much, and he was glad that Meredith had this big role and was getting to make friends with Anand's kid, but he was secretly glad, in a way that he would never say aloud, that Natalie thought the whole business was ridiculous. She had said "but isn't the music a little… *predictable?*" in a way that suggested she had substituted "predictable" for one of the insults she had learned at school and they had asked her not to say at home.

She was such a Gruber kid. Smart as the King of Siam's whip, even though she didn't show it the way Meredith did. Pulled out the truth of the musical right away. Jack would do the best job he could with the pit orchestra, but he would be as glad as Natalie was when the whole thing was finally over.

Alex didn't get to watch movies with Meredith on Fridays anymore, because Meredith was nearly always at rehearsal. Even when Meredith wasn't at rehearsal, she would call and say that her parents had told her she needed to stay home and rest, or do her homework. The three of them sat at lunch together, and Meredith and Daniel talked about the play, always having an extra inside joke that Alex wasn't aware of, something that she had to pick up in the middle of their conversation.

"Dr. Barney wants to know if a prince would really open his milk spout like that," Meredith said, her eyebrows in exaggerated imitation. Daniel laughed. It wasn't that funny.

Jackie was the youngest person in the play and she loved every minute of it. She loved remembering to breathe just the way Miss Opal said, and she loved remembering to put both Ts in "get-ting," instead of singing it "gedding," the way Miss Opal said most Midwestern people would do. "But that's why you are my very special Siamese children," she told them, and Jackie always stood in the front, because she was the smallest, and Miss Opal always smiled at her as if she were the most special of them all.

She was so special that, two weeks before the play, Dr. Barney and Miss Opal asked her if she would like to read a few lines just by herself, at the very end.

"We need someone to play Princess Ying Yaowalak," Miss Opal said, "and we think it should be you."

Jackie remembered her manners. "Thank you, but I have to ask my parents first."

Then Dr. Barney laughed, and said "I'll have to remember that one," and Miss Opal explained that her parents already knew.

Meredith also already knew, and she and Jackie jumped up and down in the hall together at the break, and then Meredith told Jackie that Princess Ying Yaowalak was a real person and she had read a book about the real King of Siam and she would read the part about Princess Ying Yaowalak to Jackie when they got home.

"It's important to know as much as possible about your character," she said, "so you can play her accurately."

But nobody ever told Jackie she was playing Ying Yaowalak inaccurately. She walked to the center of the stage, held out her letter, and said goodbye to Mrs. Anna. She put her Ds and Ts in each word just like she was singing, and after she did it the first time everybody clapped, and after she did it the second time she saw Miss Opal smile at her, and she almost smiled back except that hadn't been one of the things Dr. Barney told her to do. She saved her smiles for later, after she and the other Siamese children went offstage.

"That was supposed to be Priya," Daniel said, when he and Meredith were alone again, waiting. He said it quietly, in the under-the-breath way they had learned to talk, as they sat in the wings and watched the actors move on and off stage around them. "Dr. Barney came to our house and tried to get her to do it, but she didn't want to."

"She didn't want to be in a play? It's such a good role."

"I didn't want to be in the play," Daniel said. "But they said I had to." He didn't tell Meredith that Priya had cried, and that he had wondered if he should cry too to get out of having to do this thing that sounded time-consuming and not a lot of fun. But he was too old to bury his head in his mother's trouser leg and refuse the opportunities offered to him.

Then he realized what he should say to Meredith. He had gotten distracted again. "I'm glad I'm in it now." He looked at her face, half lit by the stage, as she kept her eyes focused on the actors. He hoped she had heard him. He wondered if he should say it again, but instead he sat quietly next to her, watching Kirkland college students pretend to be Thai women pretending to be African-American slaves. He was glad to be in the play, even though he didn't like this play very much. The part he was glad about was Meredith.

On the last night of the play, Miss Opal found Jackie in front of the makeup mirror, as a college student was darkening her face and eyebrows. "Our little princess," Miss Opal said, and Jackie tried to keep from smiling because she had to be still for her makeup. "Are you excited for closing night?"

The college student stepped away, so Jackie could turn in her chair to see Miss Opal better. "I'm excited, but I'm sad that it's the last one."

"Well, I wanted to tell you what a pleasure it has been to get to work with you," Miss Opal said. "You have a lovely voice and I hope you keep singing." She put one hand, on Jackie's shoulder, gave it a warm squeeze, then walked away. Jackie watched her leave. She didn't stop to talk to Meredith. She didn't stop to talk to Daniel. She hadn't come to talk to any of the Siamese children but her.

The college student came back and said "cover your eyes!" so Jackie put her hands over her eyes like she did every night, and heard the sound of black spray paint covering her hair. Miss Opal had come down into the dressing room just to talk to her. She had been a pleasure to work with. People always said nice things about Jackie when she was with her sisters, like their matching dresses were pretty, or they sang well at the talent show—but nobody had ever said anything like that *just to her*.

When Jackie took her hands off her eyes, she decided she would be a singer when she grew up. She'd tell Miss Opal as soon as the play was over.

WINTER 1991

33. AMERICAN GIRLS AND *LITTLE WOMEN*.

Rosemary invited her daughters into her bedroom one at a time, asking them to please not tell the others what they were discussing. She brought Natalie in first, wanting to make sure that her middle daughter never grew up thinking she was overlooked, trying to give her as many special moments as she could.

Natalie was seven years old now, her purple glasses slightly smudged, her long, wavy hair in need of brushing. Rosemary would have to trim it again, before Christmas. She had made them all Daisy Kingdom dresses to wear on Christmas Eve, red with bunny Nutcrackers and ballerinas printed at the bottom. Natalie's jeans were getting too short; they'd have to shop the sales over the holiday break, on one of the days Rosemary had off.

"Samantha," Natalie said, and Rosemary was surprised, but she thought *it's okay if we get two Samanthas*, and asked Natalie to send Jackie in.

Jackie's sweatshirt was too big for her skinny frame, and the sleeves were rolled up at the ends. Okay for a Sunday afternoon, of course, but something else Rosemary would have to think about when they went shopping. Not that Jackie wouldn't grow, soon enough. She danced slightly, putting one sock foot out and bringing it back in as if she were doing a personal Hokey Pokey. Her hair also needed brushing, and her barrette had slipped halfway down from where Rosemary had clasped it that morning.

"Molly," Jackie told her, her foot going back into an arabesque. That had been who Rosemary had thought Natalie would pick, because of the glasses.

Meredith's hair was combed straight, because she had started to take care of it herself now that she was ten years old. Rosemary watched her as she made ponytails and then pulled them out again until she got one to be perfectly smooth, with no hair bumps on the way to the rubber band. Rosemary wanted to say something, to tell her daughter *you look fine, you look beautiful*, but she usually said *you look fine, we have to leave*, which was not the same thing.

"Kirsten," Meredith said. So there wouldn't be two Samanthas after all. Rosemary asked "are you sure?" trying to figure out if Meredith had somehow talked to the other two and was sacrificing her own choice, but Meredith said yes, and her smile was genuine, so Rosemary called Pleasant Company and placed the order.

"I thought for sure Meredith would pick Samantha, Nat would pick Molly, and Jackie would pick Felicity," she told Bobbie Jo. Stephanie was also getting an American Girl that Christmas (another Samantha), and Bobbie Jo was giving her all of the schoolroom accessories as well.

"My mother had a desk like that when she went to school," Bobbie Jo said. "We have her class photograph." Rosemary knew that Bobbie Jo must have been around Molly's age in the 1940s, and wondered why she wasn't using that American Girl doll to bond with her granddaughter. She thought of what Kirkland must have been like, during the war, but all she could see was the illustration of Molly throwing her brother's underpants out the window.

On Christmas Eve, Rosemary had the camera ready to take photographs of three girls in matching dresses, their hair wrapped around their heads in matching coronet braids, opening three identical maroon boxes. Meredith knew exactly what they were from the moment she tore off the paper, but Nat and Jackie didn't realize it until they pulled the lids off the boxes and revealed three nearly identical dolls.

Each of her girls spontaneously hugged their doll, still in its box, to their chest. Jack had to get the scissors to cut the plastic ties that held down the dolls' arms, and then Rosemary asked if they could do it one more time. Her three daughters obligingly hugged their dolls, faces beaming, but they were also watching the camera.

Rosemary took another picture, later, after the three girls had gone to bed and she and Jack had stuffed their stockings for the next morning. They slept, blankets up to their chins, in their shared bedroom, each of them with a doll head poking out next to them. It felt like what Pleasant Company promised on the cover of every catalog. It felt like girlhood.

The next day they played with their dolls exactly as Rosemary had hoped they would; the picture she had kept in her head as she convinced Jack it was a worthwhile expense. Kirsten, Samantha, and Molly, loosely bracketed by a time travel device that had been Meredith's invention, were getting to know each other. Rosemary had noticed her daughters were playing together less regularly than they used to; Meredith was spending more time reading or writing in one of her notebooks, or going to watch movies with Alex or play video games with Daniel. Natalie had her friends, who always seemed to be having birthday parties or slumber parties. Jackie had whoever was around. They had ballet and piano and church and homework and the play (thank goodness that was over) and this moment of watching them all engaged with each other, creating a story with their imaginations and their dolls, now seemed rare. It had been the right year to buy the American Girl dolls. Next year might have been too late.

When Meredith called Alex on Christmas Day, she mentioned the American Girl doll only briefly, because she knew Alex didn't have one. She felt sad about that in a way that was different than feeling sad that Alex didn't get cast as a lead role in the play. She wrote in her diary:

> Alex didn't get a Last Doll. She and I never played with dolls, but I wonder if she had gotten Felicity, if we would have. I don't know if I'll get a lot of toys next year. I don't need any more toys but it feels strange to think that I'm getting too old for them. What kind of presents do you get when you are too old for toys? Clothing and books, probably.
>
> I don't want to think about what will happen when I am too old to make up stories and act them out. I don't ever want to stop playing.

The next day Meredith and Alex exchanged their gifts—both copies of *Little Women*, which they had planned in advance, each with a heartfelt inscription on the title page—and as Meredith read the story she thought about how she and Alex might play it, when they were both finished reading. She thought of how they could re-enact Amy's drowning scene, with Meredith gripping the edge of Alex's bed and flailing while Alex stood above, ready to lie on her stomach and drag Meredith out of the water and onto the bedspread. Alex was Jo of course, but Meredith couldn't decide which of the March sisters she was most like.

As it turned out, Alex couldn't either. They got together in Alex's bedroom after they had finished the book, and instead of playing the story they talked about it.

"I don't know," Alex said, "I liked Jo a lot but she was really mean sometimes."

"Beth was always good," Meredith said, "but she died. Does that mean you're mostly like Meg? She was mostly good. She was talented, too."

"Do we have to be like one of them?"

"I thought when I was reading it that you were like Jo and Meg, and I was like Beth and Amy," Meredith said.

"Amy was awful!" Alex said. "But you always fuss about your clothes and your hair and you always try to be super-polite to grownups, so maybe you are like Amy. Or Meg."

"I don't want to be like Meg," Meredith said. "All she did was get married and have babies."

"You just said I was like her!" Alex said, and Meredith thought of how something about this conversation felt a little bit off, how she and Alex weren't like mush and milk anymore. She was the one who had come up with the idea for the inscriptions, because it sounded like something someone in a book would do. When the March sisters had received their own matching, inscribed books on Christmas morning, she wanted to call Alex right away and say *they're just like us!* But they weren't.

"Did you like the second half?" she asked.

"No," Alex said. "I skipped part of it, it was so boring."

"I skimmed a lot of the chapters," Meredith confessed, and the two of them looked at each other and laughed, at this grown-up gift they had planned and prepared for, that neither of them had fully read. As they left their books behind and went into the kitchen for more of Alex's mom's fudge, Meredith thought that they felt like best friends again. It was a relief as solid as refrigerator-cold Christmas fudge, and—her mind filled in the phrase like she was writing it in her diary—just as sweet.

SPRING 1992

34. LIZ COBURN'S LAST CLASS.

At the last class, Liz Coburn did a quick warmup and let everybody dance. She played *Beauty and the Beast*, then swapped it out for a Beach Boys cassette. Meredith shook her arms and legs in tandem with Alex as the Beach Boys invited the room of ballet students to a surfin' safari. Alex kept putting her fingers on her nose and wiggling downwards; Meredith was always half a beat behind.

She watched Liz dance with Jackie and the other kindergarteners. Natalie and her friends had gotten bored with the dancing and were sitting on the floor in a circle, chatting and laughing with each other. A few parents had started to arrive, standing against the wall until the music was over and they could say *thank you* and *congratulations* and *we'll miss you.* One of the moms held a small gift bag with a stork on it.

Meredith knew that she had to ask now; that if she did not, she would miss her chance. She thought of how Posy Fossil had gotten to dance by asking for lessons, and how Pauline had gotten the role of Prince Edward by asking. It would be as easy as walking over and forming the question, and yet she had not done it. She thought she would do it at the end of this song, and then she thought she would do it at the end of the next one.

And then she did it. It felt like stepping out of the part of life where she was supposed to be, like there was another Meredith behind her still dancing with Alex. She felt the little canvas pads of her ballet slippers on the balls of her feet. Her head began to buzz; it had been a long time since it had done that, but at least it was familiar. She was doing the thing she had to do, before the class was over.

"May I ask you a question?"

"Sure, Meredith," Liz said, still swaying to the rhythm.

"If I wanted to continue taking ballet lessons, where could I go?"

"Oh," Liz said. "Sure. There's a dance studio in Delacroix. I used to teach a class there."

Meredith had seen this dance studio. They drove by it on their way to the mall. The building's windows were painted with silhouettes of ballet and jazz dancers. "Do they teach pointe work?"

"What?" Liz was partially distracted by the students who were dancing next to her, and the ones who were waving goodbye before running down the stairs.

"Pointe. I'll be eleven in the fall."

"I think so," Liz said. "I don't know. You don't want to do pointe, though—you'll lose half your toenails."

Meredith knew exactly what she might lose. She thanked Liz, went back to Alex, and whispered "I know how we can keep training." Alex put her fingers on her nose again, and Meredith followed, the two of them shimmying their way down to the floor.

"Did you all enjoy your last dance class?" Dad asked at dinner, as each of them passed their plates so he could scoop them spaghetti out of the big glass bowl.

"Yes!" Jackie said. "We got to dance to *Beauty and the Beast*."

"Jackie, that's too much parmesan," Mom said.

"I like parmesan," Jackie said.

"I asked Mrs. Coburn where we could go to continue taking lessons," Meredith said, "and she said the dance studio in Delacroix."

"That's so far away, though," Mom said, passing the parmesan shaker.

Meredith shook the green cylinder three times, and then passed it to her dad even though not a lot of parmesan had come out. There were always lumps in there, blocking the holes. "It'd be just once a week. We already go to Delacroix every other weekend, so it wouldn't be that different."

"I'm not sure that's true," Dad said.

"It is," Meredith said. "We went last Saturday to buy summer clothes, and we went two weeks ago to do that thing with the car."

"What thing?" Dad said.

Mom answered. "I think she means the oil change."

"Well, you all didn't come with me to get the oil changed," Dad said.

"No," Meredith said, "but maybe we could. We could find a dance class that was on the weekends, and we could go take lessons while you went to the mall or to the oil change place."

"We don't need the oil changed that often, Mer," Dad said, smiling at her.

"What if we traded weeks with Alex and her parents, like you did for swim team last summer?"

"Meredith, honey, I don't think it's going to work," Mom said. "That's a 40-minute drive each way."

"But I'm old enough to go *en pointe*," Meredith said.

"Meredith," Mom said again.

"You can't take lessons forever," Dad said. "It's just not how it works."

"Can I stop taking piano lessons then?" Natalie had a forkful of spaghetti halfway to her mouth, but she was more excited to ask the question than to eat.

"No," Mom said.

Dad frowned. "Do you not like piano lessons?"

"Not really," Natalie said.

"Is it that you don't like the music?" Mom asked. "Or the practicing?"

Natalie shrugged. "I don't know, I just don't like it."

"I like piano," Jackie offered.

"Well, I want you to keep doing it, at least for a little while longer," Mom said. "Do you know how many people regret quitting piano lessons? Jonetta was saying just the other day that she wished her parents had made her keep taking lessons."

Meredith watched this and stayed quiet, cutting her spaghetti without letting the knife tap against the plate, wondering why piano was valued higher than ballet. She had heard Jonetta say that thing about piano lessons when she picked Stephanie up last week, and she had heard Donna say it after she and Alex played a duet together. She had never heard any adult say they wished they had stuck with ballet lessons. The only adult she knew who had stuck with ballet lessons was Liz Coburn.

Rosemary gestured for Jack to come into the bedroom after dinner, as Jackie started practicing the piano and Meredith and Natalie cleared the table. She spoke softly; the house was full of Jackie singing along with her piano practice, but Meredith might still hear. (She knew the girls listened, upstairs, at the air vent in the dining room ceiling.)

"We can't do this, right?"

"Can't do what?"

"Drive Meredith to dance lessons in Delacroix."

Jack looked confused. "I don't know, is there any reason why we should?"

"Well, she likes it," Rosemary said.

"I don't want to drive to Delacroix every week," Jack said.

"Neither do I," Rosemary said, "and if we did it for her we'd have to do it for all of them, and they wouldn't be in the same classes."

"There are plenty of opportunities for the girls in Kirkland," Jack said, making his voice into a decision. Rosemary agreed; in the past year Natalie had done swim team, and they had all been in a play, and a talent show, and taken voice lessons and piano lessons and ballet lessons. There would be other chances for Meredith, ones that didn't involve driving to Delacroix every week. Maybe there'd even be another dance class someday. The Kiwanis building already had the barres and mirrors set up. She'd tell Meredith, before the girls went to bed, that she'd ask Bobbie Jo if she knew of any other dance teachers who lived nearby.

After the table was clear, Meredith went upstairs and put one hand on her bedframe and started practicing. *Tendu, tendu, tendu, dégagé.* Posy Fossil didn't stop dancing just because her teacher went away. She practiced on her own until another teacher arrived.

She wanted her parents to see her doing it, to notice her dedication to ballet was just as strong as her dedication to piano or math or writing, but it was Jackie who came up the stairs instead, grabbing the other bedframe and mirroring Meredith's barre exercises. The two of them were close enough to bump toes, which made Jackie laugh and made Meredith feel a little better. They practiced a few minutes more, listening to Natalie practice the piano below them, which was all they needed to do for the day. All Meredith needed to do, from now until she was an adult, was keep practicing for a few minutes every day.

SUMMER 1992

35. MEREDITH AND DANIEL LEARN BASIC.

Daniel hit Enter, and three images appeared on the black computer screen. At this point, he had played the game so many times that he had the moves memorized, and he quickly shifted the pyramid of rectangles from one base to another without ever stacking a larger rectangle on top of a smaller one. He was rewarded by three long tones playing a major chord, and an invitation to play the Tower of Hanoi again.

He leaned back on his chair to see where Meredith was in her game. The desks in the Kirkland College computer lab had little walls between them, so he couldn't see what was on her screen, but he could see that she was making some kind of map in her unicorn notebook. The corner of her BASIC workbook hung off the edge of her desk, closed.

"Meredith, I finished my game," he said. "Want to play?"

Meredith looked up. "Yes! Give me just a sec." She finished connecting two clusters in her notebook, added a few more words, then set it on her desk and scooched her chair over to Daniel's computer. He had taken everything off the screen except the little blinking cursor at the bottom.

"It's called Hanoi," he said, and Meredith typed LOAD "HANOI" and then RUN and the three images appeared. Daniel watched her manipulate the rectangles back and forth. She was a little slower at it than he was, especially now that he knew exactly where they should go, but she only had to undo one move, and she quickly got to the end.

"Da, da, daaaaaa!" she sang along with the chord, making her voice sound like the

157

computer's. "That's so great, I like it so much!" Meredith said, turning in her chair to smile at Daniel.

"How's yours doing?"

"I'm still mapping out all the story first. Then it'll be about typing everything in and connecting all the pieces so they go to the right place."

Meredith had not wanted to build any of the game ideas listed in the back of the BASIC workbook. For her first game, she built Ghost—except, since the computer had no idea whether a string of letters was considered a word, every move ended with the same question: "Is this a word? [Y/N]" Daniel's dad gave it a pass anyway, since it fulfilled the function of a playable game, and her code was correct.

So now Daniel was moving further on in the workbook, learning how to make shapes and sounds, and Meredith was working on a text adventure. His dad had warned her against that, but not too strongly; instead, he ended his lesson with "well, all learning involves experimentation!" and let the two of them continue their work in the computer lab.

They continued working, Meredith taking a break to walk in circles around the classroom, and Daniel reading the next chapter of the workbook. It was getting to be time for lunch, and he didn't want to start anything new, so he ran Hitchhiker's Guide to the Galaxy instead. It counted as experimentation.

There was a knock at the door—Daniel's dad never knocked—and it was Alex. She had come straight from swim team, wearing a pair of Looney Tunes shorts and a T-shirt over her swimsuit, and her long red hair hung straight and slightly dripping. Daniel felt a little uncomfortable looking at her, like he was seeing something he shouldn't, but he also knew Alex didn't care what she looked like.

"Mom said I should come hang out with you until lunch," Alex said.

"Are Nat and Jackie here?" Meredith asked.

"No, your dad took them home. Do you all want to hang out this afternoon?"

"Sure," Meredith said, looking over to Daniel to see if he was in. Neither of them ever had much to do in the afternoons, after their two-person computer class was over. Daniel was glad that he couldn't swim; that he got to spend his summer mornings in this air-conditioned room instead. Most of the Kirkland College buildings weren't air-conditioned, but this one had to be, because of the computers.

"What are you doing?" Alex asked, and Daniel showed her the Tower of Hanoi, and Meredith explained a bit about her text adventure.

"It's like *Alice in Wonderland*," she said, "except Alice is older now and she's figured out a way to get back in."

They looked at the clock—it was 12:15, past the time when Daniel's dad was supposed to get them for lunch—and then they started talking about video games and books and the movies they wanted to rent, and then it was 12:40.

"Should we go find your dad?" Meredith asked.

Alex said, "I think we should go find *lunch*."

Dr. Seth arrived at 12:42, bursting through the door, saying "Sorry, sorry, sorry, lunchtime, I know—but do you want to see something cool?"

It always felt weird when parents said "cool." When Meredith's dad said it, you could hear the little pause before and after, fake quotation marks denoting his opinion of the word. But Dr. Seth said it like he meant it, and she noticed that his hair was more fluffed up than usual, like he had spent more time running his fingers through it as he worked. Daniel did the same thing sometimes. She watched him from her side of the desk, wondering what he was thinking.

They went into Dr. Seth's office, stepped over a few piles of papers, and lined up behind his chair. "This"—he turned around in his seat to look at them, his eyes excited—"is the World Wide Web."

The computer looked exactly the same as any other computer.

"Let me show you," he said. Meredith watched as Dr. Seth typed, then leaned back: "We are now connected to the Library of Congress."

Meredith had seen the *Reading Rainbow* episode where LeVar Burton went to the Library of Congress and asked for a book, and they put his request into a long tube and his book rose out of the basement on a tray. "What do you mean, connected?"

"I mean that we can ask the Library of Congress to give us information about any book in the world, and our question will instantly go to Washington, DC and they will give us an instant reply." Dr. Seth's hand went to his hair again. One foot was jiggling up and down under his desk, threatening to knock over an empty can of soda. "Name a book."

Meredith waited the usual two-second pause to see if anyone else would speak up, and then took the responsibility of volunteering: "*The Westing Game.*" Dr. Seth typed it in, and the screen changed:

"*The Westing Game* by Ellen Raskin, first published 1978 by Dutton. 1979 Newbery Medal Winner. The mysterious death of an eccentric millionaire brings together an unlikely assortment of heirs who must uncover the circumstances of his death before they can claim their inheritance."

It wasn't any information that Meredith didn't already know—her copy of *The Westing Game* had the Newbery Medal printed on the cover, after all—and she had hoped it would tell her something new. But it still felt exciting to be connected directly to the Library of Congress, if that's what was going on.

"Is there, like, a librarian on the other end?" Alex asked.

"No," Dr. Seth said. "It's computers talking to other computers. My computer is asking the library to retrieve information on a specific book, and the library computer is giving me this information from its database. Daniel, say another title."

They spent a few more minutes typing their favorite books into the computer, and watching as the Library of Congress sent them information. It was a fun game—kind of like searching a card catalog—and Meredith liked that both Daniel and his father were so excited about playing it. She watched them from behind the chair, as Dr. Seth and Daniel and then Alex all leaned in close to the computer screen, and he talked a little bit about modems and universities and how soon, every school would have a computer like this. They could look up books and research papers whenever they wanted.

"This is world-changing," Dr. Seth said, and Meredith looked at Alex's half-dry hair, and the back of Daniel's neck, and the empty soda can that had tipped over and rolled into a stack of books, and focused her mind on remembering all of this, in case what Dr. Seth said turned out to be true. She would write it down later, in her diary—the way it felt to be standing next to her two best friends on a summer afternoon as they watched the world change together. She'd make it sound a little more important than it seemed to be, in case it was.

PART 2: 1997–2000

SUMMER 1997

36. THE GIRLS PLAN AN IMPORTANT PURCHASE.

After dinner they met in Meredith's bedroom one last time, to discuss strategy; then Meredith checked her watch and they went down the stairs ten minutes early, walking in the living room and standing in a line next to—but not quite in front of—the television.

"We want to ask you about something," Meredith said.

Their parents were in their usual places: Jack in his chair, and Rosemary on her end of the couch, leaving space for when their daughters would pile in to watch *The Simpsons*. They didn't all fit, anymore, so Meredith had taken to sitting on the floor, pushed up against Natalie's leg and the arm of the sofa, next to the magazine rack so she could read during the commercials.

"Sure, what is it?" Jack asked, and his voice was cheerful but also fake, like he knew he wasn't going to like whatever they said next. That was what they were afraid of; that was why they had rehearsed.

"We would like to buy a Super Nintendo," Natalie said.

Jackie knew her cue. "We've saved up the money for it. One-hundred-fifty dollars."

"Where did you get a hundred fifty dollars?" Rosemary asked, looking at them in that way that Meredith always interpreted as *why did my daughters do something I didn't specifically tell them to do?* Meredith was so tired of that look.

"I've been babysitting, and Natalie and Jackie both have birthday money."

"Natalie hasn't had her birthday yet."

"It's from *last year*," Natalie said.

Rosemary watched Natalie, wondering where she had picked up that tone. That "duh, Mom, why are you so dumb" tone that she and Jonetta laughed about, sometimes, when they saw each other at the bank or met for coffee. Rosemary had laughed because Jonetta had laughed, and because Jonetta was always talking about Stephanie—and now that same voice was coming out of Natalie's mouth, and she wasn't even thirteen yet. Not for three more weeks.

"Are you all contributing equally?" Jack asked. "Or is this more like Meredith is buying a Super Nintendo and you're helping her?"

"I mean, yeah, I'm putting more money in," Meredith said. "But it's going to belong to all of us. Equally."

"Because we're sisters." Jackie thought it would be a good time to improvise a line, since they had already gone off-script. She smiled.

"Is Meredith going to take it with her when she goes to college?"

Meredith felt her face tense up. Her parents had been talking about *when Meredith goes to college* ever since she started high school. They'd always talked about it, of course, but now it felt like they had made a plan for what she would do in college and what kind of person she would be—apparently, the kind of person who takes a Super Nintendo away from her sisters—without asking her what kind of person she thought she might become, when she left Kirkland.

So Meredith pushed her face into a smile, making sure it included her eyes too, just like they were taught in drama class. "No, it'll stay here. I wouldn't take it with me."

"Where are you even going to get a Super Nintendo?" Rosemary asked.

"From Daniel," Natalie said. "And he's going to sell us all his games."

"Is that going to cost extra?"

"No, Mom, it's all good," Meredith said. "I worked it all out with him already. He has a Nintendo 64 now, and a PlayStation, and he doesn't want his Super Nintendo any more."

"Are his parents okay with this?" Rosemary asked, and Meredith wanted to snap back *I don't know, Mom, why should his parents have to be okay with him selling his own property*, but she kept her mouth shut. The first page of her newest diary was epigraphed with Marmee's line from *Little Women*: "I am angry nearly every day of my life, Jo, but I have learned not to show it; and I still hope to learn not to feel it." She had made it her goal to get all the way through her adolescence without shouting at her parents the way teens did on television.

"They're okay with it," Jackie said. Meredith wondered whether she was speaking out of innocence or deliberately lying, because Meredith did in fact know that the Seths were okay with this transaction—it was something she and Daniel had discussed, the annoyance of still having to get permission for everything balanced with the idea of respecting their parents, at least as much as they could—but she hadn't mentioned it to her sisters.

"I'll talk to Anand," Jack said. "I'm sure it's fine."

Rosemary frowned. "What if he wants it back someday?"

"We'll figure it out then," Meredith said. "But… he won't. Or we'll figure it out. Because we're friends."

"We could just let him play with it when he wants to," Natalie said, in that same "duh, Mom" voice.

"*Simpsons* are almost on," Jack said. "How about I talk to Anand, or maybe you talk to Preeti, see how they feel about it, and maybe we can let the kids make their deal."

"A hundred fifty dollars is a lot of money," Rosemary said. It made her a little uncomfortable to think that her girls had enough extra cash to buy something expensive like a Super Nintendo. They should be saving it, instead—except they already insisted that Meredith save half of everything she earned at her babysitting job, it had been a family rule ever since the girls were old enough to get birthday checks. Natalie always saved everything, it seemed like, but Rosemary suspected that Meredith had stocked up the spending half of her cash just long enough to blow it all on a video game system. She wanted to say *you should be saving your money for something important*, except she knew Meredith would just glare at her and then hide it under a fake smile.

"It's not that much money," Meredith said, taking her seat next to the magazine rack to watch *The Simpsons*. She didn't pick up a magazine during the first commercial break because she was mentally drafting the email she would send to Daniel, after *The Simpsons* and *King of the Hill* and *The X-Files* were over:

D—

We broached the Super Nintendo Conversation tonight. Parents said they have *to talk to your parents first, so prepare them. ^__^*

Rosemary sat next to Jackie, who had her knees pulled up to her chest because her legs still weren't long enough to sit properly on the couch. She watched her youngest daughter watch *The Simpsons*, because Jackie's face was the only one that didn't seem to carry hints of irritation at the corners of the mouth and eyes, the constant adolescent frustration that they were still young enough to have parents. Her girls were growing up, but they still wanted to play together—just with a Super Nintendo now, instead of dolls. What had she played, at that age? Gin rummy, sometimes, but mostly she sat with her best friend and listened to records, and then went home to a house with no sisters, just her and her mother and the same question: *what did you do today?* and the honest answer: *nothing*.

Rosemary wanted to lean over to Jack, to whisper *I think we should let them get the Super Nintendo,* but they all had to wait until *The Simpsons* were over, and then until *King of the Hill* and *The X-Files* were over, before the girls would go back upstairs and start getting ready for bed. It was one of the best parts of the week, all of them sitting together in the living room as a family.

37. NATALIE GOES FOR A SWIM.

Natalie left wet footprints on the cement as she walked towards the diving board. She looked over her shoulder to see if Fancy Geoff was watching her, even though she knew he kind of had to because he was the lifeguard. She had pulled the bottom of her suit out of her butt before she climbed out of the water, and she paused at the edge of the diving board, bouncing slightly, before she dove in.

When she surfaced she saw that Fancy Geoff was talking to Stephanie, so she kept swimming, dipping under the rope that separated the diving well from the lap pool and getting in three laps before she hauled herself up, a little out of breath, wondering if she had beat her best time.

"Good practice, Nat!" her coach called. Swim team was over for the day, but Natalie liked to stay in the water as long as possible. It was too warm to do anything else. None of the little kids would show up until after lunch, so she and her friends had the entire pool to themselves.

"Are you staying here this afternoon?" Kimberly asked. "Because you could come over if you wanted. We could see if my mom would drive us to the mall."

"Sure," Natalie said, hanging on to the edge of the pool and looking up at Kimberly, already showered and wearing a tank top with a cherub printed on it. The cherub looked fuzzy because Natalie's glasses were tucked into her sandal, next to her swim bag. "I have to ask my parents, but they'll say yes."

"It's so *hot*," Kimberly complained. "I'm going to get sweaty."

"Get back in the pool then," Natalie laughed.

"Maybe I'll put my feet in," Kimberly said. "Over by the lifeguard stand."

They both looked at Fancy Geoff and started giggling, and then Kimberly started walking and Natalie began swimming, hauling herself up out of the pool before Kimberly could reach the coveted spot immediately to the left of Geoff's lifeguard stand. You could almost sit in the shade of his umbrella, if you leaned.

"Hey, Natty," Geoff said. The way he said her name made Natalie feel grown-up and a little embarrassed. She undid her swim cap and shook out her long, wavy hair like she was in the movies. There was a ring of sweat around her forehead, and she could feel the ends of her hair sticking to her back.

"We're going to the mall today," Kimberly said, sitting next to Natalie and dunking her feet into the water.

"Great," Geoff said. "Buy me a lip gloss."

Both girls laughed. Natalie wanted to say something, but couldn't think of anything besides *it's so hot*, which wasn't much of a conversation starter. "Did you see me dive?" The words came out as a surprise, and Geoff turned to look right at her.

"Course I did," he said. "Saw you swim those laps, too. Natty Gann, first place in the under-thirteens."

"I'll be thirteen in a week," Natalie said. She wasn't always first place, either. It had only happened once.

"I'll tell the boys to watch out."

"Geoff!" It was Stephanie, still wearing her swimsuit. Natalie had started wearing a bra that summer, but Stephanie had *boobs*. "I brought you a freezy pop. Want to split it?"

"Did you get that out of the canteen?"

"I paid for it. Quarters are on the cooler." She peeled the white paper off the orange twin pop and broke it in half, offering the bigger chunk to Geoff. "It's so damn hot."

The college had done *Kiss Me, Kate* that spring, so the tune popped into Natalie's head without her wanting it there. She felt sweat begin to gather where her hair met her neck. Geoff and Stephanie were talking again, about high school stuff, and she and Kimberly were sitting in their shadows doing nothing.

So Natalie pressed her hands against the hot cement and dropped back into the pool. She put her whole body in the water, feeling her long hair lift up towards the surface, coming up again with her head thrown back like they used to do when they played Little Mermaid. Geoff wasn't watching. She climbed out of the water, grabbed her bag of clothing, and headed towards the showers.

38. ROSEMARY GETS PROMOTED.

If Rosemary kept her stomach held in, her skirt didn't feel so tight around the waist. It hadn't been as bad when she left the house that morning, but she hadn't eaten more than a piece of toast then, and her belly always seemed to get bigger throughout the day before flattening out while she slept. It looked the worst when she sat down; she could see the round skin pop out like a drawer that wouldn't close, and couldn't tighten her stomach muscles to make it go away.

So, fine, she thought. *Time to go on a diet*. Rosemary thought about what she usually ate every day, wondering what she could cut out—no butter on her toast? One slice of turkey instead of two on her sandwich? One slice of bread? That afternoon her sack lunch was a ham sandwich with mayo, an apple, and two cookies. She'd skip the cookies, then, and tomorrow she'd skip the mayo.

Or you could buy some new clothes, Rosemary thought, knowing that in addition to being too snug, her skirt was worn thin on one side from where her purse rubbed against it. She could get some new things for herself when she took the girls back-to-school shopping, but the thought of pulling items on and off in a dressing room while her three daughters stood bored and impatient outside felt like too much work. Maybe she and Jonetta could go. If Jonetta came into the bank today, she would ask.

"Rosemary," Carolyn said. "Got five minutes?"

"Of course," Rosemary said. Bobbie Jo was at the other teller station, and nobody had come into the bank for the past half hour.

Carolyn smiled. "Come on back to my office," she said. "I want to talk to you about something."

Rosemary followed, suddenly nervous. They had a college student that spring who had worked part-time as a teller, and she had been a cheerful young girl but she was always late, and one day Carolyn had asked her back to her office and after that it was over.

"Sit down," Carolyn said, and Rosemary put her hands on her lap, hoping it would help to hide her stomach bulge. Carolyn's clothes always looked fresh and crisp and perfect. When Rosemary had started working at the bank, she had thought that her clothing would look perfect every day too. But she had three kids and a husband and a house to take care of, which meant that her family decided what would happen to her just as much as she did.

"So I don't know if you've heard yet," Carolyn said, "but I'm moving to Delacroix."

"I hadn't heard," Rosemary said. She wondered if Bobbie Jo knew, and had chosen not to share the gossip over the teller station wall for some reason that probably had to do with Rosemary getting fired. Maybe the whole bank would close. That didn't make sense, though. Rosemary kept her hands still and breathed as deeply as she could into the fabric of her skirt.

"Would you be interested in taking on the manager position after I leave?"

"Oh, wow," Rosemary said, almost laughing in her relief. "That's a surprise."

"You must have guessed this was coming," Carolyn said, and Rosemary realized that if she had been paying attention, she could have. At the beginning of the year Carolyn's father had broken his hip, and a few months ago both of Carolyn's parents had moved into the big nursing home outside of Delacroix, the one that served three different towns. Carolyn never said a lot about her family, but Rosemary knew that she had built her life around being able to care for her parents—which meant following them down the highway, moving to a place with a nursing home and a shopping mall and a movie theater and more than one bank. She wondered if Carolyn had already found a new job.

"Do you need some time to make the decision?" Carolyn asked.

"No," Rosemary said. "I'd love the job. I've always been very interested in what you do."

That felt like it might have been the wrong thing to say, but Carolyn smiled anyway. "Trust me, some of it isn't that interesting." She held out her hand, and Rosemary shook it. "Congratulations, Rosemary. I'll spend the next two weeks training you, and I can also take you through the hiring process, since we'll need to find someone to be your replacement. Now we need to have the conversation about salary and benefits."

Five minutes later Rosemary walked back to her teller station—"Hello, new boss," Bobbie Jo said—imagining the person she could become as the new Kirkland Central Bank manager. She would get to work directly with the bank president, and have her own office with her name on a little placard on her desk, and she would earn more money. She would get a fresh haircut and a new skirt suit and she would wear the pearl earrings Jack had bought her on their fifth wedding anniversary. (She hardly ever had an occasion to wear those earrings, but with this job she could wear them as often as she wanted.)

She could see herself walking into the bank in new shoes, buying her lunch instead of packing it, maybe joining Kiwanis. She'd ask Carolyn about that, before she left; whether there were professional organizations she should be a part of, events she should be attending, items to mark on the calendar. It was so exciting, to get to be the most important person in her own life for the length of an afternoon.

"I'll tell you, I knew for weeks and Carolyn said I couldn't say anything," Bobbie Jo said. "Are you happy?"

"I am," Rosemary said, although it was harder for her to say for sure if she felt happiness or giddiness or nervousness or whatever emotion represented possibility. "I had no idea... I mean... I hope I'll be good at it."

"You'll be fine," Bobbie Jo said. "You like being in charge of things."

No, I don't, Rosemary thought, feeling herself want to contradict Bobbie Jo, to say that she wasn't in charge of anything in her life, that everything would go better if she *could* find a way to be in charge. But that was what Carolyn was giving her: a chance to manage the other tellers and find her replacement and make sure there were always fresh flowers in the lobby and inkpens at the teller stations.

"It's lunchtime," Carolyn said, coming out into the lobby. "Do we want to go get sandwiches and ice cream and celebrate Rosemary's promotion?"

Carolyn hung the "Closed for Lunch" sign on the bank's door, and the three of them walked across the street together. Rosemary would order a turkey sandwich without mayo, no chips, just the pickle. Sherbet instead of ice cream, and only eat half the glass.

That ring of fat around her waist didn't belong there, it had never been there before, so she'd just be a little more careful about what she ate until it went away.

FALL 1997

39. JACK TAKES MEREDITH FOR A DRIVE.

Jack heard the noise of the Super Nintendo through the ceiling, so he went upstairs. "Meredith?"

"She's on the computer," Natalie said from her bedroom, formerly the guest room, both of his younger daughters intent on the screen and their controllers.

"Thanks," Jack said, turning around. He went through the kitchen and into the "computer room," formerly the pantry, cans of beans sharing shelf space with the bulky computer tower. Meredith was at the desk, equally focused on her screen; she tapped a key, and all the words in the document she was working on scrolled up before Jack could read them.

"Meredith, do you want to go for a drive?"

She turned around. The pantry had no windows, and Jack smelled Meredith's teenybopper perfume and hairspray and farts. *Laying it on a little thick!* he wanted to say, but he knew better. His job, as a dad, was to say nothing about his daughters' appearance that might imply he disapproved. Or, in this case, their smell.

Meredith hit another set of keys and ClarisWorks closed out, leaving the Mac screen empty and waiting for the next user to select a program. "Sure," she said.

They got in the Volvo—Jack started walking towards the drivers side, then said "whoops, I guess you're driving"—and Meredith carefully backed the car out of the Grubers' driveway.

"Don't scrape the curb," Jack said.

"I'm not going to scrape the curb," Meredith said, and she didn't.

She drove the fifteen-year-old Volvo downtown, passing the bank and the school and the church, then turned west towards the college.

"You're doing pretty good," Jack said. "Almost ready to get that license."

"Thanks," Meredith said. She didn't seem to be enjoying driving very much; she kept her hands firmly on 10 and 2, checked her mirrors, and looked bored.

"You pulled up a little too close to the intersection there," Jack said.

"What?" The car sat perfectly flush to the cross-street.

"You pulled up too close before you stopped. If there had been a person crossing the street, you would have hit them."

"There's nobody crossing the street," Meredith said.

"But you would have hit them," Jack said. "If there had been a person on the sidewalk and they started crossing the street, you would have hit them."

"If there was a person crossing the street, I would have stopped before I hit them."

"Just drive, Meredith, you can't sit at a stop sign!" There were no other cars around, but Meredith looked both ways anyway and pulled forward. The back bumper scraped against the concrete as the car drove through the dip in the intersection, and Meredith glanced at Jack as if to say *don't say anything*.

"Look," Jack said, "I'm just trying to prepare you for your driver's test. You have to know the rules of the road."

"I know the rules of the road," Meredith said. "No rolling stops. When you're at a four-way, the person who got there first goes first, unless you arrive at the same time and then the person to the right goes first. When you're on the highway, keep one car length per 10 miles of speed between you and the other car in front of you."

She stopped at a stop sign—keeping the car behind the sidewalk this time—then nudged forward slowly, her eyes snapping back and forth in both directions. Jack watched her in silence, thinking about how much she reminded him of his older sister. So focused, so determined, that same habit of getting defensive and then going quiet when something didn't go her way. It was funny that Meredith had met Anne only a few times in her life and still came out so much like her.

Jack remembered the house feeling quieter, almost happier, after Anne left for college. He wondered what it would feel like after Meredith left. Certainly Meredith was never outwardly angry; she was always polite, nearly always cheerful, her manners as perfect as the placement of her hands on the steering wheel. Anne would have said "We're done with this;" Meredith, instead, asked.

"Can we go home now?"

They had been out for about 20 minutes. After Meredith pulled the car into the driveway, checked to make sure the lights were off—even though they had never been turned on—and the parking brake was in place, then checked twice to make sure the door was locked, they went inside to find Nat, Jackie, and Rosemary in the kitchen, Rosemary standing at the counter with a cup of tea and the two girls eating Oreos. Jack reached into the package and grabbed two for himself.

"How'd it go?" Rosemary asked.

"She's doing fine," Jack said. "Aren't you, Mer?"

"I'm doing okay," Meredith said.

"Had a little issue at one of the intersections," Jack said, "but I don't think she'll make that mistake again."

"It wasn't a mistake," Meredith said. "There wasn't anybody in the street."

"Well, we'll just have to practice a little more before the big test," Rosemary said.

"Yeah, it didn't seem like you were all that into practicing today," Jack said, smiling at his daughter—who started crying. "It was your idea to practice, I was writing, I stopped because you wanted to," Meredith said, her voice steady and even under her soundless tears. Then she went upstairs.

"Teenagers," Jackie said.

Jack followed Meredith upstairs. She wasn't crying anymore, although he could hear her sniffle slightly as she stood in front of the mirror in her bedroom and brushed her hair.

"Sorry about that," he said.

"I try to do what you want me to do, and then you tell me I'm doing it wrong," Meredith said.

"Hey," Jack said. "Driving a car is like playing an instrument. You're going to play a few sour notes at the beginning. It's our job to make sure you don't play those notes in a way that could get somebody else hurt."

Meredith looked at him, started to say something, and then stopped. Jack remembered Anne doing the exact same thing.

"It's okay," she said instead. "Maybe if I'm writing next time, we could wait to drive until I'm done?"

"Sure," Jack said. That was easy enough to remember, to add to his mental list of ways to get along with his family. No comments on the perfume, no comments on anyone's body or hair, no joking about whether Daniel was Meredith's boyfriend, and no interrupting Meredith while she was writing. He remembered when Meredith was little, and how he had to teach her and her sisters not to interrupt him while he was at work. If she was a Gruber kid, she was on her way to becoming a Gruber adult, and it made sense that she wouldn't like being interrupted.

He should write Anne, or call her. Tell her how much her niece resembled her. Maybe invite her over for Christmas, or something. Jack had no idea how Anne spent Christmas these days; he imagined her alone, but he hadn't really talked to her in—how long had it been?—two years.

"What do you think about inviting Anne for Christmas?" he said to Rosemary that evening.

"She'll say no," Rosemary said.

But Jack got the email back the next day:

Dear Jack:

So good to hear from you. Thank you for the invitation. It has been too long since I've last seen the girls, so why not? I'll call you this weekend to make plans. I trust your phone # is the same?

Your sis,

Anne

WINTER 1997

40. ANNE GRUBER VISITS HER NIECES.

When Anne Gruber got out of the car, Natalie thought that she looked just like an older version of Meredith, and it felt unfair, because the house was already full of Meredith and her sixteenth birthday and her driver's test and her PSATs and her college plans. Everyone talked about how amazing Meredith was, and how much work she still had to do before she could become *even more amazing*. Now they'd have to listen to stories about Aunt Anne and Dad and how hard they had worked as kids, and how Aunt Anne had done everything Dad had done but it was harder for her because she was a woman and she had done it all in the 1970s.

The four of them stood on the front porch to meet her, even though there was snow on the ground and none of them were wearing coats and Jackie wasn't even wearing shoes. Dad and Aunt Anne came quickly up the porch steps, and Dad said "Get inside, it's freezing!" and once they were in they all had cold hugs, pressing their bodies against their aunt's too-thin jacket.

"It doesn't snow like this in Seattle," Aunt Anne said. "I'm not sure I brought the right shoes. Is there a place we could go to get some warmer clothes?"

"The mall's 40 minutes away," Jackie said, "but we have a Nearly New store."

"You'll be fine," Dad said. "It's not like we're going to go hiking or anything."

"Well, I don't know what you do around here!" Aunt Anne said, laughing. Then she turned to the girls. "I haven't seen you since you were this big," she said, holding her hand slightly below her knees. "But I've seen all your school pictures." She put her finger against her chin, making a joke out of pretending to think. "You must be… Jackie, is that right?"

Jackie put her own finger against her chin. "I'm trying to remember. Am I Jackie, or Natalie?"

"You're not Natalie, because Natalie is the one who looks like her mother. That hair," Aunt Anne said, reaching out to touch one of Natalie's golden waves. Natalie stood still, waiting for her hand to pull back. "Your father and I did not get so lucky in the hair department. Straight and thin for the Gruber kids! And now we're going gray."

"Speak for yourself," Dad said, even though the gray in his hair was already showing through, the way Natalie's blue jeans turned white when she picked at the cuffs. *Everybody has white threads inside them when they get old*, Natalie thought. She wondered how old Aunt Anne was. She was older than Dad, so forty-five, maybe.

"And you must be Meredith," Aunt Anne said, putting her hands on Meredith's shoulders. The two of them stood like an optical illusion, the maiden and the crone making a vase between their faces. They both had hair parted on the side and held back with a barrette. Jackie had a barrette in her hair too, but she didn't look anything like Aunt Anne. *If she looked like anyone*, Natalie thought, *she looked like Dad.*

"Hi, Aunt Anne," Meredith said. She looked at her aunt's face and saw the same intense eyes, the same straight hair, the same wide mouth that met her every day in the mirror. Anne was heavier, slightly, but the comparison was clear: this was Meredith's past and her future. The woman who had done it all, and the woman she would someday become.

Anne squeezed her shoulders, then dropped her hands with a sigh. "I am so much looking forward to talking with you." She turned to face the rest of the family. "In fact, I'd love to take the girls out for some auntie-niece time. Do you have a coffee shop you like to go to?"

"Not really," Jack said, "but there's a nice drugstore downtown. Coffee's terrible, but the girls can show you how to get a phosphate."

"We could get sandstorms!" Jackie said. "They're so good. Have you ever had one? It's chocolate ice cream mixed with malt and marshmallow syrup."

"There's snow on the ground," Rosemary said, "and she wants ice cream."

"I'll buy you girls anything you want," Aunt Anne said. "It's my Christmas treat."

They sat in the drugstore with their coats open, Jackie ordering a sandstorm with two scoops of ice cream because Aunt Anne was paying—she laughed that a scoop of ice cream only cost 59 cents—and Natalie ordering a hot chocolate, and Meredith getting her usual vanilla phosphate. She still loved it more than anything else on the menu. Anne had a cup of coffee that she did not drink, after the first two sips. She used it to warm her hands, flinching slightly every time someone entered the drugstore and the outside air filled the room.

"So," Anne said to Meredith. "Are you thinking about becoming the third Dr. Gruber?"

"I don't know," Meredith said. She liked the idea of earning a doctorate, mostly because she wanted to see what they taught you after you had done your bachelor's and master's programs. She hated that schools held things back like that, the way her teachers had started telling her "well, you'll learn that in college." She was tired of hearing that they were only getting a simplified understanding of how an atom worked, or that the library only had the abridged version of *Les Misérables*. She wanted the knowledge that her school was keeping from her—and she knew that when she started college, she would want the knowledge that they were keeping from her, too.

"What do you want to do after college?" Anne asked. This was another question that Meredith hated because she knew nobody really wanted to hear her answer. But Aunt Anne had her face, which might mean she would understand.

"I want to write and I want to act in plays and musicals," Meredith said. "Professionally."

Anne smiled. "Well, you can't do both. You'll have to choose."

Meredith understood that, and was slightly grateful that Aunt Anne hadn't said *well, you can't do either*. She had written it out in her diary, how it would make sense to do the acting part first, and write when she got older. She'd do it in that gap between the good parts for young people and the good parts for old people. But even as Meredith made those plans she felt like they were wrong somehow, like they were her own simplified understanding of the atom. It was hard to say what she wanted to do when she grew up when the only jobs she really knew were college professor, teacher, secretary, bank teller and manager, retail worker, and the boy in their senior class who mixed up their sandstorms and phosphates.

"Have you thought about law school? Your parents say you're very bright."

Meredith wanted to talk to Aunt Anne like she might talk to Alex and Daniel, sharing their dreams across the table in rapid conversation. Instead, all she said was "I don't know, I don't think I want to become a lawyer," and sipped at her vanilla phosphate knowing that she was not, at the moment, sounding very bright.

"What about the two of you?" Anne asked. "What are you enjoying studying in school?"

Meredith was relieved to see that both of her sisters gave the same kinds of awkward responses; Natalie said that she liked history and science and P.E., and Jackie said that she liked everything but especially music.

"I'm taking piano lessons and flute lessons at home and voice lessons at the college," she said.

"Your father said we might get a concert later," Anne said. "You all play in the band, right? Gruber kids always play in the band."

"I'm in sixth grade band, Natalie's in junior high band, and Meredith's in high school band," Jackie said. "That means during the concerts our parents don't get to leave at intermission like everyone else." She took a big scoopful of sandstorm, malt dust falling off her spoon. "Also, our concerts are in the school cafeteria."

Anne laughed, Jackie kept going—"we're playing Hot Cross Buns next to hot dog buns"—and Meredith felt awkward, like it was she who was supposed to have charmed Aunt Anne and failed. Meredith very much wanted to have Aunt Anne as a friend. There was so much she wanted to ask her, like what it felt like to live at the same time as the women's movement and the civil rights movement and Vietnam, and why she had decided to teach English, and why she hadn't gotten married or had children, and whether she would read any of Meredith's stories.

She looked at Natalie, who raised her eyebrows slightly as if to say *well, we know which one she likes best*. The two older Gruber sisters sat with their respective drinks and their respective roles, the Pretty One and the Smart One, while the Funny One jabbered away and the drugstore door opened and all of them shivered slightly, the snow blowing in and melting as soon as it touched the floor.

SPRING 1998

41. MEREDITH, ALEX, AND DANIEL EAT LUNCH.

Meredith held the stapled papers under her lunch tray, trying not to push the paper into the crevices between the rectangular pizza slice and the tiny squares of carrots mixed with peas. Part of the tray was damp, and she kept her papers away from that corner. One page had touched the damp spot before she realized, and a few words were slightly transparent.

She sat down in her usual spot next to Daniel and across from Alex. "I finished the play," she said. "I made copies for you." Meredith handed out the two copies of *The Adventures of Omar the Dwarf*, giving Alex the one with the damp front page. "Daniel, you'll play Omar, Alex, you'll play Esmerelda, and I'll play the narrator and the NPCs. We could record it at my house over spring break, if you wanted."

She let them start reading and kept her eyes focused on her pizza, cutting at the crust with the side of her fork until she gave up and picked it up with her hands. The Gruber girls got to buy lunch on pizza day, although that was a much bigger deal to Jackie than it was to her, because these pizzas never changed and she had been eating them for almost nine years. Trapped in these walls like Ariel in her tree, waiting until it was her turn to be released. It was the first thing she had thought of when she read *The Tempest*; there was a poem in her diary called "Cloven Pine," because Sylvia Plath had already taken the more obvious name. She didn't ever show her poetry to Alex or Daniel. It felt unformed, like she hadn't found all of the words she wanted yet, like she was Jackie blowing into her flute for the first time.

But writing this play had been easy. All she'd had to do was think of the way jokes worked in all the movies she and Alex had watched together. These jokes worked, too—Alex laughed, showing a mouth full of half-chewed pizza, and Meredith felt herself blush a little, because it felt embarrassing to be proud of her writing. She thought of Anne Shirley and the Story Club, and wondered if she would feel embarrassed in a different way when she was older.

"This is seriously funny," Alex said. "I could play my clarinet during the snake charmer part, maybe?"

"Oh, sure," Meredith said. "We'd need a second tape recorder for that, because Esmerelda has dialogue in that scene. Daniel, could we use yours?"

"I'm not going to be here for part of the break," Daniel said. "We're going to Chicago."

Daniel tucked the open pages of his script under his lunch tray and ate his pizza. He didn't like the play. He knew that it was set in a fantasy world, same as the Narnia books or *Secret of Mana*, and in those fantasy worlds people charmed snakes and kept knives under their turbans and had names like Omar and Esmerelda. It was just part of what you had to deal with, in stories like these—the mysterious far-away kingdom where people dressed like his grandparents and acted like *Aladdin*.

He followed Meredith after lunch, walking next to her in the hallway, which was normal, and then almost to the door of the girls' room, which was weird. "Hey," he said. "*Excuse me*," a senior girl said, pushing through the bathroom door, and he and Meredith stepped out of the way.

They were almost the same height, the two of them. Alex was taller, most of their classmates were taller, but Daniel had always felt comfortable standing next to Meredith and meeting her eyes. Right now her eyes looked impatient, because they only had a few minutes before the bell rang and she wanted to wash her hands.

"I wanted to say…" Daniel looked at Meredith, at the way the ends of her hair were repelled slightly by the electricity of her oversized sweater, at the way her rust-colored lipstick was rubbed off where her lips had touched her chocolate milk spout, at the way she stood as if she were already moving.

"My parents said I could invite you to go to Chicago with us, if you wanted. We're going to see *Phantom of the Opera*."

"Oh," Meredith said, and Daniel could see her excitement exhale into disappointment.

"My parents would say no, I mean, you know them."

The warning bell rang, and Meredith walked quickly into the bathroom, calling out "I'm so sorry, I'd love to go, thank you for asking!" Daniel stood in the hallway for another second, then started walking towards his afternoon class because he had to, because he couldn't stand in the hallway and think about Meredith sitting next to him at *The Phantom of the Opera*, the way they had sat next to each other in Meredith's bedroom and listened to the whole thing, back when they were in sixth grade, back when he and Meredith were still allowed to sit in a bedroom alone. Now neither of their parents would let them do that, even though nothing had changed.

He started the email that evening.

> *M—*
>
> *The play is really funny but it feels kind of like "Small House of Uncle Thomas" sometimes. I don't want to criticize but I know it's important to you so if you wanted, we could talk about some of the stuff like the snake charmer part and maybe change it a little bit before we recorded.*

Daniel looked at the email and thought he should give it a few minutes before he sent it, to make sure the words were exactly right. He saved it as a Hotmail draft, and started a new one.

> *Alex,*
>
> *My parents said I could take a friend with me to Chicago to see Phantom of the Opera. Would you like to go? We would leave Saturday, March 28 and come back Sunday, March 29. They want to buy the tickets soon, so let me know.*
> *Daniel*

That one he sent right away, before he could regret it. He thought of Meredith sitting next to him in the dark theater, and then he thought of Alex, and he thought it would be okay. He mentally categorized Meredith as his best friend, even though the math didn't work on that; she and Alex were best friends, which meant that Meredith was his best friend and he was not her best friend, which made him the wobbly leg in their triangle. But if he took Alex, and they became better friends, the triangle might balance. Anyway, Alex was fun. She'd be a fun person to have on the trip, no matter what happened.

42. DANIEL MAKES A DECISION.

When Daniel sat down, he put his arm on the armrest between him and Alex; a second later she did too, and Daniel quickly pulled his arm away, dropping it into his lap. Of course she should have the armrest. She was the girl. She was also his guest, the birthday present his parents had allowed him on this family trip, the friend who could come along.

The trip had already been much more fun with Alex along. Daniel loved his family in a way that was hard to clarify; the feeling was something he always carried with him, like his glasses. So it was nice to have someone who could understand his more immediate feelings: his annoyance when his mother asked if he was dressed warmly enough, his embarrassment when his father tried to take control at the train station and led everybody in the wrong direction. His sister whom he adored but who was also—and would always be—five years younger than him, a half-decade separating their interests. Alex got all of that, and spent most of the train ride up giving Daniel secret smiles or rolled eyes, letting him know that his perception of his family was not incorrect; that she also saw what he did.

They were briefly allowed to explore the Art Institute by themselves, as long as they met the rest of the family on the Grand Staircase in 45 minutes—and Alex, who was used to navigating the world on her own, led Daniel on a miraculous tour that felt, more than anything else, as if he were inside a video game. Crono chasing Marle through her castle. The experience of turning the corner and being faced with something completely unexpected and breathtaking, watching Alex a few steps ahead pointing out the naked breast or exposed penis before running into the next room. If it had been Meredith, they would have made a game out of the guards who stood at every door, trying to walk by them without attracting their attention. But it was Alex, so the game was whether the great artists of the world chose to portray naked men or naked women. She said it was for feminism.

Now they sat together in the theater, Alex on the aisle and Priya on Daniel's other side, but his sister was absorbed in the glossy white program that his parents had bought for her, to make up for it not being her birthday. Daniel leaned over to Alex. "I've never been in a place this big before." The instant he said it, he realized it wasn't true; there were photographs of him as a young child in front of the Golden Palace in Mysore, and he could picture it if he thought hard enough, all the green and pink and gold. There were buildings in Boston that had been this big. Probably the Art Institute was this big, or bigger. Why hadn't he remembered all of that before he spoke?

"Look," Alex said, "there's the chandelier." She pointed, and Daniel turned, and their shoulders touched, and Daniel flinched again but didn't want to pull away, because that would be rude. Alex was wearing a black dress with some kind of black lace over it, and thick boots that reflected purple under the light. She had taken off her cardigan, and her arms were freckled up and down. Daniel thought of what his father had said on the train, about pointillism. How, when you look at something up close, you might be surprised at what it's really made of.

Alex didn't put her cardigan back on, and when the lights darkened and the chandelier started moving and both of them turned around, their shoulders touched again. It was like he could feel Alex's skin through his jacket and his shirt and his undershirt, the heat and energy of her pressing directly into his body. When they both turned around again the connection was lost, and Daniel tried to focus on the music and the play, everything he had imagined in his head as he and Meredith listened to the soundtrack and was now seeing in real life—but his imagination was already bored with the stage and was thinking of a new story, one where he got to touch Alex's shoulder again.

He waited until the moment when the Phantom called at Christine through her mirror; then he put his arm on the armrest, just close enough for the fabric of his jacket to brush against her bare skin. Alex didn't move. As the Phantom led Christine further down, Daniel leaned slightly towards Alex, easing his body against hers. She didn't pull away. Should he look at her? Would she be so focused on the candles and the boat and the music that she wouldn't notice? Daniel was afraid to turn his head, and he stayed still, holding his breath so that he could feel Alex breathing.

Alex shifted in her chair during the applause, and her arm left the armrest and did not return. Daniel kept his body where it was, tilted in Alex's direction, because he worried that if he moved, she'd realize he was only sitting that way to be close to her. By intermission his left side felt tense and heavy, and he was glad to stand up.

"I'm going to the bathroom," Alex said.

She got up and left without asking permission, without telling anyone where she was going, and Daniel followed her. It was like they were playing the game again, but a different level; her red hair and black dress and purple boots moved quickly through the crowd, faster than the old people and the families with children, and Daniel matched the path she made. From this far away, he couldn't see the freckles on her arms at all.

The theater still felt dark, even though the lights were on. It was almost as if she were the Phantom, calling him down to what turned out to be an enormous line for the ladies' restroom.

"I'm not waiting in that," Alex said, turning around as if she knew Daniel would be there. "I'll come back when it's shorter. Do you want to explore the theater?"

"Yes," Daniel said, wondering if his parents were worried about where he was. Well, he was sixteen. It was his sixteenth birthday. He was old enough to walk through a theater by himself.

The two of them walked side by side back up the stairs and into the grand foyer, where people were lining up to buy souvenirs and snacks. Daniel wondered, suddenly, if anyone would look at them and think they were a couple. Adults, maybe, on a date. They looked like the other pairs of adults in the foyer—the man in a jacket, the woman in a short dress, waiting in line to buy something to commemorate the occasion.

"Would you like anything?" Daniel asked. "A T-shirt, or a rose?" He felt hot, and wished he had just said *T-shirt*.

"It's your birthday," Alex said. "I should be giving you the gift."

"Your presence is my present," Daniel said, hearing his father's joke coming out of his mouth.

"Happy birthday, son," Alex joked back. "We're giving you a woman."

"That wasn't—" Daniel began. "They said I could invite a friend!"

"And Meredith couldn't come."

"That wasn't why I invited you," Daniel said, and then he saw his mother and Priya step into the grand foyer and, without thinking, grabbed Alex's hand and walked in a different direction. This time they went up, climbing stairs and walking past people who were starting to return to their seats, Daniel taking the lead. He had let go of Alex's hand as soon as they had started up the staircase, but he knew that when he stopped and turned around she would be there.

"Another restroom," he said. "Shorter line."

"Well done," Alex said, and Daniel stood in the hallway and waited, and he thought about what he might say to her when she came back, and he thought about how if he said what he wanted to say, it would change everything. The day had started to feel very strange; they had all woken up at 4 a.m that morning to be at the train by 6:30, and now, standing in this room he'd never seen before, he felt like he was already in a dream. Like maybe what he said next wouldn't matter. Or what mattered most was that he said it.

Alex came out right as the chimes rang, which meant he had to make his decision. "I invited you because I liked you." That was another lie, sort of, but the reason he had invited Alex was now as blurry and vague as his memory of the Golden Palace, and the only thing that was true was this moment.

"I'd also like to kiss you," he said.

Alex smiled. "It's your birthday."

She leaned over him and their lips met and Daniel's legs started shaking so much that he could hardly feel the kiss, except that there was pressure and a little dampness, and Alex's hand stroked the side of his face when she pulled back, still smiling. The touch felt better than the kiss; as they ran down the stairs back to their seats, Daniel could feel the afterimage of each of Alex's fingers on his cheek.

"Where were you?" his father whispered, as they sat down in the darkened theater.

"Line for the restrooms," Alex said. "Huge."

The entr'acte began, which meant that nobody could ask Alex or Daniel any follow-up questions about their adventures. Daniel touched the side of his face where Alex's hand had been. Then he put his arm on the shared armrest, and Alex put her arm next to his, and they sat quietly together until the musical was over.

43. ALEX HAS A BOYFRIEND.

The Monday they went back to school Daniel sat next to Alex at lunch, instead of Meredith; she felt the weight of his hand on her thigh as Daniel talked to Meredith about one of those games they both liked to play. They hadn't really talked about what would happen after the kiss—Alex had shared a hotel bed with Priya while Daniel slept on a cot below them, and they were all too tired to say much of anything—and when it was all over Alex was glad enough to have gone to Chicago, and kissed Daniel, and seen a musical and an Art Institute and a Museum of Science and Industry, and gone home.

And then Daniel was by her locker the next morning, and by her at lunch, and his hand was on her jeans. Not doing anything, of course; just there, reminding her that they were now connected.

He removed his hand a minute later to cut his Salisbury steak, and didn't put it back.

After school Daniel was by her locker again, his collared shirt untucked over khaki pants, first trying to lean against the locker next to her and then giving it up and shoving his hands into his pockets.

"Would you like me to walk you home?" he said.

The two of them walked side-by-side, silently, matching their steps. Daniel had offered to carry Alex's jacket and she had said no, and now she was self-conscious of the weight of it over her arm, the way she had to adjust it every few minutes so it wouldn't slip down and drag on the sidewalk. Was Daniel her boyfriend now? Alex hadn't thought about whether she wanted Daniel to be her boyfriend when she kissed him. She had just thought that it would be fun to kiss him, and it was.

When they reached the MacAllister house nobody was there, and Alex checked Newton's food and water dishes before pouring herself and Daniel each a glass of milk and taking two boxes of cookies out of the cupboard; it would be nice to give Daniel a choice, since he was her guest. And maybe her boyfriend. She hadn't decided yet.

"We have Rainbow Chips Ahoy and Double Stuf Oreos," she said. Daniel took two of each, and they stood on either side of the breakfast bar, dunking their cookies and wiping their fingers on napkins.

"I don't have to be anywhere," Daniel said. "I mean, I can call my parents and tell them I'm with you."

"Do you think they know about the kiss?"

"No," Daniel said. "My mom would definitely want to talk about it if she knew."

He left his napkin wadded up on the breakfast bar and walked over to the phone on the wall to call his parents. Alex watched, wondering if she was watching her boyfriend. If this was what it was like to have a boyfriend come to your house after school. It didn't feel like what she and Meredith had talked about, on the nights when they'd finished their movie and sat, taking bites out of slices of pizza they were too full to eat, sharing daydreams about their futures.

But Alex also remembered what her mom had said, when Alex had asked her how she knew her dad was The One. "He was my best friend," her mom had said, and Daniel was Alex's best boy friend, and maybe that meant he was supposed to be her boyfriend.

"They say it's okay," Daniel said, hanging up the phone.

"Do you want to sit down?" Alex asked.

She steered Daniel towards the couch, pushing aside a pile of laundry and moving one of her mom's stacks of papers to the coffee table. Better there than her bedroom, because she didn't really think her parents would like discovering her and Daniel together on her bed. She started stroking Daniel's shoulder as soon as they sat down, to indicate *yes, this is what we're doing*, and the two of them kissed again, Alex gently running her hand around to Daniel's back, feeling the warmth of his body next to hers.

At first they only kissed, their bodies apart from the lips down, then both of them shifted position and suddenly they were closer, Alex's breasts pressing slightly against Daniel's chest. He cupped one with his hand, whispering "is that okay?" Alex whispered "yes," and they continued. She slipped her hand under his shirt and put it against his back, feeling the hairs that outlined either side of his spine. She felt her fingers trace around the roll of fat at his waistline and then quickly moved her hand back up towards his shoulders, so he wouldn't be embarrassed. She had her own fat, of course, her thighs always rubbing together and wearing out her jeans, but Daniel didn't notice. His hands were still at her breasts, gently squeezing the inch-thick padding on her bra.

They were supposed to take their clothes off at some point, but Alex pulled away instead and said "I've got to walk Newton before my parents get home," and Daniel said "Okay," and they kissed goodbye at the door, and he left. Alex walked Newton in the other direction, not wanting to go anywhere near the Seth house, pausing every third tree and trying to figure out whether she wanted Daniel to be her boyfriend.

Daniel came to her house again on Tuesday; on Wednesday she had her piano lesson; on Thursday her dad was home so they ate cookies and walked Newton together; on Friday Daniel came to her locker and asked "So, will I meet you at the Video Knight at 5?"

"Oh," Alex said. "Sure."

It wasn't like Daniel hadn't ever watched movies with Alex and Meredith—the two of them had introduced him to *Spaceballs*, after all—but Alex did not like the idea that he assumed he would be part of their Friday night ritual. With him along, they had to pick something that a boy would like, and they ended up scanning the New Releases section until they finally settled on *The Fifth Element*.

"I'm calling it," Meredith said, when they climbed back into Alex's mom's car. "The fifth element is love."

Alex no longer wanted to watch the movie. She did not want Daniel sitting in the backseat of the car next to her, while Meredith sat up front. She did not want Daniel taking Meredith's spot on the couch, then scooching over so that their thighs touched, then raising his arm so that it went over her back, half on the couch and half on her shoulder.

As the movie continued—and *The Fifth Element* turned out to be the world's longest movie—Alex thought about what she did want. She did want a boyfriend, someday.

Probably soon. Probably in time for prom. She wanted sex, too, in a way that was easier to admit now that she didn't have to think about having sex with Daniel. She wanted someone who would kiss her without being so polite about it, who would get bored with stroking the outside of her bra over her clothes.

She had really liked kissing Daniel the first time, when it was exciting and it felt like something new, instead of something that she had to do simply because they had already kissed each other once. She wanted that feeling again—the surprise of discovering what somebody felt and tasted like, somebody you hadn't realized wanted to kiss you.

But who else would want to kiss her? Alex thought of everyone in her high school, and how they already knew that she and Meredith and Daniel formed their own little group, the nerds on the edge of the cafeteria. Nobody would ever come to their table and sit down. If Alex wanted to kiss somebody else, she'd have to move over and sit with them.

"HA!" Meredith shouted. "It is love! I told you."

Who would it be? Geoff? No—everybody liked Geoff, and he only ever hung out with the hottest girls. Maybe Andy? He was in band, so they had an excuse to talk. Not like they had ever really talked before, but they could. There'd have to be someone for her in high school who wasn't Daniel. If not, what was she supposed to do? Wait for college?

They didn't sit and talk after the movie, this time. Alex said she wanted to get a head start on her homework, and then she got into the car with Meredith and Daniel, because she'd need a few minutes with Daniel alone, in the space between her mom's car and his front door.

Her mom pulled up to the Seths' house first. "I'm going to walk Daniel up," Alex said, scooting out of her seat and shutting the car door before either her mother or Meredith could ask why. She and Daniel stood just outside the car, close enough that they could smell the exhaust, and Alex said "I don't want to be boyfriend and girlfriend."

"Okay," Daniel said.

"I think we should just be friends."

"Okay."

Then Alex turned and got back in the car, closing the door and trying not to cry. Daniel walked up to his house alone, Alex's mom waiting like she always did to make sure that he got in the house safely. Alex kept her eyes away from the window until the car pulled away.

"Are you all right?" Meredith asked.

"I'm fine," Alex said. "Daniel wanted to date me, and… I didn't."

"Oh, I'm sorry," her mom said. "That's so hard."

They didn't have time to say anything else because they were at Meredith's house, and Meredith said "goodbye" and "thank you for the movie"—which Alex thought was strange because Meredith had paid for the movie that week—and then hopped out of the front seat and walked to her door. They'd talk tomorrow, about all of this. About Daniel, and the kiss, and how Alex would figure out a way to flirt with Andy during band. Maybe they'd both sit together at a new table in the lunchroom on Monday.

44. JACKIE AND PRIYA SOLVE A PROBLEM.

Jackie loved the way it felt right before a performance. She had her knees on her chair and her hands on the chair's back, poking out of the rest of the children's choir like an ostrich with her head up, watching the college students walk back and forth in the hallway. The stage manager with her headset, the soloist singing her warmups, Dr. Barney sneaking out for one last cigarette.

She watched to see if Miss Opal would come down the hall, but she didn't. Jackie had voice lessons every other Sunday with Miss Opal, and they were her favorite part of her life. She worked on her breathing and her tone and her diction, and then when all of that was finished she got to ask Miss Opal questions about New York and Italy and France and opera and how to be a real performer, someday. Miss Opal loved answering questions. She took a book off her shelf, an illustrated guide to the opera, and two weeks later she played Jackie Mozart's Queen of the Night aria. Jackie immediately tried to sing it, and Miss Opal told her "When you're older."

But Jackie sang it on her own, when she was doing the dishes or making her bed. When Dad said it might hurt her voice, she switched to whistling—the Queen of the Night aria, "Je Veux Vivre" from *Romeo and Juliet*, and of course *Carmen's* Habanera, which she already knew from *Sesame Street* and that orange with the blinking eyelashes. She had been scared of that orange, when she was younger.

The children's choir was supposed to stay in the band room until five minutes before Carmina Burana began, at which point they would walk in a line to the balcony of the auditorium and sit—"quietly!"—so they could watch Act I. Then they would walk back down to the band room during intermission, so they could do a quick vocal warmup together before taking their place on the stage.

Priya, however, walked out of the band room on her own, and Jackie-the-ostrich twisted her neck around to figure out what was going on. Just the bathroom, it looked like. Priya always had to go to the bathroom.

They were friends, though, Jackie and Priya. It had started because Meredith and Daniel were friends, and then they became friends on their own. They played Barbies together after Jackie's sisters were too old. Priya had an Indian Barbie in a pink sari, and Jackie had Dana from Barbie and the Rockers, and they pretended they were sisters, or two time-traveling girls who switched places.

Jackie saw Priya come out of the bathroom, and Priya saw Jackie; she was waving at Jackie to come join her. Jackie quickly swiveled around to see what the child minder was doing; the college student was busy with someone else, and anyway Jackie was a Gruber kid. She could go where she wanted. So she climbed off her chair and went to Priya, who immediately pulled her into the bathroom.

"I think I got my period," Priya said.

"Oh, cool," Jackie said.

"No, not cool," Priya said. "I'm going to bleed all over my costume. Can you check? Is there blood on it right now?"

Both of them were wearing long dresses with white sleeves and criss-cross ribbons down the chest. Priya turned around slowly, but Jackie didn't see anything on the back of her dress that looked like a stain.

"There's no blood," Jackie said.

"Okay," Priya said. "What are we going to do?"

"Do you have a quarter?" Jackie asked. The gray machine hung on the wall of the bathroom, offering knobs for both tampons and maxipads. Jackie had been running in and out of this restroom since she was three years old and had never seen anyone use it.

"No," Priya said.

"Neither do I," Jackie said. "So let's go ask someone."

"Wait," Priya said. "What if I bleed all over the floor?"

Jackie pulled a wad of brown paper towels out of the dispenser. "Use these for now," she said.

Priya grabbed the paper towels and quickly entered a stall, and when she was done the two of them walked out of the bathroom and away from the band room, looking for someone who could lend them a quarter. Jackie knew everyone in the Fine Arts Department, so she took the lead on asking.

"Dr. Barney, do you have a quarter we could borrow?"

"Sorry, Jackie." He didn't ask why she wasn't in the band room, because she was a Gruber kid. This building had been her home since before she could remember.

"Lori, do you have a quarter?"

The soloist paused in her pacing, said "no," and continued her warmup. She was a little weak on the top of her arpeggio, Jackie noticed. *Sounds like someone needs a little more breath support.*

Jackie knew her dad would be near the stage, so she went in that direction. Priya followed behind, walking with her legs clamped together so the paper towels wouldn't fall out. "Dad!" Jackie called out, as soon as she saw him. "Do you have a quarter?"

"No," Dad said. "Why do you need a quarter?"

Jackie turned to look at Priya, who didn't say anything. So she took Priya's hand and ran away, Priya grabbing at her crotch when she felt the paper towels slipping, both of them starting to laugh at the ridiculousness of the situation. They were outside of the band room again, close enough that someone would no doubt see them and tell them to go sit quietly with the other children. Except Priya wasn't a child anymore. She hadn't been even before that; Jackie had noticed Priya's breasts making curves against the criss-cross ribbon. They were the oldest of the children, or at least they were before this evening. Jackie wasn't used to thinking of herself as the oldest of something.

Then Miss Opal came down the hall, and Jackie smiled because she had secretly hoped it would be Miss Opal who helped them. She fantasized about Miss Opal helping her out of a lot of things—her first audition, her first rejection, the first time she had to choose between two important roles. Miss Opal was wearing black velvet and pearls and looked like an angel sent to deliver Priya from bleeding all over her costume.

"Miss Opal, do you have a quarter we could borrow?"

"Are you going to give it back?" Miss Opal laughed, fished into her purse, and gave Jackie a quarter. "You two look lovely," she said. "Break a leg."

They went back into the bathroom, and Jackie handed the quarter to Priya, who put it in the machine. "This is not the time to learn how to use a tampon," Priya said, and turned the knob for maxipads.

The quarter slid out of the machine instead.

Jackie started laughing. Priya tried again, and got her quarter back the second time. "Give me the quarter," Jackie said. "I'll be back in under a minute. Count."

Priya gave Jackie the quarter, and she ran out of the bathroom, hoisting up her long dress in one hand as she took the stairs two at a time. There were people in the lobby and they weren't supposed to see her in her costume, so she turned a hard right and ran as quickly as she could into the bathroom next to the Listening Library. There was a maxi-pad machine in that one, too—she dropped in the quarter, turned the knob, and a brown cardboard package fell out. Jackie quickly shoved it into the bodice of her costume so no one could see what she was carrying, and then ran, ran, ran until she was out of breath and delivering the package to Priya.

"Thank you," Priya said, and went into the stall.

"Was it under a minute?" Jackie asked. "Did you count it?"

"No," Priya said. "These towels are so gross."

"Put them in the little thing," Jackie said. "With the paper bag."

Priya flushed the toilet and came out. "Do you think anyone can tell?" she said, as she washed her hands.

"No," Jackie said. "You can't see the pad through the dress or anything." Priya's dress was purple, and her hair was braided in a long, thick black braid down her back. Jackie's dress was brown, and her hair was lank and clumpy from running, even though she was sure she had only run for less than a minute. Meredith always kept a comb in her purse, and smoothed out her hair in front of every mirror. Jackie wondered if she should start carrying a purse, too. She could keep an extra maxipad in it, in case Priya needed one—or in case she needed one someday.

When they opened the door the children's choir was already lining up to take their places in the auditorium. Jackie and Priya waited as the line went by, then slipped in at the end where they belonged. Jackie was sure Priya was the only member of the children's choir who had started her period. Next year they'd have to find somewhere else to sing.

45. ALEX GOES TO A PARTY.

Meredith sat at the end of the table, reading *Anna Karenina* as she ate her apple. It was the same seat she had sat in since the beginning of high school, but the rest of the table was empty; Alex was sitting next to Stephanie and the other popular girls, and Daniel was on the very edge of a group of boys, the sort of seat where you could say you were part of the table even though you couldn't hear any of its conversation.

The hardest part about having no friends was having nobody to talk to, and when Meredith wrote that in her diary she added two paragraphs clarifying that of course she had a whole family of people to talk to, and she had people at school and at church, but that was a different kind of talking. With that kind of talking, you fit in words that made sense with the conversation. This was the kind of talking where you could say both what was true, and what you wanted to be true.

Anna Karenina felt like the inside of her own head, right now; pages and pages of thoughts winding around an idea. When she started the book the idea was *how do I get Alex and Daniel back*, but after spending time with Levin and her diary it became *how do I do something both great and meaningful with my life?* She understood that many of Levin's ideas were misguided, but what was important was that he kept trying. He made mistakes with the threshers and with Kitty and with his farm and then he spent pages going over his mistakes, just like she did, until he could figure out what to do better the next time. Meredith liked the Levin chapters much more than the Anna chapters, and often held her place with one finger or a torn-off corner of her napkin as she skipped ahead to see when the next Levin chapter would start.

Because Alex was Anna. Giving everything up so she could make out with some guy.

"Are you going to Morgan's tonight?" Stephanie asked Alex.

"I think so?" Alex had not officially been invited to Morgan's party, but maybe this was how it happened. You bought a few new outfits, sat down at a table, and they let you in. Alex still felt like she was on the outside of the group, even though she had known everyone at this table since they were born and Stacy, three seats over, was her cousin. But Stacy was thin and straight-haired and never got any of her plum lipstick on the spout of her chocolate milk. It took Alex a week to figure out that was because Stacy wasn't actually drinking the milk. It took Alex another week to start straightening her own hair.

Now Alex looked like she belonged, even if she still felt like she didn't. Her hair was long and straight, with one manufactured curl right at the end. Her freckles were hidden under a layer of foundation, and her contact-lensed eyes had a shimmer of white on each lid. She set her alarm for 6 a.m. to do all of this, and it had worked, because now Stephanie was asking her if she was going to Morgan's party.

Alex wondered if Andy would be there, or Brian, or any of the other high school boys who weren't dating anyone. Or maybe someone who *was* dating someone would see her at the party and change his mind. She knew that was how it worked; there would be a party or a basketball game, and the next Monday the pairings at the lunchroom table would change. There might be a little more room for Alex on the bench, or she might be pushed so far off that she sat balanced on one thigh, giving space so Barry or Ryan or Sean could sit next to his new girlfriend. No matter how full the table got, they never asked her to leave.

Friday evenings felt different without Alex; the hours stretched on and on when there was no movie to fill them up, so Meredith asked Nat and Jackie if they wanted to play Super Mario Bros. 2, since it was one of the few games they could all play together. "We can try to beat it," Meredith said. "We won't be able to beat it without Game Genie," Natalie argued, and so they put in the Super Mario All-Stars cartridge and added the code for infinite lives.

"We should have used the invincible code," Jackie said, after she walked Toad right into a Shyguy.

"You could still die by falling in pits, though," Natalie said. "Then you'd have to start the game over."

Meredith moved Princess deftly and delicately through the level—they had always, from the beginning, played Mario/Toad/Princess without any argument—but her mind was winding itself around an idea that had forced its way in as soon as they had started the game: *copyright 1988*. They were playing a game that had been around since Meredith was six years old, and at the same time, maybe at *this exact moment*, Alex was walking into Morgan's party. Alex was moving forward and Meredith was playing a game she had played dozens of times. It wasn't even like they had a new game system; by the time they bought the Super Nintendo from Daniel, it was old. Everyone else was playing Final Fantasy VII on the PlayStation; Meredith went online sometimes and lurked on the forums where they discussed whether Cloud should date Aeris or Tifa, because even that game was all about dating.

It was as if the whole world was telling her to grow up, and it didn't matter how many books she read or how well she could play the piano because the one thing that did matter was whether she was spending this Friday night at a party with the rest of her class or whether she stayed at home re-playing a childhood game with her sisters.

Alex had never been to one of Morgan's parties, so she didn't know what to wear; she ended up picking a babydoll dress with sunflowers on it, because the long sleeves would hide her freckles and the loose skirt would hide her hips, and the neckline was low enough that you could see the edge of her bra if she bent forward.

She also didn't know what time the party started, so she arrived at 8:30. There were already cars parked in front of Morgan's house, and Alex felt like everyone would see her mom pull carefully down the gravel driveway and remember that she wasn't sixteen yet, that she still had to be driven to parties by her parents. That would all change if she got a boyfriend, though. If she started dating an older boy, he could drive.

"I'll be back at 11," her mom said. "But call me if you need to. I can always come get you early."

Alex got out of the car and walked towards the front door, then changed her mind and followed the noise towards the back. It was clear that the party had already started, since the bass was thumping so loudly that Alex could feel the back door vibrate as she opened it; she carefully walked down the dark stairs and there she was, inside Morgan's party, in the middle of everything.

Except no one noticed her. Alex hadn't expected Morgan to walk up to her and offer to take her coat, the way Alex's mom did when they hosted parties, but she had expected someone to say "hi, Alex!" and invite her onto the dance floor. She had hoped it would be Andy. Instead the music beat against her ears and she shrugged off her coat into a pile on the floor and backed up against the wall, a few steps away from the middle of everything. There were people dancing; it was hard to tell who they were, because there wasn't a lot of light, and there was a punch bowl and a bag of chips. There was definitely a couple making out in the corner. Alex studied the bodies; it looked like it could be Stacy and someone, although she didn't know who.

Alex didn't see anyone else standing against the wall, though. That meant she had to do something else, something to prove that she belonged here. Her eyes went to the punch bowl first, but it stood unattended. So she walked into the center of the basement, into the cluster of people, and started dancing.

Meredith was in bed, reading *Anna Karenina*, when her mom knocked on the door. "Can I come in?" "Sure," Meredith said, quickly memorizing *page 883*.

"Preeti came into the bank today," Rosemary said. "She said she missed seeing you at their house."

Meredith ran through a handful of responses and picked the one that seemed the most appropriate. "We've all been so busy lately."

"She wondered if you had gotten into a fight, or if Daniel had done something wrong. She said Daniel invited you to go see *Phantom of the Opera* with him and you said no."

"Well, it was in Chicago."

"You said no because it was in Chicago?" Rosemary asked.

"You wouldn't have let me go," Meredith said.

"I would have loved for you to go to Chicago with the Seths," Rosemary said. "I would have bought you a new dress."

"You would have let me go to Chicago? With the cost of the show and the train and everything?"

"Why wouldn't we?"

Because when I asked for a PlayStation you said it was too expensive, Meredith thought, then discarded it. *Because it's an overnight trip with a boy.* Maybe. *Would you have let me go to Morgan's party tonight, if I had been asked?* Irrelevant, and anyway too late—Meredith was already crying.

"I wish you'd asked us," Rosemary said, reaching out to hold Meredith, pulling her daughter's head onto her shoulder. She would have made it work, to see her daughter get the chance to go to Chicago with Daniel. Rosemary had carried the picture of the two of them, in tuxedo and prom gown, ever since Meredith and Daniel had first become friends.

"You should talk to him," Rosemary said. "I'm sure he misses you."

"You don't know anything about this," Meredith said, and Rosemary held her daughter and held back her own thoughts, wanting to say *I know more than you think* and *why do all of my children assume they know everything about me* and *why am I always treated like the person who says no?* This was not the moment to get into a fight with Meredith. They had never quite gotten into the fight that hung at the edges of nearly all of their interactions, and neither of them wanted to.

After her mother left Meredith opened her diary.

> *Tonight I beat Super Mario Bros. 2 with my sisters, while Alex went off to dance in some guy's arms. It's like we're separating into two different stories.*
>
> *Mom said she would have let me go, which means it was my mistake not to have asked. Am I even sure that would have happened, though? It is an easy decision to make now that it isn't actually a decision. Now that everyone is wondering if Daniel and I are no longer friends.*
>
> *The whole thing about being in high school is that everyone is after you to not make any mistakes that might ruin everything. E.g. I wouldn't be allowed to go to Morgan's party because I might get drunk or get into a car with someone who is drunk or get pregnant or something. Not that I would get pregnant at the party, but some series of events might start there, like me meeting a senior guy, or Anna meeting Vronsky. And then later you end up pregnant, but you can trace it all back to that one initial error, so might as well stay home and see what happens when you play all of the levels in SMB2. A safe form of risk, especially with the Game Genie.*

But this mistake ruined everything too, because now Mom is sad that I didn't ask her first and Daniel's mom is disappointed that I said no, and I guess I lost both of my best friends, which doesn't seem like something that is actually my fault but there it is, one event leading to another.

And I could have said yes to Daniel, because he asked me to go with him, and I could have said yes to Alex, because she asked me to go with her. And I said no to both of them for two different reasons, and maybe neither of them were good reasons. Maybe they were both mistakes.

But if I said yes to Alex when she wanted to sit with the popular girls I would probably have been asked to Morgan's party and my parents for sure would have said no, and Alex would have still gone without me and I would still be here. All of my paths lead me to this same moment, which must mean that this moment is important somehow.

Meredith closed her diary. She didn't know if she believed in turning points, they were the stuff of bad stories, but she wanted to turn herself towards something. Her parents and sisters had gone to bed, so she walked quietly down the stairs and into the pantry. She kept the light off but turned the computer on, opening up ClarisWorks.

The four of them—Maymorgan, Reed, Kip, and Eirwyn—had been on the train for an hour before it stopped.

She wasn't quite sure what would happen, but as soon as she wrote the four names she knew who these characters were, and what they wanted, and the rest would all come out as soon as they got out of their seats and went to see what had happened with the train. If it was good enough at the end—and if, by the time she was done, they had become friends again—she would show it to Daniel.

46. ROSEMARY CALLS HER MOTHER.

Rosemary waited until after Natalie had finished the dishes; then she leaned against the kitchen counter and dialed California. The phone rang seven times, but Rosemary knew to wait. Sometimes it took her mother a while to pick up.

"Hello?" She used to say "Hello, this is Nancy," or "Hello, you've reached the Little residence," which is what Rosemary had also been taught to say, back when she was small. She was glad enough to hide that surname behind Jack's, because she had never really stopped being small and used to get so angry when men—always men—would tease her about her name. Now she looked in the mirror and thought she looked both small and old, and then she called her mother and was reminded what old really was.

"Hi, Mom. It's Rosemary."

"Rosemary!" Her mother drew out the name so it sounded like a the creak of a door. Rosemary could hear the cadences of her mother's voice before she spoke, waiting for the two-syllable "well" and the sorrowful descent of "oh, I don't know."

"I wanted to call and see how you were doing."

"Oh, I don't know," her mother said, and Rosemary wondered how four words could take up so much space, so much time. Meredith was at the piano practicing the Moonlight Sonata, and her mother seemed to be speaking as slowly as Beethoven's melody, with just as many mistakes.

"I guess I'm doing well. I had a nice breakfast the other day, with the girls." These were the women who had come in and out of the house when Rosemary was a child, the ones

218

who used to sit around the kitchen table and talk while she practiced her own sonatas in the living room. "Phyllis couldn't have the orange juice because of her diabetes, but the orange juice was real good."

"I'm glad," Rosemary said. "I like orange juice." The responses she could give her mother had diminished, over time. "I hope Phyllis is doing well."

"Oh, I don't know," her mother said again. "She goes to the doctor all the time. There's a nice girl from church who drives her."

"That's good," Rosemary said, wondering who would drive her mother to the doctor if she needed to go. The girl from church? Would her mom even ask?

"You know Arlene had pneumonia."

"How's she doing?" Arlene's pneumonia had actually been in February, but it had come up in nearly all of their phone calls since.

"Well, she's at home and Jim is taking good care of her," her mother said. Jim was Arlene's husband, and Rosemary pictured him, skinny and slightly bent over, caring for his wife. Who would care for her mother if she became sick? This was the question Rosemary thought, but did not ask, during each of their conversations.

"I watched *The Price is Right* today," her mother continued.

"Did someone win the showcase?" Rosemary already knew what her mother would say next.

"Oh, I don't know. Then I had lunch, I made myself a bologna sandwich with mayonnaise, and then I went for my walk. You know I'm supposed to walk every day. The doctor says."

Rosemary thought of her mother, who was as little as she was, carefully making herself a bologna and mayonnaise sandwich. She wondered how often her mother bought groceries, whether there was very much bologna on the sandwich and whether any of it had expired. She thought of all the work she did in a day to keep her household going—the shopping, the planning, moving food and plates and laundry from one room to another—and could no longer imagine her mother doing any of it.

"I'm glad you're walking every day," Rosemary said.

"You practiced the piano," her mother said, "and now I practice my walk."

"Would you like to talk to the girls?" Rosemary asked, knowing that each of her daughters could be counted on to spend at least three or four minutes with their grandmother, telling her that school was going great and that they had a lot of friends. She waved Jackie over to the phone first, and stood in the kitchen doorway as each of the girls had a near-identical conversation. *We have to go visit her this summer*, she thought. *Make sure she's doing okay.*

"Well, it's been great talking to you," Rosemary said afterwards, because her mother no longer ended long-distance phone calls, when she ran out of news to share she said "well..." and then remembered something else she had eaten, telling Rosemary about her TV dinner or the cookies they had after church on Sunday. Rosemary had previously counted that as a sign of health; surely her mother was okay if she was going to church, and going to breakfast with the girls, and sharing her opinions on Lean Cuisine. *We need to plan a trip*, she thought again.

"I'm always glad to hear from you," her mother said. "And the girls."

"I'll call you next week," Rosemary said. "Bye, mom. Love you."

"I love you too."

SUMMER 1998

47. NATALIE GOES TO THE MALL.

Natalie and Kimberly sang, their voices louder than the radio that accompanied them. They waved their arms in a seatbelted dance, mimicking Natalie Imbruglia in the music video. Kimberly's mom glanced at them through the rear-view mirror and smiled. Parents liked it when their kids sang in cars, Natalie had noticed. Unlike her own parents, Kimberly's mom did not care whether they sang in harmony.

"I'll be back in two hours," Kimberly's mom said, dropping them in front of the Delacroix mall. Two hours was not enough time to see a movie, but it was enough time to try on clothes and shoes and put them back, and dig through the 10 for $10 earring bins, and buy a pretzel and share it while they sat, cross-legged, on the wide edge of the mall fountain. They'd throw their leftover pennies in, if they had any. They'd make wishes and refuse to say what they were, because saying your deepest desires only worked when you were a little kid, when everyone said you were cute for wanting something you'd probably never receive.

Now both of them had to work at being cute, had to spend their mornings dealing with pimples and period blood and the leg stubble that grew overnight, not even giving them a day's rest. Natalie went to bed with legs that were just beginning to scratch, and woke up with tiny black hairs sprouting from ankle to knee. She shaved above the knee too, because Meredith had warned her.

They climbed out of the car, Natalie feeling the smack of the concrete through the soles of her sandals as she jumped from the minivan to the pavement. The sticky afternoon began to collect on her skin, her upper lip starting to sweat in the time it took for them to walk from the car to the mall doors, pulling them open as fast as they could, dunking their bodies into the air conditioning.

"Where do you want to go?" Natalie asked. Mom had taught her to always ask the other person what they wanted to do first, whether you were a guest in their home or they were a guest in yours. It was the kind of advice that didn't make sense when two people did it, and when she went to Chrissy's house they often went through three rounds of "well, what do *you* want to do?" before they finally agreed on something. But Kimberly was the kind of person who would say "Let's go look at earrings," and so they went.

It was a good first stop because the store had a lot of mirrors, and Natalie and Kimberly both knew how to walk by a mirror and do a quick check, make sure their lips were still glossy and their bra straps weren't showing. "My hair looks so gross," Natalie said, after seeing her still warm face and running her hand over her upper lip.

"Nat, your hair looks gorgeous," Kimberly said.

"It's stuck to the back of my neck," Natalie complained. She hauled her thick hair into one hand to check and felt the slight pull as it detached itself from her sweaty skin. Why was it always so hot, every summer?

"You could get a clip," Kimberly said, holding up a giant claw clip molded in the shape of pink flowers. She snapped the clip's jaws right in front of Natalie's face. "I want you to wear me!" she said, in a monster voice.

"No flowers," Natalie said. "Too girly." She wasn't that kind of girl, the kind that wore pink and flowers and those little butterfly clips that looked like they had been dipped in glitter. She wanted to look like the girls in the Delia's catalog, the ones who who wore striped tank tops and olive-green cargo pants and stared at you from behind their cropped hair.

"Okay," Kimberly said, digging into a bin of flavored lip gloss and coming up with two closed hands. "Pick one."

Natalie pointed, and Kimberly opened her left hand. "Sweet Peach," she said, holding out the lip gloss. She opened her other hand. "Candy Apple. Ugh."

"Want to switch?"

"No, I want Passionberry," Kimberly said. "Because I'm *passionate*."

"What does a passionberry even look like?" Natalie asked. She was holding both lip glosses now, as Kimberly raked her fingers through the bin in search of the elusive flavor, scooping up handfuls of tubes and dropping them back in again. "Purple," Kimberly said, finally grabbing the one she wanted. "Which one are you getting?"

"I don't know." Natalie secretly wanted to try the black lipstick that was against the wall with the chokers and the goth stuff. She didn't want to be goth, but she didn't want to be a sweet peach or a candy apple either. She wanted to see what she looked like with actual color on her lips, instead of this shiny goop that made a little slick sound every time she opened her mouth. But all the moms had agreed: no real makeup until high school, and the summer before high school didn't count.

"I think I'll get two," Kimberly said. Then she whispered in Natalie's ear, her face as close as the claw: "Jenna's sister says nobody will notice if we walk out without paying."

"I don't want to steal anything."

"Chicken," Kimberly said, closing her hands around Passionberry and Sassy Strawberry. "Go," she whispered again. "But not too quickly."

The two of them walked out and, just like Jenna's sister had promised, nobody noticed. Once they were two stores away, Kimberly held up her stolen merchandise and laughed, and Natalie wondered if she should have tried harder to talk Kimberly out of stealing, or if she should be refusing to walk next to her right now. She could go to one of the payphones and call home, just like her parents had told her to do. *We'll come get you, no matter what.* But she couldn't imagine making the call over two tubes of lip gloss. That wasn't really what her parents had meant, right?

The day felt spoiled, like Natalie had failed at being a friend and now she was failing at being herself. Maybe this was just what almost-fourteen-year-olds did. Teenage rebellion. Maybe she really was chicken. Maybe she was failing at being a teenager too.

They got their pretzel and they sat by the fountain and they took turns dipping the chewy, almost raw dough into the cream cheese frosting, and then they threw their pennies in and, like always, asked each other what they had wished for.

"I'm not telling," Natalie said, which was what she always said, except this time Kimberly said "Chicken."

"Fine," Natalie said. *I wish you hadn't stolen those lip glosses.* "I wish I could get my hair cut."

"Let's do it!" Kimberly stood up, and pointed at the salon across from the mall fountain. "There's no line."

Something felt not right about this plan, but the day had felt not right for a while, and Natalie hated the way her hair felt against her skin, and it only cost $9. She had $15 in her purse for the afternoon, plus the crumpled dollar bill she had put towards the pretzel. She could do this.

"What kind of haircut are we getting today?" the girl asked, snapping Natalie into a green apron and spraying her thick hair down with water.

"Do you know Natalie Imbruglia? Like in the "Torn" music video?" It felt strange to say her own name aloud.

"Oh my god I *love* that song," the girl said. Her own hair was jagged, with a layer of black over what looked like butter yellow. "So it's like a short cut with some long side bangs, stacked in the back?"

Natalie didn't know what it meant to stack hair, but she said yes anyway. Within a minute there was a pile of her golden, sweaty hair curling on the floor, and within ten minutes she could tell that she was going to have a very short haircut, although it was hard to tell what it was going to look like because her glasses were balanced carefully on her lap, under the robe.

"You are *so lucky*," the girl said, in between blasts from the blow dryer. "You have such gorgeous hair." Apparently that's what everybody said about her hair, even when most of it was cut off.

"I'm going to shave the back of your neck," the girl said, and Natalie felt the last few pieces of hair unstick themselves from her skin. She couldn't remember what it felt like to not have hair against her neck. Even when she wore a ponytail, her hair still found its way to her neck and face, clinging to any part of her that was sweaty or moist or covered in flavored lip gloss.

When it was time to put her glasses on, Natalie loved what she saw in the mirror. She had a haircut just like Natalie Imbruglia and the Delia's girls; two longer pieces in the front and cut to the top of her neck in the back, with shorter layers that she could see when she shook her head from side to side.

"Your mom is going to say you're *so cute*," the girl said. "Is she paying?"

"No," Natalie said. "I am." She suddenly wondered what her mother would think. Well, she was *so cute*, right? She looked older, maybe. She wanted more time to stare at the mirror, to look at the back of her head, to get used to seeing her neck and her ears. But Kimberly was waiting, and the girl was waiting, and the receipt Natalie received had a line for a tip, so instead of staring at herself she stared at the piece of paper and wondered how much a tip should be. She had a $10 and a $5 and didn't know if it was appropriate to ask for change, so she gave the girl the entire $15 and ran back to the fountain.

"Wow, don't you look chic," Kimberly's mom said, when she came to pick them up.

"Thank you," Natalie said, remembering to be polite. "I wanted it for summer."

"I got lip gloss and a new tank top," Kimberly said, showing her mom her bag.

Kimberly's mom laughed. "I can smell the lip gloss," she said, in that way parents did that was kind of nice and kind of mean at the same time. The things they only said to their daughters and not to their daughters' friends, even though Natalie had also applied her half-finished tube of Watermelon Splash as they stood outside and waited for the car, knowing her hair would no longer blow in the wind and stick to her mouth.

When they got back home Natalie was excited to show off her new haircut, and to maybe get a few minutes in the downstairs bathroom where, if you opened the doors on the medicine cabinet just the right way, you could see both the front and the back of your head. She hopped out of the car, landing on grass this time, and thanked Kimberly's mom for driving them. Then she went inside, called out "I'm home," and saw her mother's face.

"What did you do to yourself?" Mom asked.

"I got a haircut," Natalie said. "For summer."

"You cut your beautiful hair."

"It's okay," Natalie said, wondering why it wasn't okay, knowing that she should have known that it wouldn't be okay. "It'll be good for swimming. I'll save seconds off my time."

"Don't," Mom said. "Where'd you get it cut?" It was that voice that sounded like yelling even though Mom wasn't speaking loudly at all.

"At the mall."

"And how much did it cost you?"

"Nine dollars," Natalie said. Then she felt guilty. "I mean, fifteen with the tip."

"You gave a six dollar tip."

"It was my money," Natalie said. She didn't know why a six dollar tip was wrong. "And my hair."

"What's going on?" Dad asked, coming into the room. "Nice haircut, Nat."

"No it isn't!" Mom said, and Natalie realized her mother was crying. "She cut her gorgeous hair and some idiot at the mall let her do it, and who lets a thirteen-year-old get her hair cut without her mother?"

"Hey," Dad said. "It's just hair. It'll grow back."

"It was so hot," Natalie said. "It was sticking to my neck."

Mom was still crying, sniffling and almost wiping her nose on her arm before catching herself. "Go upstairs. I don't want to talk to you."

Natalie almost did as she was told, but then she stopped. "It's my hair and my money," she said. "And maybe I don't want to talk to you either."

Then she ran upstairs and sat on her bed and cried. She was a rebellious teenager for sure now, even though she could never tell Kimberly she had been brave enough to yell back, because she wasn't going to talk to Kimberly ever again.

"Nat," Meredith said, standing in the doorway. "Can I come in?"

Natalie lifted her head, and Meredith immediately said "I love your haircut!" which only made her cry again. "Mom hates it," she said. "She yelled at me and said it looked terrible."

"Mom's stressed out right now because of Grandma," Meredith said.

"Is Grandma okay?"

"She doesn't think so," Meredith said, and the two of them sat together on Natalie's bed, Meredith going to the bathroom and coming back with a roll of toilet paper, until Natalie was done crying and was ready to wipe away the strands of hair that had stuck to the edges of her eyes.

They heard Jackie come up the stairs, humming, still unaware, swinging into the room with one hand on the doorway. "Mom says you can come down now," she told Natalie. Then she smiled. "You got your hair cut!"

Natalie was almost going to cry again, but she decided not to. She also decided she wasn't going down. If she had her penny to wish again, she wanted her mother to come up the stairs to her, to say she was sorry she had yelled.

"Are you okay?" Jackie asked.

"Yeah," Natalie said.

The three of them sat together, and it took about a minute for Jackie to start humming again, and Meredith, always showing off, started humming the harmony part, and Natalie just sat there until Meredith looked at her like *come on* and she joined in, the three of them quietly singing together like they used to, and then Natalie heard Mom's footsteps on the stairs and sat between her sisters and saw her mother's face and realized that sometimes her deepest wishes could still come true.

48. ROSEMARY AND JONETTA EAT NACHOS.

"I don't know what happens," Rosemary said. "You have these cute little girls, and then…"

"Your girls are still cute," Jonetta said, reaching into the casserole dish and pulling out a chip. A second chip came with it, connected by the layer of baked cheese and black olives.

"Jackie never brushes her hair, Meredith brushes hers too much, and Natalie cut hers off. I still don't understand why she did it. She looks like a boy."

"She looks fine. Anyway, you've got good kids. I'm the one who has to worry about what my daughter is up to. Have you put Meredith on the pill yet?"

"No," Rosemary said. "Is Stephanie?"

"I made an appointment," Jonetta said. "Had to have the talk with Stephanie about it—that was a fun evening—but I am not going to be somebody's grandma. Not until she's out of high school."

Not college? Rosemary thought, but didn't say anything. Instead she eyed the dish of nachos and wondered if she could take another helping. It wasn't like she was ever going to be skinny again, not like she used to be. *This is what letting go is,* Rosemary thought. *A haircut. A new pair of pants.* She took the serving spoon and dropped a pile of nachos onto her plate, then reached for the plastic tub of sour cream.

"My mother never took me to the gynecologist," she told Jonetta. "I had to figure it out when Jack and I got married. Of course my mom never really took me anywhere."

"How's she doing?" Jonetta asked. "Y'all are going to visit her in a couple weeks, right?"

"Yeah." Rosemary knew that Jonetta already knew the details, that they had been passed down through Bobbie Jo. It was hard to believe that their mothers were the same age. "We leave a week from Tuesday."

She paused, and sighed, and felt her belly press against her waistband. "I don't know what I'm going to do. She's not going to be fine, I know that. So I'm going to have to do something. Do I bring her out here? Do I stay and take care of her? What do you do, when your mom lives a thousand miles away?"

"Bring her here," Jonetta said. "She'd probably love it."

"Then what do I do with all her stuff?" Rosemary thought about her mother's house, every surface covered with magazines or knick-knacks or discarded items of clothing. "I always knew this would happen and yet I never thought it would happen."

"What?"

"All of this. Her getting older." She broke a chip in half, broke the larger piece in half again. "Next week I'm putting three teenagers into a car and we're all driving to California."

"Hey, I've never been to California," Jonetta said. "It's beautiful, right?"

"The most beautiful place in the world."

49. THE GRUBERS DRIVE TO CALIFORNIA.

This was how Jack did the math: they could get to Fresno in two days if they really pushed it. Two days would only mean one night in a motel. They could pack the cooler with bread and lunch meat and eat at rest stops.

The girls were old enough, now, that they could sit in the back without anyone needing too many bathroom breaks or getting carsick. They'd just have two miserable days, and then they'd be there.

Meredith pushed her fingers into the points right below her eyebrows, where her eyes and sinuses all met up. She couldn't tell if it was helping; sometimes it felt like her headache eased slightly, but it always came back. She tried her sinuses, her temples, and the back of her neck, pushing her fingers against the weight of her skull and massaging the tendons. She tipped her head forward, making sure she could still touch her chin to her chest. It wasn't meningitis.

She would have stretched a little more, rolled her head from side to side, except she was sitting right next to Jackie and didn't want to enter her space any more than they had to. The family rarely used the car all at once; they walked to church, or to the college, or only two or three of them would drive to Delacroix. Now the three Gruber sisters sat together in the backseat, quietly avoiding each other, becoming invisible in the silence.

But Meredith spoke, in that way you had to do in cars that was just loud enough to be uncomfortable. "Mom, do you have any Tylenol?"

"Are you sick?" Rosemary's voice came back, anxious and exhausted.

"No," Meredith said. "I have a headache."

"Just lie back and go to sleep, then."

Meredith didn't want to lie back and go to sleep, because she already had to pee a little bit, and she knew that the next hour—maybe the next two hours—would be about trying to forget that she had a headache and needed to use the toilet. If they stopped at a gas station, she could buy some Tylenol on her own.

Jackie watched Meredith rub at her neck, and then she looked at Natalie half-asleep next to her, and then she looked straight ahead, at the road. She didn't like reading in cars, so she had nothing to do but wait until she fell asleep by accident or something, or until Mom or Dad turned the radio on. They had left early enough that nobody had wanted the radio, and then it became what this trip was about, silence and waiting and thinking.

Okay, then what would she think about? Grandma, probably. She knew that they were going to visit Grandma to see how she was doing, and she got the idea that maybe Grandma wasn't doing well. Was Grandma going to die? Thinking about it made Jackie sad in a way that felt like her own body telling her that death was terrible—but above that, the way the five of them hovered above the wheels and the concrete, her brain told her that she wasn't sad. Or that she was a little sad because someone in her family might die, and she was a little sad because her mom was sad, and she was definitely sad when she thought of Grandma being in pain. But she wasn't sad because she was going to miss her grandmother, because she didn't miss her right now and she hadn't missed her yesterday.

So Jackie sat in the car and thought about everything she knew about Grandma. Her name was Nancy Little. She liked going for walks and watching TV. She used to work as a secretary, but she hadn't done that in a long time. There was a picture of her on the bookshelf, with golden-brown hair just like Mom and Natalie. Jackie knew that picture was from when Grandma was younger, because her hair was gray now, but she could never tell how much younger. The golden-brown curls were puffed out around her head just like all of the old ladies Jackie had ever seen—except Miss Opal, of course.

Jackie thought that she would be sad if Miss Opal died, and then she felt sad about being sadder about Miss Opal than about her grandmother. Then she started to imagine Miss Opal's funeral, and how she would fly back from singing opera in Europe to be there. She pictured herself in a black dress and high heels and one of those hats with the little black veil that hung over one eye. She was tall and thin and had blonde hair, because Jackie always imagined her future self with blonde hair. She walked to the podium, looked down at Miss Opal in her casket, and began giving her eulogy. *I loved Opal Lancaster. She was my favorite teacher.* Then Miss Opal sat up, because she wasn't really dead, and the two of them began walking around the cemetery, and they started looking for a snowcone machine, and then Jackie realized she might actually be asleep—so she did what she always did when she knew she was dreaming. She jumped into the air, squeezed her legs together, and began to fly.

Natalie looked over Jackie's slumped body, her head bouncing up and down to match the movement of the car, and raised an eyebrow at Meredith. Meredith smiled, because yes, Jackie did look ridiculous. Of course she was in the middle seat, where there wasn't anywhere to lean. Natalie was glad that Jackie would always be smaller than her, that there would always be someone else to take the middle. She was also glad that whatever arrangement they had decided upon when they were very young children, that moment when one seat in the car became permanently *theirs*, put her behind Mom instead of Dad. Mom was shorter, so her seat was always moved forward. Natalie could shift position, scootch down in her seat a little, and almost get her legs completely straight. It was the most fun thing she would be able to do for the next two days.

She looked up to see who else in the car was sleeping. If it was just Jackie, they could turn the radio on; if Mom was sleeping too, they probably couldn't. Dad would want public radio, but the trip was long enough that there'd have to be some place where there wasn't any public radio, and then someone else could choose the station. Natalie already knew that this wouldn't be a trip where anyone sang in the car. When they were getting ready that morning, Mom and Dad were talking about taking turns driving, and Meredith had asked if she could take a turn. Both of them said "No," and it was the kind of *no* that puts a separation between the adult world and the kid one, sticking Meredith back on the kid side even though she had her license now. This trip wasn't about them. It was about Mom and Grandma, and the three of them had to be good kids who sat in the backseat and waited for the whole thing to be over.

And Natalie wanted to be a good kid. She hadn't really felt like a good kid since she got her hair cut, or maybe since she got her period, or maybe since she knew they would have to stop—she'd have to ask them to stop—soon or she'd start to leak blood out the sides of her pad and onto her shorts. They'd all have to stop soon, because it had been hours, but one of them would have to ask for the stop. One of them would have to say *I can't wait anymore.*

Rosemary opened her eyes, stiff and uncomfortable in her seatbelt. She had no idea where they were. She felt a little nauseated, and she couldn't tell if it was from the driving or from not eating anything. It had been too early when they left, and now she wanted french fries or chips or anything that wasn't that clammy lunch meat they had back in the cooler.

There was a box of granola bars at her feet, and she pulled one out for herself, leaning over to offer the box to her girls. "Anyone want a granola bar?"

"Can we stop?" Natalie asked.

"Can we stop at a gas station?" Meredith immediately followed.

"They want to stop at a gas station," Rosemary said to Jack, passing the message forward.

"We've got plenty of gas," Jack said. "Tell them there's a rest area in about 40 minutes."

Rosemary leaned back. "There's a rest area in about 40 minutes," she said. Her girls looked back at her with silent eyes, impatience and frustration under a mask of good behavior, and said nothing.

This was how Jack did the math: even if they did fly they'd still have to get up at four in the morning to make it to St. Louis, and that would be if they wanted to take a flight that left around 10 a.m., not one of the really cheap ones that left before dawn. They'd have to spend three hours in the car and at least eight hours in planes and airports, because they'd probably do a layover in Denver, and then they'd have to rent a car in Fresno. The entire day would take them 14 hours, just like today. There wasn't any way to get halfway across the country without at least one miserable day—and if they were going to be miserable, they could do it without spending two grand.

Rosemary twisted back into in her seat, ate her granola bar, and waited, her own face matching her daughters. Her bag was in the trunk next to theirs, with extra clothes packed in case she needed to stay. Would she stay? *We'll see how Mom's doing,* she thought, knowing she had the rest of the day and all of tomorrow to get through before she could make that decision. Until then, she would lie back and go to sleep.

50. ROSEMARY MAKES A DECISION.

"I like the green beans with a little butter in them," Rosemary's mother said.

"Well, I didn't cook these with butter," Rosemary told her. "Just plain."

"They're great," Meredith said.

"Yeah, Mom," Natalie echoed. "Great."

You let your butter go rancid, Rosemary thought, *and you criticize my cooking.* She and Jack had spent the morning cleaning out her mother's refrigerator and cupboards, and buying all new groceries. The girls had wanted to help, but Rosemary sent them on a walk around the park instead, slipping Meredith some cash so they could buy sodas or ice cream, anything that would keep them—and her mother—outside.

"I'm so glad you could visit," her mother said again. She used that sentence to fill any silence that lasted longer than it took to chew a mouthful of beans.

"We wanted to see how you were doing," Jack said, and Rosemary thought *don't make it obvious.* This would only work if her mother didn't think anything was wrong. She hadn't noticed the stack of Lean Cuisines in the freezer yet; hadn't said anything about the bunch of bananas on the freshly-scrubbed countertop. What had she noticed? Jackie said, when they got back, that Grandma had asked her how school was going three times.

"Well, I'm so glad you could visit," Rosemary's mother said, and then they continued eating, Rosemary trying to think of any kind of conversation that was left to them, since she had already asked about how her mother was feeling and whether she'd gone out to lunch with Phyllis recently and if she'd seen anything good on TV.

"The chicken is good too," Natalie said. Her girls. She was going to miss them, because she had to stay—of course she had to stay, there wasn't any way she was getting out of this house until she made her mother a doctor's appointment and probably some kind of follow-up appointment and cleaned everything, the toilet and the bedsheets and the cluttered coffee table. She'd take her mother to the doctor, she'd mop the floors, and then she'd figure out what to do next.

"How long do you think it will take?" Jack asked, both of them getting ready to sleep in Rosemary's childhood bedroom. The girls had the guest room next door, and Rosemary kept her voice down.

"Between two weeks and two years?" It was a joke, sort of. "It probably all depends on what the doctor says, and what our options are."

She paused. "You know I'm going to have to call the bank on Monday."

"I know."

And there it goes, Rosemary thought. *There it all goes.* She'd call the bank on Monday, and on Tuesday her family would get into the car and leave her behind, as if her entire adult life had never happened.

"I love you," Jack said.

"I love you too."

51. MEREDITH GOES TO THE LIBRARY.

Meredith walked quietly down the stacks, tracking the numbers as she passed them. When she got to the 790s she stopped, paused on the edge of her foot, and then kept walking. Now she knew where they were.

She passed more numbers, more rows of books, listening for any noises besides the sound of her closed-toed shoes against the cement floor and her own breathing. She could hold her breath, though; she did it without thinking, especially when she *was* thinking. Stopped the air in the back of her throat and kept moving.

Library: books on writing, books and movies on theatre, she had written in her notebook that morning, along with all of the other tasks like *get gas* and *ask Jackie what birthday cake she wants*. Meredith had started making lists again, now that Mom was gone, because if she didn't write down *laundry* she'd get to the end of the day and it wouldn't get done. Dad had said they were old enough to do their own clothes, now. They had become old enough to do a lot of their own things, that summer.

Meredith continued to walk around the third floor of the Kirkland College library, wondering if anyone would come down the metal stairs and see her standing there, with her still-damp hair and worn out clothes. She had come straight from her job washing dishes in the college cafeteria, checking off *work* before *library* and *get gas*, and she felt embarrassed to exist in the world with her sweaty face and gross old sneakers and her T-shirt that pulled a little too tight at the arm holes. Too many people knew her as

Meredith Gruber, Dr. G's whip-smart oldest daughter; she didn't want them to know her as this person, too.

She also didn't want them to know that she was ducking into the 790s and 800s to look at books on theater and creative writing. Her father had occasionally checked out Kirkland College books on her behalf, and her job in the cafeteria had entitled her to a library card of her own, and now she felt like she was making a secret desire public, that taking these books and movies off the shelves and stacking them up on the checkout desk so Mrs. Francis could stamp their cards would start a chain of conversation: *Meredith Gruber wants to be a writer and an actor. She checked out all the books on how to do it.*

Maybe it wouldn't be Mrs. Francis, though. Maybe it would be one of the college students whom Meredith didn't know. She could walk halfway up the stairs, her head just peeking up into the main floor, to check. If she saw someone she knew, she could turn around.

The thing was that Meredith had to check out books from the 790s and 800s if she wanted to learn anything, because what she knew so far from two years of high school was that she'd already read all the books, she could already do all of the math, and their science teacher was so clueless that she wrote the words "grass, rat, cow" on the overhead projector and said it was an example of a food chain.

Her Language Arts teacher wrote "A+" on her papers without leaving any other comments. The drama program had been cut for budget, and because the drama teacher went on maternity leave and never came back. If Meredith was going to get herself ready for college, she had to do it on her own—and she had to announce, maybe to the entire town, what she wanted.

She walked into the row marked 790 and squatted down so she could see the books. Her shoes smelled like dishwater and her hands smelled like grease. She started taking titles off the shelves: *Audition* by Michael Shurtleff, *An Actor Prepares*. She wondered if there might be actual college students who wanted to read these, and if she was taking something away from them instead of waiting her turn. But they weren't there, nobody had come down into the stacks the entire time Meredith had been there, and so she could have these books for just a few weeks, until she had taken everything she could out of them the way she and her sisters sucked the last drips of soda up from their straws. "International waitress call," Alex had said, back when it was Meredith and Alex.

Meredith missed Alex. She and Daniel had gone back to being friends, although there was a new boundary between them, the way Mario Kart 64 had walls all around the edges of each course even though the game made it look like you could drive anywhere you wanted. The two of them had spent an entire Sunday afternoon seeing how far the cars could go before they ran into rock walls or blocked paths. When their arms accidentally bumped, they both flinched and then Daniel scooted slightly to the left so it wouldn't happen again.

When Meredith had her books, and when she had gone down one more floor to take VHS copies of *Into the Woods* and *Carousel* out of the video section, she climbed back up the metal stairs to see who would be waiting for her at the top and whether she would have to make small talk about her choices and dreams. But it wasn't Mrs. Francis after all; just another student who swiped Meredith's books the way Meredith had washed her dishes earlier that day: uninterested, waiting for her shift to be over.

"Thank you," Meredith said. She carried the stack of books and videos in one arm as she reached into her back pocket for her little notebook. Walking out the library doors, Meredith balanced the notebook on top of *Into the Woods* and crossed out *library: books on writing, books and movies on theatre.* Next was *get gas,* and then she could go home.

52. THE GRUBER SISTERS GO BACK-TO-SCHOOL SHOPPING.

"Okay," Meredith said. "Music store first, then the mall."

Jackie leaned her cheek against the car window, feeling the vibrations enter her skin and travel through her teeth. She opened her mouth slightly and exhaled a slight "ahhh" sound to see if it would make her voice hum the way it did when she talked into the box fan.

"Haircuts before clothes?" Natalie asked.

"Makes sense," Meredith said. "Unless there's a line or something."

Jackie twisted her head so her ear pressed against the glass. It was easier to hear the car that way, and she only had to half-hear Natalie and Meredith. They were going back-to-school shopping the same way they did every year. Jackie would look at opera scores while Natalie picked out reeds for her clarinet, and then she would stand quietly while Meredith and Natalie tried on clothes, and then they'd stand quietly while she tried on clothes, and then they'd all go to the school supply store and walk past the notebooks with glitter and unicorns on them so they could pick the cheap ones with plain covers. Maybe Meredith would say she could have one notebook with cartoons or dolphins or hearts on it, the way Mom used to. But they had less money now. That's what Dad had said when Mom stayed in California, and that's what he told Meredith that morning.

Meredith parked the car with a jerk, the way she always did, and they went into the music store to get Natalie's reeds. "It's the Gruber girls!" the man said, the one with the name that Jackie could never quite remember. She had been too young, when they were first introduced, to pay attention.

"I'm looking for a couple boxes of Vandoren B-flat 2.5s," Natalie said. "Maybe two boxes to start?"

"It's that time of year," the man said, pulling open a skinny drawer and taking out two blue boxes. "Excited for marching band?"

"Sure," Natalie said, even though Jackie knew that she and Meredith both hated marching band, that there was nothing fun about wearing wool uniforms on 80-degree days, or getting on the school bus at 4 a.m. to travel to a parade. Jackie had to leave at 4 a.m. too, all of the parents and siblings following the bus to the parade route. This year she'd be marching with the junior high, and Dad would follow the band and talk to the band directors about recruiting their students for Kirkland College, and maybe Mom wouldn't be there.

"How's the flute doing?" the man asked her. He could remember that she played the flute, and Jackie felt a little ashamed that she couldn't remember whether he was a Bob or a Bill.

"It's going well," she said, lying just like Natalie, because the truth was she was only adequate at flute, she had thought that she would put it to her lips and it would be as easy as singing or playing the piano, and it wasn't. She wasn't terrible at flute, but she wasn't good—and it was much more interesting to practice at something where she was already good, where she could think about tone and expression instead of just hitting the notes. Of course she didn't practice piano much anymore, since Mom had stopped teaching lessons. Meredith kept banging through Schumann and Beethoven, as loud and forceful as the way she parked the car, but Jackie spent her practice time putting her hand against her diaphragm and singing "Sure on this Shining Night," trying to stretch her breath to the very end of the line. When she finished practicing Meredith would sit with her and play the accompaniment, and Jackie would think of Mom and Grandma as she sang, articulating her love with every consonant. Miss Opal had told her she had to find her own meaning in the words, since they didn't make sense on their own.

"And the French horn?"

"I'm going to prep the Larghetto from the Mozart Third Horn Concerto for contest this year," Meredith said, "although that's only if my lips survive playing the trumpet in marching band."

Jackie let Meredith stand there, talking to Bob or Bill like she was an adult, making her silly fake jokes the way parents and adults did, and turned away to the rack of opera scores against the wall. That was what kids could do: walk away in the middle of the conversation. She pulled out Humperdinck's *Hansel and Gretel*, wondering how old she'd have to be to sing Gretel's part, knowing that it would all depend on someone deciding to stage the opera in the first place. Maybe Miss Opal would let her learn it anyway. So much of practicing was about music that you would never get to perform.

"Jackie, we're ready to go." She almost sounded like Mom, only it was Natalie this time instead of Meredith. The two of them leading the way back to the car, sitting in the front seats, deciding where they would go next.

"I'm hungry," Jackie said. "Do you want to get ice cream?"

"We don't have money for ice cream," Meredith said.

"I have my allowance," Jackie said. "We could get three Dilly Bars for three dollars."

"Let's do it," Natalie said. "I'll throw in my allowance and we can get Blizzards."

"We should get Blizzards!" Jackie said, because they had always been plain notebook, single-scoop kids, and she knew Mom would say *don't waste your money*, but Mom wasn't here.

"Fine," Meredith said, and Jackie heard her put the turn signal on. And then, because she knew Meredith, she waited.

Meredith began singing. Kirkland College had put on *She Loves Me* last fall, which meant even Natalie knew the words. As the car pulled into the Dairy Queen drive-thru, the three Gruber sisters pulled worn-out dollars out of their pockets and purses and sang about ice cream, Meredith making up a harmony part and Jackie jumping up an octave just because she could, just because she was so happy that they felt like sisters again, and because she was going to get to try a Blizzard for the first time.

53. ROSEMARY COMES HOME.

When the plane landed Rosemary stood up right away, pulling her purse out from underneath her seat and clutching it to her stomach as she waited for the aisle to fill up and then clear, walking as quickly as the person in front of her until she was off the airplane and could run, her feet echoing against the jetway as she pushed past the other passengers and made it to the gate, out of breath, searching for her family.

There they were. Jack. The girls. Right as close as they could to the flat black rope, and Rosemary stopped and breathed and hugged them, not even knowing who she was hugging, and somebody bumped the back of her leg with their bag and she realized she was in the way, and Rosemary ducked under the rope and hugged them all again.

She was crying, but Meredith had a tissue in her purse, and even though Rosemary had a tissue in her own purse she took the one her daughter offered her, and they all made their way to baggage claim and got her bag, the same one she had packed at the beginning of the summer, and then they all got in the car again, the same seats they had taken at the beginning of the summer. It was like they were finishing a journey together.

Except they weren't; this was only a temporary break. Rosemary would go back to Fresno in three weeks, to check on her mother again and clean the house. Until then she had a neighbor who had promised to go visit every evening, as if her mother were a pet and she was away on vacation.

"Are you excited for the first day of school?" Rosemary asked, leaning her body halfway into the backseat.

"I'm excited to not have to work in the cafeteria anymore," Meredith said.

"Nat? Jackie?" Rosemary said, touching each of their knees as she said their names. "High school and junior high!"

"I guess," Natalie said. "It's not that big of a change."

"You get to do music contest this year," Rosemary said. "Have you thought about what you're going to play?"

"I don't know. Dad and I have been working on some stuff. I got some new reeds for school."

"Oh, I was going to get you reeds," Rosemary said. "But I got you a birthday present. And one for you too, Jackie. I can't believe I missed your birthday! I want to hear about everything that happened this summer."

The car was silent, for a moment. The girls had called their mother every week. There wasn't anything that had happened that they hadn't already told her, in the ten-minute calls where she said, again and again, "What else? Tell me more!"

"I worked a lot," Meredith said, at the same time that Jackie blurted out "I got my locker number for school!"

"What is it?" Rosemary asked.

"31."

The car was silent again, and Jack said "Turn around, that's not safe," and Rosemary did, reluctantly. Then she twisted back, just one shoulder this time.

"We should go back-to-school shopping tomorrow."

"We already got our supplies," Natalie said.

"But we could go again," Meredith said, quickly.

"Yeah," Natalie said. "We could go to the mall."

"And maybe get Jackie's hair cut," Rosemary said.

The girls looked at each other. "I got it cut," Jackie began, hesitantly. "Last week." Then she mugged at her mother, sticking her fingers into her hair and pulling it in front of her face. "Guess I forgot to brush it this morning, huh!"

"You always forget," Natalie said.

"And you don't have any hair to brush!" Jackie returned, and Rosemary was glad of her girls, so glad of them and Jack and the car and the highway taking them all home.

The next morning Rosemary slept in, and when she came downstairs she saw Meredith, in a pair of too-short pajama bottoms and a shirt from the sixth-grade math contest, cracking eggs into a bowl. Meredith's posture and hair were perfectly straight as always, her head bent like a ballerina on a music box as she dropped the yolks and whites into the bowl and put the shells into a separate bowl, to take out to the compost afterwards. She turned to the sink, squirted dish soap onto her hands, and washed them. Then she ran the bottle of dish soap under the water.

"Are you making breakfast?" Rosemary said. "That's nice of you."

"Yeah, I mean, I've kind of gotten into cooking." Meredith opened the refrigerator and pulled out a block of cheese, which she began grating over the bowl. "I tried to make Jackie's birthday cake from scratch. You know, not a mix? It didn't turn out, though."

"Baking from scratch is hard," Rosemary said. "I don't think I ever really learned how to do it. It's not like my mom ever made anything that didn't come out of a box."

"How's Grandma doing?"

Rosemary shrugged. "I don't want to talk about it."

Meredith kept grating. "She still had a good cake, though, because I went to the store. Got a Funfetti. She wanted green frosting, so I used food coloring. I've got a chocolate cake mix for Natalie that I was going to make tomorrow."

"I'll make it," Rosemary said, and Meredith noticed the catch in her voice, the yearning that sounded like a demand. "I brought you a present too, by the way. I didn't want you to feel left out."

"Thank you," Meredith said, smiling. "I didn't expect a present. I'm excited to see what it is." She sounded adult, more grown-up than she had been when Rosemary left, making breakfast for everybody in her outgrown clothes.

"Maybe we should get you some new pajamas," Rosemary said, "when we go shopping. I didn't know you needed them."

"I don't," Meredith said. "It's just that all of the other ones are in the wash." Rosemary realized that the washer had been running all this time. Had she not noticed it? Had she forgotten the sounds of her own home?

"I figured I'd do ours while you were asleep, and we could do yours when you woke up," Meredith said, putting the cheese back into its sandwich bag and turning on the stove.

She grabbed a frying pan, took a knife out of the drawer, and sliced off a pat of butter before dropping the pat onto the pan and the knife into the sink.

"Don't let it get too hot," Rosemary said.

"I know how to cook eggs."

Rosemary watched Meredith take a wide turning spatula out of the drawer and move the rapidly melting butter around the pan. She took a saucer out of the cupboard and rested the greasy end of the spatula on the saucer, then turned to her bowl of eggs and cheese. Rosemary wanted to help, to tell Meredith to go sit down, to offer her all the mothering she had missed that summer.

"Have you tried whisking it with a fork?" Rosemary asked. Meredith had the bowl of eggs over the frying pan, ready to pour. She set it down and took a fork out of the drawer. The frying pan suddenly smelled like burning butter, and Meredith lunged for the knob.

"Do you want me to do that?" Rosemary asked, and Meredith said "No," whisking her eggs and pouring them into the frying pan and hearing the washing machine slow its hum to a halt, wishing her mother to keep silent and not suggest that the clothes needed to go in the dryer. She knew how to cook eggs. The butter would have been fine if she hadn't had to get the fork. It didn't make sense to whisk the eggs before you poured them anyway, because the first thing you did, once they were in the frying pan, was grab the spatula and stir them around.

That afternoon they opened presents and then Rosemary wanted to hear them play everything they had practiced that summer, so Meredith played Schumann and Jackie sang Barber and Natalie unpacked her clarinet and played Brahms—or at least the exposition, which was as far as she had gotten in the sonata.

"Remember when we played that?" Rosemary asked, putting her hand on Jack's thigh.

"The F Minor?" Jack said. "We were in college."

"It was our sophomore year," Rosemary said. "I thought you were so cute. Did you know your dad was cute, once?"

Jack grinned, and put his hand over Rosemary's. "Hard to believe. Right, kids?"

"You could play this when you're in college," Rosemary told Natalie.

"She could play it next year," Jack said. "For contest."

"It's a hard piece, though," Rosemary said. "I remember we practiced it forever."

Jackie looked at her parents and raised an eyebrow. "There may have been another reason for the practicing."

When it was all over and the kitchen was clean and the clothes were folded and put away, Meredith sat in her room, her chin on one knee, *Little Women* open in front of her. She re-read the chapter where Mr. March comes home, taking the section where he tells each of his daughters how well they've done and letting the words turn to half-images in her mind, as if they had happened to her instead of the March sisters. She imagined her mother saying "I see in the burn on your small hand that you have worked hard and learned much, this summer," but she knew that Mom was just as likely to say "be careful!" and tell her, with fear and love and authority all mixed up in her voice, how to avoid getting burned the next time.

Then Meredith remembered there was another chapter to re-read, the one where Marmee returned. It was funny how she had forgotten about that, and how different it was from Mr. March's homecoming; Marmee told Amy she was too young to wear the turquoise ring that Amy had started wearing in her absence, and spent the rest of the chapter planning Meg's future even though Meg—it said right in the text—did not love John Brooke "yet."

It was like *Little Women*, then, after all. Mothers had been mothers ever since Marmee, and probably earlier than that. Meredith closed the book and opened her diary but found that she couldn't write; instead, she sat on her bed and listened to the quiet house below her, her parents and her sisters all asleep, and just felt instead, like a stream of thoughts buzzing out of every part of her body but without words. She loved her mother. She loved her whole family. She felt different and separate and growing up and sad and strange and wrong and full of possibility and aching to connect and wanting to cook her own eggs because she *knew how*, she did not need to be told anymore. She wanted to make her own plans for her own future—and it was over, she was thinking again, she was Meredith crafting sentences in her head like her life was the novel she was writing in the pantry.

Downstairs Rosemary lay next to Jack, letting herself feel everything too. Trying not to cry, because everyone she loved was asleep, and she did not want to wake them.

FALL 1998

54. JACK AND JACKIE SPEND SATURDAY AT WORK.

Jack moused over to the "check email" button and double-clicked. Eudora was scheduled to automatically check email every five minutes, but he was impatient. As soon as the "no new messages" notification popped up, he double-clicked again.

Jackie, now finished with her voice lesson, poked her head around the door. Jack smiled and waved her in. She sat in the chair generally reserved for students, the one they used as they put together or took apart their clarinets and oboes and English horns. Jackie shifted position, tapped her fingers against her sternum as if it were her flute, and looked like she was putting together and taking apart an idea.

"Whatcha thinking, Jacks?"

"Can I go to Kirkland College when I grow up?" Jackie asked. "I mean, when I graduate?"

"Sure," Jack said. "You could go to college and live in the dorms, or you could go to college and live at home. It's a great way to save some money and get a world-class liberal arts education."

"And I could keep taking voice lessons from Miss Opal," Jackie said.

"Yeah, you probably could."

"Then could I go to New York or Chicago, like she did?" Jackie's legs were now hanging off one arm of the chair, and her finger-drumming traveled down to the seat, found the one piece of yellow foam sticking out of the corner, and began picking at it.

"We send kids on internships to Chicago, sure. You could do a summer program."

"What's an internship?"

Jack checked his email again. "An internship is a chance to learn how a business works. You get to observe the business, do a little work, and meet people who can help you get a job someday."

"I don't want to do that," Jackie said. "I want to sing opera."

"That's a pretty big goal," Jack said.

"I practice every day. Miss Opal says I'm doing really well."

"I'm sure you are," Jack said. "But even if you practice, there's still going to be a lot of competition. You might need to make a Plan B."

He watched his daughter, uncharacteristically unimpulsive, consider this. "Was this your Plan B?" she finally asked, looking at him to see if she had said the wrong thing.

"You mean teaching? No, I always wanted to teach. There aren't a lot of jobs for full-time musicians, so I knew that if I got into teaching I'd be able to keep my chops up, and perform, and make a living."

"Why aren't there a lot of jobs for musicians when everything around us is music?"

Jack put on his Dr. G voice. "Care to elaborate?"

"I mean, we have music in our heads all the time, and all that music was written and performed by people. Every time we go to Sam Goody there are new CDs, and there's music in commercials and TV and movies and on the radio. Every city has a symphony, every college has an orchestra, every school has a band. There should be enough jobs for all of us."

"Well, not every college has an orchestra," Jack said. "But think of it this way. There are, what, forty people in junior high band? And only one band director."

"But of those forty people, only one of them's going to *want* to be a band director. I bet I'm the only kid in Kirkland in the past *seventy years* who's wanted to be an opera singer. Why shouldn't there be a job for me, if I keep practicing?"

"Well, for starters, you might not have the right physicality," Jack said, hoping he wasn't treading on dangerous ground. "Operatic sopranos tend to be... larger. Big ribcages. Lots of room for the voice. You're small. And skinny."

"I can sing fine, though," Jackie argued. "And it's not about the ribcage, it's about the diaphragm and the breath support. And diction and pitch and tone." She paused. "And interpretation. And feeling. And being able to communicate an idea even if the audience can't understand the words."

Jack thought about what he could say next, to help Jackie understand. "You know even Opal didn't make it as an opera singer."

"Yes she did. She has pictures in her office."

"That's from a very short period in her life, though. It wasn't her career."

"So maybe I'll do opera first," Jackie said, "and then teach. I could come back to Kirkland and take Miss Opal's job when she retires."

Jack smiled. "You're going to have to go to graduate school before you can teach at the college level," he said. "And even if you do, Kirkland probably isn't going to hire you. You grew up here."

"Dr. MacAllister grew up here," Jackie said.

"Well, she got hired a long time ago, when things were different. There are a lot of people applying for professor gigs right now. There's a lot of competition."

"Everything has competition!" Jackie said. Gruber kids didn't whine, so her voice sounded firm and forceful instead. "Maybe I'll just have to do something that has competition and figure out how to be the best at it."

Jack's computer chimed, and he turned to look at his email. He saw the news in the first line: *Subject: Department Chair Decision*, followed by *Jack, we are pleased to announce.* He felt like he could breathe for the first time since Rosemary quit her job.

"Maybe you will, Jackie," he said, opening the email. "Sometimes when you work hard, good things happen."

55. ALEX AND STEPHANIE GO CRUISING.

Stephanie slowed down as they came, once again, to the four-way stop outside the bank. They could see the boys' car pull to a stop behind them; Alex turned to wave before Stephanie drove through.

The boys caught up by the time they reached the gas station, their headlights lighting up Stephanie's rear-view mirror and, Alex thought, *reflecting their interest.* She kept thinking about what she would say when they finally stopped, not on this circuit of the school and the bank and the road that led up to Dos Bandidos, but maybe on the next one. When Stephanie finally decided to pull over.

Stephanie had the music going so loud that they didn't have to talk; Alex leaned her head back and watched as Stephanie turned onto the two-lane road to Dos Bandidos and hit the accelerator, because nobody ever took this road unless they were taking Driver's Ed or cruising. You could get to Dos Bandidos from Main Street, and from there you could get to the highway, and from there you could get to the rest of the world.

But Alex just wanted to get to the gas station, because Geoff and Andy and Sean were in the car behind them and she wanted Geoff to buy her a Frozen Coke. Stephanie had gone out with Geoff, but now she was going out with Sean, which meant that Alex could maybe go out with Geoff if he was interested, and she'd know he was interested if he bought her a Frozen Coke. That was how it worked. That was how these things started.

So Alex leaned against her seat and watched for her favorite moment, the part where Stephanie made a left turn at Dos Bandidos and Alex could suddenly see the entire town lit up below her, the windows and the streetlights and the distance making it look bigger than it was. She could only see it like that for a few seconds, before Stephanie drove onto the road behind the college, because the point of cruising was to use the roads less traveled for as long as you could, to fill your car with the dark and the music and the speed before you had to turn onto Third Street and stop the car in front of the bank and slowly pull forward.

When Stephanie did pull into the gas station she did it in a smooth move without using her turn signal, because the only people behind them were the boys, and because it was fun to catch the boys by surprise. That was why Stephanie had kissed Sean at Morgan's goodbye party, right before school started and Morgan went to college. Alex wondered what would happen if she kissed Geoff, right there in front of the gas station next to the cooler full of ice. She thought of opening the cooler, grabbing a loose piece of ice, and running it across Geoff's collarbone. Was that something boys liked? She had carefully peeked into a magazine at the dentist's office and ice cubes were on a list of 101 Spice-It-Up Sex Tips, but it also seemed like the kind of thing her cousins did, back when they were younger. Ice down the back of the shirt. A bad joke.

Alex got out of the car and saw the boys' car coming from the other direction; they had to pull a U-turn, and the bass from Geoff's stereo got louder as they drove up. In the summer, they cruised with the windows down. Now, it was just cold enough that Alex decided she wouldn't try the ice thing.

Instead, they all went inside, standing in a cluster next to the racks of Rand McNally atlases and camouflage caps. Stephanie stood next to Sean, her hand in his butt pocket and his arm wrapped around her. *They looked like they were made for each other*, Alex thought; both of them with white-blonde hair like the Dollanganger siblings in *Flowers in the Attic*. Or a pair of Precious Moments dolls. Sometimes Alex wondered why she was here, why she spent her evenings sitting in a car while Stephanie drove her around. Sometimes she thought about all of the days she would have to get through before she could do something new.

But maybe Geoff would be her something new. Alex started walking towards the fountain drink section, the new Frozen Coke machine slowly swirling. The group followed. Geoff might even have followed first.

"Have you tried one of those Frozen Cokes yet?" Alex asked.

"I have," Andy said, but Alex wasn't interested in Andy anymore, and he always sat in the backseat when they went cruising anyway. Alex used to sit in the backseat. She knew what it meant. So she turned towards Geoff instead.

"We should try one," she said, watching to see if he was surprised by the *we*.

"Sure, why not?" Geoff said, taking a 16-ounce cup off the rack and putting it under the Frozen Coke spout. Alex watched as the cup slowly filled, Geoff making sure to add a little extra at the end so there'd be Frozen Coke pressed against the clear dome of the lid. "You have to get your money's worth," Alex said, and then felt embarrassed, because that didn't sound like flirting.

But Geoff smiled. He grabbed a thick blue straw, took a drink, and then passed the cup to Alex. She thought of her lips touching the same straw as his, her hands wrapped around the same cup, and barely noticed the taste.

"How is it?" Geoff asked.

"Frozen," Alex said. "Cokey."

"So… not what you were expecting, then," Geoff teased, and Alex thought about how he was so much more interesting than Sean or Andy, and how the two of them could maybe be perfect together, the way Sean and Stephanie were perfect together.

"Do you want another sip?" Alex said, holding the cup towards Geoff. "I mean, with this stuff I don't think you sip it. I think you slug it."

Geoff laughed, and his fingers brushed against Alex's as he took the cup, and after he took a long pull from the straw he said "Slug it? You can't slug a slushie."

"It's not a slushie," Alex said. "That's trademarked."

"Sorry, sorry," Geoff said. "A *Frozen Coke*. Drink technology completely unrelated to the Slushie Beverage."

He gave the cup back to Alex and went to the counter to pay for it. Alex followed, standing next to Geoff as he pulled two dollars out of his wallet and left a penny in the tray, and then she followed him out to the parking lot where they all stood with their drinks and their Slim Jims and talked until the cold made it too uncomfortable. Stephanie snuggled up against Sean and Andy crossed his arms tightly and shifted from one foot to another and Alex looked at Geoff and said "It's freezing out here."

"You picked the wrong day to try Frozen Coke," Geoff said, and before Alex could be surprised that he had referenced *Airplane!* he said "How about I take you home?"

They had to drop off Andy first, but that was what you always did with people in the backseat. Alex sat in the front, the Frozen Coke cold and melting condensation into her hands, knowing that as soon as Andy got out of the car, her entire life might change. Geoff pulled up to the four-way stop, flicking on his turn signal. Alex waited.

SPRING 1999

56. ALEX CALLS MEREDITH.

After Geoff drove away Alex went inside, said hi to her mom, avoided stepping on the stacks of graded and ungraded tests that surrounded the couch and the coffee table, and opened the freezer. She untwisted the plastic at the end of the sleeve of Thin Mints and slid out two cold cookies, putting one in her mouth and carrying the other one back to her room.

She glanced at the mirror, then put the other cookie in her mouth and grabbed her brush to fix the back of her hair. Then she put on extra deodorant, and then she decided to change her underwear.

Alex grabbed her chemistry textbook and her notebook and went back out into the living room. "I'm going to do my homework in the basement," she said.

"Okay," Donna said. "I'll holler if I need you."

Alex went downstairs into what her parents called the "half-finished" basement because it was both half finished and *half-finished*; they had planned on turning it into a fully functional living space, but they got as far as a sofa and a table and stacks of boxes that wouldn't fit anywhere else. Alex often did her homework in the basement, because there was more space for her to spread out her books and papers, and she also often used the phone in the basement to call her friends. It was far enough away from the main floor—something she and Meredith had tested, the afternoon in third grade when they pretended to be spies—that her parents couldn't overhear her calls.

Alex started to dial Stephanie's number and then stopped and hung up the phone. She couldn't call Stephanie. Stephanie used to date Geoff. That would be weird, to call Stephanie and say *guess what?* even though Alex knew that in any other situation Stephanie would be the right person to call. They were kind of best friends now, in that they hung out after school and sat at the same table at lunch. But they weren't real best friends. There was something missing, the sort of thing that made Alex happy enough when Stephanie was around but always a little relieved when she was gone. It was like she had to pretend to be like Stephanie, when they were together—otherwise they wouldn't have anything to talk about.

So Alex called Meredith instead. Her hand hesitated and then punched in the number as quickly as it had done when they were younger, and the phone rang, and Alex heard Natalie say "Hello, you've reached the Gruber residence, this is Natalie." *The Gruber way and the MacAllister way.*

"Hi, Nat," Alex said. "Is Meredith there?"

"Sure, hang on," Natalie said, and Alex heard the soft thud of the phone against the end table, and then she felt nervous, like maybe Meredith wasn't the right person to call either. But then she heard Meredith say "Hey, what's up?" and Alex realized how much she had missed talking to Meredith.

"Hey," Alex said. "Did you do that last math problem?"

"What—" Meredith started, and then she paused. "No, I didn't do that last math problem."

It was Alex's turn to pause and listen, to make sure her parents hadn't picked up the phone extension in the kitchen or the one in their bedroom. It was a code they had created, years ago. "I didn't do it either."

"Good to know," Meredith said. "What's going on?"

"Geoff and I…" Alex knew nobody was listening, but she dropped her voice anyway. "had sex." She was glad that she had not said "did it," even though that was how she and Geoff had joked about it, when they made the plan.

"Oh wow," Meredith said. "Um… congratulations? Is that what you say?" She laughed slightly and then said "How about I go upstairs? Call me back?"

Instead of shuffling around with extensions—especially when you had two younger sisters who didn't always hang up the downstairs phone when requested—they had worked out that it was easier for Meredith to hang up, go upstairs, and to grab the phone on the first ring. They did the math problem check again, and then Meredith said "Okay, so what happened?"

"Well, we had been talking about it for a while, and then today after school we... you know, *did it.*" There it was. "In his car."

"Oh *wow*," Meredith said. "Very *Titanic*. Did you do the thing with your hand?"

That was Meredith, always checking to see if life fit into a story. But it felt comfortable, like Alex could finally be herself. "Of course not. My hands were otherwise occupied."

"Well then," Meredith said. "Was it..." and then Alex waited for Meredith to sort through her thoughts, because part of being on the phone with Meredith was waiting until she worked out, in her mind, what she was going to say. "I want to ask *was it good for you* but that is a cliché, so: was it what you wanted?"

"It was," Alex said, smiling, because it had been. It had been exactly what she wanted. "Geoff was so nice. He made sure I was comfortable, he brought the, uh, condoms, he's just the best boyfriend. I really like him. I love him."

"I'm glad," Meredith said. "I'm so happy for you. Is that the right thing to say?"

"I don't know," Alex said. "I'm happy too."

"Then it's good," Meredith said. "Congratulations. You have had"—she dropped her voice to a whisper in case any sisters were around—"*the sex.*" Then she started laughing. "Oh wow, you're going to have it *again.*"

"What?" Alex said, and then she started laughing too. "Oh my god, I *am.*"

"You're going to have so much"—and Alex heard Meredith quickly pause and put an idea together—"*pizza.*"

This was why they were best friends. "You're right. I'm going to have pizza at home, and I'm going to have pizza in the car, and I might have pizza at Geoff's house."

"Just make sure you have plenty of napkins."

They talked for a few minutes more, and then Alex hung up, and then Meredith hung up and went into her bedroom and took out her diary.

Alex called because she and Geoff had sex which is great for them and I'm glad it went well but seriously she has not talked to me in forever and now she called to tell me this. She let her hand move faster than her mind. *Are we friends or are we not because I want to be friends I think but you can't just call me after not being my friend.*

Meredith closed the diary because her hands were moving too fast for words. She went downstairs and began to play the piano, letting her fingers go and her head buzz, putting what she couldn't say into the music and playing as loudly as she could.

SUMMER 1999

57. MEREDITH AND JACKIE PREPARE FOR AN AUDITION.

When Meredith and Jackie asked their father if they could audition for the Delacroix Community Theatre production of *Into the Woods*, they knew he would say yes. Asking Dad wasn't like asking Mom; he never said "I worry that you might spend too much money" or "I worry that you won't be safe." *Dad focuses on the practicality of the present moment,* Meredith wrote in her diary, pleased with both the alliteration and the assonance. So she presented him with a very practical plan.

"I'll work lunch shifts at the cafeteria and we'll leave when they're over. I'll pay for the gas. I've been driving to Delacroix at least twice a month for over a year. This'll also be good for my college applications, since there's no drama program at the high school anymore."

"Sure, fine, see what happens," Jack said. "You know you still have to get cast."

But Meredith had a very practical plan for that, too. She knocked on Miss Opal's door and asked if she and Jackie could have a special voice lesson to prepare, and when it was time for the lesson she arrived with Cinderella's song, "On the Steps of the Palace," note-perfect.

"It seems like you already have this down," Opal said. "There's a line in the bridge that we could tighten up a little—" and they did, and then it was done. Jackie worked on her audition piece, for Little Red Riding Hood, and then Meredith asked if Opal wanted to hear the duet that the two characters sing at the end of the musical.

"I'm not sure they'll need that at the audition," Opal said, "but I'm always happy to hear the Gruber girls sing together." So they sang, their voices blending into a single divided tone, and Meredith wondered if there would be a way, after all, to make sure this was part of the audition.

"How did you get your song right without practicing?" Jackie asked, as they walked home.

"I practiced," Meredith said. "I sang along with the cast album."

"But it was like you knew the whole song, after you sang it once."

"I sang it more than once," Meredith said. "I just remember things well." She looked at Jackie, who seemed disappointed. "It's like things just go into my brain."

"I wish things just went into my brain," Jackie said.

"Well, you're the one who's going to be the opera singer, though," Meredith said. "You're a vocalist. I can sing. There's a difference." She didn't mention the conversation she had heard, years ago, through the vent in the ceiling: Mom wanted each of them to have a special thing, and since Natalie had swim team and Meredith was learning computers with Daniel and going to the Math Olympiad and winning the DAR's American History Essay Contest and being invited to play the piano at the Kiwanis pancake breakfast—Meredith had too many special things—Jackie would get voice lessons. It had been just as much babysitting as anything else, back then.

"I wish Delacroix had a community opera," Jackie said. "Or even a light opera."

"You get what you get," Meredith said, imitating their mother, "and you don't get upset." Rosemary was in Fresno again, helping their grandmother. Their high school didn't have a drama program and its choir was an unbalanced nine people, with Meredith accompanying at the piano and singing simultaneously. They couldn't have everything they wanted or needed, but they could audition for this show.

When Meredith walked into the Delacroix Community Theatre—DCT, of course, it was DCT instantly, as if she had always been there—she felt like she had stepped through a doorway into a magic world. The stage was big, bigger than the one at the college, and there were people everywhere in black T-shirts and stretchy clothes, and they all looked smart and put together and interesting, and whenever anyone looked in her or Jackie's direction, they smiled.

After they signed up, they went towards the front of the house and stood on the edge of the cluster, the vocal warmups and stretches all mixing together next to them, and

Meredith whispered "we should sing." They got four bars into the duet before someone called out "do I hear the Gruber girls?" and a man came through the crowd with a face that almost seemed familiar, and then Meredith remembered, her brain pushing the information towards her. *David.* He had been a freshman in college, the year they moved to Kirkland. He still had the same floppy hair, the same serious-but-happy expression. *Intense*, Meredith thought. Then: *That's the same word people use to describe me.*

"I can't believe it's the Gruber girls!" David said. "I knew you when you were really little! I bet you don't remember me."

"David, right?" Meredith said. "You were a student at Kirkland."

"Of course Meredith remembers," Jackie said.

"Meredith, okay," David said. "And I don't remember which one you are," he said to Jackie. "I know there were three of you."

"I'm Jackie," Jackie said. "Jacqueline." It felt weird to say her full name out loud like that, but it's what she had written on her audition form, and what she and Miss Opal had agreed would be her "professional name" some day.

David smiled. "Jacqueline, of course. Like your dad. How's Dr. G?"

"He's doing well," Meredith said, wondering if she was doing an equally good job carrying on this conversation. She was also doing math, working out how old David was now. "He's the department chair."

"He was a great teacher," David said. "You can tell him that. And somebody taught the two of you to sing."

"It was Miss Opal," Jackie said.

"Is Opal still there?" David asked. "I remember her. I don't think she liked me all that much. Hey—we should sit down. You want to sit down?"

The three of them sat together in the second row as the director and musical director walked onto the stage and began explaining the audition process. Everyone would sing one song, and then they'd do a short movement activity together. There'd be a short break, and then the director would split people up for scenes.

"What part are you going for?" David asked.

"Cinderella," Meredith said.

"And Jacqueline must be Little Red," David said, leaning over to smile at Jackie.

"I'm hoping for the Baker, but I'll take whatever they give me. DCT is so great. I'm so glad I found this place."

So am I, Meredith thought. Then the first name was called, and the three of them sat quietly together, waiting for their turns to sing.

58. *INTO THE WOODS.*

As soon as Jackie walked into the theater she became Jacqueline. It was as simple as that, and something she hadn't even thought of when she wrote her full name—generally only reserved for end-of-the-year state-wide multiple-choice tests—on the audition form. Miss Opal pronounced it the French way, but at DCT they called it out in two syllables: Jack-leen, easier to say than to spell.

Becoming Jackleen was almost as interesting as becoming Little Red, and Jackie was still figuring out who both of these people were. "Everybody gets sex in the woods," their director had said at one of the early rehearsals, and so Jackie asked herself: was Little Red attracted to the Wolf in *that* way? The scene suggested that there was a reason Little Red stayed, instead of sticking to the path where she belonged. When you want someone, you want to talk to them. You want them to talk to you.

Meredith had forgotten what it was like to be in a place where she wanted to talk to everyone and everyone wanted to talk to her. She and Jackie started leaving earlier and earlier, arriving at DCT a half-hour before rehearsal started just so they could be there, so they wouldn't have to spend that time anywhere else. There were always a few people who came early: the director and the stage manager of course, but also David, as the Baker; Angie, who played the Baker's Wife; and Carla, who played the Witch. They'd sit in the Green Room and eat bags of food from Taco Bell or Dairy Queen, and after the first week Meredith and Jackie started packing their own dinners, usually sandwiches with thin slices of ham or turkey smashed next to a layer of cream cheese—"because we need the energy,"

Meredith said—and they sat together and watched as everyone else they loved came in through the stage door.

They all loved each other but they all had their favorites, and Meredith's favorite was David and Jackie's favorite was Elizabeth, who played Rapunzel. Elizabeth was a true soprano, with both the wide ribcage and the cascading hair. The costume designer was working on a wig that would go under her blonde locks instead of over it; "I am *not* crushing that hair under a wig cap," he said, and Meredith and Jackie repeated his emphatic statement at home, whenever they had something that they were *not* going to do.

Jackie did get to crush her hair under a wig cap, because she needed a set of blonde ringlets and it was obvious that her thin hair would never curl. It was one more way that she was different, at rehearsal, than she was at home—even though she only got to try the wig on once, it wasn't like the rehearsal skirt they gave her to wear every day. When she had the wig on she twisted around, and the costume designer said "hang on, I'll get a mirror so you can see the back," but she wasn't looking at herself; she was looking to see if Elizabeth was in the room, and if Elizabeth would smile at her.

Meredith also got a wig—"you Gruber sisters did not win in the hair department," and Meredith did not tell the costume designer that there was a third Gruber sister who did, it was almost like Natalie and Dad and Mom didn't exist when they were at the theatre—and with the soft dark waves framing her face she felt prettier than she had ever been. They gave her glasses, too, because the costume designer's inspiration owed a lot to the American Playhouse videorecording of the Broadway production, and when Meredith put them on she wondered if they had cast her because she looked smart and intense and—what was the right word? *hesitant? self-contained?*—the way Kim Crosby had been in the video. That, and she could hit all of the notes in "On the Steps of the Palace," which everyone kept saying was hard.

She knew she was good in the part and she also knew that she wasn't really acting; she was putting emotion and nuance into the lines, and going after her objectives, but she was doing all of these things as herself, not as another person. She tried to do everything she had read about: writing out backstory, creating collages, standing in front of the mirror until she stopped seeing herself and started seeing Cinderella. She still felt like the play was the story of Meredith Gruber, a smart young woman who spent her days cleaning up after other people—literally, because she worked in the Kirkland College cafeteria nearly every afternoon—and who dreamed of finding a place where her intelligence and her beauty would be recognized.

And she had found it. *DCT is the best thing that ever happened to me*, she wrote in her diary. It was the first place in her life where she was popular. It was also the first place where people wanted to really dig into her work and help her make it better; instead of getting A+ papers with no handwritten notes besides "good job," Meredith got dozens of notes every evening, and she wrote them all down and took them home to study before the next rehearsal.

There was also David. Meredith knew that she could never date David because he was a full decade older than her, but she could sit next to him on the couch in the Green Room, and watch him work on his scenes with Angie, and imagine, every time they reached the end of the play, that Cinderella and the Baker would someday fall in love. One day Angie had to miss rehearsal and Meredith sang the Baker's Wife's part in "It Takes Two," because their musical director could not sing and play the piano simultaneously, and they needed someone to fill in the gap. She looked at David and tried not to blush. *David isn't the person I'm going to marry*, she wrote in her diary. *But someday I'm going to meet someone and it's going to be like the conversations I have with David. I wish I were older, so it could be him, and now.*

Jackie always blushed, when Elizabeth sang. It was just something that happened. It was also something that she had started to think about. Only when she was Jacqueline, of course. Not at home, when she was Jackie.

Not when she was Little Red, either. Little Red was curious about the Wolf and Jack and a world that contained both bread and knives. Jackie understood that Little Red started the play as a person who thought she knew what to do but didn't, because she was only doing what she had been told. Then she left her mother's house and met other people and started to figure out who she really was, now that she had strayed from the path that had been set for her. Jackie wondered what it would be like when Little Red started calling herself by her real name. She knew she was supposed to figure that name out on her own, and write it down, but she felt like she needed to be Little Red a little bit more. They had two weeks of rehearsal left. She'd get it—and if she didn't, maybe it wasn't as important to her character as it was to her.

59. MEREDITH FINISHES HER NOVEL.

Meredith wrote the last sentence quickly, because she had been thinking about it for weeks. She double-clicked on Save, and then double-clicked again to make sure. Then she sat, all 225 pages of *The Door at the End of the Train* open and complete in front of her, and smiled. She double-clicked Save one more time.

It was done. She had done it. She had written a novel. She had thought about that last chapter and that last sentence but she had not thought about what would come afterwards, the moment where her heart and breath kept pulsing as fast as her fingers had typed, the realization that she'd have to click Save again and then Close and then her words would disappear and then she would have to do something else, and what she wanted to do was go outside and run, but it was dark and everyone else was asleep and so she sat and smiled and clicked and saved and closed and went upstairs and did thirty pushups in her bedroom. Then she stood in front of the mirror and waved her arms around and grinned at herself, at the idea that she had written *an entire novel*, she had done it and it was done. She would always have written a novel, no matter what else happened to her.

She emailed Daniel the next morning.

> *D—*
>
> *I finished TDATEOTT. I'd love for you to read it, if you wanted. I have to do four emails because it's too large to send as one file, so I'm sending it over in four parts.*

It's so weird to think that I've finished it. I hope you like it. I thought of you as I was writing it

Meredith hit delete and watched the letters disappear. She had thought of Daniel as she was writing *The Door at the End of the Train*, but she had also thought of David, especially in the last few chapters when the face she imagined reading her story shifted. She could never send her story to David, though. Daniel and Priya had come to *Into the Woods* on comped tickets. So had David's girlfriend.

*It's so weird to think that I've finished it. I hope you like it. I know you just saw me do this big creative thing but this is even bigger and creativer so… give it a read. ^__^*
M

She sent the four emails, waiting for the computer to slowly load each document. Meredith knew she'd have to get off the computer after that, to give someone else a turn to use the phone or check their email. Part Two would have to wait until the evening, when she got back from the cafeteria.

Dear Aunt Anne,
How are you? I hope you are well. I'm going to start my senior year in a month, which is exciting.

Meredith thought of all the other things she should mention in a letter: they had been in *Into the Woods*, Natalie had done swim team again, Mom and Dad were talking about whether they needed to move Grandma to Kirkland or find a place that would take care of her in Fresno. "You can't fly out to California every month," Dad had said, the three sisters trying not to listen, the words coming up through the ceiling vent anyway.

I have a favor to ask of you: For the past year and a half I've been working on an epic fantasy novel titled The Door at the End of the Train. *I just finished it and I was curious if you'd be interested in reading it. I'd love to know your thoughts.*

I have to send this email in four parts because the novel is 225 pages long and it won't fit in one email. So if you see three more emails after this one, that's what they are.
Thanks,
Meredith

After she sent the four parts she checked her email one more time, to see if Daniel had responded yet. He could have read at least the first part by now. Maybe the whole thing, if he didn't have any other plans that afternoon. She checked her email again, to make sure.

FALL 1999

60. ROSEMARY PLAYS SUPER NINTENDO.

After the funeral they all flew back together. Rosemary sat next to Jack and put her hand on his when the plane started to jerk like a scratched record. "It's just the Rockies," she said, as he gripped the armrest. She had flown so many more times than he had, now.

She hoped the girls were okay, all three of them sitting across the aisle. They had to be taken out of school, and they'd have to go back to school tomorrow. They'd be exhausted. They had all been so helpful, going with Jack to buy the cans of Hawaiian Punch and the vegetable trays, helping to serve casserole and make conversation with people they hardly knew, her mother's friends who had only seen them in wallet-sized photographs. She wished they hadn't had to do any of it.

They'd stayed with one of Rosemary's mother's friends, she and Jack in the guest room and the girls in sleeping bags in the den, because Rosemary hadn't wanted to sleep in her mother's house. The house she grew up in, the house she came back to, the house in which her mother fell, one afternoon, coming out of the bathroom. Rosemary had been in her mother's kitchen, making lunch, only a few steps away but not close enough to catch her. It wouldn't have made a difference even if she had, because it had been a stroke. That is what everyone told her, the people who came in the ambulance and the doctors and all of Rosemary's mother's friends.

They also told her, after the funeral, how well she had taken care of her mother, both in that house and in the hospital. Then they told her, even though it was a question, that she should feel sad about her mother but also glad that she could go home, back to

Jack and the girls. Except she wasn't done, death and being a daughter didn't end at the funeral. She would go back in a month to begin cleaning out the house.

Her girls had asked if they could help. They could come over Christmas break, they had said. Rosemary had said no, quicker and sharper than she meant to, and they did not mention it again. She hadn't wanted any of them there, for any of this. She had wanted them in Kirkland, going to school and swimming and being in a play and studying for the ACTs and doing all of the things they were supposed to do. They'd have good memories of this year, instead of the memories Rosemary had.

When they were home Rosemary felt like a person in a dream, watching everything move around her like blurred shapes. She heard Natalie laugh. She heard Jackie sing. She sat down at the dinner table so Meredith could serve her a grilled cheese sandwich, black ash on the edge of the bread and it tasted like nothing.

She thought she should hear Meredith play the piano, it had been months since her last lesson, and Meredith played everything she had learned on her own and Rosemary said "fine, good, I can tell you've practiced" because she didn't want to say "I didn't hear you, I can't pay attention." Natalie played the clarinet and Jack said words and Rosemary nodded and smiled and said "you're really doing well" because she couldn't say "I love you so much it's like a flashbulb in front of my eyes."

She wanted to be alone but she also wanted to be with her family, so she sat with them in the living room and watched episodes of *The Simpsons* and *The X-Files* and let everyone tell her how she was supposed to feel, and then didn't feel any of it. They did the laughing for her, at the jokes she missed. They explained why *The X-Files* wasn't good anymore. It was because they'd gone to California.

One day Rosemary woke up from a nap and couldn't remember where she was; the room was dark and she thought she was back in Fresno, and then she thought she needed to go check on her mother, and then her eyes adjusted and she saw the bedspread and the wallpaper and the wedding picture. She was in Kirkland and her mother was dead.

She went upstairs because her girls were upstairs, they were all playing some game that they had bought from Daniel Seth years ago, before any of this had happened. She sat on the edge of Natalie's bed and watched, looking at the backs of her daughters' heads and the way they talked with each other so easily, these three beautiful girls who had played together since the days they were born.

"Do you want to play?" one of them asked.

"No, it's okay," Rosemary said. "I'll watch you play."

"The game has room for four people," Meredith said. "We could start over. We're only on the first world."

"You've never played Super Mario, right?" Natalie asked. "We could teach you."

"It's Super Mario 2," Jackie corrected, "and we play it with infinite lives so there's no way you can die."

"Unless you fall in a pit," Natalie said.

"But you don't really die," Jackie said. "You just start over."

"Here," Meredith said, putting a controller in Rosemary's hand. "You get first pick of the characters."

"Oh, I don't know," Rosemary said, pushing buttons and watching the arrow move back and forth. "How do I choose one?"

"Press A," Natalie said, and Rosemary pressed A, and a figure turned from gray to green and raised his hand.

"Awww you picked Luigi!" Jackie said. "That's perfect! I always play Toad, and Natalie always plays Mario, and Meredith always plays Princess."

"Peach," Meredith said. "She has a name now."

"Woo-hoo-hoo," Natalie said. "Feminist Mario."

Rosemary didn't know what any of this meant, but she watched as Natalie took the first turn, opened a door, and immediately began falling.

"Wait, is that bad? I thought you said if you fell you died." *I remembered something,* Rosemary thought.

"This is okay," Natalie said. "That's how you start the game."

"Just don't fall into a pit later," Jackie said. "Jump over them."

"We'll show you when it's your turn," Meredith said.

When Natalie beat her level the screen changed and it was Rosemary's turn to open the door and let her little green man drop to the ground. His legs swiveled, like he was panicking. "You're going to be okay, little guy," Rosemary said. "I've got you."

"His name's Luigi," Jackie said.

"Jump over the pink guys!" Meredith said.

"How do I jump?" Rosemary said.

"A," all three of her girls called out, and Rosemary pushed A, and her green guy swiveled his legs and came back down and the pink guy walked right into him.

"Sorry," Meredith said. "You need to push A and to the right. On your D-pad."

"What's a D-pad?"

"Just explore," Meredith answered. "You've got infinite lives. You'll figure it out."

"How did you all figure this out?" Rosemary asked, after she walked into a second pink guy and her turn ended.

"Practice," Natalie said.

"Gruber kids know how to practice," Jackie said, imitating their father, and they all started laughing. Rosemary laughed too. It was a little late, but it was real. She was real, and her girls were real, and Jack was real, and she had to pay attention because soon it was going to be her turn again.

61. NATALIE WANTS TO GO TO A PARTY.

Natalie dropped her backpack on the floor underneath the row of coat hooks, then hung up her jacket. She heard the television in the living room; Mom, no doubt, curled up on the couch watching *Oprah*. Jackie had walked home with Priya, and Meredith was doing ACT prep at school. Natalie went into the kitchen, shook a handful of Cheez-Its into a napkin, and took them into the living room. Mom scooched her feet up so Natalie would have room to sit.

"Cheez-Its?" Natalie said, holding out the napkin. Mom shook her head.

Natalie waited until the commercial to ask her next question. "There's going to be a party after the Homecoming dance. Can I go?"

"I don't think so," Mom said. "Won't it be late?"

"We might not stay for the whole dance," Natalie said.

"Who's we?"

"You know, me, Ben, Jenna, Mark, Kimberly, Stephanie and Sean, I think the whole court's going."

"Who's hosting this party?"

"It's at Jenna's. And yes, her parents will be there."

Mom frowned. "I worry about you being out that late."

"It's the same late as everyone else," Natalie said.

"We'll talk about it later," Mom said, turning back towards *Oprah*.

Natalie kept watching until she heard the back door open. Dad was home. She got up and took her crumpled-up napkin into the kitchen to throw it away, and to say "Hey, Dad."

"Hey, Nat."

"Do you all care if I go to a party after the Homecoming dance? It's at Jenna's, her folks will be there, and everyone on the court's going. I could be back by 11:30." She made it as casual as she could, bending over partway through the question to pull the overflowing trash bag from its under-the-sink can and tie the ends together.

"Have you talked to your mother?"

"Yes," Natalie said, holding the garbage bag, the visual symbol of her responsibility.

"And what did she say?"

"She said we'd talk about it later."

"Then I guess we'll talk about it later," Dad said. "Thanks for taking out the trash."

Natalie knew that she couldn't bring up the party first thing at dinner; it would sound desperate, and anyway they had to hear about Meredith's practice ACT and Jackie's homework and Dad's meeting and Mom's—well, Mom mostly listened. So after all of this, when everyone's plates were nearly cleaned and there were only a few kernels of canned corn or flecks of hamburger remaining, Natalie said "So there's going to be this party."

"I already said you couldn't go," Mom said.

"You said we'd talk about it later," Natalie said.

"What party is this?" Dad asked. "This is the Homecoming party?"

"It's after the dance," Mom said, as if that were reason enough to say no. "It's too late."

"What if I was back by 11:30?"

Dad mashed a piece of corn under his fork and ate it. "Where is this party?"

"It's at Jenna's," Natalie said. "Her parents will be there, and the whole court's going."

"You can't break up the set," Jackie joked. Natalie's inclusion on the Homecoming court had surprised her parents, because it was so... *un-Gruber-like*. It had almost surprised Natalie, even though she had contacts now, and wore makeup, and had grown her hair out into a cute Drew Barrymore flip. "It isn't because you're pretty," Meredith had said, when they walked home from school after the announcement. "I mean, sure, it's a little bit because you're pretty, but it's also because everyone likes you." "You're the Teen Choice Award," Jackie had said, laughing.

"So there will be seniors there," Dad said. "It's not just a sophomore party."

"Sure, there'll be a lot of people there," Natalie said. "Stephanie'll be there, I think Alex is going."

"Is Meredith invited?" Mom asked.

Natalie granted herself the power to invite Meredith. "Yes."

"Do you want to go to this party?" Dad asked Meredith. Natalie matched eyes with her sister, and Meredith got the message and came through: "It might be fun. Natalie and I could both go."

"You let Meredith and Jackie go to that cast party this summer," Natalie said.

"Well, nobody asked me about that," Mom said. "That was your father's idea."

"It should be fine," Meredith said. "I can watch out for Natalie, and make sure she's back by 11:30."

"I still think that's too late for a fifteen-year-old," Mom said.

"*ELEVEN*, then."

"No need to use that voice, Nat," Dad said. "Now, when does this dance end?"

"Ten," Natalie and Mom and Meredith all said at the same time.

"So you'd go and you'd have to come back right away."

"But I'd still get to go," Natalie said. "Everyone on the court is going. Stephanie and Sean said they'd give me a ride."

"I don't like Sean," Mom said.

"Well, if Meredith's going, you won't need a ride," Dad said.

"So can we go?" Natalie asked.

"Your mom and I will think about it," Dad said, "and we'll let you know."

Natalie cleared the table and started on the dishes, wondering how long she had to wait. She was probably the only person on the Homecoming court whose parents hadn't said yes right away. Maybe the only person who even asked her parents, instead of just going. They had to let her go. It would be embarrassing if they didn't. Everyone would know, and then they'd never pick her for anything like this again.

Dad walked through the kitchen on the way to the computer room. "Improve your attitude," he said to Natalie as he passed her, in that annoying parent sing-song. So the way she was doing the dishes, *by herself*, wasn't even good enough. At school everybody liked her. At home nobody did.

They told her the next day at dinner. "I called Jenna's folks," Mom said, "and they said it'd be fine if I came along. I'd stay upstairs, you all would be in the basement, and I could drive you home at 11:30."

"Well?" Dad asked. "Does that sound like a workable plan?"

"I don't know," Natalie said, looking at her plate.

"Eleven thir-ty," Mom said in that same parent sing-song, making it sound like a question even though it wasn't. It was a warning.

"I guess," Natalie said.

"You don't sound very happy," Dad said. It was also a warning.

Natalie wondered which would be worse: to miss the party or to have her mom upstairs the entire night. "I'm not happy," she said. "I don't have to be happy, and you shouldn't make me feel bad for not being happy."

"You shouldn't make us feel bad for wanting you to be safe," Mom said, and Natalie knew she had lost.

"Fine, I'll go," Natalie said.

"Maybe you shouldn't go," Mom said.

Dad said "How about we *let* it go," and he reached across the table for more leftover hamburger and macaroni, and Natalie thought that she'd have to tell everyone on the Homecoming court how awful her parents were, so they'd understand that the reason her mom came to the party was because her mom was overprotective and weird, not because Natalie needed someone to look out for her. She could make it okay, at school. Everybody already liked her there.

62. MEREDITH GETS A 34.

It was rude to ask, but they all knew anyway because the parents and the teachers told; Daniel scored a 33 on his ACT, Alex had a respectable 31, and Meredith got a 34, the highest score Kirkland R-IX had seen in years. She came home from school to find a piece of computer paper taped to the door; Mom had written "34!!!" on it. Meredith carefully peeled the tape off the door. It had been a long time since Mom had been excited about anything.

The guidance counselor, who had previously treated Meredith with the same "you'll be fine" dismissal that characterized her high school experience, interrupted Meredith's American History class to drop a stack of college brochures onto her desk. Meredith already had these brochures at home, she had received new brochures every week since she took the PSAT/NMSQT and got on National Merit's potential scholarship list, though she wouldn't know if she was eligible for a scholarship until she took the SAT in December. She and Daniel were planning to take it on the same day; they had to go all the way to St. Louis, and Daniel's father would drive them.

"Maybe it's time to think about expanding your college search," the guidance counselor had said, but Meredith thought about it in terms of contraction; starting with the colleges that every smart kid had heard of, like Harvard and Yale, then moving down to the ones she had read about in books, like Oberlin and CUNY, then going online and typing in the name of a small liberal arts school that was within a day's drive, looking at the pictures of students reading under trees and crowding next to a mascot, trying to imagine herself at one of these places.

She wanted a school with a good theater department and a good English department, and she started clicking away from every college whose students showed too much "actor face"—wide eyes, open mouth—in their production photographs. One school posted its students' undergraduate theses online, and Meredith discounted the entire institution after reading an English thesis on The Awakening that claimed Kate Chopin was a relative of Frédéric Chopin.

Her parents' search criteria came down to a single data point: does the college offer a full-ride scholarship? This included both the Tuition Exchange colleges, at which Meredith would be allowed to attend for free due to her father's status as Kirkland College professor, and the handful of Midwestern colleges offering comprehensive scholarships. The colleges and universities suggested by the guidance counselor did not make either of those lists, but Meredith carried her brochures home and added them to the stack next to her bed, the stack she knew was designated "colleges I cannot attend" but still looked through anyway. They were her dreams; all the trees she wanted to sit underneath were in those thick, glossy pages.

Daniel was going to Columbia. His father had gone to Columbia, and he was applying Early Decision. His application was already complete, now that his ACT score had come in; Anand would fly out with him in two weeks, to show him the campus and meet with his old professors. For Daniel, taking the SAT was extra; if he got National Merit, he'd get a little extra scholarship cash to put against his loans. For Meredith, taking the SAT and getting National Merit meant she might be more attractive to full-ride-scholarship schools. It wouldn't move any brochures out of the "colleges I cannot attend" pile, but it would prevent her having to move more brochures in.

The day before Meredith's eighteenth birthday, a brochure from Juilliard arrived in the mail. She had searched the school online and then, feeling both daring and rebellious, dropped her name and address into the request form. She saw the brochure when she came home from school but let it sit on the dining room table with the bills and newspapers, waiting to see if her parents said anything.

At dinner the pile of mail got moved to the couch, and Meredith went upstairs after helping with the dishes to see that someone had tossed the brochure, face-down, on her bed. She picked it up and opened it, reading the words *Lincoln Center* and *New York* and feeling like she already belonged there just because she had read those words so many times before.

She heard Dad on the stairs. "Meredith?" He stood in the doorway and smiled at her. "Your mom and I think it's time to start planning some college visits."

"Daniel's going to New York," Meredith said. "We could go with him. Check out Columbia and…" She held up the brochure with her finger still inside, marking her page, not wanting to say the word aloud.

"We're not going to New York," Dad said. "It's time to put away the brochures. We'll drive to a couple of good schools, check 'em out, maybe catch a play or a band concert, and then we'll decide where we're going to apply."

Meredith didn't say anything. She couldn't. Her fingers slipped against the slick paper of the Juilliard brochure and she tried not to cry.

"Mer, you have the chance to go to some of the best small colleges in the country *for free*," Dad said. "Your mom and I aren't going to let you throw that away."

Meredith nodded.

Dad started to walk away, then turned back around. "You'll thank us later," he said, and Meredith wondered if it were true, and if she ever would.

WINTER 1999

63. JACKIE AND PRIYA MAKE A TOAST.

Their arms were cold, because the T-shirts had been cheaper than the sweatshirts, but they stood next to each other in the Methodist church lobby and waited with smiles until the pastor finished welcoming another guest and turned back around to take their picture.

"Take another one," Rosemary said, looking out from between Natalie and Jackie.

"I'll take a bunch," the pastor said. "Do y'all want a silly one?"

They let the question hang for a beat too long. "Let's do a silly one," Jackie finally said, and they all grinned and made bunny ears for the photo that none of them wanted. Rosemary could pull it out later, toss it into the shoebox instead of the album. How long had it been since they were all photographed together? She had plenty of pictures of the girls, albums of Daisy Kingdom dresses and swim team uniforms and the piano recitals she used to hold in the living room. Meredith with her head tilted to one side; Natalie with her friends; Jackie always in motion, one part of her body slightly blurred. So, when she saw the T-shirts at the grocery store, she bought five. She kept the image in her mind—all of them together on New Year's Eve—and remembered to bring her camera.

"Let's hope the film isn't affected by Y2K," the pastor said, passing the camera back. Rosemary put it in her purse, hoping that at least one of the photos would turn out, that it hadn't been a mistake to insist that they all wear matching "2000" shirts. The girls had protested that their shirts were too big, and Meredith and Natalie were already covering theirs up, Natalie grabbing the flannel that she had left on the arm of a chair and Meredith putting on a cowl-neck sweater. Meredith had French-braided her hair before they left, the scent of the hairspray trailing along with her as they got into the car to go to church, and Rosemary knew that it was for this moment, so she could pull a sweater over her head and not end up with hair floating electrically around her ears. Meredith thought Rosemary did not know her, and she was wrong. Rosemary knew all of her daughters. She knew that Jackie would leave her arms bare all night and never get cold.

Meredith held her lips inside her mouth as she put on her sweater so her lipstick wouldn't stain the inside of the neck. The T-shirt felt oversized and bulky underneath, but they had their picture and she had helped make her mother happy. Now she felt like herself, or at least the person she was supposed to be for this party: the rising senior who would talk politely about her ACT score and her college plans before offering to organize an activity for the younger children. As they walked into the Fellowship Hall, Meredith scoped the room; she was the oldest one here who wasn't an adult. Even though she was, technically. She was eighteen now. She wondered what would happen if she claimed a place next to her parents and their cluster of Kirkland faculty and staff, and let Natalie deal with the babysitting.

"Is it midnight yet?" Natalie said, standing next to Meredith with her two cookies and her paper cup. There would be sparkling cider at midnight, but until then it was pink punch and cookies and a single vegetable tray, the same thing they had every year. The cookies were the best part, because most of them were homemade. This year Meredith and Rosemary had baked the Grubers' share together. They had talked about doing sugar cookies with icing and "2000" squeezed out of one of those cake topper tubes, but they ended up doing peanut butter cookies at the last minute, their fork prints uneven, hoping the cookies would cool enough so that the tops wouldn't stick to the underside of the wax paper.

Meredith clinked her paper cup with her sister's. "Five hours to go."

Natalie had been invited to another party, but Mom and Dad had said no. That party wouldn't start for another two hours, and she had already heard that they were going to have beer and wine coolers and peppermint schnapps, which Kimberly said tasted like liquid candy canes. Kimberly was in charge of bringing her mother's half-empty bottle. Ben was in charge of the beer. Natalie would have to go to school next Monday and hear all about it, the parts that they'd tell her as well as the parts that she'd figure out just by listening, by sitting next to all of the conversations. They'd all know what peppermint schnapps tasted like. They'd know what it felt like to drink, to get that buzz that was the first step on the chart towards death, the one they all had to memorize in health class. Natalie thought it was idiotic that anyone assumed they would drink all the way to the end of the chart. You could eat your way to death too, and nobody did that, except for that one guy in the Brad Pitt movie. Natalie hadn't been allowed to see that either. Kimberly and Jenna had watched it together when Jenna's mom wasn't home and told Natalie about it later. That was how she learned about the world.

Jackie finished her cookies, went to the end of the Fellowship Hall, and sat down at the piano. She began to pick out a melody. It was that song Meredith liked, the one she bought on CD and played out of her bedroom every morning. Jackie wasn't sure of the words because she only ever heard it through Meredith's wall—and because Sting didn't sing all of his Gs—but she knew it was a song about *tonight*, about the one night in all of their lifetimes when they'd get to see a new millennium, so it felt like the right thing to play. Plus she didn't have anything else to do.

Jackie started playing chords to match the tune. At first her left hand jumped too far down, and the notes she hit didn't match the ones in her head, but after a few times through she started to get it. She hadn't ever thought that playing the piano could be like singing, where you felt the pitches you wanted and your body knew how to create them. She felt like someone had kept something from her that she was just starting to figure out.

She switched from chords to a sort of rolling bass line, do-sol-do, matching her melody to this new pattern. Her foot dropped onto the damper pedal to connect the bass together, since her hands were too small to play the notes like Mom used to teach her, each finger lifting from the key as the next finger pressed down. Like her hands were her breath. It was funny that she hadn't put that together before.

"What are you playing, Jacks?" It was her dad, leaning on top of the piano.

"That song Meredith likes," Jackie said. "The one about New Year's."

Dad sang in a fake scoopy voice: "Should auld acquaintance be forgot..."

"Not that one," Jackie said. "I forgot about that one."

She felt with her fingers, hoping she could find it without any mistakes. It wasn't quite right—her left hand was still stuck on the other song, and one of the chords didn't match—but she got the melody.

"Are you playing that by ear?" Dad asked. "When did you learn how to play by ear?"

"I don't know," Jackie said, suddenly embarrassed. Then she grinned. "Just in time for the new millennium!"

"We're getting together a game of Trivial Pursuit, if you want to play," Dad said. "Your mom said I should ask."

"Do I have to?" Jackie said. "Can I stay here?"

"Do whatever," Dad said. "We've got a lot of time to kill before midnight."

So Jackie continued to play, picking through the Auld Lang Syne song and then finding all of the notes in "Last Midnight" from *Into The Woods*, because that song was kind of about New Year's too, everyone joking about the Y2K bug ruining everything. Planes crashing out of the sky. They had turned off and unplugged the computer before they left, just in case.

After she had played for a while she looked up and the grownups had all sorted themselves into Trivial Pursuit teams, and half of the cookies were gone, and it was 8:30. She got up and went to find Meredith and Natalie, but the two of them were in the nursery with a bunch of little kids watching *The Lion, the Witch, and the Wardrobe*—a good choice, because it was three hours long—and so she left them to their movie and kept walking. The phone was at the end of the hall, and nobody else was around.

Priya picked up on the third ring. "Hello, Seth residence."

"It's me," Jackie said. "I'm at the church. It's so boring. I learned how to play by ear."

Rosemary was trying to remember which king witnessed the signing of the Magna Carta when her daughter came racing into the Fellowship Hall, the smack of her feet against the floor echoing against the high ceilings. *No running*, she thought automatically, but she knew she couldn't say it anymore, not if she didn't want her girls to glare at her. "Do you care if Priya comes over?" Jackie said, out of breath. "Her parents say she can stay until midnight."

"How did you talk to Priya's parents?" Rosemary asked.

"I called them," Jackie said.

"On the church phone?"

"It's a local call," Jackie said. "Can she come?"

"Tell the Seths they're all welcome," Dad said, and Jackie ran back to deliver the news to the phone that she had carefully placed on the church hall floor.

In the end Anand and Preeti and Priya came, bringing a bottle of champagne and two bags of Doritos, and Daniel stayed at home to play video games. Jackie wondered if Meredith would be disappointed, when she came out of the nursery to find all of the Seths except Daniel. They could have stood awkwardly, side-by-side, at midnight, and not kissed.

But Jackie and Priya made plates of cookies and chips and took them up to the choir room, Jackie bringing along a deck of cards from the grownups' table so they could play Speed, their hands flipping and slapping at the cards, the cookie crumbs scattering on the carpet.

Jackie watched Priya shuffle and deal the deck. Priya was wearing a white hoodie with GAP stitched across the front in purple, which meant they were almost dressed alike. It was funny how that had happened and they hadn't planned it. Priya looked so pretty, with her dark hair falling against the white sweatshirt. Jackie suddenly wanted to reach out and give Priya a hug. It felt strange. Her fingers hit against Priya's as the two of them went after the same card, and Jackie thought that maybe she shouldn't do that; that the feeling inside of her body would come out through her hand and give her away.

"Do you want to go outside?" Jackie said, as soon as the game was finished. "It feels weird to stay inside on the night of the millennium."

"It's not the real millennium," Priya said. "It's just the millennium for people who can't do math."

Priya explained it as Jackie got the coats; if the first year was Year 1, then the year that came two thousand years after Year 1 would be Year 2001. Jackie laughed because that made the whole thing even more ridiculous; the T-shirts, the photos, the ceremonious unplugging of the computer.

"We have to spend all night at the church for something that isn't even the real millennium!" Jackie said, holding the door for Priya as they went outside.

There were lights in front of the church sign—"The Bible Is Y2K Compliant"—and snow on the ground, and as they walked their shadows fell against the snow like Priya's hair against her hoodie, and Jackie felt like she couldn't stop looking at her, so she looked at their shadows instead, where she could keep watching Priya without her noticing. If they moved too far away from the light the shadows looked the same, two girl-shaped blurs.

It was quiet outside, and cold, and they walked around the church with their footprints behind them and their breath in front of them, and Jackie finally said "I think I want people to call me Jacqueline. Could I say it's because of the fake millennium?"

"I think you could say it's because it's your name," Priya said. "Do you not like being called Jackie?"

"I don't mind it," Jackie said. "But it's what my folks called me when I was a baby. Maybe I want my whole name."

"Jacqueline sounds like you. It's kind of funny but it's pretty at the end."

"It sounds like it could be an opera singer's name," Jackie said, seeing the words "opera singer" leave her mouth like a dream; solid and real only when it was inside her head.

"We should go to college together," Priya said. "We could be roommates. I'd be pre-med and you'd be pre-music."

"Prima donna," Jackie joked, and Priya laughed, and Jackie felt like going outside was the best idea she had ever had. This whole boring night had been worth it just so she and Priya could stand in the snow together.

"I'm glad you're here," Jackie said. She wondered if she should follow up with *why*. She wondered if there was a why, besides Priya being Priya, her best friend.

"Me too," Priya said. She smiled at Jackie. "Jacqueline."

Jack's team had trounced everyone at Trivial Pursuit, and they had switched over to Monopoly, Anand moving on from his long-winded explanation of "the real millennium" to an eager discussion of the true Monopoly rules, not the house rules that everybody played, and how that made the game both mathematically more interesting and "to what I know will be everybody's relief, *shorter*."

"We're in no hurry," Jack said. "Let's play the long version."

Some of the parents had already started to collect their kids and go home, and Natalie had given up on the nursery after the movie ended and was sitting next to Rosemary at the table, gamely organizing Monopoly money into piles. Meredith stayed with the few remaining children, parading them all into the Fellowship Hall for one more cookie each before putting in *Prince Caspian* and beginning to collect the Little People and Sorry pawns that had scattered over the nursery floor.

"Have you seen Jackie?" Rosemary asked.

"I'm sure she and Priya are around here somewhere," Preeti said. "They don't want to hang out with old people like us."

At ten minutes to midnight they all gathered, the adults and the children, and the pastor went into the kitchen to get the sparkling cider and the unexpected champagne. There were still only paper cups, but the plastic sleeve went around and everyone took their cup, and the parents helped pour the sparkling cider for their children, and Meredith thought they might pass her the champagne bottle but they didn't, because she still wasn't an adult at eighteen and because even the real adults had to follow the rules.

Jackie and Priya came in late, almost missing it, and the champagne and cider bottles were next to each other on the table, beside the vegetable tray with its warm plastic bowl of French onion dip. Priya lined up two cups and poured from the champagne bottle, not the sparkling cider one. Jackie took her cup and their eyes met and both of them smiled.

They were on the outside of the circle because they had arrived last, and each of them held their cold, waxy, illicit cup of champagne and counted along with everyone, and then they toasted, and then they drank, and then they kissed.

Jackie didn't know why Priya had kissed her, or why she and Priya had decided to kiss each other at exactly the same time. Everyone was kissing each other; Mom was kissing Natalie on the cheek, and Meredith was blowing a kiss at one of the little kids, and half of the adults were doing the French kiss-kiss thing, where they put their faces on either side of each other without touching. But she knew why she had kissed Priya.

"To the millennium!" the pastor said. "Hallelujah!"

"To the fake millennium!" Jacqueline and Priya said, adding their secret word to everyone else's cheer and raising their empty glasses.

SPRING 2000

64. ANNE GIVES MEREDITH ADVICE.

Meredith got the reply two days after she sent the email. She saw the subject line: "Re: College advice" and was nervous to open it, so she quickly clicked, taking in the entire email in one gulp:

Dear Meredith,

It was good to hear from you. I am well, and thank you for asking. I have a stack of midterms to grade, and I'd much rather answer your email than deal with them!

However, I'm sorry to say that I cannot be very helpful. I'd give you an opinion if I had one, but I don't know a lot about the schools you're considering; Midwestern liberal arts colleges are not my area of expertise. If your father says they're good schools I'd trust his judgment, and of course it's hard to turn down a full scholarship.

I do know that you're going to get a good education wherever you go. You're smart and you're a hard worker, which already puts you ahead of most of your classmates. Keep doing what's gotten you this far and you'll be fine.

As for how to identify a strong English department: the truth is that you're already strong in the English department (pun intended) and you may be one of those students who has to wait until grad school to start learning things they don't already know. I'm guessing you've already read most of what's on the standard survey of American and British literature. You'll have to challenge yourself, because your classes may not, especially during your first year.

If you want to be a writer, the important thing is to keep writing. I must confess that I haven't read the novel you sent me, but I'm sure it is good, and it's impressive that you finished it. Keep at it. That's the best advice I can give.

Your (wildly impressed and proud) aunt,

Anne

After Meredith saw what it said, which was to say *nothing*, she read it again more carefully. Aunt Anne didn't think one school was better than the other. She didn't even say how to tell whether one English department was better than another, which Meredith thought wasn't fair; Aunt Anne had been teaching in an English department for years, so she should know what to look for in a good professor vs. a bad one.

And what Meredith wanted, more than anything in the world, was a good professor who could become her mentor. Last summer Meredith had read a biography of Stephen Sondheim, hoping to learn more about *Into the Woods*, and at the beginning the biographer explained that a teenaged Sondheim wrote a musical and gave it to Oscar Hammerstein II to read, and Hammerstein spent an entire day taking it apart and telling Sondheim how to make it better. Meredith had thought Aunt Anne might be her Oscar Hammerstein.

But Aunt Anne hadn't read her novel. Which Meredith already knew. More importantly, Aunt Anne thought Meredith might be bored in her first year classes and might not learn anything new until grad school and until then would just have to challenge herself, keep working hard on her own, keep writing novels that were probably good even though nobody would read them and tell her for sure.

If that's what she could expect for the next four years, then the decision was easy. She'd take the full scholarship plus room and board. It was hard to turn something like that down, after all.

65. THE DISTRICT MUSIC CONTEST.

Some part of Meredith must have woken up when the phone rang, because she was already awake when her mother knocked, softly, on her door. The red numbers on her clock radio read 3:47, almost 45 minutes earlier than she had set her alarm. Mom, of course, wanting to make sure they were up, make sure they wouldn't miss the bus—or worse, be the last ones there.

So Meredith thought she would stay in bed, at least until her alarm went off; then she thought she had better go downstairs and use the toilet before everyone started taking showers. They still kept the stair light on, and when Meredith pushed her sleep mask up on her forehead she saw Mom and Jackie and Natalie at the top of the stairs, and Mom was crying.

"Stephanie's dead," Mom said, and Meredith stepped in next to Nat and Jackie so Mom could pull the three of them close to her, a grasping group hug of grief and crushed arms. That had been the phone call, then; the news passing from one house to another in the night. Stephanie Dillard was dead.

When they arrived at the school, Meredith could tell who knew and who didn't; the people who got out of their parents' cars tired but game, instrument cases and uniform bags in hand, and the people who had all of that plus a box of tissues, who immediately clustered with their friends to cry together and share what they knew: Stephanie's car had been hit by a truck on the highway out by Dos Bandidos.

The parents clustered, too, moving in a pack to every new car, sharing their most important detail: *no, Stephanie wasn't drinking.*

It was an important detail, Meredith thought as they boarded the bus, her mind trying to organize her thoughts by turning them into a story. *If Stephanie was drinking, it was something that could happen to Stephanie. If she wasn't drinking, it was something that could happen to any of us.*

Their music teacher stood at the front of the bus before they left, all of them hunched into their coats like pillows, mostly quiet, the night still around them like a darkened room. "I know this is a sad day," he said, after telling them all, once again, what had happened. "But we've decided we're still going to go to Contest—and we're going to do our best, for Stephanie."

Meredith wondered who was on the other half of his "we've decided;" if he called up Principal Howard to ask, or if she called him, or if he made the decision on his own. There were people still crying in the back of the bus, where Stephanie would have sat. Natalie was in the middle somewhere with her friends. Meredith was in the second row, next to a freshman who had arrived minutes before they left. Maybe his mother had assumed they wouldn't be going. Maybe there had been a second phone call, traveling from home to home, telling everyone that Contest was still on.

And maybe it should be, Meredith thought, although it didn't matter to her, she had her college acceptance letter and her first-year information packet sitting on top of her dresser. The way she played the piano or sang was now completely irrelevant, except to add one more achievement to her list. The way the band and choir performed might be more important to somebody, though. Maybe the school. Maybe all of them, because they had practiced—but it didn't seem to be, anymore. Meredith wasn't sure what you were supposed to do when one of your classmates died. It had never happened before. She couldn't remember it ever happening in a book. When people died in books they were close, like sisters or best friends; or they were bad, because the book wanted to teach you not to drink or do drugs. Stephanie wasn't either of those things. She was a person they knew. Meredith might have said that they were friends, if someone who didn't know either of them had asked, but the truth was that they weren't.

Meredith had known before she went to bed that she'd spend the entire music contest exhausted, her eyes itchy, sweat on the back of her neck, her mind instantly forgetting the hallways and cafeterias so it could focus on the few minutes of performance. That was how Contest always was, every year. This year Stephanie was dead, but the day had always felt unreal, so in that way it didn't feel *different*. Meredith wondered if she should feel different. She held her French horn and the band did its best for Stephanie and Meredith still thought of it as a story that she was both watching and writing at the same time. *We left an empty chair for her, in the clarinet section.*

Then it was time to strip off the wool band uniforms and put on the dresses they had rolled into their backpacks, the ones they knew wouldn't wrinkle, and brush their hair out in the bathroom. Meredith stood by the mirror closest to the door because she was singing in half an hour, which gave her just enough time to warm up and run through her pieces before she had to go stand in line.

The practice rooms were always in the same place, and Meredith closed herself into the tiny white pod and quickly warmed up with the piano. Then she began the piece she had been working on for months, both at home and with Miss Opal:

When I am laid, am laid in earth...

She stopped, her breath caught just behind her throat. She could not do this. She could not sing these words. Meredith felt all at once what death was, and what it meant, and how everything about Stephanie had ended and would always be gone, and how sudden it must have been, a truck on the highway at night, how it could end like that at any moment for any of them. Then she started grieving Stephanie herself; not the idea of death but the truth of Stephanie, everything she had known of her, for nearly all of her life. Her eyes were slick and smeared with tears.

Meredith opened her choir folder and took out a tissue. She wiped her eyes, let her feelings sink into her so they couldn't get out and disrupt the performance, and sang.

After it was all over everyone carried their instruments and their uniform bags and their backpacks back to the bus, the sun low in the sky, two hours to go before they were home. The day felt both too long and like it had never happened. The band director stood at the front of the bus and told them that he had called Peg Howard and learned that there would be a gathering at the Baptist church when they got back, for anyone who wanted to go.

Meredith was one of the first people on the bus. Natalie took the other half of the seat, and Meredith wondered how her sister's day had gone; if she was feeling as strange and sad as Meredith was and if she had also swallowed it all down to make it through. Natalie would call Stephanie a friend and mean it, after all. *Would have*, anyway. Meredith realized how quickly they would all start talking about Stephanie in the past tense.

"So we made it through," Meredith said.

"Yeah," Natalie said. "I'm going to the church thing when we get back."

"Me too," Meredith said.

The bus was moving now, the sun enormous and orange like a painful throb, like Meredith's head and the tears that had never made it out of her eyes. "You remember the night Mom and Dad went out and Jonetta and Stephanie came over and we played board games and then we watched *Peter Pan*?"

Natalie nodded. "Stephanie thought we were going to watch the Disney one."

"But she liked it," Meredith said. "We got up and danced to all the songs. I keep thinking of the four of us, dancing."

"She used to come over for piano every week, and we'd have snacks together and play Barbies before our lesson," Natalie said.

"That's right," Meredith said. "You had lessons together."

"Do you remember that talent show?" Natalie asked. "We made up those words for that piece she played."

Meredith sang, softly. "Oh, the thing about chips that are neato…"

"Don't sing on the bus, Mer." Natalie poked her sister, teasing. "Don't be the weirdo."

"I'll always be the weirdo," Meredith said. "You'll be the Homecoming Queen." Then she thought of it, and because it was her sister next to her, she said it. "And Stephanie will be the one who died."

"Yeah," Natalie said. She sniffed, and dug into her backpack for more tissues. "I'm going to miss her," she said, balancing the handful of tissues on the thigh that was closer to Meredith, so they could share.

"Me too," Meredith said again, even though she knew she didn't mean it the way Natalie did. But she could miss everything Stephanie had been, and everything she might have become. She pulled a tissue out of Natalie's crumpled wad and held it, wondering if everything she had felt in the practice room would come back, or if that had been her one chance to grieve and she had chosen to sing instead.

66. JACK HAS COFFEE WITH NATALIE.

"You going to try one of the cappuccinos?" Jack asked, as he and Natalie walked towards the coffee shop. "That's coffee with steamed milk in it."

"Maybe," Natalie said.

"I'm going to have a caffe latte," Jack continued, letting the four syllables come out like timpani beats. "You can ask for a shot of syrup, if you want. That's what Opal told me this morning."

The sign above the door read The Place, in hand-painted purple letters; everybody just called it the coffee shop. It had been open for a week, in the building that used to be a bait store.

"We'll have to get you driving soon," Jack said. "You know your mother's... not ready yet." It wasn't fair to put it all on Rosemary, but it was easier. They had both had the discussion, after Stephanie's death. Rosemary called Jonetta every day, to see how she was doing. She baked casseroles, wrapped in foil, until all their dishes were at the Dillards'.

"It's cool," Natalie said.

"Walking's good for you," Jack said, holding the door for his daughter. They were the only customers in The Place.

"I'll have a small caffe latte," Jack said. He knew that the woman behind the counter was named Angel, and that she had two kids, a young boy and a girl. They lived in the apartment above the store. Rosemary would know more about them, probably. They were new, the small family with the dream of bringing fancy coffee to Kirkland. Well, he'd give them a try. It was the neighborly thing to do.

"How about you, Natalie?" he asked.

"Do you have, like, a soda?"

Angel smiled. She was young, her hair pressed into sticky curls and pulled back into a high ponytail. "I could getcha an Italian soda," she said. "Or we got cans of Pepsi or Sierra Mist."

"Try the Italian soda," Jack said. They couldn't walk all the way to The Place to get a can of Pepsi.

"Okay," Natalie said.

"What size?" Angel asked.

"Um... small?"

"What flavor?"

Natalie looked at the menu board, which was painted in the same handwriting as the sign. "What flavors do you have?"

"Gosh," Angel said. "Vanilla, hazelnut, cherry, mint, almond, there might be some blackberry left, you want me to go in the back?"

"No, um, cherry's fine."

"All right, then," Angel said. "One small caffe latte and one small Italian soda with cherry. That'll be $7.25."

Jack pulled cash out of his wallet and then led Natalie to the table in front of the window. Might as well sit where other people could see them, let them know that The Place was the place to be. Of course, after giving Angel $8.00 for two small drinks, he wasn't sure if this was the kind of place that would last. "That's some spendy coffee," he said to Natalie, his voice low so Angel wouldn't hear. "You won't be able to come here every day."

"I wasn't planning on it," Natalie said.

"I don't know," Jack said. "You might. I think she wants this to be a youth hangout."

"Yeah," Natalie said. "Lots of youth here right now."

Angel brought out the two drinks, Jack's in a thick white mug with a chip in the handle and Natalie's in a glass. Jack sipped his drink and thought that Opal had maybe hyped this up a little too much. But that was Opal for you. She had one caffe latte in Italy twenty years ago and now she was an expert.

"Do you like your Italian soda?"

Natalie shrugged. "It's kind of like a phosphate."

"Yeah, I don't know why you'd come here when the drugstore's down the street and you can get a cup of coffee for 89 cents," Jack said. That was almost too loud; he had forgotten to be careful. So he changed the subject. "I wanted to talk to you about your future."

"What about it?"

"Well, it's time to start thinking about college. Have you given any thought to what you might want to major in?"

Jack watched Natalie play with her straw, pushing it back and forth against the edges of her glass. He and Rosemary had known Meredith would be an English major for years—"English major and theater minor," Meredith had started correcting everyone, when they asked—and Jackie was headed for music, maybe music ed if he could talk her into it. They needed good music teachers around here, and she could be a great one. But he didn't know what Natalie was interested in. He realized he was a little nervous about what she might say.

"I was thinking maybe business?"

"Why business?"

"I don't know," Natalie said. "Because I'm probably going to work in a business?"

"The point of college isn't just work, Natalie. You go to college to learn. You could learn about anything. Theology, science, literature, art, music—you're really an outstanding clarinetist, you know."

Natalie smiled slightly at the compliment. "I can still play in the band. You don't have to be a music major to play in band."

"Okay, sure." Jack said. "Sure. So... what interests you about business?"

Natalie swiped at her straw a few more times. "I'm not going to be a professor like you, and I'm not going to be, like, a writer or an opera singer, so I'm probably going to work in a business, like Mom did. And it was kinda cool when she was the manager, and maybe I should learn how to do that."

"You know your mom didn't have any business background at all," Jack said. "She was a music major. You can get any job you want, if you're smart."

"So are you saying I should major in something else?"

"I'm not saying anything," Jack said. "Only that I want you to really think about what you want." That was what worried him about Natalie; she'd done fine in school, Gruber kids always did well in school, but she didn't seem to be passionate about anything. He'd never seen her read an extra book just to read it, or practice beyond the half hour set on the timer. *Maybe every family has a Christopher*, he thought. So far Natalie hadn't been much of a party animal—they hadn't let her—but that could all change once she left home, and she could still end up like his brother. Which wouldn't be that bad; Christopher had a few wild years and then got an ordinary job working for some insurance agency somewhere. But that wasn't what he wanted for Natalie. He wanted her to get excited about something and start working towards it.

"What's your favorite thing you've ever done?" Jack asked. "The thing that's most interested you."

"Swim team," Natalie said.

"So are you interested in maybe learning more about phys ed? Or maybe physics! There are a lot of physics in swimming. Arcs, angles, motion."

"I liked being on a team with my friends," Natalie said. "And I was a good swimmer."

"Okay," Jack said. "It sounds like you like working with people. Maybe you should think about psychology, or one of the social sciences."

"Sure," Natalie said. "I can think about that." Jack knew that his daughters only said that to get him to stop talking, the way he used to say "we'll see" when they were younger and asked him for ice cream or toys. He knew that Natalie wasn't going to go home and type "psychology" into Yahoo. She wasn't even asking him what the social sciences *were*, the way Meredith or Jackie might have done.

"Well, you don't have to decide today," Jack said. "You've still got a little while. You know, you don't even have to decide your first year of college. You can go in undeclared, take a bunch of different classes, and see if anything strikes your fancy. Colleges can change lives that way, you know."

"Did it change your life?" The two of them were standing up now, their cup and glass half full and unfinished on the table, walking towards the door.

"No, I always knew I wanted to be a music major," Jack said. Then he smiled. "I guess it kind of did. 'Cause I met your mom."

He held the door for Natalie as they left, feeling like he'd done the right thing by talking to his daughter, glad that they could have a little bit of time together, and glad that there was still time left to help Natalie make some smart choices about what she wanted, and where her future might go.

67. MEREDITH GOES TO PROM.

Rosemary held the camera, waiting for Meredith to come down the stairs. It was The Moment, she knew she was supposed to wait for and capture this moment, and in many ways she had been waiting to capture this moment for years. Since Meredith was a baby. She had thought of their weddings most often, the photos where she'd be standing next to her daughters, maybe both of them at a vanity with their faces reflected in the mirror, but definitely the one where they would be side by side, Rosemary with each of her girls in turn.

She never pictured herself in the prom photos; mothers didn't get dressed up for prom, it wasn't their moment the way a wedding was. (Nobody sold Mother of the Prom Queen dresses, although they probably could, people would pay for them.) But she never pictured Meredith alone, either. The photo on the stairs, that would be all right. Girls always came down the stairs by themselves on prom night. But the one in the yard, before they left—she hadn't ever thought it would be just Meredith. For the longest time she thought it would be Meredith and Daniel. Then she hoped it would be Meredith and *anybody*.

Rosemary thought of Jonetta, who would have been standing in her own apartment waiting for Stephanie to open her bedroom door. There weren't any stairs, but Stephanie would have had a date and a corsage and they would have gone out and posed in front of the apartment building, the row of bushes instead of the front yard, and then Stephanie would have gotten into Sean's car and Jonetta would have spent the rest of the night worrying about them being safe.

Rosemary wasn't sure how to talk to Jonetta anymore. It had been easy at first, when she could bake casseroles and commiserate about funerals, when it was about helping Jonetta get through the day and letting her cry when she needed to. (Then coming home and crying in the bathroom where nobody else could see.) Now Rosemary didn't know what to say. Everything about her life seemed to highlight Jonetta's loss. *Meredith is going to prom and Stephanie is not. Natalie keeps rolling her eyes at me and Stephanie is dead.*

There would be a moment of silence for Stephanie during prom, even though Stephanie wasn't a senior. But she had been dating a senior, and Sean had bought Jonetta and Bobbie Jo both corsages. Meredith had said that it was the Student Council's idea, and Rosemary wasn't even sure it was a good one—she felt like if it were one of her girls, she wouldn't be able to look at the flowers—but it was something. She hadn't been able to call Jonetta yet, not today anyway. She wouldn't call tomorrow either, not when everything in her mind would still be about whether Meredith enjoyed prom and how late she stayed out and how tired and grumpy they both were because Rosemary had of course waited up for her. She could call on Sunday, though. That would be all right. Maybe by then she'd know what to say.

Meredith was taking too long. Rosemary wanted to go up and check on her, but she didn't want to miss her picture on the stairs. She called out instead, her impatience serving as vocal amplifier: "Meredith! Are you okay?"

Meredith stood in front of her bedroom mirror. She kept her eyes wide open, so her eyelashes wouldn't smash together and leave black filaments of mascara on her skin. She kept her mouth open, too. She screamed from the inside but blocked the sound with a glottal stop, just like Miss Opal had taught her. Her diaphragm was engaged. Her shoulders were straight. Her fists were clenched.

She had known this moment was coming and she was prepared for it and she could still not bear it. Which was to say she knew she could bear it. She knew that in a minute she would have to walk down the stairs and walk into the yard and get into the car and have her mom drive her to the school, and then she'd have to walk under the silk-flowered archway that the juniors had built, and Principal Howard would say her name but no one else's because she would do all of this alone.

And Meredith *would* do all of this. But first she would stand in front of the mirror and make silent screaming faces.

Daniel was not going to prom. That was the worst part. If Meredith had to sack up—literally—his parents should have made him go too. She had asked him twice if he would go with her. The second time felt embarrassing. Not the fake kind of embarrassing when you spill food on yourself or walk around with your bra strap showing, but the real kind. Meredith's brain still cringed when she thought of it, and she saw the cringe come through her eyes as she continued to scream.

There would be no magical moment for her tonight. No long-time crush announcing over the microphone that he wanted the next dance. No mysterious stranger catching her eye. It wasn't going to be Jo and Laurie, it wasn't going to be Betsy and Phil Brandish, it definitely wasn't going to be Lizzie and Darcy. It wasn't even going to be Kitty hoping Vronsky would dance with her instead of Anna because there was nobody Meredith cared about that much, there wasn't a single person she wanted to dance with besides Daniel, and even then she wanted to joke with him about the dancing as much as she wanted to actually dance. About how ridiculous prom was, as a tradition.

But she also wanted the tradition. She wanted the corsage, and she wanted to walk down to the grocery store and buy the boutonniere, the old ladies who had watched over decades of proms telling her they already knew what Daniel had chosen for her and they'd make sure the flowers matched. She wanted Daniel's arm under the archway. She wanted his name next to hers. They had been friends for so long.

You couldn't force a friend to go to prom with you. You also couldn't convince your parents to let you ask a college student from your dual credit class—that had been Meredith's second idea, and it hadn't worked either. What she had to do, the only option left to her, was to walk down those stairs alone.

So Meredith unclenched her fists and slipped her feet into her cheap, ice-blue strappy heels and picked up the tiny purse that almost matched and walked down the stairs. She kept her eyes open just as wide, so they wouldn't blink against the flash, and tilted her head slightly to the right.

"One more," Rosemary said. "Keep smiling."

The next day, when Meredith checked her email, there was a message from Daniel.

M—

I read your book. You are really talented. It reminded me of Final Fantasy III/VI, which is the highest compliment I can give. They could definitely make it into an RPG.

How was Prom?

D

This was better than prom. He had read her book. She had so much she wanted to tell him. Meredith's thoughts fell into a shape that felt perfect, something she knew she'd have to shatter into pieces as soon as she started writing them down. That was always how it was, but she'd have the fun of looking at the pieces and picking out the best ones to send Daniel. She'd tell him everything, and he'd read it and they'd be closer than ever. It didn't matter that he hadn't wanted to go to prom with her. All that mattered was what she'd write as her reply.

68. MEREDITH AND ALEX HAVE COFFEE.

Meredith still looked both ways before she crossed the street, even though Alex had already started walking. They were going to have coffee at The Place. Alex had asked, and Meredith had said yes, and now she felt awkward, half-running to keep up, her backpack slung over one shoulder and smacking against her hip.

"I haven't been in here yet," Alex said. "I heard it's fancy."

"Dad said it was bohemian," Meredith said. *La vie bohème*, she thought, but didn't say anything because she didn't think Alex knew *Rent*. "He also said it was expensive."

"That sounds like your dad," Alex said, and Meredith wondered what that meant. They went inside, stared at the menu, and both ordered cappuccinos.

"Do you think this is trying to be, like, Central Perk?" Alex asked. They sat at a table in the corner, both of them choosing to avoid the sofa with the tuft of white filling poking out of a tear on the arm.

"It is The Place to be," Meredith said. She had just thought of the pun and it already felt as tired as the sofa.

Alex sipped her cappuccino, leaving a red-brown lipstick mark against the white mug. They had both been given spoons with their drinks, precariously balanced on stained saucers; Meredith used hers to scoop out a taste of foam, then put the spoon down. That didn't seem right. She wasn't sure how a cappuccino worked.

She also wasn't sure what to say to Alex, who sat across from her like a familiar stranger. Alex was beautiful, her red hair in thick, loose curls and her makeup porcelain and perfect.

When Meredith tried to do her makeup like that she looked like a clown, her skin white to the edge of her jawline. Alex wore a blue lace camisole and her eyeshadow looked like silver glitter. Meredith was wearing a dress from two summers ago, the kind that you could wad up and tie into a knot, the crumpled material promising to never wrinkle or wear out. It felt like the promise Meredith had made to everyone.

"Are you doing that theater thing again this summer?" Alex asked.

Meredith considered the best way to answer this. "No," she said. "Mom doesn't want me on the road every day, late at night." It was true and it felt wrong in two ways—first because she could have answered it without mentioning her mother at all, and second because she was leaving out the night she had asked one more time and both her parents had yelled at her and her mother had cried. "But I'll be able to audition for shows in college." The days felt like wet curtains she had to push through, a summer of heat and work sticking to her skin. She had thought she would write another novel but she had no ideas—just pages of paragraphs that would not turn into stories.

"I went to Stephanie's grave, once, after the funeral," Alex said. "By myself. It felt weird. It felt like I was walking into her family's house."

Meredith looked at Alex and loved her. "I don't think Ms. Dillard would mind if you went," she said, because she could not say *you have always been one of the smartest and best people I've known.* Then she said "I wish I had known Stephanie better," because she knew Alex and Stephanie had been close, and because she could not say *I never thought of going to her grave. Some days it's like I forget she died because I forget she was ever alive.*

"She was a good friend," Alex said, and they drank a little more of their cappuccinos, and Meredith wiped foam off her upper lip and then wiped her hand on her indestructible dress. Their coffee had not come with napkins.

"Have you written your speech?" Meredith asked. Daniel was valedictorian and Alex was salutatorian and Meredith was third, because she had gotten two Bs in gym. Meredith had also gotten the full ride scholarship, which is what her parents had said to her at dinner, to make the disappointment not matter. Nothing about high school mattered at all, any-more—except Meredith still had to get through it, and through an entire summer.

Alex shrugged. "I started it. I feel like if I said what I wanted to say, the school wouldn't let me give the speech. Like, there's so much of what happened in high school that our parents and teachers don't know anything about, and that was all the important stuff. That's what made us who we are."

Meredith thought of her novel and *Into the Woods* and her trips to the library, listening to CDs at night with her headphones on and reading everything she could about writing and structure and style. The afternoons she spent surfing the web, hoping nobody would need to use the phone, looking up theater reviews and photos of cities and biographies of the people she wanted to become someday. There was so much of the world she'd only seen through a browser window.

"You could write that," Meredith said. "Maybe write that what happened at school was important, but what we learned from life was important too. And that's what we'll have to remember after we graduate." She was already putting the speech together in her head. "Some of us are going to college, but all of us are going to learn from life, and our friends, and our families. This isn't the end of our education—it's the beginning."

"Can I steal that?" Alex laughed. "I always wished I could write like you."

I always wished I could be like you, Meredith thought, and then immediately knew it wasn't true. Yes, she had often longed to do things "the MacAllister way." But she wanted something different from her life, something that would take all the Gruber in her to accomplish. She wanted to be herself, more than anything. *We were never Betsy and Tacy*, Meredith realized, pressing the sentence into her mind so she could remember it for her diary. *We were always Emily and Ilse.*

The door opened, and Natalie walked in. Ben, who had held the door for her, followed. Meredith and Alex had chosen a corner table, and Nat and Ben did not seem to know they were there. Meredith put her finger to her lips and gestured Alex's eyes towards Natalie, who was placing her order while placing her hand in Ben's back pocket. He put his arm around her as if they had been doing this for weeks, and Meredith suddenly wondered if they had.

"Let's go before they see us," Meredith whispered, and she and Alex got up quietly and walked towards the door, waiting until it closed behind them before running and laughing down the street, the way they used to do when they were best friends.

69. THE GRADUATION.

The Grubers and the Seths took up half of Row H. They could have had the whole row, if they wanted it; each of them were entitled to eight graduation tickets, but neither of them had any other family coming that evening. The extra tickets had been given to Meredith and Daniel, who had passed them along to classmates who needed them for double sets of grandparents or a few extra cousins.

The MacAllisters, a few rows ahead, had twelve seats together—but Rosemary knew that was also because people like Deanna Russell (née Cory) had tickets for herself and her husband because she was a teacher, and they had brought the new baby, whose cries ricocheted to the top of the cacophony of people. The graduation was held in Kirkland College's auditorium, which gave them the benefit of both space and acoustics.

"Do you remember when Meredith and Daniel were in *The King and I*?" Preeti asked. *And me*, Jackie thought, but she didn't say anything. The conversation was between her mom and Priya's mom, the two of them talking over Jackie and Priya about Meredith and Daniel and college and memories and everything that was going to happen next. Priya leaned her head towards Jackie and whispered "It's like they're the first people who ever graduated." Jackie felt the warmth of Priya's body next to hers, as if the molecules of air were kissing each other on their behalf. Priya had set her up for the perfect response: "To them, they are."

Jackie and Priya had started having sleepovers, which both of their moms had agreed should be limited to once a month—and only on Friday nights—to ensure the girls didn't fall behind on their sleep or their schoolwork. That meant there had been four sleepovers since New Year's, which meant Jackie and Priya had kissed four times. More like thirty-two or forty times, since each kiss multiplied like the exclamation point they had learned in algebra. They put on their spaghetti-strap pajamas, watched their movie, ate handfuls of that crisped rice snack Priya's mother made, sat up talking until they got tired, and then they both got into Priya's bed, pulled the covers up over their bare shoulders, and kissed.

They both liked to see what happened if they kissed the parts you weren't supposed to kiss: earlobes; the bend of the arm right above the armpit; the skin next to the thumb, both loose and stretched taut—taut was better. They ended up giggling, always, and eventually they went to sleep. Jackie slept happiest when she was next to Priya. Not *best*—she was always tired the next morning, just like their moms said they would be—but happiest.

The auditorium lights flashed, but did not dim; they needed to be up as the high school band, minus its most senior members, performed Elgar's March #1, Trio section, aka "Land of Hope and Glory," aka "Pomp and Circumstance," and Natalie knew that she was the only person whose father had explained all of that over the dinner table. The sheet music simply said "Pomp and Circumstance (The Graduation March)," and Natalie kept her mouth shut about the rest.

Natalie hadn't thought she would miss Meredith after she left for college, but she was starting to realize that she would. It wasn't like she and Meredith had ever fought, because they never had, not once, but they were so different. Meredith was the one who thought it was cool that the American graduation march had been written for some British king's coronation. She and Dad collected facts the way little kids collected Pokémon.

So yeah, Meredith was a huge dork. But she was Meredith. She had always been around. Natalie could have had a worse sister.

Jack watched Peg Howard welcome the graduates and their families before introducing the first of too many speakers: the art teacher, whom he could tell was going to say something she thought was profound but was in fact as cliché as her flowing tunic and abundance of beads. He sat through a graduation every year. He had even given the faculty speech last spring—his was better.

He knew Rosemary thought it was his fault that Meredith was not giving a valedictory speech this evening. There were two gym teachers—one who coached girls' basketball after school and also taught chemistry, and one who coached boys' and taught civics—and Meredith got the mean one and Daniel and Alex did not. They could have called Peg Howard and made sure Meredith was in the right gym class, the one where everyone got an A unless they cussed out the teacher or something, because it wasn't like his kid was any worse at sports than Daniel Seth. Alex, sure. She could hit a ball. But Meredith and Daniel were more of the "good hustle!" types. Not that there was anything wrong with hustle. Meredith's hustle was going to get her anywhere she wanted to go, but it wasn't going to get her an A in gym. Unless she was in the other gym class, but she wasn't.

But then Peg Howard had asked if Meredith wanted to play a short piano piece after Daniel and Alex had given their speeches—the high school graduation always had music, if there was someone talented enough to play—so Meredith was going to get her moment too. Not that graduation needed to be any longer than it already was, but it wasn't Jack's job to comment on the length of the ceremony. It was his job to be supportive.

"Each of us has someone to thank, a parent or a grandparent or a teacher who's supported us as we've achieved this goal," Daniel said, perspiration collecting between his shoulder blades under the layers of undershirt and dress shirt and suit jacket and graduation robe. He had practiced his speech so many times that he could almost smile when he said it. He had also written "smile" at the end of a few paragraphs, just in case he forgot. His dad had ordered a digital camera from a catalog, so they could email the photos—and the speech—to his grandparents as soon as they got home.

It was kind of a cool moment, undermined slightly by Daniel's embarrassment that yes, the Indian kid was the valedictorian. He wondered if they'd even remember his name at the ten-year reunion, which he already planned not to attend. "Who was our valedictorian?" "The Asian kid." "Oh, *of course*." But—and Daniel looked up from his speech and smiled— fuck them all. He'd be gone by August, and Kirkland would become a story he could tell when people asked him where he was from. Or he could leave it out completely.

When Alex gave her speech she smiled at her family and at her friends and at Geoff, who had given her a pair of promise earrings two days ago. "Everyone else does promise rings," he had said. "But you're special." They were also smart enough to know that the tiny diamond earrings could slip into Alex's ears and stay hidden. A ring would prompt conversation about how they were too young, that college was a time to explore. But they were going to explore together. They had made a promise, and Alex wore her hair pulled back so it would sparkle against the light.

Meredith waited until Alex's applause started to dim before standing up and taking her place in the aisle. She walked up the left-hand steps as Alex walked down the right-hand ones, waited at the edge of the stage for Peg Howard to announce that Meredith Gruber would play a short piano selection, and then took her seat at the piano. The bench was cushioned and adjustable, but Meredith did not want to waste any time figuring out how the knobs worked. She knew that everyone was waiting for this part of the ceremony to be over. Best to get to it.

She played Samuel Barber's Excursion #3, because she loved it and because it was showy and because it was the one thing Meredith knew nobody else could do, it was another one of those pieces that everyone said was hard but wasn't, not in the way people thought it was. The hard part was hitting all the right keys, it had taken work to memorize where every finger should go, but the part everyone said was hard was the meter, eight beats in the left hand against seven beats in the right. It wasn't hard at all once you'd heard it, once you stopped thinking of it as seven against eight and started thinking—or stopped thinking, really, and let the notes fall in between each other where they belonged. It used to make her brain buzz when she played it. It was one of the few things that still did, and then she learned it well enough that it didn't, and now she could play the whole thing and think about why she was playing it at the same time.

Meredith knew she was playing this as a demonstration of accomplishment, in both the contemporary sense and the *Pride and Prejudice* sense. *Look at how accomplished this young woman is, with her ability to play seven beats in the right hand and eight beats in the left. Think about how far she'll go.* But Meredith knew, as each note struck and echoed and disappeared, that this accomplishment wouldn't last. She wasn't going to take piano lessons in college. She was the only person who'd kept them up all through high school—even Jackie had quit taking real lessons that spring—and now she was playing this beautiful and difficult piece for everyone, and then she'd put the sheet music away and never play it again. Maybe once or twice, just for herself, the way Jackie still sat down at the piano and played by ear, the house filled with Mozart and Sixpence None the Richer. But Meredith wouldn't have a house to fill. She'd have to walk from to her dorm to a row of practice rooms, in a building where she wouldn't even be a music student, and sit down to play a piece that would have one more wrong note in it, every time.

It seemed like such a waste—and a heartbreak. Meredith tried to put the heartbreak into the few measures she had left, the diminuendo and the ritardando and the careful placement of each last note, seven beats against eight, until they collected themselves into chords and were immediately forgotten in the applause. She bowed. Then she walked down the stairs and back to her seat, ready to line up with her class and process across the stage.

Rosemary knew you weren't supposed to stand up when it was your graduate's turn, but you probably weren't supposed to hoot and holler either, and you definitely weren't supposed to crouch in the aisle with your video camera, and she decided that she was going to stand. Or half-stand. Just enough so that she could get a good picture, without the backs of anyone's heads.

Meredith was near the front, because they went alphabetically; Rosemary felt her heartbeat start to race as her daughter got closer and closer to the steps, and when it was Meredith's turn she stood, her knees half-bent and shaking, her hands pushing the button and advancing the film and pushing the button and then it was gone, Meredith had shaken Peg Howard's hand and was walking down the left-hand stairs and it was someone else's turn.

"I got some too," Anand whispered, when Rosemary sat down. He held his digital camera towards Rosemary, Meredith's face on a tiny screen. "I'll email them to Jack."

They should have bought a digital camera. They were going to buy the school photos, the ones the professional photographer took as every graduate accepted their diploma, but they should have bought a digital camera too. Why hadn't she thought of that? She'd get one for this summer, for Meredith's move-in and the photo she wanted of the whole family in front of Meredith's dorm. Then one of the three girls. Then one with Jack and Meredith together, so she could have one with her and Meredith together. The photo that said *I got you here safe*. The photo that meant *I love you*.

Rosemary started crying, and dug into her purse to grab her packet of tissues. She saw Jackie look up at her, that quick glance to confirm whether to be concerned or embarrassed, and Rosemary smiled at Jackie as if to say *Moms, right?* Jackie smiled back, and Rosemary wiped her eyes, and then she reached for Jack's hand and gave it a quiet squeeze as if to say *We did it*, and then she took her camera and checked again to make sure the film was advanced, so she could take a picture of Daniel when it was his turn. It was important to return the favor. She'd take one of Alex too, since the girls had been such good friends. She hoped they'd all stay in touch after they went to college. Rosemary hadn't stayed in touch with any of her high school friends, she couldn't remember most of their names, but Meredith and Daniel and Alex would be different. They'd email each other. She'd have to get Meredith to set up a Hotmail account for her before she went to college, so Rosemary could email her daughter every day.

FALL 2000

70. MEREDITH MATRICULATES.

Meredith heard the door open. It was Daniel; she saw *sethiroth* ungray itself and appear under Buddies, and Meredith wiggled her mouse so *maymorgan* would appear ready to chat. Everyone in Meredith's dorm had downloaded AIM the night before, as soon as they set up their new computers, as soon as their parents took their photos and cried and said goodbye. Meredith wasn't sure she liked it—she hated being interrupted—but it was new, and it was fun to make away messages.

Her current away message read "I'm eighteen years old and I don't need *in loco parentis!*" It puzzled her, how quickly and how often she had heard those three words in the eight hours between when she and her family arrived on campus and when her parents and her sisters began the drive home. The perky administrator who spoke at the parent-student lunch used it, which made sense—but then the chair of the honors department had said it too, later that afternoon when everyone was getting tired and Meredith was wishing she could go back to her new dorm room and it was clear that her mother was wishing she didn't have to leave.

Meredith didn't want her college to be her parent. This was supposed to be the first time in her life when she could be herself *without* the continuous eye of a parent. She was Meredith Gruber when she called her family and when she emailed them—and she had done all of that last night, and emailed her mother again this morning—and after that she was Meredith, just Meredith, adult and alone and finally able to figure out who she could become.

Except she didn't think that's what college wanted for her.

> *maymorgan:* this place feels like summer camp
> *maymorgan:* we played chubby bunnies last night, CHUBBY BUNNIES
> *maymorgan:* now our RA wants us all to walk to matriculation together, like
> we can't find the auditorium on our own
> *sethiroth:* what's chubby bunnies

How did Daniel not know what chubby bunnies was? Meredith had never even *been* to summer camp and she still knew about stuffing marshmallows in her mouth. She typed quickly, and then her RA knocked on her door, and she and her roommate both turned from their computers—"let's GO, girls!"—and Meredith changed her away message to "matri-C-U-later" and slipped her feet into black ballet flats. Her lanyard was already around her neck, key and keycard dangling. She was wearing a *lanyard.* That hadn't been in any of the college brochures.

Meredith had dressed up for the matriculation ceremony, wearing the same black skirt she had worn to her grandmother's and Stephanie's funerals paired with a tangerine blouse that looked silky but was really polyester. The outfit was sticky and hot and wrong; nearly everyone else she saw was wearing shorts, or short skirts. There was another first-year Meredith recognized who wore one of those long hippie skirts tied with a drawstring; she looked comfortable and interesting and like someone Meredith might want to get to know. She already knew she didn't really want to get to know her roommate, beyond a general pleasant civility. They weren't even walking together, even though other roommate pairs had stuck close, like it was nice to have a friend in the crowd.

The auditorium, just like the auditoriums back home, doubled as a basketball court. Students filled the bleachers and the balconies and the folding chairs set on the floor, and the fans circled frantically above them and the air did not cool.

As they sat, half-listening to welcoming words from deans and presidents, Meredith thought about how she might describe the scene to Daniel when she got back to her computer. She liked the phrase "fans circled frantically," which had popped into her mind as soon as she saw them, spinning so fast their stems quivered, and tried to commit to memory—but it was so noisy and so hot. *The hot day made her feel very sleepy and stupid,* Meredith thought automatically, and then she thought that she should always carry a notebook with her, like she did that one summer, so that she wouldn't have to remember everything she wanted to write later. (She'd write about that summer someday.)

The faculty speaker was from the music department, which Meredith thought was appropriate—for her, anyway. She'd have something to tell her parents, when it was time to talk to them again.

"Every generation has had a defining historical tragedy," the speaker began, "except yours."

Meredith thought that couldn't be true. She started doing the math along with the speech: World War I, World War II, Korea, Vietnam... were they counting the Berlin Wall, before it came down? "You have not been asked to go to war," the speaker continued, "and you have not been asked to take a stand in the name of civil rights. You have no unifying moment, as we did with the moon landing or with the Kennedy assassination or the assassination of Dr. Martin Luther King Jr., where you'll always remember where you were when it happened."

Princess Diana, Meredith thought, because she remembered where she had been when she heard the news. She and Alex had walked to the drugstore together for ice creams. They pushed open the door and everyone was listening to the radio. Or maybe Columbine, except she couldn't remember where she'd been when she first learned what had happened; only the jokes everyone made afterwards.

"You are a peaceful generation, a prosperous generation, some would say an entitled generation. You've had access to more than any generation before you, and we have asked less of you. The question is: what will you do with this privilege you've been given? What will you make of this world?"

Art, Meredith thought, instantly and with her whole body. *I am going to work as hard as I can to make art—novels and plays, and maybe I'll act and sing and play the piano, and I'll find my mentors and collaborators and we will work together and it will be extraordinary.*

She didn't listen to the rest of the speech because she was already making plans. College could matriculate her however it wanted. She had just matriculated herself. As soon as she got back to her dorm she would turn off AIM and then she would look at her schedule and block off two hours every day just for her, and she would call those hours Hat Time after *Sunday in the Park With George* and she would use them to make art. She'd start by writing a play. By the time she was done she would have new friends, and they would stage it together.

Meredith didn't know what would happen after that, but she didn't have to think about it yet. That would be next year. Today she would block off her hours, say hello to the girl in the drawstring skirt, and buy a notebook. Tomorrow, she'd go to class and then get to work.

ABOUT THE AUTHOR

Nicole Dieker is a freelance writer, a senior editor at The Billfold, and a columnist at The Write Life. Her work has appeared in Boing Boing, Popular Science, Scratch, SparkLife, The Freelancer, The Toast, and numerous other publications. *The Biographies of Ordinary People* is her debut novel, if you don't count the speculative fiction epic she wrote when she was in high school.

Learn more about Nicole at NicoleDieker.com.

Get updates on *The Biographies of Ordinary People*, including the forthcoming sequel, at tinyletter.com/NicoleDieker.

ACKNOWLEDGEMENTS

Thanks first to my family, who are not the characters in this book but who inspired me to create them because I wanted so much to write about being a little kid in rural Missouri surrounded by musical theater, piano practice, and wind ensembles. (I believe that music, as much as books, shapes who you become.)

Thanks second to Patreon and more specifically to my patrons, who supported me both financially and emotionally as I drafted this project. I could not have done this without you.

Then, thanks to Pronoun. This publishing service appeared right when I needed it, and exceeded all of my expectations. Thanks also to Veronica Ewing for creating the beautiful paperback layout.

Thanks to Boing Boing—an early chapter of *Biographies* appeared on the site in 2015—and thanks to The Billfold, which both taught me how to write these kinds of stories and gave me my readership.

Lastly: thanks to you, for reading this. I hope you read the next one.

READ A CHAPTER FROM
THE BIOGRAPHIES OF ORDINARY PEOPLE,
VOLUME 2: 2004–2016

Meredith climbed the stairs to Gina's office. She could hear the box fan in Gina's door before she turned the corner, which meant she was in her office; it also meant that she couldn't hear whether Gina was on the phone. The paper slipped into the plastic square by Gina's door read *Gina Christakos, Theatre; Office Hours MW 1:00-2:00,* but sometimes Gina would be in the middle of a call, putting one hand over the receiver and asking Meredith to wait—and it was embarrassing to stand outside the door, trying not to listen to half of a private conversation.

Sometimes it wouldn't be a call; Meredith would hear the conversation and then hear another voice, usually a professor. On those days Meredith turned around and walked back to her dorm, depending on who the voice belonged to and how she felt about them seeing her, standing in the hallway. She had crushes on the beard-and-sweater English professors and kept her body still, in class, so they wouldn't show; she had crushes on the grad students who rehearsed the altos in the popcorn-ceilinged room before sending them back to the choir, and let herself stare at their precise hands and expressive faces because it was okay, she was supposed to watch; she waited to have crushes on boys her own age but it never happened.

But today Gina was not on the phone, and no one else was in the office, and she welcomed Meredith as she stepped awkwardly over the box fan. "What's on your mind today, Meredith?" Meredith never knew if she came to Gina's office hours too often, so she tried to only come once every other week, although she had started coming every week now that there were only a few weeks left until graduation. Meredith rarely saw other students knock on Gina's door, so it wasn't like she was taking anything away from anyone else, but it still felt—well, she knew she was asking for more time and attention than was her fair share. But she had to get everything she could out of college while she was still here.

Meredith had started her college career with a plan—write a musical, ask for student activities funding to workshop her musical, seek out a mentor and ask her questions during office hours—and quickly discovered that no one else was expecting her to take this much initiative. Her first faculty adviser had suggested she learn to write scenes before trying an entire musical, advice to which Meredith would have paid more attention had the adviser bothered to read the musical and listen to the score that Meredith had recorded in a practice room on cassette, singing all the parts and overdubbing the harmonies. But Gina helped Meredith navigate the funding application, and sent the email that got her permission to stage the project in the theater department's basement, and sent another email to a visiting professor who helped get one of Meredith's scenes into an anthology of student writing—a published one, for which Meredith was paid $50 and a copy of the book. In return, Meredith brought Gina all of her questions about art and life.

Including this one.

"Everything we've studied—in theater, and in my English classes, and in art history and music history and everything else—has been about famous people."

"Okay," Gina said, smiling. Sometimes Meredith looked at her and saw the person she hoped she might become, smart and calm and patient in an office surrounded by bookshelves that reached up to the ceiling. Meredith expected she would have students someday—it was one of the better ways for artists and writers to make money—and she thought about what she would put in her own office. The students who came to visit her might see all the books, memorize the titles, and look them up later, just like she had done.

"And then when we go to the library it's the same thing. There are all these biographies of famous people and how they lived their lives, but most of us aren't going to be famous. It's like we've gotten these models for life that aren't applicable." Meredith didn't need to think about how to phrase her thoughts, because she had planned them out before she climbed the stairs. "We've learned about all of these well-known artists and how they did their work, but we don't ever study how the rest of us do it. Where are the biographies of ordinary people?"

Gina didn't answer right away, and when she did she said "I don't know," and Meredith could tell that it wasn't a question she had ever really thought about before. "There's Studs Terkel—"

"Well, sure—"

"But that's not what you mean. I'm not sure they exist. Maybe it's something everyone has to figure out on their own."

Meredith left Gina's office a few minutes later, not wanting to overstay her welcome. She pulled out her notebook as she walked down the stairs, writing *The Biographies of Ordinary People* so she wouldn't forget. Once she'd figured it out, she could write a book about it, a true story about non-famous people making art, and then the libraries would always have it for the students who were looking.

CPSIA information can be obtained
at www.ICGtesting.com
Printed in the USA
BVOW04s0618240517

485004BV00014B/39/P